This work gives an 'inside' view of Chinese theatre and the actor in performance for the first time. In doing so it also challenges western theatre artists such as Brecht, Grotowski, Barba and Schechner, who have extracted from Chinese theatre elements which might enrich their own theatres. Jo Riley writes from her personal observations of and dialogue with Chinese actors and her first-hand experiences of the theatre world of China in general, none of which were possible before 1980. She uses not only *jingju* (so misrepresented as Peking opera) but also exorcism, puppet theatre and ancient animation rites at the tomb to provide models for exploring the process of creating presence on the Chinese stage.

Each chapter takes one moment from a performance by the *jingju* master Mei Lanfang to show the articulation of the actor's body through metaphorical or actual dissection in training and initiation which releases the life-giving force of *qi* and movement as the manifestation of presence. Riley follows these discrete series of actors' movements and the overall action on stage and uses them to illustrate the essence of Chinese theatre. The book is well illustrated with photographs and diagrams and is accessible to anyone interested in theatre, even those with no knowledge of Chinese or Chinese theatre.

Chinese theatre and the actor in performance

CAMBRIDGE STUDIES IN MODERN THEATRE

Series editor
Professor David Bradby, *Royal Holloway, University of London*
Advisory board
Martin Banham, *University of Leeds*
Jacky Bratton, *Royal Holloway, University of London*
Tracy Davis, *Northwestern University*
Richard Eyre, *Director, Royal National Theatre*
Michael Robinson, *University of East Anglia*
Sheila Stowell, *University of Birmingham*

Volumes for Cambridge Studies in Modern Theatre explore the
political, social and cultural functions of theatre while also paying
careful attention to detailed performance analysis. The focus of the
series is on political approaches to the modern theatre with attention
also being paid to theatres of earlier periods and their influence on
contemporary drama. Topics in the series are chosen to investigate this
relationship and include both playwrights (their aims and intentions set
against the effects of their work) and process (with emphasis on rehearsal
and production methods, the political structure within theatre companies,
and their choice of audiences or performance venues). Further topics will
include devised theatre, agitprop, community theatre, para-theatre and
performance art. In all cases the series will be alive to the special cultural
and political factors operating in the theatres they examine.

Books published
Brian Crow with Chris Banfield, *An introduction to post-colonial*
    theatre.
Maria DiCenzo, *The politics of alternative theatre in Britain,*
    1968– 1990: 7:84 (Scotland)
Jo Riley, *Chinese theatre and the actor in performance*

Chinese theatre and
the actor in performance

Jo Riley

CAMBRIDGE
UNIVERSITY PRESS

PUBLISHED BY THE PRESS SYNDICATE OF THE UNIVERSITY OF CAMBRIDGE
The Pitt Building, Trumpington Street, Cambridge CB2 1RP, United Kingdom

CAMBRIDGE UNIVERSITY PRESS
The Edinburgh Building, Cambridge CB2 2RU, United Kingdom
40 West 20th Street, New York, NY 10011–4211, USA
10 Stamford Road, Oakleigh, Melbourne 3166, Australia

First published 1997

Printed in the United Kingdom at the University Press, Cambridge

Typeset in Trump Medieval 10.25/14pt, in QuarkXpress™ [GC]

A catalogue record for this book is available from the British Library

Library of Congress cataloguing in publication data

Riley, Jo.
    Modern Chinese theatre and the actor in performance / Jo Riley.
        p.   cm. – (Cambridge studies in modern theatre)
    Includes bibliographical references and index.
    ISBN 0 521 57090 5 (hardback)
        1. Theater – China.   2. Operas, Chinese – History and criticism.
    3. Acting.   4. Acting – Study and teaching – China.   I. Title.
    II. Series.
    PN2871.5.R56   1997
    792'.0951—dc20   96–31554 CIP

792.0951
Rie

Contents

vii

CONTENTS

Illustrations

Plates   *Page*

Diagrams

* Redrawn by Jane English

Introduction

Chinese theatre has always been viewed by Western theatre artists and scholars as the experience of *difference* which might offer a source of inspiration to their own theatre. Each practitioner approaching the Chinese theatre has identified elements within its aesthetic which have confirmed his own projected (unattainable?) theatre model. Bertolt Brecht found his theory of gesture and *Verfremdungseffekt* confirmed in a series of performances that he witnessed in the Soviet Union, in 1935, and recorded his impressions in several articles.[1] On the same occasion, Vsevolod Meyerhold praised the sense of theatre memory or tradition in Chinese theatre[2] and Sergei Eisenstein discovered his technique of montage echoed in the way the Chinese actor moved like a 'dancing skeleton . . . whose arms and legs fall apart and come together again'.[3] In the 1960s, Jerzy Grotowski explored the concept of breath (*qi*) and voice control in Chinese theatre[4] and, along with directors such as Peter Brook and Richard Schechner, turned to Chinese and Oriental theatres in search of a universal language of theatre.[5] In the 1980s, Eugenio Barba founded his ideas on training for the theatre on Chinese and Oriental models[6] and Ariane Mnouchkine's epic-folk theatre adopted some elements of Chinese theatre, amongst others, in order to defamiliarise Shakespeare.[7] Thus the broad, contemporary, Western view of the Chinese theatre is composed of a mixture of these

---

[1] For example, Brecht 1964: 91–9.   [2] Banu 1986: 156.

[3] Eisenstein 1988: 777.   [4] Grotowski 1969: 117–24.

[5] Grotowski 1969; Williams (ed.) 1991 and Schechner 1985.

[6] Barba and Savarese 1985.

[7] Fischer-Lichte, Riley and Gissenwehrer 1990: 281–2.

individual perspectives, gained, in most cases, from single performances observed in the West either live or on video, or in some cases during workshop situations with Chinese actors that lasted no more than a month.[8] Moreover, such perspectives are not aimed at mediating the Chinese theatre *per se*, they rather seek to identify elements in the other theatre which might inspire and reform the own theatre.

While the pre-occupation of such important artists with the Oriental and Chinese theatres has brought some awareness of them to the Western theatre world at large, the nature of each artist's own specific interest means that the focus is turned inwards, back towards their own theatre. Some theatre practitioners looked for techniques of *distancing* in the Chinese theatre, while others searched for *universals* of theatrical language. Each opened up one small window on the Chinese theatre, one or two aspects which the artist *felt* (since none were literate in Oriental languages) confirmed his own pre-conceived idea of what theatre should try to be.[9]

The situation has been enlightened greatly since the 1970s. Sinologists such as William Dolby[10] and Colin Mackerras[11] have systematically mapped the historical and social context of Chinese theatre. Elizabeth Wichmann[12] and Gerd Schönfelder[13] have elucidated the music of Chinese theatre. Such works have greatly supplemented the earlier, descriptive works by Cecilia Zung,[14] Tao-Ching Hsu,[15] and others who have listed the costumes, make-up, movements and plots of some plays. The sinologists are, however, largely reliant on Chinese sources reflected through a cultural-evolutionary concept of the development of theatre,[16] not to mention certain theatre professional taboos and political restrictions.

As a challenge to the Western theatre practitioner who looks to China for the experience of difference and finds only his own theories and visions confirmed, and in an attempt to escape the evolutionary-historical presentation of the Chinese theatre, this work shall try to

[8] At the International School of Theatre Anthropology 1980–5, for example, or at the Cardiff Laboratory Theatre in 1986, 1987 and 1988.

[9] See for example Pronko 1967.   [10] Dolby 1976.

[11] Mackerras 1972, 1975 and 1983.   [12] Wichmann 1991.

[13] Schönfelder 1971, 1974.   [14] Zung 1937.

[15] Hsu 1985   [16] Zhou Yibai 1980.

show, for the first time, a Chinese perspective. My account is drawn from inside the theatre world in China, as an initiated participant. It is based on many years of study in China at the Central Drama Academy in Beijing and in the field, in rural China. It shall draw upon personal experience of training for, performing[17] and spectating various kinds of performance art in China, as well as from personal encounters with teachers and actors across China.

My point of departure is not the viewpoint of a Western spectator, the *outsider*, who sits inside a Chinese theatre, or of a scholar pouring over ancient documents in a Western library; instead it asks the question: What does the Chinese spectator, an initiate, or *insider*, expect to see even as he stands outside the theatre before the performance has even begun? Is there a body of shared knowledge about each actor – his heritage, his training – and what about the play itself? Is it known? Does it have a performance history, and how does the Chinese spectator apply this knowledge to the performance he observes?

Once he is inside the theatre, what does the Chinese spectator *see*? How does he interpret the actor and the role being played? What tools of knowledge must the Chinese spectator have to crack the surface codes of a Chinese performance, and how do they operate? Some elements may be read in terms of their historical or aesthetic contexts, but others depend on philosophical, even genetic contexts. The Westerner perceives the process of life (of time and space) as a sequence which moves from position A to position B. Does the Chinese view differ? Is there a different (vertical, in depth?) way of reading the theatre, as Pound and Fenellosa suggested of Chinese poetry?[18] What happens when the spectator investigates the actor below the costume, music, make-up, movement, layer by layer, meaning by meaning? The Chinese teachers say that before an individual may speak out (articulate meaning), he must first absorb the form of speech. What is the *form* of the Chinese per-formative body? How is it composed? How does it prepare?

In the Year of the Dog (1983) I travelled up from the south of China towards Beijing, by train, by boat, by bike, by foot, crossing great river

---

[17] As the wine seller in *Zuida shanmen* (*Escaping from the Monastery*) with Ma Mingqun and the Beijing *jingju* 2nd Company, for example.
[18] Fenollosa 1969.

beds empty of their waters, green-brushed mountains dry and strangely peaking out of rice fields, brown and yellow dust bowls of interminable plains, searching for 'Chinese theatre'. The hot days were filled following the image of film cameras dotted across the map of each city showing cinemas and theatres, buying tickets, unknowing. The cool evenings and nights were spent sitting on hard wooden benches in the square, in the park, the tea-house, circus tent or on upright chairs in theatres, numbered odds to the right, evens to the left, watching. I saw everything. From spoken Western-style theatre, traditional theatre, socialist cinema, music concerts and variety shows, to comic dialogue, sing-story-telling and disco. My ticket allowed me hours of programme, once inside. I could get up, walk about, eat, come back, find my seat occupied by a grandmother selling a brood of chicks from a basket on her lap, or an old gentleman dreaming with his pipe and spittle. They would move, or I would, and a busy woman in little white cap would come by with an enormous steaming kettle of hot water to fill our tea jars, before filling those on stage for the musicians and performers. My ears filled with noise and chaos. Of people talking, shouting, eating, laughing. Of the rough percussion on stage and the performer's song. Of piglets snorting and hens clucking, of babies suckling, grandpas spitting. My eyes filled with the colour, movement and shape of bodies on stage, of bodies off stage, of bodies back and forth behind and ahead, carrying kettles, baskets, an instrument, a prop, a pipe. For hours and hours, a gentle chaos, a sleepy bustle, and then a pause, a stop, a breath, a concentration, an involving passion for the moment on stage, as the female role tosses a sleeve over her shoulder, cries, exits, dragging the white silk on the floor behind her, trailing it for the dead hero to catch it and call her back, before being released again by the crack of sunflower seeds in the mouth of my neighbour before the shell flies to the ground, my feet, the earth.

The goal of my journey was Beijing, the capital city, the pure, the north, the citadel, the 'original' model, as I thought, of all this, the 'true' theatre, *jingju*, known to Westerners as 'Peking opera'. But when I arrived there, it was September, the middle of the Campaign Against Spiritual Pollution, and after checking in, my bags were deposited outside the hostel in the street and I was told 'there are no foreigner travellers in Beijing now'. I left China via Shanghai, city of lust and

4

splendour, of lemon meringue pie and European quarters, without my theatre.

When I returned, the following year, it was to the Central Academy of Drama in Beijing. The pure source, the theatre in Beijing, was not what I had dreamed. The stalls were half-filled with old grey men, their eyes closed, nodding, tapping their long yellow fingers to the beat, muttering; five white-shirted youths leaned lugubriously over the gallery resting their heads on their arms, languidly watching the flickering digits on their silver quartz watches. On stage, thirty minutes of this play, an hour of that, an interval and another thirty minutes of something. The actors played their play like automata, the only real movement was the shifting strip of characters displayed on either side of the stage giving the text. Without it, the figures on stage are dumb to the spectator, even with it, the text is unforgivingly classical, few can follow its intricacies (and I wondered which spectators could read anyway) but a summary is provided in red ink on tissue paper programme notes. Night after night it was the same scenario, the same twenty or so plays moved from theatre to theatre, unchanging, for two whole years: acrobatic spectaculars such as the Monkey King favourite *Sun Wukong danao tiangong* (*Sun Wukong Stirs up Trouble in Heaven*) and episodes from the saga *Baishe zhuan* (*The White Snake*); martial spectaculars such as *Sanchakou* (*Where Three Roads Meet*) *Yangjia jiang* (*The Yang Family Generals*), *Mu Kezhai* (*The Mu Family Axehandle Stockade*) and plays taken from stories of battles in the Three Kingdoms such as *Changbanpo* (*The Battle of Changban Hill*); historic romances such as *Yu Tangchun* (the tale of the wronged prostitute, Yu Tangchun), *Shi yuzhuo* (*Picking up the Jade Bracelet*), *Changshengdian* (*Palace of Eternal Youth*) and *Bawang bieji* (*The King Takes Leave of his Concubine*). Though the same plays are regularly offered to Western theatrical entrepreneurs, who believe the repertoire has been adapted for them to simple plots with eye-catching acrobatics, in fact they are produced to capture the failing Beijing audience. Specifically designed for the foreign market are the numerous Shakespeare adaptations,[19] and productions using children from the *jingju* school performing in English – anything to excite someone, anyone. Actors graduating with poor skills

[19] Li Ruru 1988.

turn to the blossoming black markets at night to deal in leather jackets and lamb kebabs. Actors graduating with excellent skills do the same, practising English at street corners and dreaming of *kung-fu* films. Older actors, frail and sad, in worn, buttoned up Mao suits and caps as unchanging as their weary expressions, moan into their jars of tea, fished out of black plastic handbags, the cadres' key accessory.

The form *jingju* had its heyday at the turn and beginning of this century. It was a product of certain theatrical styles which met in the capital city and influenced each other. It was performed in the city at court as well as in tea and guild-houses, and later, in specially built theatres. One of the best known *jingju* actors of the early 1900s was Mei Lanfang. Mei performed the female *dan* role. He experimented with, and developed, *jingju* in all its aspects – costume, set, text, movement repertoire and song. Mei was a great *jingju* star in the 1920s and '30s; he 'declined' to perform during the Japanese Resistance, but returned to the stage in the 1950s in the changed arena of the Communist regime. He was given support by the government, which he reflected in visits to soldiers guarding the Chinese frontiers to Vietnam and Korea, as well as in performances for miners, workers and farmers across the land. But (this changed) Mei Lanfang died in 1961; and the Cultural Revolution of 1966–76 destroyed all that was left of the gasping theatre tradition, both *jingju* in Beijing, and the other theatres in the regions beyond. All cultural monuments and ideas were overturned. All that had been China, her writing, religion and theatre was eradicated at one blow. During those years, nearly every trace of the theatre tradition was erased. Most actors were sent to labour in the countryside and the few that remained performed eight politically correct plays over ten years to a bound audience. In the early 1980s, after the creation of the new culture along with its New Speak (*xinhua*), some attempts were being made to revivify the theatre by reintroducing certain traditional plays – rewritten according to recommended, thoroughly discussed and ratified lines. Mei Lanfang was used as the ghostly model, the prime spiritual recoverer of the lost golden age of theatre. *Jingju* began to travel to the West again; we were told of its 'ancient traditions', its 'deeply significant, codified movements'. But what came was not the *jingju* of before; the new *jingju* has been created under different political and social circumstances; it has a different history.

But now, from Beijing, with an official Work Unit Card that showed I belonged to the Guild of Theatre Schools, I could travel again – this time extensively, and empowered with the language – south to Fujian and Guizhou, north-east to Shanxi. The theatre of the surrounding countryside and cities away from the capital was far more alive, more a part of the people's lives as they participated on and off stage, and I found the myth that the Beijing theatre (*jingju*) *is* Chinese theatre was being elbowed out by a vibrant tradition of making and watching performance of all (other) kinds in all (other) places. The capital has lost its central significance for theatre.

This was the search for the 'missing' theatre. The theatre people of my generation East and West had never seen, a theatre not coloured by the designs of those new theatre makers. It was an attempt to find a Chinese theatre by travelling back temporally and spatially to the outlying areas of China; to uncover the writings, religions and passions that made the theatre.

In the yellow plains of poorest Shanxi, I found ancient theatre stages from the twelfth century in temples transformed into schoolhouses, homes, granaries. In the coastal region of Fujian, a vibrant puppet tradition thrives as clans compete to outdo each other in skill and variety of repertoire. The representation of man, through the figures, and the manipulation of such human figures by men, raised all kinds of questions about performance and being, about life and death, or the real and other, fictive, theatrical worlds. In the southern province of Guizhou, among a population of eight ethnic nations: Han, Miao, Buyi, Dong, Shui, Yi, Gelao, Yao, a form of theatre called *nuo* (to cleanse, exorcise) performed at the lunar New Year, autumn harvest festival and – in the event of drought, sickness, infertility – at the desire of any villager. The performers are male clan members, villagers, mostly farmers. Their theatre cleanses, celebrates and reconfirms the clan community.

The *nuo* performance arena is marked by a passageway of red banners, leading to an open space at the heart of the village. Guizhou is cold at New Year, not the minus temperatures in white sun that make Beijing winters bearable, but a creeping, cold dampness that never clears from the layers of clothes that swaddle each body. The spectators stand close to keep warm. The very first day of New Year, I walked to the village of Wujiaguan, just outside Anshun. The village has no *dixi* troupe of its own (the local form of *nuo* theatre), but invites a troupe from distant Zhanjiadun to perform on its behalf, who arrive at midday, in costume with drums, having marched several hours, singing. The troupe follows the red-bannered path, the waiting spectators gather to greet them. But before they are permitted to enter the performance area of Wujiaguan, the actors face a test. On a table, barring the entrance to the village, stand tiny porcelain cups of spirits and rice. The village elders congregate behind the table and offer the cups to the troupe leader and his deputies, singly, to drink and offer propitiation, respect and libation to the earth round which they are about to enter. One by one an actor approaches and is given a riddle. He must puzzle it out in verse, singing, or withdraw, singing. The first riddle was the character *quan* (spring, source) with a picture of a leaf above it. It was quickly solved as 'fresh, green spring', a good omen for the coming spring crops. The second riddle was an unfinished literary quotation from the *Saga of The Three Kingdoms*; the third also tested the literary scholarship of the invited actors. These riddles were easily solved, and celebrated with yet more libations of wine and song. The fourth riddle was 'two colts galloping side by side'. One actor came forward, then another. The actors became agitated. The village elders waited. An hour passed. The troupe sang and sang – the feathers in their head-dresses tossing and quivering. The village elders conversed, edgily watching me. Finally they agreed that my presence allowed them to move the barrier and welcome in the troupe, despite the final riddle remaining unsolved. Under normal circumstances, the troupe must guess the riddle before they may perform, no matter how long it may take. Later, a hoary voice whispered to me, across the din of duelling generals 'this is the year of the horse, midday is the hour of the horse – the first moment of the New Year, the time of performance, should have been like the two horses galloping in'.

What other spectators demand so much of their performers and so challenge the actors' literary scholarship? It was a contract between partners which continued throughout the performance. A wrong movement, a mispronounced text, a badly executed sequence was criticised by a circle of old women sitting at the edge, nodding, gossiping, tut-tutting.

In the early 1900s, *jingju* spectators talked of going to 'hear theatre' (*tingxi*). They were as critical, as initiated, as the old women in the countryside. Mei Lanfang's reputation was based on modifications he proposed which such knowledged, sharing audiences ratified. But where was he now? No disciples continued his tradition (the representation of female *dan* roles by males was abandoned in the 1950s), the plays he performed were stripped of 'unsuitable' content (whether superstitious, feudal, bawdy, spiritual or religious), and the theatres are barely filled with men who barely remember their part of the contract, while those who would have been initiated, who would have joined their elders, sat in bars drinking beer from white plastic jugs and playing pool.

Mei Lanfang, and all that he once represented, the mythical *jingju* that I never experienced in the 1980s, has become the empty centre of this study. He is the one figure that unites all kinds of theatrical performance occurring in China; elements of his art are reflected in all theatrical events, from puppet theatre, mortuary ritual and *nuo* masked theatres, and I found that the examination of all these other performance events illuminates, reflects and fulfils the image of the great master.

In the *nuo* theatre, the actors orientate their performance around a mathematical, magical matrix known as the Luo diagram. It consists of three rows of three cells, numbered in such a way from 1–9 that any route along a straight line of three renders the same digit, 15. The *nuo* performers place certain values onto the matrix related to the macrocosm, and their dance across the performance space becomes a recreation of perfect (mathematical and cosmological) harmony. In the matrix, the central cell, bearing the digit 5, with its magical relations to centrality, medial control and harmony, is the key element combining all other outlying digits with each other. Each route across the Luo diagram exploits and transgresses the magic, unifying centre, the axis of recreation. In this study, the model of the Luo diagram has been applied to the whole of Chinese performance in general. The figure Mei Lanfang stands at the centre of the study as the model around which presence in performance, the articulation of the performing figure, can be analysed. Through one play, *Guifei zuijiu* (*The Favourite Concubine Becomes Intoxicated*) aspects of Mei Lanfang's performance art are analysed. Each moment, from the discussion of the role outside the theatre among the queuing spectators in chapter one, to the first entrance pose, three minutes later in chapter five, opens a path towards other forms of performance and back. The focus of the study could have been any play from the *jingju* repertoire. The method of analysis can be applied to all plays. This particular play was chosen simply because it is better known, because more materials are widely available – in film and text and because it became identified more than any other play, with the actor Mei Lanfang.

The eight chapters of this work take Mei Lanfang as a starting point, as central, unifying figure to illuminate a different aspect of performance. Chapter one, 'Family', begins with the moment outside the theatre and the known history of the performer and the play shared by the initiated audience. It deals with the tradition of performance within the clan or adopted family and the breakdown of such traditions in modern China. The second chapter, 'Appearance', analyses the first pose of the actor on stage, and explores systems of meaning in the cut and colour of costume and dress and, finally, the system of meaning in the body underneath the costume: how the body is transformed, manipulated or recreated as an actor. In chapter three, 'To sever', methods of transforming, cutting, articulating the body for performance are analysed. Training methods, actual physical dismemberment and masking are parts of this process in Chinese theatre. Chapter four, 'Identity', explores the spoken and sung text of performance and the shifting sense of identity portrayed by the acting figure. Key issues of Chinese performance such as self-narration, self-manipulation of the articulated body and distance from the role being played are discussed. In chapter five, 'Life', the model of the mortuary figure, placed in the tomb to provide life in the underworld, is related to the performing figure in theatre. The processes in China by which inanimate figures of wood, metal, porcelain and paper are animated for the other world of death are closely related to similar processes of animation of the role by the actor in the other world of theatre. Chapter six, 'Presence', continues this discussion and explores the movement of such animated figures in detail. What kinds of movement show presence? How is movement represented by such figures to give the idea of presence? The mathematical-magical matrix of creation, the Luo diagram, is the centre of chapter seven, 'To unify'. In this chapter, specific examples of movement sequences from *jingju* and *nuo* are given to explore the significance of the movement of the rearticulated body in a defined space of cosmological meaning. Chapter eight, 'Round', illuminates the key aesthetic criterion of *jingju*, the quality of roundedness in all movements, and relates this to the cosmological conclusion of the articulated, presenced body moving in space in all Chinese performance.

Like the digital values of the Luo diagram, the eight chapters of this work could be read in any direction. All routes pass the central, unifying figure of Mei Lanfang. The passage across the work is not intended to be linear, but multi-layered, interconnected, like a spider's web. The structure of the eight chapters thus replicates one of the most profoundly significant concepts of Chinese performance – the congruence of the performing body, and the space around it, to a mathematical, spatial, temporal matrix of *creation*, the Luo diagram, the key to understanding the source, control and articulation of *presence* by the actor on the Chinese stage.

1

Jia
(Family)

The price of a ticket in 1985 was generally less than half a Yuan, the main unit of Chinese currency, depending on the theatre and the performance. An average wage was about forty Yuan; a theatre ticket cost about the same as a lunch-time meal but a jug of beer was twice as much. The price was low enough to allow spectators to attend at least once a week; theatre fans came several times a week. Tickets are issued from the box office on the morning of, and just before the performance; at least a third are handed out free of charge by the work unit. One bitter February morning,[1] I joined a queue for a performance of *Yuanmen zhan zi*[2] (*Execution of the Son at the Great Gate*) with Yang Huimin in the title role of Mu Guiying outside the Jixiang (Lucky Omen) theatre in the Jinyu (Gold Fish) Alley. It was unusual to have to queue for tickets – the performance had aroused much interest, and the queue buzzed with excitement. It was made up almost entirely of men over the age of fifty – only a few women of the same age were present. The conversation passed back and forth along the queue in broad Beijing dialect over my head: What was the actor's greatest talent? Was she taught by this master alone or that master as well? Was she better than another actor in singing? Or worse than another actor in technique? Was she contemporary to this actor? Or had she learnt from that actor's performance?

---

[1] 4 February 1985. The performance was by the Beijing jingju santuan (Beijing Opera Third Company); the second piece in the programme was a newly adapted play *Tong tianhe* (*Crossing the Heavenly River*).

[2] All Chinese titles and terms are transcribed in the *Hanyu pinyin* system, including those used in citations from other works, to help the non-sinologist reader. A character list and glossary of Chinese terms can be found at the end of this work.

Then, under my fur-lined, deep-collared coat, hat and scarf, it was real-
ised I was a foreigner, a girl, under fifty. First they expressed amazement,
what could I possibly be doing there? Then, they gently scorned me for
being an outsider, for not knowing the complex performance history
of the actor. Finally, in a rush of voices, they fought to tell me their own
versions of it, losing themselves in the fine details of a performance-
biography whose complex construct extended as far back as they wished
in any direction they desired.

What are the expectations of the Chinese spectator as he stands
outside the theatre? What knowledge does he bring to the performance?
How does he interpret the performance?

On the simplest level, the Chinese spectator is at least acquainted
with the style of theatre he is about to see – *jingju*. *Jingju* is conven-
tionally translated as Beijing opera, though its literal translation is
'theatre of the capital'. It is one of many different styles of theatre in
China and has very little to do with opera. The Chinese words *xi* and *ju*,
meaning theatre performance, describe a performance art which is made
up of four basic performance skills: *chang* (singing), *nian* (recitation) *da*
(military skills and acrobatics) and *zuo* (doing, 'acting'). *Jingju* is only
one of over three hundred different styles of theatre in China and each
is defined as a particular style by the type of melodic and/or percussive structure. Each form reflects, to a certain extent, the geographical
and cultural influences of a particular area of China. Thus *chuanju* is
the form known in Sichuan, *huangmeixi* is from Anhui and *gezaixi* is
performed in Fujian and Taiwan, for example. *Jingju* is composed of
elements from several different melodic structures: *qinqiang* from the
Shaanxi area, *xipi* from Hubei, *yiyangqiang* and *erhuang* from Jiangxi
and *erhuang* from Anhui after different travelling companies from
those areas brought their local styles to the capital from the mid 1770s
to 1830.[3] *Jingju* is distinguished by the two main melodic systems
erhuang and *xipi*. Both systems use an orchestra composed of the drum,
large cymbal, small cymbal, and double cymbals, *huqin* (spike fiddle),
erhu (second spike fiddle) and *yueqin* (moon lute). The main aria accompaniment in *jingju* is the *huqin* spike fiddle.[4] *Jingju* is based on

---

[3] See Gissenwehrer 1983 and Mackerras 1972 for a detailed history of *jingju*.
[4] See Wichmann 1991 and Schönfelder 1971 and 1972.

sheng (male)

jing (*hualian* or painted face)

dan (female)

chou (comic)

Diagram 1   The four role types

a melodic system quite different from another form of theatre that was performed in the Beijing imperial court and among the literary circles, *kunqu*, a southern style based on the *kun* melodic system which depended on the flute as principal accompaniment. The *kun* theatre contrasts strongly with the more popular forms which flowed into *jingju*.

The *jingju* actors train for and perform specific role types. The four main role types are depicted in Diagram 1. Within these role types are certain subdivisions. The male role type subdivides into: *xiaosheng* (young gentleman, scholar), *xusheng* (mature gentleman), *laosheng* (old gentleman, scholar) and *wusheng* (martial, or warrior). The female role type subdivides into: *qingyi* ('blue robe', women of high social status and dignified behaviour), *huadan* ('flower' *dan*, younger, vivacious female), *huashan* (between the *huadan* and *qingyi*), *laodan* (elderly female), *wudan* (martial female), *daomadan* ('knife and horse' *dan* – light martial female). The painted face role type divides into: *tongchui hualian* ('copper hammer' – big voice painted face), *jiazi hualian* (stance, or posturing painted face), *laohua* (*heitou* or elderly painted face) and *wu hualian* (martial/acrobatic painted face). The comic roles (also called *xiao hualian* (small painted face) sub-divide into *wenchou* (civil comic) and *wuchou* (martial/acrobatic comic) roles. The civil comic roles include officials, scholars, innkeepers, guards, and the *caidan* (comic female) role.

Jia (Family)

In the past, the Chinese performer was socially disregarded; no person from an acting family could rise to an official post, and actors were listed on the social scale below beggars and thieves. The actors lived and worked in separate entertainment quarters outside the city gates as social outcasts. Before 1920, the *jingju* troupes were made up of either all male or all female performers. The female troupes performed in brothels and were mostly prostitutes. In the male troupes, boys trained from a young age under severe conditions as apprentices to performers or retired performers who then reaped the income from the boys when they were good enough to go on stage. After 1949, the social position of actors improved; the training schools and professional companies became State controlled. Girls and boys train and perform together; and all students are guaranteed an income on graduation regardless of how often (if at all) they are required to perform.

Jingju uses no set other than a table and chairs which may represent the inside of a palace, inn or home. The tables and chairs are also used to indicate a mountain, a bridge, a well, or a bed if such is needed. The scene is set by the text spoken by the performer. To indicate the passage of time or space, the performer makes one circuit of the stage, *pao yuanchang* (running the circle). To suggest the performer is riding on a horse, the actor holds a silk horse whip; a carriage is shown by two square flags with wheels painted on, when showing travelling in a boat the actor takes a paddle in one hand. Flags are also used to indicate circumstance: black flags portray wind, or a storm; blue show the sea or a river.

From the late 1800s to the 1930s, many outstanding actors achieved immense renown and admiration across China including: Tan Xinpei, Zhou Xinfang and Ma Lianliang (*laosheng*, old gentleman, scholar), Yang Xiaolou (*wusheng*, martial male), Xiao Changhua (*chou*, comic), Jin Xiushan (*hualian*, painted face) and Yu Zhenfei (*xiaosheng*, young gentleman). But it was not until one actor, Mei Lanfang, travelled to Japan, the Soviet Union and America, that *jingju* came to be known outside China. Mei Lanfang was considered to be the sole representative of *jingju* to the West over a period from 1930 to his death in 1961. He performed in the Soviet Union before Stanislavsky, Meyerhold, Tretyakov, Brecht, Piscator and others, while Eisenstein made a film of elements of Mei's performance. Mei was photographed with Stanislavsky and with Charlie Chaplin as the Chinese performer *per se*.

The individual person, Mei Lanfang, whoever that was, is of little interest. Mei Lanfang so incarnates the idea of the *jingju* performer (both in China and in the West), and *jingju* is so representative of Chinese performance in general, that one performance by Mei Lanfang can provide a springboard from which to examine the performer in China. The chosen performance is as the concubine Yang Yuhuan in the play *Guifei zuijiu* (*The Favourite Concubine Becomes Intoxicated*). Any other performance by any other actor would provide an equally rewarding model of analysis, but this play, and the man who made the role so entirely his own that his interpretation of it has remained unchanged offers an example of the epitome of what Chinese performance is all about. The role stands for all roles as Mei Lanfang stands for all *jingju* actors, as *jingju* stands for most forms of Chinese performance. Mei Lanfang is *the* Chinese performer.

Embodying the family

Mei Lanfang (1894–1961) was born into a theatre family. He literally embodies a whole tradition of performance passed on to him by bloodright through his performing family. Mei Lanfang's family history shall be reconstructed in the first part of this chapter. Mei Lanfang also earned a body of performance knowledge, by adoptive right, through his training and apprenticeship into the system of *jingju* performance. A discussion of the masters who trained Mei Lanfang forms the second part of this chapter. Mei Lanfang can be described as a vessel which is composed of all that his ancestors were, both his acting family and the various masters and other professionals who passed down their own traditions to him by example, and both these traditions are visible to those who watch Mei Lanfang perform on stage.

Who are those who watch? Before turning to Mei Lanfang, the object of the spectator's gaze, a brief diversion shows that the spectator is only qualified to watch and judge after undergoing a certain apprenticeship himself (most of the spectators are male). The spectator coming to see Mei Lanfang perform has been *initiated* by his own family since childhood by a parent or grandparent into the traditions of the performers he watches. The gentleman scholar and *ximi* (theatre *afficionado*) Qi Rushan, who has written ten volumes on Chinese theatre, for example, was initiated into the world of theatre by the male members of his family. Qi's great-grandfather, Qi Zhengxun, was a government official who associated with other scholars who cultivated private and amateur performances: 'In those days, the scholars carried drum, gong, fiddle and flute around with them, and started up in the tea-houses when they had nothing else to do.'[5] Qi Zhongqing, Qi's grandfather, carried on the tradition and became a government official who could sing over a hundred roles. His son, Qi Mingchen, Qi Rushan's father, could also sing all the major arias from plays such as *Xixiangji* (*Tale of the Western Wing*), *Pipaji* (*Tale of the Lute*), *Changshengdian* (*Palace of Eternity*) and *Taohuashan* (*Peach Blossom Fan*). Not only was the practice of amateur singing and playing a vital part of any scholar's life in China; all the villages had their own troupes and temple performances, so that ordinary life in China was also thoroughly permeated by the theatre: 'We used to say that in some villages even the dogs howled as if they were singing *gaoqiang* melodies. I frequently went to the theatre, and though I cannot sing, I can probably sing better than those howling dogs.'[6] Qi Rushan, like all the village boys, also joined a *wushu* (martial arts) club in the village which, he claims, initiated him into the art of movement on the stage. 'Because we boys spent half the day watching the *wushu* in the village, when we went to watch martial plays, we were even more fascinated, and became absolute fans of the theatre.'[7] Qi Rushan was born in 1877. In 1991, I filmed a *wushu* (martial arts) club training in the village temple in Zhong Suo village in Guizhou under their master Lu Huamei, who was also the head of the village theatre company. Lu teaches Tang Quan style, which is in the middle level range of skills, and over three hundred villagers train regularly with him (nowadays girls included). Six small boys also take part in the training, the youngest of whom is ten years old, and the skills they learn from Lu are also observed from standing on the stage with the village theatre company when they perform. As in many villages, from Qi Rushan's day to the present, the village temple, martial arts training and performance indivisibly form the cradle of acting in and spectating theatre.

---

[5] Qi Rushan 1979, vol. 10: 6094. Sources, unless otherwise stated, are translated by the author.

[6] Ibid.   [7] Ibid., vol. 10: 6095.

The initiated Chinese spectator reconstructs Mei Lanfang's performance-biography even before entering the theatre. When watching the performance on stage, the initiated spectator *sees* the various members of Mei Lanfang's performance-biography come alive in Mei's performance. It is as if all the family members and teachers behind Mei Lanfang are also present on the stage – he is a performer of many shadows of presence. For the uninitiated spectator, a brief family tree and performance biography of the actor Mei Lanfang are set out below. Both biographies are thoroughly visible and present to the spectators waiting outside the theatre before the play begins as well as at each moment of performance.

Mei Lanfang was born into the acting profession. Both his father and grandfather were actors married to the daughters of other actors. The male line of the Mei family went on stage; the female line married into the profession and gave birth to male performers and female marriage parcels to be married off to other actors. Those in the acting profession were social outcasts. They intermarried with other acting families and lived beyond the main city gates as a group of outsiders, a clan of professional performers.

Mei Lanfang's grandfather, Mei Qiaoling (1842–82), was a *qingyi* performer. He was the eldest son of a shop keeper in Jiangsu and sold to a childless man in Suzhou at the age of eight, named Jiang. Jiang later married again, and the second wife bore him a son, so Mei was sold to a trader who bought and sold children for the theatre, and finally sold into the Fushengban Company[8] to study the *dan* or female roles. Mei Qiaoling was skilled in a wide range of *dan* roles from *qingyi* to *huadan* and this breadth of skill brought him some fame despite his somewhat unattractive appearance in costume due to his large size – hence his nickname, Pang Qiaoling (Fatty Qiaoling). At the age of thirty, Mei Qiaoling became the leader of the Sixiban Company and seldom appeared on stage after this, devoting his time to the management of the troupe and training of the younger students. However, in 1908, the funerals of both the emperor Guang Xu and the empress dowager Cixi Taihou, who died shortly after him, imposed a mourning period of

---

[8] The name of the company literally means 'Rising Fortune'. All the troupes had similarly propitious names which, however, are not translated individually in this work.

one hundred days without the sound of music. The company was prevented from performing and the long break nearly ruined the Sixiban Company. Mei Qiaoling died in penury.

Mei Qiaoling's wife, Mei Lanfang's grandmother, was the daughter of the *kunqu* male role actor Chen Jinjue. They had two daughters; one of whom married the martial role actor Wang Bashi, and gave birth to the *dan* actor Wang Huifang (cousin to Mei Lanfang), and they also had two sons, Mei Yutian and Mei Zhufen (see Diagram 2). Mei Zhufen (1874–97), Mei Lanfang's father, was known on stage as Mei Mingrui. He briefly performed as a *dan* actor before he died, aged twenty-three. Mei Zhufen was married to Yang Changyu (1876–1908), who was the daughter of the martial role actor Yang Longshou.[9] On the death of his father, Mei Lanfang was given into the care of his uncle, Mei Yutian (1869–1914),[10] who was the eldest son of Mei Qiaoling. Mei Yutian was an accomplished *jingju* musician. Originally he played the flute and had three hundred *kun* melodies in his repertoire before changing to the *huqin* (spike fiddle) and becoming renowned as a *huqin* player, the private accompanist to the *jingju* actor Tan Xinpei. Mei Yutian married within the profession, Hu Shi, the daughter of the *dan* actor Hu Xilu. As uncle and substitute father, Mei Yutian was responsible for the training and upbringing of Mei Lanfang for the *jingju* stage, for he had no children of his own.

The *jingju* performer can always be identified in terms of the clan or family to which he belongs, whether he was born to it, as Mei Lanfang, or sold into it, as Mei Qiaoling. In some other systems of Chinese performance (generally amateur), the family connection is so vital that only the members of one particular family have the right to perform at all. In Anhui's Nantong city and the region around Fenhe in Dong county, an exorcism event known as *Zhong Kui xifu* (*Zhong Kui Dances with the Bat*) is performed annually.[11] Zhong Kui is a mythological figure who has the power to exorcise demons. He is represented

---

[9] In *Zhongguo jingjushi* 1990, vol. 1: 480–3.

[10] The *Zhongguo dabaike* 1983 gives two different sets of dates for Mei Yutian. On page 244, the dates are given as 1865–1912 and on page 247 as 1869–1914. The latter dates are also given in a lengthy eulogy to Mei Yutian in *Zhongguo jingjushi* 1990, vol. 1: 585–88.

[11] *Zhongguo minzu minjian wudao jicheng* 1980: 1582–613.

Key

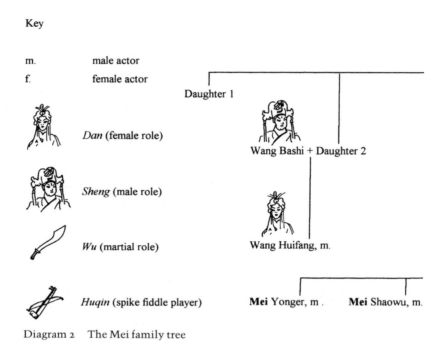

m.   male actor

f.   female actor

Dan (female role)

Sheng (male role)

Wu (martial role)

Huqin (spike fiddle player)

Daughter 1

Wang Bashi + Daughter 2

Wang Huifang, m.

Mei Yonger, m .   **Mei** Shaowu, m.

Diagram 2   The Mei family tree

in all kinds of theatrical performance from marionette to *jingju* as a red-faced, black haired, hunchback or cripple. In this piece, the figure Zhong Kui dances with a figure of a bat made of paper, accompanied by an assistant spirit. The significance of dancing with a bat is that the title of the piece makes a homonym of the phrase 'Zhong Kui brings fortune'. In the Anhui dance, one performer dresses as a spirit and ties a large puppet construction representing the exorcist figure Zhong Kui to himself with false arms so that it appears as if there are two perform-ing figures. In fact, the performer operates and manipulates the Zhong Kui figure in front of him with his hands which are inside the figure (see Diagram 39a, b and c on p. 217). The dance of Zhong Kui is owned by the Fang clan – only members of the clan may perform it. The clan recounts its origin from two Fang brothers who came to the area about 350 years ago. Now that the clan is very large, several groups of the

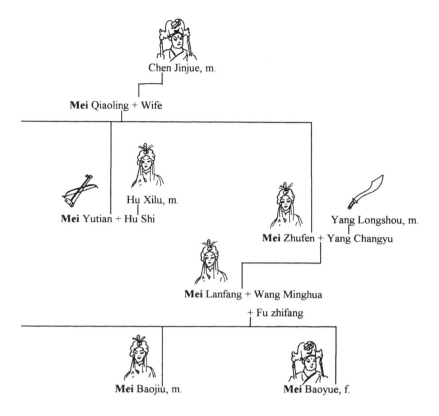

Fang family have formed who perform independently of each other in different villages.

A similar situation can be found right across the *nuo*[12] (exorcism) theatre: in Tangguan town, in Guizhou, where the form *dixi* is performed, the two families Lou and Zhang totally dominate the troupe; only two other different families, Du and Ye are represented. The troupe consists of three generations of Lou, two generations of Zhang, two generations from the Du family and one from the Ye family. This divergence from the main clan stem occurs when no male children are

[12] The term *nuo* means 'to exorcise'. The *nuo* theatre is one element of an exorcism event at New Year and harvest festivals, for example, held by a community. Most forms of *nuo* theatre use fixed masks; the performers are not professional actors but male members of the community initiated for the duration of the event, and directed by a master of the event.

born to learn the part, so that the right to perform passes along the matrilineal line. Because the Chinese naming system requires that all children born in the same generation – that is, cousins and cousins however many times removed – are given the same first personal name, one generation of performers can be easily identified.[13] In the same area of Guizhou, another village, Zhanjia Dun, records sixteen generations of performers in the Zeng family. The current troupe includes lead actor Zeng Tiaotong (68 yrs), his son and second lead Zeng Yuhua (31 yrs) and his apprentice son Zeng Xiaopi (7 yrs).

The concept of each performer embodying a whole family of professionals who have gone before him is also the rule in marionette theatre. The hand-puppet company from Zhangzhou in Fujian has passed through five generations of the Yang family: from Yang Wuxian (b. 1801) to his son Yang Hongchang (b. 1848), to his son Yang Gaojin (b. 1863), to his son Yang Quansun (no date), to his younger brother Yang Xiansui (no date), to his son Yang Chun (b. 1911) to his son Yang Feng (b. 1942).[14]

Imitating the master

Mei Lanfang was born into the Mei professional acting family, but he was also educated by other actors and masters in the profession. The system of training for *jingju* depends upon the (fatherly) relationship of master and disciple. The student served the master at table, as well as obeying the master entirely in the training hall. The method of teaching simply requires that the master do and the student imitate. The latter element of the compound *laoshi* (master, teacher), *shi*, means 'to imitate'. A student who fails to reproduce the movement correctly is told to watch again. The master shows the movement at performance speed; it is seldom broken into smaller parts for ease of learning. The student is simply expected to copy – as a child – without thinking. Once the student has mastered the physical outline of the movement, the teacher withdraws his model and merely corrects the student – forms the student into the correct mould.

---

[13] Author's field notes: Lou *Qi*xian, Lou *Qi*yi = one generation; Lou *You*liang, Lou *Xiu*ping = two generations; Zhang *Shao*quan, Zhang *Xin*hua = two generations; Du *Hai*an, Du *Chun*xiang = two generations; Ye *Zhao*ming = one member of the Ye family (strangely, Ye was one of the troupe managers).

[14] Author's field notes, 1984.

There is no philosophical or aesthetic text on training for the Chinese theatre such as the *Natya Sastra* in India, or Zeami's writings in Japan. Rather the master incorporates the performance knowledge in his body. This is passed on to the student by the process of imitation. In training for actual role pieces (rather than learning the basic repertoire of movements, or training physical strength and flexibility) the master stands next to the student as model, giving the correct pattern of movements (see Plate 1). In the rehearsal rooms, the student is literally shadowed by the presence of the master who has taught him the role, and by his master's master who taught him the role. On the stage, the performer is visibly shadowed by these presences in the mind of the spectator.

Mei Lanfang's performance is impressed with the style of many masters who taught him (see Diagram 3). Wu Lingxian, a *qingyi* performer, taught Mei Lanfang at his home on the recommendation of Mei Yutian. The *qingyi* role was the role played by Mei's grandfather, Mei Qiaoling. The term *qingyi* (blue robe) possibly refers to the typical robe worn for such roles – a long, plain, dark blue or black robe over a long white skirt. The robe has *shuixiu* (water sleeves) – white silk sleeve extensions which traditionally cover a woman's hands from view. The *shuixiu* sleeve on stage is generally between a metre and a metre and a half beyond the cuff, depending on the skill of the actor. The greater the skill, the greater the length of the sleeve. The *qingyi* role is renowned for skill in manipulating these sleeves; the actor folds, throws, and catches them in performance in a multitude of ways to express aspects of the role. The other skills a *qingyi* must have are singing, recitation and the ability to dance gracefully.

From 1908, Mei Lanfang joined the Xiliancheng Company and trained with the *dan* actor Qin Zhifang, his uncle. At the same time, he also studied the role *huadan* (flower *dan*) under Hu Erqing, also an uncle, who was a *chou* (comic role). The term *hua* (flower) is widely used in many different theatre vocabularies. It can mean 'brightly coloured,' 'patterned'; in this case perhaps indicating the colourful costume of the *huadan* as opposed to the sombre dress of the *qingyi* (blue robe). Before various governments implemented certain reforms on the *jingju* theatre in the first part of this century, the flower *dan* represented a vivacious, licentious young woman of lower social status. As a

Plate 1   Role training at the Zhongguo xiqu xuexiao (China Theatre School)

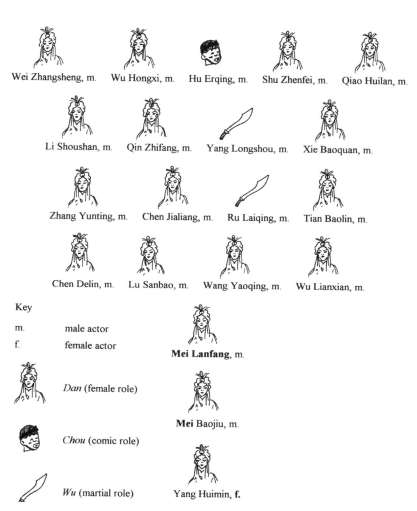

Wei Zhangsheng, m.   Wu Hongxi, m.   Hu Erqing, m.   Shu Zhenfei, m.   Qiao Huilan, m.

Li Shoushan, m.   Qin Zhifang, m.   Yang Longshou, m.   Xie Baoquan, m.

Zhang Yunting, m.   Chen Jialiang, m.   Ru Laiqing, m.   Tian Baolin, m.

Chen Delin, m.   Lu Sanbao, m.   Wang Yaoqing, m.   Wu Lianxian, m.

Mei Lanfang, m.

Mei Baojiu, m.

Yang Huimin, **f.**

Key

m. male actor
f. female actor

Dan (female role)

Chou (comic role)

Wu (martial role)

Diagram 3   Map of masters

mischievous, sexy, often comic role she was the very opposite of the *qingyi*. These aspects of the role have now been toned down to mere coquette. She may wear trousers and a short jacket or a robe and long skirt, but seldom water sleeves. The main skill a *huadan* actor must have is the ability to present the life and verve of the role. Individual technical skills are less important.[15]

[15] See *Zhongguo jingjushi* 1990, vol. 2: 632–40.

25

Mei Lanfang's formal teaching days ended here. He had been introduced to two different styles of *dan* acting and began to perform at the age of eleven in minor parts. At the same time, however, he continued to learn from other performers and masters on a private basis. Each teacher would pass on the knowledge of how to perform a specific role. For example, Mei learnt the role of the concubine Yang Yuhuan (from the play *The Favourite Concubine Becomes Intoxicated*) from Lu Sanbao, and the role Dong Fangshi (from the play *The Rainbow Pass*) from Wang Yaoqing. At this level, the teachers were still performing themselves. Though they also embodied the knowledge of performance handed down to them by their own teachers, most of the following masters listed below made their own creative extensions of the tradition which were recognised as individual *liupai* (schools) or styles of performance.

From Chen Delin (1862–1930),[16] Mei Lanfang extended his repertoire of *kundan*, and *qingyi* roles. Chen Delin was the son of a trader and, like Mei Qiaoling, was sold into a theatre company – and became Mei Qiaoling's own disciple. He was first taught the *kundan* role before learning *qingyi* in the *jingju* style at the age of nineteen from Tian Baolin. Such was the quality of his voice that his style of singing was established as its own school, the Chen style.

Wang Yaoqing (1881–1954),[17] another of Mei's teachers, also studied *qingyi* under Tian Baolin. As a child, he was sold into the Sanqingban Company where he studied martial skills under Chong Fugui. He was injured and at the age of twelve changed role types to study *qingyi* from Xie Shuangshou. From Du Dieyun, he studied the *daomadan*, female light martial role. Wang was one of the first actors to break the convention of the time that different role types were not to be mixed. Most standard works on *jingju* insist that the role type is fixed for life, and that performers seldom cross role types. However, if a performer, like Wang, was injured, or his voice unsuitable after it broke at puberty, the student was often forced to change role type. Where the student was particularly talented, this resulted in an unusual breadth of skill. The performer might introduce new aspects to the role type, combining skills associated with one role type with those associated

---

[16] See ibid., vol. 1: 489–92. [17] See ibid.: 492–9.

principally with another. The examples of Wang Yaoqing, Mei Lanfang, and most of the performers who specialise in the role of the exorcist figure Zhong Kui (see below) demonstrate that combining elements from different role types is actually seen as an important step in the creation of a new style. Mei Lanfang adapted the *qingyi* role of the concubine Yang Yuhuan to that of *daomadan*, making the role less sombre and more athletic. The Mei school or style of performing Yang Yuhuan as a *daomadan* role is now widely accepted as the standard one.

Mei Lanfang learned a wide range of skills from teachers of many other role types than his own *dan* role. The list of masters who taught him includes Ru Laiqing,[18] who was a *wusheng* (male martial role) and a disciple of Mei Lanfang's maternal grandfather Yang Longshou; and *kun* actors (rather than *jingju* actors, for example): Qiao Huilan, *kundan*, disciple of Zhang Yunting; Shu Zhenfei, Li Shoushan, Xie Baoquan (whom he invited to Beijing from Suzhou) and Chen Jialiang (the grandson of Chen Jinjue and Mei Lanfang's grandmother's nephew).[19] Moreover, his spike-fiddle-playing-uncle taught Mei several pieces (it was not unusual for a musician to teach a performer); Qian Jinfu taught Mei yet more martial roles (which he performed with Yang Xiaolou, also a disciple of Mei's maternal grandfather and a contemporary of Chen and Qian, from the Sanqingban Company); Li Shoushan, a *kundan* and *hualian*, also taught Mei various roles.[20]

Mei Lanfang learnt the role of the concubine Yang Yuhuan from Lu Sanbao. Lu was a *huadan* actor, though originally he had studied *xusheng* (mature male) – yet another example of an actor forced to change role types. As a *xusheng* actor, Lu was known as Yang Hui. Because he had difficulties with his voice,[21] he changed roles to perform *huashan* roles (that include elements of both *huadan* and *qingyi*),

---

[18] Mei Lanfang and Xu Chenjuan 1961, vol. 1: 34–5. Ru is pictured with Mei Lanfang on page 36.

[19] Dong Weixian 1981: 149–60.

[20] Mei Lanfang and Xu Jichuan 1961, vol. 1: 103–5.

[21] Since the boys began their training at the age of seven or eight, the period after the child's voice had broken was extremely crucial. If the student's voice was no longer suitable for performance, the student was either transferred to another role type, or engaged as servant, dresser or stage manager to the rest of the company.

and later moved towards roles which demanded more physical skill such as the *daomadan* – female light martial role. In costume and make-up, Lu was said to have an unattractive, tragic or stern look and so he was particularly suited to roles which involved him killing or dying – the so-called *sharenxi* (murder plays) – which were banned from the repertoire during theatre reforms carried out by various governments from the 1900s.[22]

Yang Yuhuan is the title role of the play *Guifei zuijiu* (*The Favourite Concubine Becomes Intoxicated*). In the play, which is a short piece lasting an hour, the concubine prepares for a banquet to welcome the emperor who has chosen her for the night's rendezvous. She soon learns, however, that the emperor has decided to visit a different concubine, and so Yang Yuhuan drinks alone to drown her disappointment before returning to her own quarters. Lu Sanbao (1877–1918) taught the role to Mei Lanfang at a time when Lu himself no longer performed it. Mei was for a time in the same company as Lu, the Yiwenshe Company, and admired Lu's performance: 'I often watched him perform, and I found his style meticulous, his skill well and truly deserving of his reputation.'[23] Thus, in one performance of the role of the concubine Yang Yuhuan, Mei Lanfang incarnates all the styles of his various teachers and their various styles, as well as embodying the particular style of Lu Sanbao and his teachers (see Plate 2).

The master-father

Within the acting profession, actors address each other by terms which reflect generational relationships. Thus the actors fully perceive themselves within a 'family' situation. Not only was the master addressed as *shifu* (the characters literally mean master-father) but also directly as in a familial relationship. Thus Mei Lanfang addressed the *laosheng* actor Tan Xinpei (who was contemporary to Mei's grandfather) as *yeye* (grandfather). Even in a situation where the relationship was less formal, the terms of address remained familial. Wang Yaoqing ought to have been addressed by Mei Lanfang as 'uncle' because Wang was thirteen years older than him:

[22] Dong Weixian 1981: 182–3.
[23] Mei Lanfang and Xu Jichuan 1961, vol. 2: 19.

Plate 2   Mei Lanfang with his teacher Lu Sanbao in *Jinshansi (Jinshan Monastery)*

[Mei Yutian] decided I was the right age to study the role in *The Rainbow Pass*, and he discussed the idea with Wang *daye* [*daye* means father's older brother]. One day, he took me to Wang's home and told me to light incense and formally *ketou* [pay respect to] Wang. Wang was quick to answer: 'According to the rules of the generational differences, we are the same generation, so we don't have to follow the strictures, just call me elder brother, and I shall call you younger brother Lan.' Mei Yutian knew what a modest man Wang was, and that there was no use trying to persuade him, so although our relationship was one of master and disciple, from that moment on, we addressed each other as brothers.[24]

Thus every actor performs each role according to the 'family' way of doing it. Just as Mei learnt the role in *The Rainbow Pass* from Wang Yaoqing, so Wang learnt it from his teacher, who learnt it from his, and so on. All these 'role ancestors' are present when Mei Lanfang (the present incarnation) performs. If an actor makes a mistake on stage, he is said to have *naogui* (disturbed the ghosts/spirits) as if the actor has offended these presences.

Such presences can even be traced back to an 'original ancestor,' one of the earliest recorded *dan* actors, Wei Zhangsheng (c. 1744–1802). Wei is included in the biography of Mei Lanfang because he is the farthest back in the family tree it is possible to go. Wei and his troupe brought the *qinqiang* style of opera to Beijing which contributed to the founding of *jingju* as a whole. Wei came from Sichuan, and was immensely popular in Beijing despite being banned from the stage in 1782 because his performances were considered bad influence (lewd and bawdy). However, in 1791, the author Shen Qifeng complained that even the *kundan* actors copied his style, 'even among the *kunqu* actors there are some who have turned their backs on their teachers and learned from him'.[25] Wei Zhangsheng left the capital to return again in the late 1800s, when his style had become more agile and included martial skills. Wei provides yet another example of the way in which successful performers have extended the boundaries of so-called fixed role types in a line of actors that has continued through Mei Lanfang's teachers such as Wang Yaoqing to Mei Lanfang himself.

Nor does the performance biography end with Mei Lanfang. Rather he stands as one link in a long and continuous chain of *dan* actors. After 1949, no male students were permitted to take up the *dan* role, and females were allowed to perform on stage instead. This means that the performance of the *dan* role by male actors technically stops at

[24] Mei Lanfang and Xu Jichuan 1961, vol. 1: 105.
[25] Mackerras 1972: 95.

the generation of Mei Lanfang. He is at the end of one tradition and (after declining to perform during Japanese occupation) at the beginning of a new one where he is a male model for future female *dan* actors. This is with the notable exception of his younger son, Mei Baojiu.

From 26 October to 2 November 1984, a special series of twenty-one anniversary performances was arranged in conjunction with the Ministry of Culture, Chinese Theatre Association, the China *Jingju* Academy and the Beijing *Jingju* Academy, among others, to celebrate the ninetieth anniversary of Mei Lanfang. Star of the occasion was naturally his son, Mei Baojiu (then in his fifties) who seldom performs nowadays, as well as his daughter, Mei Baoyue, who plays male roles.[26] Of the other seventeen *dan* performers, less than half were male actors (two of those came from Hong Kong and New York and all were over the age of forty), but all consider themselves as descendants of Mei Lanfang and his school of acting, though in most cases the accuracy of the actor's interpretation of the Mei school was much disputed by the spectators.

Not only Mei Lanfang and his disciples in 1984 stand shadowed on stage by their many teachers and family of professional performers. The role of the concubine Yang Yuhuan in the play *Guifei zuijiu* (*The Favourite Concubine Becomes Intoxicated*) has itself a history of performance related to the styles of performance in which it was traditionally presented. It was created in one style of theatre before being absorbed into others including *jingju*. The role is composed of trace elements of these other forms which are visible to the initiated spectator. Mei Lanfang stands on the stage as a composite body of his ancestral heritage in a role which has its own complex biographical history of interpretation.

According to Mei Lanfang, the role of Yang Yuhuan was brought to Beijing by the *hanxi* (Hubei theatre style) actor Wu Hongxi in July 1887. The first record of the role was in the Qianlong era (1736–96) as a *huabu* piece, i.e. any form but *kunqu* which is based on the melodies of

---

[26] This extraordinary paradox is inexplicable unless Mei Baoyue simply does not have the right voice or manner for *dan* parts. Though Mei Baojiu has gained enormous popularity in Hong Kong and Singapore on account of his father, in Beijing it is said that neither he nor his sister have achieved the same level of perfection as Mei Lanfang.

the flute.[27] *Huabu* was the popular theatre as opposed to the courtly *kun* theatre and was considered by admirers of the latter to be somewhat vulgar in comparison.

However, another author suggests that the movement of the role was yet more complicated than this, passing from *kun* through *huabu* before being absorbed in the new *jingju* style:

> The theatre of the capital continued to some extent to absorb the Hubei repertoire. Perhaps the most famous example was *Guifei zuijiu* . . . This play, originally a *kunqu* piece, had been adapted to Hubei opera by the Dao Guang period (1820–50). It was introduced to Peking by Wu Hongxi, the famous *dan* of the Hubei opera early in the 20th century and remained popular in the capital until very recently . . .[28]

After Wu Hongxi's performance, the *jingju* actors also followed in performing the role.[29] The play *Guifei zuijiu* is currently performed in *huiju* (Anhui), *hanju* (Hubei) and *chuanju* (Sichuan) styles. Thus the role, starting with Wu Hongxi, has itself a biography of performers who have interpreted it in their own various styles of theatre.

Initiation – eating the ancestors

The *jingju* performer Mei Lanfang is a composite body made up of his real family, his teachers and his teachers' families and teachers throughout generations. The professional ancestors that shadow his performance are visible to the initiated spectator but *different* from the spectator. The spectator does not belong to the same family system as the performer, though he may know and appreciate it; the actor is outcast in relation to the spectator. In the *nuo* (exorcism) theatre, the knowledge of performance is embodied in one man who *stands for* the spectator; he is a composite body deriving from the *same* family to which the spectators of the community belong; the actor is in-cast(e) in relation to the spectator.

---

[27] *Zhongguo xiqu quyi cidian* 1983: 572.
[28] Mackerras 1975: 155. Mackerras is writing in the mid-seventies, when the play was not performed for political reasons.
[29] Mei Lanfang and Xu Jichuan 1961, vol. 2: 36–7.

In different parts of China, the leading *nuo* performer is called by different names: Fashi, Saigong, Shigong in the south; Duangong in the south-west; Zhangtanshi in Sichuan for example. All these titles contain the element *gong* which is a title of respect, or *shi* meaning 'master'. *Shi* also carries the sense of 'to imitate'. Thus the master sets the pattern for the disciple to imitate – this is the process of learning, as in *jingju*. Both elements *shi* and *gong* show the sense in which the one man is held to be someone in possession of special knowledge – he is a kind of sage, or elder, worthy of respect. In Dexian county in Guizhou province, the master is known by the title Duangong which literally means, 'master of the doctrines/principles/beginnings' or 'master of the centre'. The term Duangong is recorded in the Tang dynasty as the name given to a *wu*.[30] A good deal of scholarly debate has gone into the discussion of what a Chinese *wu* actually is.[31] Yet more scholars have tried to analyse the meaning of the character used for *wu*.[32] For the purposes of this study, however, the *wu* is most appropriately defined as an initiate in certain techniques, knowledges and practices which can change a situation of disease or disaster into a better one. This definition deliberately avoids any collision with the term 'shaman' which is often given as the translation of *wu* and which, in the context of performance, is somewhat confusing (for example, the Chinese *wu* in the *nuo* event does not necessarily enter a trance, nor make a spiritual journey).

In Dexian, the Duangong is given yet another name, Tulaoshi, which means 'master of the soil'. The title refers to the boundaries of the community – whether village or town. The Tulaoshi is responsible for managing the area defined by the community as its own. Since the communities are clan-based, the territory belonging to each clan is, by implication, an ancestral territory passed down from generation to generation, kept apart from land handed down by other ancestors in other clans. The Tulaoshi is thus more than merely a keeper of geographical boundaries. He is also the keeper of the ancestral heritage, the clan

---

[30] *Zhongguo fengsu cidian* 1990: 784.

[31] See for example, De Groot 1982, vol. 6: 1187–323; Hawkes 1985: 42–51; Waley 1955: 1–19; Elliott 1955.

[32] See for example, Chan 1972; Hopkins 1920.

identity. *Laoshi*, as a title of respect literally means 'old master'; *gong* can mean 'father'. The Tulaoshi, or Duangong is like the oldest member of the community – he is the 'father' of the community; he connects with the ancestors.

A *nuo* performance company is known as a *tan* or altar – a group of people who associate themselves around the ancestral-territorial clan altar. Only the Duangong is a professional in the sense that he is always a Duangong. The rest of the company is made up of clan members who, for the duration of the performance only, are initiated into the performance methods and are known as *linshi* (temporary masters). The rest of the time, when no theatre is performed, the *linshi* are sworn to secrecy. They 'pretend' to have forgotten. Only the Tulaoshi may remember, and he keeps the performance texts (if there are any), the masks and the mask trunks hidden in his own home.

The process of initiation into the performance troupe shows how closely the ties of family or clan are bound in the *nuo* theatre. The chief element in the initiation process is the giving of rice – an important ingredient in all ancestral rites.

The following example comes from the initiation of a performer into the *tiyangxi nuo* theatre[33] in Sichuan. Here, the aspirant must donate one *dou* (peck – measure)[34] of rice to the master. The giving of rice as part of the contract or dowry by which an initiate becomes accepted in the group is a common phenomenon in various initiation processes in China from secret societies to Daoism. Daoism is also known as the *wudoumi jiao* (five-*dou*-of-rice religion) as this was the quantity required of the initiate. In the case of *nuo*, several significant associations are to be made concerning this gift.

1   The first is a pun on the word *dou* which means 'ladle' or 'scoop' and puns on the same word meaning the stellar constellation *Ursa Major* or Big Dipper. This constellation is associated with the creation myth explored in chapter three. The constellation represents the

---

[33] On this form of *nuo*, see Riley 1991: 4–20; Xiong Feide, Wang Yansheng and Wang Xingzhi, and Hao Gang in *Nuoxi wenxuan*, ed. Li Yuanqiang (no date); Hao Gang and Tao Guangpu 1993: 149–69.

[34] A *dou* is about 10 litres or 1 decalitre.

constancy of the centre (the north pole) around which everything turns in a cyclical sequence. As such, it expresses the pattern of change in the cosmos in which all things come round, in which new life refreshes old. The cosmos is viewed in this constellation as a perfectly balanced, unified world where sickness, death or drought have no place. Moreover, it sets the initiate in the position of the dipper in relation to the centre (the master-ancestor) which never moves. The initiate is mortal, the history of the ancestors represented by the generations incarnated in the master is not.

2   The second association in the gift of the *dou* measure of rice is contained in the offering of rice as uncooked (yet-to-be transformed), nutritional matter. The relation of uncooked to cooked food in ancestor and mortuary rituals has been examined by Emily Ahern, who states, 'Supernatural beings are offered food that is less transformed, and therefore less like human food, according to their difference from the humans making the offering.'[35] Thus the Tulaoshi is in some way differentiated from and distant to the initiate (he is the embodiment, the ancestral representative) and this determines the kind of gift offered.

3   Thirdly, rice is considered to be the most basic, vital nutritional stuff: rice is the key food substance shared by members of a family. The eating of rice together in a real sense demarcates the family unit and reinforces kinship bonds.[36] Thus the sharing of rice is an acceptance of new bonds, a new clan or family (guild) to which the new initiate will belong.[37] The strength of the idea that those who share the rice meal are bonded is apparent in the communist principle of the *tiefanwan* or (iron rice bowl) – a socialist bowl big enough to feed the whole population of China.

4   Finally, the term *dou*, also denotes a bucket which takes exactly that measure of rice, which is one of the key items in mortuary ceremonies. The bucket is filled with various things – coins, grain and nails, and put on top of the coffin:

---

[35] Ahern 1973: 166–70.   [36] Thompson 1988: 71–109, 92.

[37] The character for rice, *mi*, is like an eight-pointed star. It is said to represent the eight directions of the Luo diagram, the grid of creation (examined in chapters three and seven) and is thus an important item in the symbolic repertoire of props required by the *nuo* event. This aspect is explored more closely in chapter three. See Berglund 1990: 222–35.

If we examine what the *dou* contains in the course of a funerary ritual we can list the following: rice, which is put in a (red) cloth wrap on top of the coffin; the temporary ancestral tablet; the 'five grains', coins and nails, symbols of fertility; short sticks of bamboo, said to represent the sons and grandsons of the dead person. When the son pulled the progeny nail from the coffin with his teeth, he deposited it in the *dou* bucket. My reading is that the items contained in the *dou* are interchangeable, all being facets of agnatic stuff. Pushing the symbolic logic further, and given that the bag of rice on the coffin is an aspect of the deceased, then it follows that the descendants by consuming rice, an agnatic substance [Yang] are metaphorically indulging in endonecrophagy. The substance of one generation is represented as the source of life and substance for next generations.[38]

Thus each initiate becomes a member of the performing troupe by establishing his association to the family or community clan leader (father) and, at the same time to the ancestral history of that clan. The performer becomes a direct descendent of the ur-ancestor. In the same way that Mei Lanfang embodies all the histories of his father and grandfather and his teachers, the *nuo* performer embodies his clan ancestors which, in this case, are also simultaneously the ancestors of the spectators.

The example of Mei Lanfang has shown that the system of family distinguishes a *jingju* performer, it provides his performing identity. This is even more apparent in the case of those *jingju* performers who, unlike Mei Lanfang, were not born into the family, but were adopted into one, or initiated into one, in a similar fashion to the *nuo* initiate performers.

From the beginnings of *jingju* to about the middle of the nineteenth century, boys were bought from their families to be sold to companies or private teachers who took them to train as performers. The contract generally stated that the teacher was now responsible for feeding and clothing the child and any income which the boy's later performances might bring over a specified number of years belonged to the teacher. If the child failed in his training, or ran away, was wounded

---

[38] Thompson 1988: 94.

or the voice was no good after maturity, the teacher relinquished his responsibility towards him. However, during training and the period of performance, the child was the sole property of the teacher. The contract between master and (generally poor) parents was, in effect, a document of purchase. One such document, made by the actor Li Wanchun, took the following format:

> Zhang Huiqing, as head of the household, gives his son Zhang Yushan, age nine, to the master Li Wanchun, to be his student. The next seven years shall be devoted to his training in the profession of *jingju*. All income he may produce during this time belongs to Li Wanchun. The student is forbidden to return home without reason, neither may he withdraw from training during this period. The sum of 500 Yuan must be provided if the student breaks off his training, or has run away and cannot be found. Sickness and suicide are the will of Heaven and neither party shall be held responsible.
>
> In gratitude to Li Wanchun. This contract was agreed by free will and not through the use of force. Signed Zhang Huiqing, Li Wanchun. Witnessed by Bai Yonggui and Jiang Tielin. Scribe: Ren Yinan. August, the twenty-seventh year of the Republic [1938].[39]

Pupils were generally bought every few years with the view to building a complete troupe. On graduation, the boys were given the same (specially chosen) name, just as in the clan system where each generation shares the same first personal name (Zhang Yushan named in the contract above was given the name Zhang Minglu on graduation). In the theatre school system, it meant that each actor on stage could be identified as belonging to a specific generation of a specific school or master's teaching. A typical 'year' photograph of some members of the apprentice troupe Fuliancheng Company managed by Ye Shaoshan, for example, depicts Sun *Sheng*wen, Zhang *Sheng*lu of the 'Sheng' class; Xiao *Lian*fang, Wang *Lian*ping, and Zhang *Lian*bao of the 'Lian' and Wang *Xi*xiu, Liu *Xi*yi, Hao *Xi*lun from the 'Xi' class.[40] Plate 3 shows a

---

[39] Gissenwehrer 1987: 141.   [40] *Fuliancheng sanshinian shi* 1933: 38.

Plate 3   Mei Lanfang (age 14, front row, second from right) with fellow students at the Xiliancheng Company

similar photograph of Mei Lanfang's own year class at the Xiliancheng Company. The situation changed in the 1940s, after which time students of a particular year are not given a generational name but are simply known as the class of '55, for example. This reflects, in a way, the attempt to demystify or defamiliarise the profession, to make it 'scientific', as any other system of training or schooling.[41]

[41] This has had severe implications on the profession as students no longer serve a discipleship to a master. Although the negative aspect of ownership has been done away with, the master-disciple (father-son) relationship contributed enormously to the quality of performance.

In all the above examples, the performer is part of a family, whether his natural family or his adopted one. This fact obliges him to certain responsibilities towards that family (loyalty, obedience, etc.) and it distinguishes him from other members of the community who do not belong to the family. The performing family is generally in possession of the right to perform, i.e. that family possesses the *knowledge* of how to perform. This knowledge is passed on, and is only accessible to, those within the family. It may not be the eldest son, or any direct son of the family who is chosen. In the marionette family cited earlier, the sons of the fathers who continue the tradition are not all the first born; in one case, the tradition passed to a younger brother and then through to his sons. Similarly, in the *nuo* example, the families represented in the troupe consist of uncles and nephews, second and third cousins, granduncles and so on. As for the *jingju* example, the family members accorded the school or generational name were originally not related to each other.

The issue of family ancestry is crucial to Chinese performance and embraces the paradox of the actor's position as master-outcast. On one level, it lends a sense of authority to the performer – the performer does not stand for himself alone, but as the incarnation, or embodiment of the lengthy tradition of all others who have acted before him. It suggests a system of élitism – only those within the family have the right (knowledge) to perform – which is also ex-clusive; the actor is other, apart from the community in general.

The concept of family naturally extends to the idea of professional guild, like the medieval guilds in Europe who held the rights to perform certain plays. The annual exorcism at the Song court (960–1279 AD), held on the eve of the New Year according to the lunar calendar, was presented by various members of the performance profession alongside officials who were not professional performers, but who, as in the *nuo* example above, were temporary members of the guild by virtue of the fact that they, like the performers belonged to the guild 'official':

[41] *(continued)* There is a striking contrast between the attitude towards and quality of performance between those raised in the 'scientific' way and those trained in the 'family' system.

When it comes to New Year's Eve day, the Great Exorcism Rite is presented in the Forbidden City, and the personal attendants (i.e. eunuchs) of the Imperial City are used together with the various squadrons and columns [of the Imperial Guard]. They all wear masks and coloured clothing that has been embroidered or painted, and they hold golden spears and dragon flags. The Deputy of the Court Entertainment Bureau, Meng Jingchu, was big and strong in physique, and he dressed up as a general in a full-length brass-plate armor gilded with gold. They also used two Guardian of the Palace Generals decked in armor and dressed as door spirits. Nan Hetu, of the Court Entertainment Bureau, ugly and repugnant, big and fat, dressed up as the Judgement Official of Hell. Others dressed up as Zhong Kui and his little sister, as gods of the earth and of the kitchen stove and the like. There are altogether more than a thousand men, and they drive the evil spirits out of Nanxun Gate to Twisting Dragon Bend.[42]

For the duration of the performance, the real guardians of the gates to the palace dressed up as mythical guardians of the gates, the door gods or spirits. Only those who belonged to the guild of door guards may enact mythical door guards at ritual ceremonies.

A similar concept is seen in the exorcist figure, the Fangxiangshi, who was the official imperial exorcist in the Zhou and Han dynasties (BC 1066–220 AD). The *shi* in the title of the Fangxiangshi is not the character meaning 'master' used in *jingju* and *nuo*. Instead it means 'family', 'clan', or 'guild' so that the Fangxiangshi is one of those 'who perform the duties of the Fangxiang'.[43] The Fangxiang was registered as an official, registered on the civil list of employees at court.

Disembodied performers

Despite the fact that Mei Lanfang represented a kind of actor no longer wanted on the Beijing stage after 1949 (the male *dan* actor), his reputation was great enough to survive the various political changes that have occurred in China this century. In most other cases, the sense of the performer as the sum of his ancestry has disappeared entirely. A near contemporary of Mei Lanfang, the *wusheng* (martial role) Li Huiliang,

[42] Idema and West 1982: 122.   [43] Bodde 1975: 79.

who specialises in the exorcistic role Zhong Kui, provides the sad example. Plays that were superstitious, exorcistic, bawdy, or supportive of the feudal system were progressively dismissed by various government edicts over a long period from the 1920s. Zhong Kui, one of the chief exorcist figures at the annual cleansing of the stage ceremony, has all but been cast out of the repertoire of performable plays. Thus actors who once specialised in this role were prevented from performing or teaching it. The exorcist figure Zhong Kui dies with its performers (as many other roles have done).

My first encounter with a performer of the role Zhong Kui was October 1984 in Beijing. I had lost my wallet and was sent erroneously to the police station nearest the place of loss[44] – the theatre quarter around Qianmen where I had been wandering. I sat for two hours in a tiny, filthy room and was occasionally interrogated and then left alone. A bored official was playing with the knobs on some kind of radio receiver in the back room, and once or twice a plain clothes policeman in black leather jacket and jeans pushed his handcuffed catches through the room to the passage outside. Much shaken by the experience I raced to a prearranged meeting at the opera rehearsal rooms.

Li Huiliang is small in height. He was then about sixty years old, slightly balding at the front, a pigeon chest, and wicked, sparkling, unusual, narrow, almond eyes. He seemed almost feminine, surreal, barely noticing the other minor actors, the director or the musicians but sparing fleeting, flirting glances for the four foreign students gathered there to witness his rehearsal. A rehearsal (*pailian* literally means 'to arrange, set out and drill') in *jingju* is simply a 'walk through'. This is because all the roles are already learnt in training. Each performer, no matter what troupe or what area of China he comes from will be able to perform on the stage with any other performer. All that needs to be done in a 'rehearsal' is confer about the timing of certain passages – it is principally the occasion for the lead actor to inform the musicians how he intends to take the tempo. In the past, a lead actor would usually bring his own spike fiddler and lead drummer with him wherever he performed – lead martial role actors would also bring their own

---

[44] At that time foreigners were sent to a special central police station rather than local Chinese ones.

fighting partner to accompany them. Li Huiliang always employed his own fighting partner in performances of another play, *Changbanpo* (The Battle of Changban Hill). The role of messenger played by Li's partner should be a *hualian* (requiring a big voice). Instead, though dressed and made up as *hualian*, the fighting partner sings *laosheng* (old man role) which is less demanding to the voice – after all the actor is only there to complement Li in the fighting routines.

Li Huiliang wore the inevitable thick, blue track-suit trousers and layers of dull coloured, home-knitted, shapeless waistcoats, cardigans and pullovers[45] (it was October, becoming chilly, and there was no heating). He was magical, creating open pathways through the room as people stepped back sensing him approach; he was tyrannical, dominating the atmosphere, while appearing sweet and gentle. He donned the black high boots of Zhong Kui and began turning on the carpet – a giant square of green shorn carpet that all Peking opera actors rehearse and perform upon for its firm, soft, non-slip texture. Li's pupil, Ma Zhongjun stood at a distance from us similarly transfixed by the master on the carpet.[46]

The orchestra dispersed – the rehearsal was finished, Li Huiliang had shown them when and where and what he wanted. It had taken about fifteen minutes. He has no voice, it was a relief not to have to hear him struggle against the percussion, which resounded in the bare room as if we were standing inside the very cymbals. Ma stepped forward, executed a few movements. Li corrected him, executed a few of his own. Ma followed. Li got cross, took a large white handkerchief from his pocket and put one corner in his mouth, the rest hanging down like a bib in front of him. By blowing it from underneath, by tossing his face to the side and catching the handkerchief with his upper arm, he showed Ma the movements and control of Zhong Kui's heavy beard. Ma had a real (stage) beard, thick, heavy, black, impressive. But

---

[45] The outer waistcoat was maroon in colour. This was a much prized shade in Beijing at the time, and difficult to obtain (most articles were blue, brown, army green or grey).

[46] The carpet defines the play area. This is so even of Tang dynasty *daqu* dance cycles which were performed on richly decorated carpets imported from along the silk route. See the Dunhuang Tang mural no. 172, 'Xifang jing tubian', illustrated in Liao Ben 1989, colour plate 5.

Li's white handkerchief outdid it for power, expressivity, magnificence. Another fifteen minutes passed in this way, Ma doing increasingly more, Li increasingly little, until he stood at the edge of the carpet as if uninterested. The class was over. Ma thanked him, Li approached us, we spoke, took the photograph.

Li Huiliang is not mentioned in any of the reference works on *xiqu* theatre actors, though he is well known and revered by his public as one of the best interpreters of Zhong Kui. He is also one of the few actors who dares to play the martial role of Zhao Yun and the painted face role of Guan Yu in the same play (*Changbanpo*), crossing two role types and combining the martial skill and technique of the *wusheng* with the power and force of the *hualian*. Li Huiliang is a difficult figure, a thorn in the side of the contemporary *jingju* scene. The hint of scandal surrounds him; he was many years in prison under the communist government. Li came to Tianjin after 1949 with his father, who was the head of a troupe known as the Lijiaban Company. Between 1966 and 1976, Li Huiliang was arrested for being the Nationalist leader Chiang Kai Shek's 'sworn son'. He was rehabilitated in October 1984 prior to the thirty-fifth anniversary of the founding of the People's Republic. A series of performances had been arranged for him, as a kind of welcome-back-last performance.[47] The ambivalence towards him was apparent in all the official *jingju* teachers I spoke to, no one was quite sure if he really had been reinstated or not, if it was safe to judge him as a great actor. He is not a Beijing man, he came from the south. He did not train in any of the regular *jingju* schools of the time, but studied with private teachers, his last teacher being of as disreputable reputation as that now accorded him. It all felt highly irregular, the theatre world was unsure, the wicked genius had returned to the stage.

His performance as Zhao Yun, a heroic warrior from the play *Changbanpo* was impressively sad. Towards the end of the play, Li must make a rapid backstage change and reappear as the red-faced Guan Yu,

---

[47] From the 20th November 1984, for three days, Li Huiliang was invited by the Experimental *Jingju* Company and the China Theatre Academy to perform at the Concert Hall in Zhongshan Park. He performed four pieces in rotation: *Yanyanglou* (*Tower of the Bright Sun*), *Changbanpo* (*The Battle of Changban Hill*), *Tiaohuache* (*Fighting Against the Chariots*) and *Zhong Kui jiamei* (*Zhong Kui Marries Off His Little Sister*).

God of War. The change describes the magical metamorphosis of the warrior Zhao Yun into the fighting dragon god as he finally defeats the enemy, Cao Cao. Li Huiliang's *tuigong* (leg skills) were excellent, one leg easily reaching the ear as he posed for the long seconds of a *liang-xiang* (pose); bearing the four flags of a general on his back and a spear in one hand and a horse whip in the other he spun and somersaulted as the horse beneath him 'died', but his voice was weak and hoarse and very ugly. In the past, Li had been known for a spectacular double backward somersault off the edge of a chair representing a well, when he saw that the lady he was attempting to save had jumped into it in martyrdom. Trying to catch her, he grasps only her coat which flew through the air with him like her ghost (see Diagram 77). Now, the spectators counted the beats before each spear-throwing trick, poised to applaud with shouts of 'hao' (good) regardless of the moments of self-doubt when the older face of the actor penetrated the thick layers of the warrior's make-up with the sweat and strain of his efforts.

Li Huiliang's Zhong Kui, on the other hand, was masterful. All the spectators knew what lay behind the figure of Zhong Kui that night – the personal disappointments and the bitterness of the injustice of becoming an old man who, for too long, has been prevented from performing, and is now physically unable to, interspersed with moments of remembered inspiration, brilliance and awe. The mythical figure he plays, Zhong Kui, gained top position in the imperial examinations and was denied his post because of his ugly, deformed appearance. He committed suicide and was shown pity in the underworld by the gods and given the power of exorcism. The figure of Zhong Kui has a long history of representation in the fine arts and literature by scholars and artists who felt themselves similarly mistreated by the authorities. The personal fate of Li Huiliang, the actor, well matched the role he presented that night.

Although the role of Zhong Kui is a singing role (it is based on the form *kunqu*) nonetheless, Li's gruff voice seemed to fit this wicked, sad, figure, the disfigured, crippled scholar. And one quickly forgave the lack of breath after strenuous sequences, the struggle under the heavy costume, for here was an actor who also spat fireworks from his mouth over the stage, who blew fire across the front rows. It was the first time I, and many others, had seen such techniques, techniques

that belonged to the 'golden age' of *jingju* at the beginning of this century, when the repertoire consisted of many such spiritual and godly
figures.[48] Li Huiliang dared us all, captivated us all, disturbed many a
conscience.

The biographies of the actor Li Huiliang, and those actors before
him who have performed and passed on the tradition of playing the role
of Zhong Kui provide a stark contrast to the sparkling record of Mei
Lanfang and his teachers. The tradition that ends with Li Huiliang is
full of names of actors about whom nothing is known. Even the recent
history of Li Huiliang is not to be found in the theatre source books.
Neither his teacher, Yan Yuanhe, nor his teacher's teacher, Xiao Gui-
guan, are recorded in any of the standard reference works on Chinese
theatre. Of thirty-two performers who apparently performed the role,
only seven are recorded in the standard reference works, and only four
of these are mentioned in relation to the role of Zhong Kui. This may
stem from the fact that the role is partly a *kun* role and some of these
actors came from the south, so they are not so readily recorded among
the standard (northern orientated) texts. However, the style of reference in each case seeks to paint the picture of a dedicated socialist actor
as if to compensate for the 'superstitious, feudal content' of the role
Zhong Kui.

Unlike Mei Lanfang, who passed on a legacy of performance
celebrated in anniversary performances by many contemporary performers, Li Huiliang is no longer able to teach the role; it will die with
him. His student Ma only had time (and the training) to learn shreds
of it. The same historical and political decisions that maintained the
Mei tradition (politically undesirable male performers of female roles)
though in subtly changed form (i.e. the *dan* role is now only played by

---

[48] Mackerras 1975: 164–74 defines seven phases of communist reform in the
theatre from 1942 onwards which slowly eliminated plays which contained
ghosts, spirits, superstitious, religious or lewd scenes, feudal kings, slaves
and so on (the vast majority of the repertoire). Over this period, figures
such as Zhong Kui could not be presented on stage. Instead, a policy of
presenting the 'three prominences' was introduced: 'Among all characters,
give prominence to positive characters. Among positive characters
give prominence to heroic characters. Among heroic characters give
prominence to the main heroic character.' See also Mackerras 1983: 167.

female actors) have completely destroyed the tradition of Zhong Kui (politically undesirable figure of exorcism). Such apparently superficial reforms have radically obstructed the process of tradition, of the transmission of knowledge: the actor is cut off from his own tradition.

The role of Zhong Kui, a *kun* part, falls into five different styles, each with its own representatives. According to another performer of the Zhong Kui role, Hou Yushan, the following actors all performed Zhong Kui.[49]

1   The first school is known as the southern style, and includes Mao Song, Zhu Chuanling and Shen Chuankun who are not mentioned in the sources though two further actors, Lu Souqing and Xu Lingyun are provided with brief biographies.

Lu Souqing[50] was born in Suzhou, Jiangsu Province as the son of the *hualian* (painted face) actor, Lu Xiangrong. Between the years 1875–1908, he performed with the Suzhoudaya kunban Company and the Kunyiwuban Company. Later, he moved to the Quanfuban Company. His style was noted for its fiery, blazing quality, but the source dictionary does not mention him playing the role of Zhong Kui. It does state, however, that as an old man, he was invited to perform alongside Mei Lanfang in the role of a comic, or *chou* in the play *Fengzhengwu* (*The Mistake of the Kite*, later known as *The Phoenix Returns to the Nest*). Here is yet another example of an actor who crossed role types. Lu's heritage was the painted face role but he crossed role types from painted face general to comic minister. Xu Lingyun (1885–1965) was born in Zhejiang province and also excelled at several quite extreme role types: male, female, painted face and clown roles. In 1921, when the Quanfuban Company (of which Lu, above, was also a member) dispersed,

> [Xu] proposed to set up an institute of classical *kunqu* with the *kunqu* scholar Mu Ouchu and others and gave benefit performances in order to gather funds. After 1949, he revised many short excerpts from the *kunqu* repertoire and published them in three volumes. He also wrote a lengthy work, *Sixty Years of Theatre-Going*.[51]

---

[49] Hou Yushan 1984: 17–33.   [50] See *Zhongguo dabaike* 1983: 231.
[51] *Zhongguo xiqu quyi cidian* 1983: 349.

2   In the second school of representation of Zhong Kui, the northern style, the actors Sheng Qingyu, Zhao Deyu, Xiao Deyin, Jing Rongqing and Shang Changchun all apparently performed Zhong Kui in the 1930s. A sixth actor, Liu Kuiguan (1894–1965) was a *jingju* actor born in Kaifeng, Henan province. At the age of six, he learned basic martial skills from his father Liu Changqing before applying to several masters to learn the role of martial painted face and *hongsheng* (red face male, such as Guan Yu) roles.

He was known for his resounding voice, steady and firm technique and excellent leg skills. After 1949, he became the deputy chairman of the China Dramatists Association in Yunnan and head of the Yunnan *jingju* school, becoming a Party member in 1959.[52]
The northern school further subdivides into two substyles.

2a   The *nanjing* northern style was represented by Zhang Zijiu, Qiu Cheng, Shao Laohei and Yu Qusheng who are not recorded in the source dictionaries. Hou Yilong (1889–1939)[53] who performed this style was a Hebei man noticed for his suppleness of back and leg movements which were both strong and vigorous. This skill is said to have come from rehearsing over the winter vacation outside in deep snow without a shirt. He could 'tumble three consecutive somersaults and terrify the first four rows'.[54] In 1917 he led the Rongqingshe Company to Beijing and died in straitened circumstances at the age of about fifty during floods in the Sino-Japanese war in Tianjin. Another actor from this style was Hou Yushan (b. 1893)[55] (no relation). Hou is also a Hebei man from the same county as Hou Yilong. It is from his article that the tree of Zhong Kui performers is composed. He performed up until the Sino-Japanese war and then returned home and 'often aided the Eighth Route Army by repairing their fortifications and sending them grain'[56] while also teaching a new generation of *kunqu* students. In 1949, he returned to Beijing where he became a teacher at the Beijing People's Art Theatre and at the Literature and Art Work Troupe of the General Political Department of the Chinese People's Liberation Army. At the age of 64, he

---

[52] Ibid.: 331.
[53] Ibid.: 349; *Zhongguo dabaike* 1983: 121 and illustration.
[54] *Zhongguo dabaike* 1983: 121.   [55] Ibid.
[56] Ibid.

was still able to perform Zhong Kui and in 1957 became a teacher at the newly founded Beifang kunqu juyuan (Northern Style Kunqu Academy). Hou is skilled at performing several role types: painted face, martial, comic martial and old man. He can somersault onto the back of a chair and in the 1930s at the age of 40 could somersault over three other performers at a great height from the floor. His portrayal of Zhong Kui 'startles the very gods' and he was known as the 'living Zhong Kui'.[57] Finally, in the same style, belongs the actor Sun Yuanbing (1925–).[58] Sun was born in Beijing to a family of actors. His great-grandfather was a well-known martial role performer at the end of the Qing dynasty, Yu Chusheng. Sun is described as a 'gaunt-faced, diminutive, 52 year old man clad in pyjamas'.[59] Sun originally trained in the martial role before learning the painted face role and has performed the role only four times in Taiwan since arriving there in the 1940s. Two actors of the next generation who performed Zhong Kui in this style, Hou Xinying and Hou Guang (son of Hou Yushan) are not recorded in the source materials.

2b The second substyle, the *dongjing* northern style was represented by the actors Zhao Sanshi and Li Yizhong, who was the first to bring the role of Zhong Kui to Beijing, as well as Tang Yigui, all of whom are totally absent from the theatre books.

3 Finally, another style of Zhong Kui came into being known as the *pihuang ban* style, or *jingchao pai*. Both names refer to the melodic style of performance associated with *jingju* or northern *bangzi* styles. In these styles, the percussion is dominant as opposed to the flute in the *kunqiang* style which dominates the four styles above. It is to this tradition of Zhong Kui that Li Huiliang belongs.

The first representative of this style, and simultaneously the most well-known Zhong Kui performer, was He Guishan. This may be a reflection of the popularity of the northern style (the southern forms may have been less well regarded in the north, particularly Beijing) or perhaps the heavily percussive, rough style lent itself better to the figure Zhong Kui.

---

[57] Ibid. [58] Shi Song 1976: 42.
[59] Ibid.

He Guishan (1841–?)[60] was performing at the end of the Qing dynasty. He was a Beijing man, trained in *jingju*. He was a member of several early renowned troupes in Beijing, the Sanqingban Company and the Chuntaiban Company. His voice was simple but vigorous and he did not think much of ornamentation in singing. His eye skills were startling, he seemed to make them protrude. He carried on the tradition of the *ershisi shi menshen jiazi* (twenty-four Door-God stances). These poses derive from the fact that Zhong Kui is considered to be an effective guardian spirit, and the image of Zhong Kui in one of these guardian poses is consequently pasted outside the doors of houses to protect the inhabitants from demons.

As if to compensate for the superstitious, politically precarious nature of the role Zhong Kui, a legend was built around one of He Guishan's performances in Beijing in 1914 which proved him to be *nonetheless* an 'honest and upright man'. After the performance the manager gave him four silver coins. He Guishan shook his hands in disapproval and said, 'It's not right.' The manager, thinking he had given too little, prepared to explain, but he interrupted, 'My wage is two silver coins. If I take four coins now, I'll never be able to sing four coins worth again!'[61] He still performed Zhong Kui at the age of seventy-four.

The next generation of Zhong Kui actors, He Peiting, son of He Guishan, Ye Zhongding, Ye Fulai, Zhao Xikui and He Lianshou are not recorded in the reference works; only one actor in Hou's list, Qian Jinfu, is mentioned. Qian Jinfu (1862–1937)[62] was a Manchu born in Beijing and trained in *jingju*. In 1883, he entered the Sanqingban Company and progressed from there, on its dispersal in 1890, to the Chuntaiban Company. In 1896, he started his own small school, the Changqingban Company, and in 1909, he entered the Chunqingban Company. He often performed next to Yang Xiaolou and Tan Xinpei and became famous for his skill in face painting. Apart from all the other qualities shared by the previous performers – strong voice, excellent physical skills – Qian was noted for his skill in performing with weapons. In this style must

---

[60] See *Zhongguo dabaike* 1983: 111 and illustration at the foot of the page; Dong Weixian 1981: 203–6; and *Zhongguo jingjushi* 1990: 526–31.

[61] *Zhongguo jingjushi* 1990, vol 1: 530.

[62] See *Zhongguo dabaike* 1983: 286 and illustration at the bottom of the page.

be included, though not mentioned in the dictionaries, Yan Yuanhe, Li Huiliang's teacher, and Li Huiliang.

Li Huiliang suffered the discontinuity of tradition enforced on him as an actor by political circumstances such as the so-called Great Proletarian Cultural Revolution of 1966–76, when actors were invited to work in the countryside to reform their thinking, as well as the consequences of the fact that his speciality, the role of Zhong Kui was itself not desirable in the context of the political climate of the time. What exonerated Mei Lanfang and broke Li Huiliang and many others, was a cultural–political decision that cannot be redeemed – *jingju* has changed its very being. In the 1990s, the system of training and perform-ance based on the master-student relationship has all but vanished entirely.

Li Huiliang teaching his disciple in the rehearsal room is not by any means the only broken *jingju* master vainly attempting to pass down his art. Since many actors spent long years working in the fields in the countryside, or in other environments than the theatre during the years of the Cultural Revolution, they were not able to keep in physical form. *Jingju* is so demanding of physical suppleness and strength that, like ballet, it must be continuously practised. Jin Zongnai, a teacher at the Central Drama Academy, and former martial role (*wusheng*), was just one example of the many actors who were not able to return to performing and were lucky to find work in the classroom or backstage. Not only was a whole generation lost, since those actors who were too young before the Cultural Revolution to become masters were too inexperienced on returning to the stage, but, moreover, those older masters who did return to teaching were generally unable to provide the 'model' themselves any more. The whole system of training which depends upon the master doing and the student following was entirely disrupted.

Zhang Chunhua, a *wuchou* (comic-martial) role, of the China *jingju* Academy (he was born in 1925 or so, he is not sure) narrated this tale of the difficult process of applying to be taken on by a master:

> I went to the theatre each night the actor Ye Shengzhang performed, and watched him. Then, one night, after many months, I approached him. I said, 'I have the skills you need,

teach me!' Ye turned to me and asked, 'Have you studied my performances?' I said, 'I have.' He barely looked at me, and said, 'Are you lying, or is that the truth?' I told him it was the truth, and showed him some movements. He stopped me, 'Did I do it like that?' I answered, 'No.' Then he said, 'Go back and watch some more.'[63]

Full of disappointment, the young actor followed Ye's advice and practised Ye's special skill – holding one foot and jumping with the other leg through the space made by arm and foot, back and forth, over and over again (see Diagram 79). Then he returned to Ye, and said, 'If you jump once, I'll do it twice; if you do it three times in succession, I'll do it four times in succession.' And he promptly did and was accepted by the master.

Zhang has no special student, or apprentice under him. He is bitterly disappointed that no student he has yet encountered is fit to become his student. He says this is because if a student has the physical ability to perform, it is only because he has been trained like a sports gymnast.[64] The student seldom goes to the theatre to watch and learn and thus lacks any idea of the expression, motivation, or 'acting' that lies behind the physical skill of a part. If, on the other hand, the student has some talent in acting, he will have found a more profitable outlet for it than performing, such as merchandising. Zhang told me of the difficulty of arranging rehearsals around times when the actors are not at the market selling various goods. When they are at rehearsals they watch the clock not the master.

Zhang Chunhua maintains that no more schools or styles of performance will be created because the whole system of master-student apprenticeship has collapsed. There is no chance for a student to develop from the pattern given by the model (master). Instead, Zhang insists, all students follow what he calls the *xiangpai* (video school). The students are forced to watch video films of past performances and

---

[63] Author's field notes 1989.

[64] Visitors to the training classes at the China Theatre School are told with pride of the scientific approach to training. This includes a special diet and an employment policy which favours teachers who have been trained in sports and gymnastics.

either reproduce these verbatim – without the nuances of interpretation that would have been given them if they had had personal tuition, or simply give up – there is no awesome master to discipline, cajole, encourage. Top graduate Liu Zewei is seldom given the chance to perform, his friend, Xia Lang, has long ago left the acting profession (see Plate 4).

A modern performer stands on the *jingju* stage alone. He is shallow, empty of tradition, disembodied. The spectators who gathered to see certain actors perform and discussed the performance biography of each actor no longer come to the theatre – to see the same roles performed in the same empty (video school) way.

The lack of continuity that has killed the *jingju* performance tradition has also affected the *jingju* spectator tradition. It has become a theatre with no initiated (knowledged) spectators. In 1985, the audience was mostly composed of males over the age of fifty whose numbers seldom filled the theatre. The next generation of spectators were 'lost' in the Cultural Revolution when only eight revised, socialist plays were performed. During this time, the public was obliged to attend the theatre. The children of such spectators have not been encouraged back into the theatre despite, or because of, attempts to revive the old tradition by bringing back some of the old repertoire in a greatly revised form.

In 1986, the struggling *jingju* troupes were re-organised. Six troupes were condensed and refined – many actors found themselves without a company, though still ensured a wage, and thus without any means of performing. In order to increase the numbers of spectators attending performances, the troupes no longer moved from theatre to theatre to ensure that each locality was served with a variety of performances and companies. Instead, specific types of performance and troupes were allocated to specific theatres and a greater percentage of tickets were issued through the work units. The Jixiang (Lucky Omen) theatre, where I stood queuing for several hours in the bitter cold, now only presents short martial or acrobatic excerpts for the benefit of the brief visits of tourist delegations, uninitiated and hungry, on their way to and from the neighbouring Peking Duck restaurant.

Plate 4   The top graduate and the disenchanted: Liu Zewei (left), top graduate
1987, and his friend Xia Lang

2

Biao
(Appearance)

Mei Lanfang begins his performance of the concubine Yang Yuhuan in the play *Guifei zuijiu* (*The Favourite Concubine Becomes Intoxicated*) by singing 'bai jia!' ('the court is moving!') off stage in one continuous ascending and then descending tone before entering. The audience always applauds the technique required to sing this phrase. The percussion and spike fiddle play a short introduction, and Mei Lanfang steps on stage from left back[1] to thunderous applause.

The first element of the Chinese compound *biaoyan* (to perform) literally means 'to show', 'to display'. It is this that the spectators are applauding – Mei Lanfang's costume, make-up, carriage – the outward appearance of the role (see Plate 5). All aspects of the performer's appearance articulate the role, both singly and in combination with each other: the colour, shape, pattern and material of the costume, which have been the same for each role over many generations. All that the actor articulates about the role is contained in the very first moment of his appearance on stage. The point of entry embodies (in visual signs) all that will happen from now until the point of departure when Mei Lanfang exits. Thus, the point of entry is, for the spectator, a kind of re-cognitive process – who is this figure? what does the figure do in this play? If the performer has chosen appropriate elements of appearance, i.e. those that have been ratified by spectators over the centuries as those belonging to the role being played, he shall be commended. In the past, Zhang Chunhua recalled, some actors were booed off the

---

[1] Most entrances on the Chinese stage are from upstage left *shang changmen* (to mount the stage) as most exits from upstage right *xia changmen* (to descend from the stage).

Plate 5   Mei Lanfang as Yang Yuhuan in *Guifei zuijiu* (*The Favourite Concubine Becomes Intoxicated*)

Diagram 4   *fengguan* (phoenix head-dress)

stage at this point if their dress was incorrect. The actors have a saying 'chuan po bu chuan cuo' (wear tattered, but never the wrong costume).[2]

Dressing as empress

All the signs or elements of Yang Yuhuan's costume lead to the meaning 'empress'. Yang Yuhuan is not an empress, she is one of many concubines. But for the evening with the emperor she is *like* an empress. Mei Lanfang as Yang Yuhuan wears a *fengguan* (phoenix head-dress). It is constructed in the shape of a phoenix with the head and body at the centre and decorative pearls and beads extending out from it as wings and tail (see Diagram 4). The *fengguan* head-dress is worn on the *jingju* stage by concubines and imperial wives because the phoenix is a symbol of

[2] See also Mei Lanfang 1962: 49.

56

the emperor's spouse. The phoenix is often depicted with the dragon, which represents the emperor, to signify connubial bliss. The phoenix is commonly embroidered on ordinary wedding gowns to suggest that the bride is 'empress for a day'. The phoenix is also a symbol of female beauty. Yang Yuhuan's gown and cape are also decorated with embroidered phoenixes.

The symbol of the phoenix as emperor's spouse derives from the fact that the bird embodies various classification systems based on the number five. It is said to be a bird of five qualities: duty, virtue, ritually correct behaviour, humanity and reliability and this is echoed in the five colours of its feathers: red, white, black, green/blue and yellow which are also the colours of the five cardinal directions.[3] The phoenix is said to be five cubits in height, and the feathers of its tail like the five Pandean pipes, as its song which has five modulations.[4] The classification of elements into groups of five represents the four cardinal directions surrounding the centre which is an image of completeness, the world. The phoenix represents the idea of the empress near to the emperor who stands in a central position to control all the directions, to master the cosmos.

The phoenix head-dress also has five long tassels on each side which hang down the front of the costume. The tassels on Mei Lanfang's head-dress are yellow, the emperor's colour, suggesting proximity to the imperial throne. The etymology of the word *fenghuang* (phoenix) implies that the bird is the emperor of all birds. The second element of the compound depicts the character for 'emperor' encircled by the wind.

In the first half of the play, Mei Lanfang wears a *numang* (female *mang* robe) over a long white skirt (see Plate 4). The robe is scarlet which indicates a government or palace official of high status. It is embroidered with patterns of clouds (immortality, deity), peonies (beauty), phoenix (empress) and sun (proximity to the emperor) specially designed for the role Yang Yuhuan by Mei Lanfang.[5] Yang Yuhuan's gown has a deep border of water pattern completing the design at the bottom. Yang Yuhuan is like the empress in that she masters the cosmos from the clouds (heavens), to the seas (earth).

---

[3] Eberhard 1986: 236.   [4] Williams 1941, reprinted 1976: 324.
[5] *Zhongguo xiqu quyi cidian* 1983: 152.

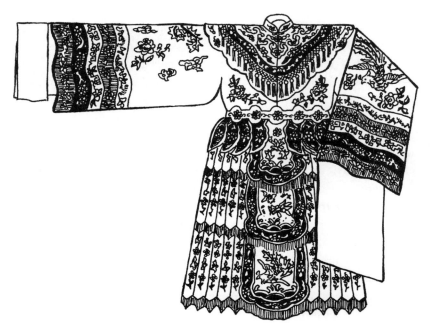

Diagram 5   *gongzhuang* (palace robe)

A short red cape, *yunjian*, with two flying phoenixes embroidered at each shoulder (the flying phoenix represents immortality) and fringed with yellow (imperial) tassels is worn over the gown. A *yudai* (jade belt) circles Mei Lanfang's waist, indicating the high rank of Yang Yuhuan at court.

In the second half of the play, Mei Lanfang wears a *gongzhuang* (palace robe) which is a multi-coloured gown whose lower part consists of three layers of five and ten ribbons in five different colours – red, white, black, green/blue and yellow. The sleeves of the gown are constructed of rings of the same colours, and the cape over the shoulders repeats the five colours in a phoenix design (see Diagram 5). This gown, like the *numang*, also represents an empress or concubine, but its system of imagery is different to that of the *numang*. The system of five indicating the empress represented in the *numang* by the phoenix, is signified here by the use of groups of five streamers of five colours to represent the five cardinal directions: red – south, white – west, black – north, green/blue – east and yellow – centre. The wearer of all five colours can master all the directions, which is equal to mastery of the cosmos. Thus, Yang Yuhuan is represented as the wife of an emperor. Contemporary actors presenting the role as, for example, Shen Xiaomei, have even changed the colour of the five tassels hanging on the head-dress at each side from plain yellow (the imperial colour) to the five cardinal colours (the imperial colours by analogy).

Both the *numang* and *gongzhuan* robes are fitted with *shuixiu* (water sleeves) typical of the *qingyi* role indicating a young to middle aged woman of good social status who is dignified and demure in her behaviour.

Mei Lanfang's teacher of the role, Lu Sanbao, wore *caiqiao* blocks (literally 'stamping, stepping out on tiptoe') in performing the role. These are wooden blocks attached to the feet of the actor in imitation of bound feet – a sign that the lady in question was of high rank (could do no menial work). Mei Lanfang learnt the technique of walking on such stilts:

> I remember that in my youth I would train on a long bench, and on the bench was a rectangular brick. I put the blocks on my feet, and stood on the brick for the length of time it took for one stick of incense to burn to the end. At first, I trembled with fear and it was very painful, my legs weren't used to it, so I couldn't do it for long, and wanted to get down. But as the days passed, the muscles in my back and legs were strengthened and I could stand firmly.
>
> In the winter, when there was ice on the ground, I practised weaponry skills and *pao yuanchang* (running the circle)[6] with the blocks on my feet. If you're not careful, you'll fall. But if you can run around on ice on blocks, when you are on stage without blocks, then you'll find it effortlessly easy. In everything you must progress from the difficult to the easy, from the bitter to the sweet.[7]

[6] The actor runs one circuit of the stage to indicate the passage of time or space. The *dan* actor must not show his feet, neither must the head and upper body appear to move. The actor must seem as if he is on wheels. In order to achieve this, the actor takes the strain of the movement of running into his knees. It is an extremely strenuous skill even without such blocks.

[7] Mei Lanfang and Xu Jichuan 1961, vol. 1: 32.

However, Mei did not use the technique for this role. The use of these blocks was associated, to an extent, with a vulgar style of performance. It was a custom apparently made popular by the actor Wei Zhangsheng in the late 1700s. It seems no coincidence that commentaries describing both him and his successor Chen Yinguan, relate wearing such stilts to a coarse style of performance. 'Chen was . . . considered lewd on the stage and loved to make bawdy jokes. He carried on Wei's custom of wearing false feet on the stage.'[8] On the contrary, actors such as Liu Qingrui (performing in the early 1800s) who were considered 'elegant and radiant and [endowed with a] loveliness without parallel' did not wear them. 'In demeanour he is dignified and correct and his voice is clear and beautiful . . . He is not used to false feet'.[9]

Thus each of the signs with which the performer chooses to bedeck himself has a highly complex structure of meaning. Even though the two costumes used to represent the role Yang Yuhuan are different in appearance (the *numang* is an outer robe, the *gongzhuan* for wearing inside the palace), the symbolism of each results in the same assessment of the concubine as empress, as beauty, as marital (legal) partner to the emperor, as a lady of rank, status and dignified behaviour. However, Yang Yuhuan is not even an empress for a day. All the signs in her appearance are ironic in the context of her real position. She is a mere concubine (servant), another concubine is favoured for her beauty over her this night, she is not the single, legal, marital partner of the emperor, she is not a lady of rank, she is not dignified, she becomes drunk.

The sheer outward appearance of the performer manifests various aspects of the role as well as the *content* of the piece he is about to play – the concubine is demoted and gets drunk. The appearance of the role embodies the point of departure (the outcome of the play – drunkenness, demotion) at the very moment of entry. Mei Lanfang covers his performing body with signs that every spectator can read and analyse as those that embody the *role* of Yang Yuhuan and *what happens to her*.

Dressing as exorcist
The *nuo* performer, or Fashi, may not dress as 'role' but he does dress in a way that signifies his position as mediator between the worlds of

---

[8] Mackerras 1972: 99.   [9] Ibid.: 137.

Diagram 6   *touza (nuo* performer's head-dress)

earth and heaven, and as controller of the cosmos. As exorcist, he must situate himself in this position in order to put the world back to rights after sickness, death or disaster and he does this by adopting various elements of cosmic symbolism into his outward appearance.

The *nuo* performer wears a bound crown *(touza)* made of hide with five sections or leaves (see Diagram 6). Each of the sections are decorated and, in the case of the Dejiang Tulaoshi, bear the characters for earth, sun, heaven, moon and water (from left to right). However, if the characters are read from the centre outwards, in both directions, the central sign, heaven, leads to sun (Yang – light) and moon (Yin – dark) which in turn lead to earth (Yin) and water (Yin). Symbolically, the head-dress represents heaven, the all-creative power at the top. From heaven stem the two principles of Yin and Yang (moon and sun) and from the two principles stem all other things, i.e. the mortal world – Yin (earth and water). The head of the Tulaoshi in this sense, is the object of mediation, for the head-dress is tied like a fan or crown whereby the furthest tip is the point of heaven, which is yet connected through the other four sections in rays fanning out, to the earthly body's head.

Over the long blue *qipao* (gown), still worn daily in this part of Guizhou, the *nuo* performer wears a *fayi* (see Diagram 7). The term *fa*, often misleadingly translated as 'magic', refers to a doctrine or philosophy, way of doing things. Thus the gown might be called a 'professional' robe. It is a loose fitting kimono-style robe. A similar gown is illustrated in De Groot,[10] where the author suggests that the structure

[10] De Groot 1982, vol. 6: 1264–7.

Diagram 7   *fayi* (*nuo* performer's gown)

of the gown – a square piece of material with a circle cut in the centre for the head, poncho-like, reflects the concept of heaven as round, earth as square. Thus the wearer of such a gown might be in a good position to mediate between the two. Of Daoist priests, who wear a similar gown, it is said, 'Above, he does not touch the heavens, below, he does not touch the earth.'[11]

The gown is embroidered with patterns of flowers in the colours of the five cardinal directions. The character *hua* (flower) puns with a similar character *hua* (to change, to transform). Thus the wearer of the gown is associated with the power of changing all the world from his position in the centre – he controls the world and is able to cause change in the pattern of the cosmos. This is the power of the exorcist.[12]

Under the gown, which is shorter at the front than at the back, the performer wears a blue cloth skirt with a white belt tied at the waist and five patterned streamers falling from the waist (see Diagram 8). The waist ribbons echo the symbolic significance of the five cardinal directions expressed in the dress and the head-dress, and possibly reflect the concept of soul banner identified in the ribbon board he carries (see Diagram 9 below).

Another exorcist figure, the historical exorcist known as the Fangxiangshi, was an official at court in the Zhou and Han dynasties.

[11] Schipper 1966: 93.
[12] See Berglund 1990: 72 for the relation of similar gowns to the Luo diagram.

Biao *(Appearance)*

Diagram 8   *nuo* performer's skirt

He was engaged in divining, healing practices, astronomy and exorcism. During the exorcism, like the *nuo* performer, he wore a specific costume, the essence of which – bearskin, gold eyes, red and black garments – is repeated in every historical record of the Fangxiangshi as exorcist:

> In his official function, he wears (over his head) a bearskin
> having four eyes of gold, and is clad in a black upper garment
> and a red lower garment. Grasping his lance and brandishing
> his shield, he leads the many officials to perform the seasonal
> Exorcism (*Nuo*), searching through the houses and driving out
> pestilences. When there is a great funeral, he goes in advance of
> the coffin, and upon its arrival at the tomb, when it is being
> inserted into the (burial) chamber, he strikes the four corners
> with his lance and expels the Fang Liang.[13]

The Fangxiangshi wears a black upper garment and a red lower garment, or a black outer garment and a red inner one.[14] The colours red and black are noted with emphasis in every passage concerning exorcism ritual:

> One day before the La there is the Great Exorcism . . . one
> hundred and twenty lads . . . aged ten to twelve . . . all wear
> red headcloths, black tunics . . .[15]

---

[13] *Zhouli*, trans. in Bodde 1975: 78–9. The Fang Liang is only one of many evil spirits exorcised by the Fangxiang.

[14] Hsu Tao-Ching 1985: 196.   [15] *Houhanshu* trans. in Bodde 1975: 81.

A youthful troupe, ten thousand of them, with red heads and black clothes . . .[16]

The principal term for red, *chi*, used in these passages also means 'to expel, to exorcise'. Daoist priests were known as 'redheads' if they specialised in exorcisms[17] just as the Fangxiangshi's assistants wore red turbans. In terms of Yin and Yang, red is the colour of Yang, of light, male, the creative principle. Red is thus the colour of the south, it represents the element fire, the fire-bird, and it is the source of life or creative power.[18] Red is also the colour of transition – it is the dominant colour of weddings, for example, where the bride compares herself to making the transition to the world of the dead:

> Everything remotely suggesting poverty and barrenness, death and decay is purged . . . She calls the groom's family *yinren* ('dead people' or 'shades') or even *gui* (ghosts). Their house is a *sangjia* (house in mourning) or *lanwu* (broken home). The head of the household, the father-in-law, is mocked as *Yanwang* (King of Hell).[19]

In both the marriage and funerary journey, the colour red keeps the bad things away. It is not, as generally assumed, used at weddings because it is a 'happy' colour. The colour red only 'brings happiness' in that it expels bad influences. Moreover, the colour red is vital in its exorcist function during the dangerous passage of transition between states – unmarried and married, alive and dead.

Black, on the other hand, is the opposite colour of Yin, of the dark and cold north. It represents the element water, and the creature tortoise. Black is the sign of the warrior – the Fangxiangshi's physical ability to combat evil demons.

---

[16] *Dongjingfu* trans. in Bodde 1975: 83.   [17] Eberhard 1986: 249.

[18] And the Communist Party; however, the colour red is seldom worn in Communist society. In 1984, the play *Jieshang liuxing hongqunzi* (*Red Skirt Fashion on the Streets*) by Ma Zhongjun and Xia Hongyuan was performed at the Beijing People's Theatre. The play concerns a female factory worker who dares to wear a red skirt and is at first vilified by her co-workers and then commended for stepping out of the drab uniform colours of the day.

[19] Blake 1978: 13.

In the Song dynasty (AD 960–1279) the original Yin-Yang symbol was recorded for the first time in the colours red and black, for the combination of these two colours represents the idea of opposites in balance, of universal harmony. In the combination of red and black, therefore, the opposites north and south, water and fire, land animal and bird, winter and summer, death and life are represented in a diagram of continuous exchange and flow.

The Fangxiangshi wears a mask with four golden (metal) eyes. Gold represents the element 'metal' for the Chinese term *jin* can mean either gold or metal. Metal, in turn, is associated with the knife, with the annual harvest in autumn, the time of approaching death (it was the period of execution in ancient China). Thus it is associated with death, with killing, echoed in the large *ge* knife-axe with which the Fangxiangshi executes evil demons. Because of its colour, gold is also associated with yellow, the colour of the centre and the all-powerful god-emperor who is positioned there. Gold represents deity, the power of one who controls and recreates the cosmos. Gold also provides the link between the pair of earthly opposites red and black. Instead of representing all the colours of the directions, the Fangxiangshi is dressed in colours of two extremes, balanced by one centre. Thus the Fangxiangshi is neither all Yin nor all Yang, he combines elements of both, is the mediator between extremes, both worlds, just as the *nuo* performer positions himself in the centre of the cosmos by adopting all the cardinal colours in his appearance to manifest the fact that he can regulate and control the cosmos.

The same elements of dress that signify 'exorcist' can be seen in a paper figure of the exorcist, the Kailushen (god who opens the way) who leads the burial procession to the grave in modern China:

> The pavilion contains an image, composed of a hollow frame of bamboo splints covered with variegated paper. This is never more than three quarters of a metre high . . . Its appearance is, according to Chinese conceptions, exceedingly terrific and therefore well fitted to strike the whole host of evil spirits with terror. The face, of a blood-red colour, has two large eyes, from which black, protruding eyeballs cast about terrible looks; a third eye stands perpendicular in the middle of the forehead,

and a long purple beard of woollen threads heightens the intimidating aspect. The dress is that of a warrior . . . A long red gown hangs down from underneath the armour . . .[20]

The paper exorcist is comprised of elements which are red, black and variegated (patterned, or the five colours), representing the power of the figure to cleanse the way for the procession in the same way as the *nuo* performer or the Fangxiangshi. This figure also wears full armour, representing the military skill with which he can kill evil spirits.

Another exorcist figure, this time from *jingju*, the figure Zhong Kui, also adopts elements that have been identified as belonging to the exorcist both in the *nuo* performer and the ancient Fangxiangshi. The role Zhong Kui is interpreted in the northern style as a warrior-exorcist. In the southern style, Zhong Kui is presented as the scholar exorcist, one who has the power to exorcise because he is imbued with the classics:

> A learned man means a man imbued with the classical doctrine which keeps mankind in the path of the normality, correctness or rectitude of the Dao . . . so that he cannot but exercise a contrary and destructive influence upon everything which is *xie* or abnormal, incorrect and bad . . .[21]

However, whether dressed as the northern style warrior or the southern style scholar, the figure of Zhong Kui is bound to the colour system of red and black associated with the Fangxiangshi. Zhong Kui is a *hualian* (painted face) role, generally presented with a painted face based on a style known as the *sankuai war* (tri-part tile)[22] face. The tri-part tile pattern divides the face into three areas – the two cheeks and the forehead. It has the effect of making the face extremely broad and large. These dominant three areas are painted crimson – a colour which the *jingju* masters say represents the qualities of loyalty and honesty, but which also is the colour of exorcism.

The northern style of figure (warrior-exorcist) wears a martial

---

[20] De Groot 1982, vol. 1: 160.   [21] Ibid., vol. 6: 1153.

[22] The word *war* literally means 'tile'. However, it also implies 'made of baked clay' as tiles are, i.e. earthenware. Does this indicate that this style referred to another, coarser technique of simply smearing the face with mud?

style *mang* (gown) in red and black. This Zhong Kui (warrior style) wears a martial-style hat known as the *bawang kui* (overlord's helmet) also known as the 'reverse tassel hat' It has a red tassel hanging down at the back and it is worn by warrior roles, confirming that this interpretation of Zhong Kui is as a martial role, *wusheng*. Over this gown, Zhong Kui wears a martial sash which is tied in front so that the two ends hang over one another to ankle level at the front. There is a repertoire of martial movements solely concerned with performing with such a sash, as kicking it with the foot and catching the end in one hand, and so on.

The southern-style Zhong Kui (scholar-exorcist) wears a civil *mang* or gown like that worn by scholars or officials which is also red, with a black jade belt. Zhong Kui the scholar-exorcist does not wear a martial hat, but one known as the Pan Guan hat. Pan Guan is, along with Zhong Kui, one of the most important Daoist gods of exorcism. He is considered to be responsible for life in the underworld. In wearing a Pan Guan style of hat, the southerners declare Zhong Kui to be in the tradition of Daoist exorcists. Zhong Kui also wears a *shiliu* (pomegranate flower) in his beard. The pomegranate is a symbol of fertility, creativity, for it is full of *zi*, (seeds/children) and the term for pomegranate, *shiliu*, puns with *shiliu* meaning 'the generations shall continue forever'. The exorcist Zhong Kui is, thus, simultaneously a bringer of new life. Furthermore, when a pomegranate bursts open, it is said to resemble a grinning/gaping mouth full of teeth – an image of exorcism as a laughing (unifying) and consuming (regenerating) mouth, explored in detail in chapter seven.

Instead of the warrior sash of the northern style, the southern Zhong Kui (scholar-exorcist) wears a *yudai* (jade belt). It is made of stiffened silk over a firm hoop which has a circumference a great deal larger than the actor, making it stand out from the costume. The jade belt is worn by scholar officials emphasising Zhong Kui's rank as the best scholar in the land – the best exorcist in the land.

Just as the two different costumes of Yang Yuhuan, one of phoenixes (*numang*) and one of the five cardinal orientations (*gongzhuang*), resulted in the same meaning – empress, so the two different representations of the role Zhong Kui, martial and scholarly, result in the same interpretation – exorcist (see Plate 6).

Plate 6   Li Huiliang as the exorcist Zhong Kui

Dressing as ancestor

In the *nuo* theatre, the Fashi, Duangong or Tulaoshi, always appears on stage with a *paidai* (ribbon board), a hollow piece of wood with thirty-six coloured and patterned streamers or ribbons attached to it (see Diagram 9).[23] During certain parts of the performance, it is held in the hand. At other times, it is balanced over the shoulder of the performer. The *paidai* ribbons are made in the five cardinal colours and may be decorated with flowers, or abstract designs, but they must be decorated, for the term *hua* (flowered, or patterned) is a pun on the term meaning 'changes'. The Fashi is someone who can control the five cardinal directions and make changes in the cosmos. Similar multi-coloured streamers are used in burial rites, where the soul of the deceased is called into a streamer, known as the soul banner, on the way to the grave before it comes to its final resting place in the ancestral

[23] In other forms of *nuo*, it has a different name. In Xiangxi, Hunan province for example, it is called a *liujin* (flowing skeins, strips of cloth) and consists of twenty-four or twenty-six strips in pairs. See *Xiangxi nuowenhua zhi mi* 1991: 302–3.

68

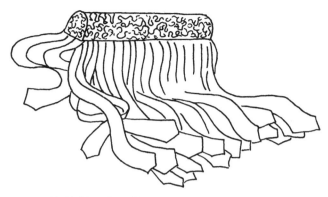

Diagram 9   *paidai* (ribbon board)

tablet.[24] The soul banner used at funerals bears the name of the deceased on it (to mark the banner for the soul as its own) and must be carried by a scholar or person of rank in the funeral procession because scholars are natural exorcists. In performance, each actor has a ribbon board and each performer is a kind of *wu* who can call upon, or communicate with, the 'spirits' of the other world. The analogy of the soul banner seems to suggest that the ribbons of the ribbon board are the soul banners of the performer's ancestors – that the performers are invested with the presence of the ancestors. Indeed, the ribbon boards are passed down from each performer to his son and represent the spirit of all the performers in the ancestral clan before him. Before each performance event, the Fashi calls the presence of his own master(s) or predecessor(s) into his body, and this is manifested by the flowing ribbons of the *paidai*.

In Buddhist terms, the soul banner is thought to contain the souls of various gods or spirits. In rites used to save souls in Fujian at the turn of the century, De Groot describes a similar Buddhist ribbon board and identifies the colour system not only with the cardinal directions, but also with a particular Buddha. 'Thanks to the streamers, the spirit of each of the six mighty saints is present . . . and may exert its beneficial influence.'[25]

The nuo performer stands on stage as the representative of the

---

[24] De Groot 1982, vol. I: 175–7.   [25] Ibid.: 123.

69

ancestral clan and all the ancestors that have gone before him right back to the original ancestor/creator. He is a direct descendant of the clan, called by the same name and, through the *paidai*, he carries the visual/physical sign of those ancestors' presences just as any contemporary *jingju* actor adopts the visual signs of the role and its past interpreters in his costume and make-up.

Certain aspects of the historical exorcist's, the Fangxiangshi's, appearance also suggest various mythical figures which have to do with original ancestors, or original creators of the world. Thus, the Fangxiangshi, like the *nuo* performer, probably physically manifested signs of the presence of such ancestors in his appearance.

The Fangxiangshi is described in the *Zhouli* as 'wearing' a bearskin.[26] Later documents from the Sui and Tang dynastic histories, however, record that the bearskin was worn over the head and as a kind of mask.[27] The Fangxiangshi is described as a head and face covered in bearskin. The only features described are his four gold eyes. Hairiness over the human face suggests the concept of a body which is part-man, part-beast. Like the werewolf, the exorcist performer is viewed as someone who is not all human, but embodies some animal (spiritual/ancestor) parts. Moreover, the beast element has particular connotations in the context of exorcism, for the beast is seen as a destroying, consuming power. The mythology of the bear, related to three creative figures, provides some clues as to the possible identity(ies) of the ancestor(s) represented by the Fangxiangshi exorcist.

The first, Yu the Great, is a mythological figure who was given a special document known as the Luo diagram, inscribed on the back of a tortoise which rose out of the Luo River. With it he could stop the great flood and create the world. The Luo diagram is a grid of nine cells arranged in three rows of three, discussed in detail in chapters three and seven. Yu's father was known by the sign for bear, and legend recounts that Yu himself turned into a bear in order to divide land from the seas and create the world. Yu told his wife to bring him food at the sound of the drum. He changed himself into the form of a bear and, as

[26] See Hopkins 1943: 111–17 for one approach to the meaning of the bearskin.

[27] Granet 1959: 301 n. 2.

he danced the Luo diagram by hopping and dancing from stone to stone, he accidentally knocked the drum. His wife approached, saw him in his changed form, and was turned to stone.[28]

The Fangxiang is linked to Yu the Great by the bearskin which he wears over his face. Moreover, the Fangxiangshi carries out the exorcism by piercing his lance in the four cardinal directions inside the tomb, in a similar leaping and hopping act of creation as that carried out by Yu in his metamorphosis as bear.

The second, concerning another legendary figure known as Chi You has also been linked to the Fangxiangshi through the use of the bearskin. Legend recounts that Chi You was a rebel who challenged the authority of the Yellow Emperor. There ensued a terrible cosmic battle during which a drought, sent by the Yellow Emperor, was quashed by floods sent by Chi You. Chi You came to be regarded as a god of rain and is depicted as a dragon (water-spouting not fire-puffing), or snake. In his battle with the Yellow Emperor, Chi You was ultimately defeated and the blood shed in the battle flowed a hundred *li*.[29] Thus Chi You can command cosmic powers, and he is associated with the bringing of rain – in agricultural terms, a fertility god (by implication a god of creation, like Yu). The concept of Chi You as creator also derives from the myth that he was the inventor of metallurgy, or metal casting for weaponry. The myth recounts that:

> Huangdi, after deliberating with Bo Gao, cultivated the teaching (of virtue) for ten years, and then the mountain of Gelu opened up and water came forth and metal (copper) followed it; Chi You took it and worked it and made the *ji* lances of Yonghu and the dagger axes of Rui.[30]

Yet again, the exorcist figure is composed of symbols of death and execution parallel to those of creation and fertility (harvest). In pictorial representation, Chi You is shown with five weapons – spear, dagger, sword, knife, bow and arrow or crossbow.[31] However, recent archaeological discoveries have found images of Chi You with the five weapons

---

[28] Hentze 1941: 20.   [29] Karlgren 1946: 283.

[30] Ibid.

[31] The system of five indicates his power in the cosmos, echoing the systems of five colours, etc. examined above.

in tombs not as the usual reptilian (water-spouting – fertility) figure, but as a 'roly-poly bear-like figure'.[32] The tomb sculptures date from the Han dynasty (when there was a revival of the Chi You cult) and they are positioned on the north wall of the tomb, facing south, over the entrance. The figure of Chi You is represented as exorcist and protector who prevents or terrifies evil away from entering the tomb. Moreover, the conception of Chi You as bear-like, suggests that he is perceived as a figure who shall come back to life out of the darkness of the cave-tomb (the bear hibernates over winter). He is the promise of new life, a figure of new creation.[33] The Fangxiangshi, with his bearskin, shares some elements of the Chi You figure for both operate as exorcists in the tomb. Masks or busts of the Fangxiangshi or Chi You were positioned over the entrance of the tomb to protect the deceased from evil spirits.

And thirdly, the Fangxiangshi may be related, through his bearskin, to a third legendary figure, the Taotie. The Taotie is a mythological figure represented on ritual and mortuary food vessels. The figure is some kind of animal of prey, sometimes tiger-like, ram-like or owl-like,[34] with a gaping mouth and two protruding fangs. The Taotie is often considered simply as a glutton, one who eats or consumes sacrificial offerings in the vessels on which he is depicted. However, Hentze proposes that the Taotie is a kind of regenerative beast as well. In gulping down the old, the dead, for example, the Taotie also spits out the new. The figure is often depicted with a child, man, or cicada (an insect which was thought to regenerate spontaneously from the earth) in his jaws. The figure of the Taotie is also found over the entrances to tombs in a similar position to the mask of Chi You or Fangxiangshi. The

---

[32] Bodde 1975: 122 and Liu Mingshu 1942: 341–65.

[33] Some scholars have gone so far as to connect the Fangxiangshi directly to Chi You and others maintain that Chi You is the original myth behind *nuo* theatre with its twelve animal masks. See Chen Duo 1989: 19–26, Qian Yi 1990 and Yu Yi 1990. Some of the arguments concerning the myth of Chi You can be found in Bodde 1975: 120, Gu Poguang 1990, Cheng Te-k'un 1958: 45–54. For some depictions of Chi You as a bear or tiger-like figure, see Finsterbusch 1966 and 1971, vols. 1 and 2, especially plate 78: 294, plate 97: 329c and 329d, plate 159: 601 and plate 243: 16.

[34] Berglund suggests the Taotie is a tortoise, 1990: 200–21.

image seems to suggest that the deceased shall arise again *literally* through the jaws of the Taotie at the entrance to the tomb into the new world of death.[35]

The myth of the Taotie indicates that the concept of bear can and should be extended to all kinds of hunting animals in general. The presence of hair, particularly facial hair, suggests a hunting animal which has the power to re-create out of destruction or even by destruction. Moreover, that destruction is carried out through the mouth – by eating or consuming. The example of the Fangxiangshi's exorcism shows the same image of tearing apart and consuming in order to cleanse, bring in (spit out) the new year:

> Then the Palace Attendants of the Yellow Gates start a chant in which the troupe joins: 'Jiazuo devour the baneful! Feiwei devour the tigers! Xiongbo devour the Mei! Tengjian devour the inauspicious! Lanzhu devour calamities! Boqi devour dreams! Qiangliang and Ziming, together devour those who, having suffered execution with public exposure, now cling to the living! Weisui devour visions! Cuoduan devour giants! Qiongqi and Tenggen together devour the gu poisons! May all these twelve spirits drive away the evil and the baneful. Let them roast your bodies, break your spines and joints, tear off your flesh, pull out your lungs and entrails. If you do not leave at once, those who stay behind will become their food.[36]

The term translated here as 'devour' is the Chinese word *shi* meaning not only 'to consume' but also 'food, rice'. In this way, the exorcism is closely linked to the idea of nutrition in the sense of continuation, growth, just as the imagery of rice operates in ancestor and *nuo* initiation rituals described in chapter one. One generation feeds on the last. In general performance terms, such metaphorical endonecrophagy (eating the ancestor) is merely the expression of the fact that the performer *contains* the presence of the ancestors within him.

The sign 'bearskin' – indicating the power of the exorcist to

---

[35] On the possible relation between the Fangxiangshi and the Taotie see Zhou Huawu 1991.

[36] *Houhanshu* trans. in Bodde 1975: 81.

consume and regenerate worn by the Fangxiangshi – is also adopted by the *jingju* exorcist figure Zhong Kui, who wears a full *rankou* black beard with extra tufts of hair at the corners of the mouth, the moustache and the eyebrows, which no other role in the *jingju* has. Thus, the exorcist, whether Fangxiangshi, Zhong Kui or Chi You is associated through the sign 'hair' with at least three mythological figures who, in turn, are associated with original creation. There is a case to be made that the Fangxiangshi, like the *nuo* performer, is 'ancestor dressing' – he adopts elements of, for example, Yu, Chi You or Taotie, in order to have the appearance of – embody – ancestor/creators in order to call their presences (powers) into the exorcism in hand. The exorcist Fangxiangshi, with his full head or face-covering of bear-skin is associated, through these ancestral/creative myths, with the idea of one who consumes in order to recreate. The performer's body is represented as the *locus* of the creative principle. The performer consumes the ancestral/creative powers in order to give them anew.

The de-(re)formed body

The human performers in the examples above embody certain traditions that articulate the presence of various ancestors and the destructive/creative powers of exorcism when they take to the stage. The manufactured performance artefact, the puppet, is similarly conceived as merely the present embodiment of certain traditions or lines of ancestry. In this, the human body and the manufactured body are identical. Each calls the tradition of exorcists/performers into its body for the duration of the performance, each is the temporary locus (reincarnation) of traditions of creation and exorcism.

In Taiwan and parts of Fujian, the marionettes are known by the marionette troupes as *zun wangzi* (honourable diseased person) rather than by the terms meaning either string puppet (*tixian kuilei*), rod and string puppet (*zhangxian kuilei*) or simply, puppet (*ouren, kuilei, muou*). The term *wangzi* deserves some attention, for according to ancient documents, the word was used to describe the elderly and/or infirm who were used as sacrificial victims to move the gods to pity in the case of drought, for example, and thus to restore harmony on earth.

Several sources mention the use of *wang* as sacrificial victims. The *Liji* records a certain Prince of Lu who wanted to offer up *wang* in

639 BC and the same tale is also mentioned in the work *Zuozhuan*.[37]
The term *wang* in the following source links the *wangzi* to the *wu*:

> In a year of drought, the ruler Mu (BC 409–377) called Xian Zi
> and asked him as follows,
> 'Heaven has not sent down any rain for a long time; I will expose
> some *wang* to the sun, do you agree?'
> 'Exposing such unsound children of men in the sun . . . when
> Heaven does not give rain is an act of cruelty . . .'
> 'Well then, I will expose some *wu*, has this your approval?'
> . . .
> 'Heaven does not give rain, do you expect rain from silly
> wives?'[38]

De Groot comments,

> Those 'infirm or unsound' *wang* were non-descript individuals,
> evidently placed on a line with *wu*, perhaps queer hags or
> bedlams, deformed beings, idiotic or crazy, or nervously
> afflicted or ascribed to possession . . .

And continues with a quotation from a commentary on the above passage by Jing Kangqing from 2 AD,

> Mu would expose the *wang* to the sun in the expectation that
> Heaven would compassionate them [sic] . . . and as the *wu*
> had received a *shen* [spirit] into themselves, Heaven,
> compassionating the latter, would send down rain.[39]

In the *Zuozhuan*, the gloss states that *wang* are 'personnes émaciées, le
visage est tourné vers le Ciel et qu'un diction dit que le Ciel, par pitié
pour elles, ne veut pas faire tomber la pluie dans leur nez'.[40] Furthermore, the *Cihai* dictionary[41] lists the *Lushi chunqiu jiushu* as explaining, 'all *wang* are people with bent backs' while the commentator Gao
Xiu notes, '*wang* have a chest that sticks out and they turn their faces
upwards in sickness'. The same dictionary reports a passage from the

---

[37] Granet 1959: 315 n. 3.　　[38] *Liezi*, trans. in De Groot 1982, vol. 6: 1193.
[39] De Groot 1982, vol. 6: 1194.　　[40] Granet 1959: 316.
[41] *Cihai* 1979: 1514.

Mingli that *wang* are 'blind, bald people with bent backs' and from the *Qie jingyinyi* that *wang* are 'weak'.[42]

Here, the very shape of a body defines its performative function. The infirm or abnormal body is perceived as a body which is marked by some external, invisible power or spirit. Such imperfect bodies contain that spirit – are already in a position of mediation between this world and the world of spirits. Not only is the marionette figure seen to be a figure which is imperfect (not of this world – its feet do not touch the ground, it moves stiffly, for example) but also the exorcist – the one who cleanses, who re-orders the cosmos into harmony is imperfect, not wholly human. Zhong Kui, for example, has a hunched back, a cleft hand and a slight limp. In *jingju*, the performer of Zhong Kui wears a bundle of padding over the buttocks and another over one shoulder under his costume. This gives him a bustle-like protrusion at the back and a hunchback, both of which distort the movements he makes on stage from the patterns of movement dictated by the conventions of *jingju*.

Several of the mythical exorcist/creative figures examined above are associated with the idea of a body which is crippled, hunchbacked or other in some way. Yu the Great hopped on one foot to recreate the world after the flood, and the same kind of dance was repeated by the one-legged, mythological exorcist figure Gui, the master of music. Gui 'chef de la musique royale, savait en touchant les pierres sonores, faire danser à l'avis les cent animaux'.[43] The radical of the character *wang* carries the meaning of those who are 'épuisées, qui trâinent la jambe'[44] and even pictorially seems to represent the dragging foot (see Diagram 10). Chi You, the fertility god/exorcist/creator associated with the Fangxiangshi, contains an indication of the abnormal (different) body in the etymology of his name. The second element of his name could imply 'cripple' (see also Diagram 11): 'You . . . (premier, extraordinaire) équivaut à *guai* (prodige), et contient l'idée de "néfaste". On admet qu'il ne se distingue guère du caractère *wang* et tous deux donnent l'idée d'une marche lente et trâinante . . .'[45] The same element describing the dragged foot in the name Chi You is also present in the character Kui

---

[42] Schafer 1951: 130–84.   [43] Granet 1959: 505, 506 n. 2.
[44] Ibid.: 551.   [45] Ibid.: 357 n. 1.

Diagram 10 a   The dragging foot radical

b   The character *wang*

Diagram 11   The character *you* (in the name Chi You)

Diagram 12   The character *kui* (in the name Zhong Kui)

Diagram 13   The character *kui* (large) used for marionette

used for the exorcist figure Zhong Kui who performs on the *jingju* stage (see Diagram 12). The hopping, stamping, dragging and jolting movements of the feet are discussed more fully in chapter six. The second element in the character *wang* used for the marionettes indicates 'king'. The character *you* used in the name of Chi You may mean 'special', 'particular'. The second element of the character *kui* used in the name of Zhong Kui is 'head'. All three terms indicate a sense of a limping, hopping foot (deformed) and some extra special (god-like) quality – a physical paradox explored fully in chapter seven. From these examples, it is clear that the performing body is marked as a body which is other.

Not only body shape, but also body size is an important signifier of the quality 'exorcist'. The more usual collective term for puppets (sometimes used, however, specifically for marionettes) *kuilei*, indicates a body, like the *wangzi*, which is in some way de-(re)formed. Pictorially it is composed of the 'standing man' radical together with the element meaning spirit (see Diagram 13 and note the 'dragged leg' in the element meaning spirit). The *Shuowen* dictionary interprets the compound *kui* as meaning 'huge'. Over-large size suggests that the exorcist/performer is non-human (more than human). De Groot describes a statue of a Kailushen, at the head of a funeral procession:

> In some instances its size is enormous. It is then often wheeled along the road on an open cart, no pavilion being large enough to contain it. When so big, it is usually stuffed with the heart, the liver, the paunch and other intestines of a pig. In Java, where the Chinese inhabitants are nearly all descended from natives of south-eastern Fujian, there are frequently to be seen Kailushen higher than the roofs of two-storied houses; but in most provinces of the empire such gigantic figures cannot be used, because the streets are too narrow.[46]

One of the few sources which directly interprets *kui* as noun, the work *Xunzi* says, '*Kui* is [something which is] almighty and [which] has nothing to fear from heaven or earth.'[47] The *kuilei* is something which is large, unpleasant to look at, and can move between the two worlds of heaven and earth.

The same importance laid on size, or physique, is apparent in the *nuo* theatre where, among the members of the clan who perform, certain men are given certain roles according to their physical stature. In Guizhou province, Anshun county, the company who perform *dixi* in Taoguan village have chosen Ma Guochang to perform the part of Guan Yu (another important martial-exorcist roles). Ma is 1.80 metres tall – head and shoulders above the rest of his colleagues. At a performance celebrating the lunar New Year in 1990, Ma did not perform but, as the most important actor in the troupe, was obliged to join me among the spectators[48] to help me interpret the performance. One

---

[46] De Groot 1982, vol. 1: 160–1.   [47] *Xunzi*, chapter *Xing e*.

[48] The spectators at a *nuo* performance, which generally takes place on an open piece of ground, give only vague attention to the performance (which may last several days to a fortnight) except where the action is particularly exciting. Most villagers do not even need to attend to know that a replacement Guan Yu is not satisfactory: only if the correct actions are carried out in the correct way by the correct person is the performance deemed good and effective – otherwise it is not. A *nuo* performance does not *need* the community to witness it.

spectator later told me that he was afraid the performance was not as effective as in past years when Ma performed, for his replacement was too small to be taken seriously by the gods.

A third element of the composite meaning 'exorcist' alongside body shape and body size is the quality 'ugliness'. The second component of the term for puppet, *lei*, is given in the *Shuowen* dictionary to mean 'dead, withered'. A later dictionary, the *Jiankang zidian*, confirms this interpretation of *lei* explaining it as something which is 'foul, or disintegrated in appearance' and the *Liji* mentions '*lei* is something which looks as ugly as the dead'. The compound term for puppets, *kuilei*, thus seems to contain the idea of something which is not only huge, it is also horrid, ugly, foul to behold and associated with death.

The annual exorcism carried out at court in the Song shows that certain performers were chosen for their huge and ugly appearance to play certain exorcist roles:

> The Deputy of the Court Entertainment Bureau, Meng Jingchu was big and strong in physique, and he dressed up as a general in a full-length brass-plate armour gilded with gold . . . Nan Hetu, of the Court Entertainment Bureau, ugly and repugnant, big and fat, dressed up as the Judgement Official of Hell.[49]

Ugliness (like the dead – a body from the other world) is the sign of an exorcist. Not only is the role Zhong Kui hunchback, hairy and limping, but the right hand wears the sleeve tightly bound at the wrist of the right hand, while the left hand wears the long water sleeve. Some say that this is to show that Zhong Kui has the power to 'tie up' the evil demons, just as his hand is tightly bound, others maintain that the bound hand hides a magical sixth finger which must be tied up out of sight. The function of the opposition between bound and loose hand, just as the opposition between scholar/warrior and hunchback/cripple, however, points to Zhong Kui as an exorcist composed of signs meaning one who is different, other, ugly and terrifying.

The terrifying aspect of the exorcist body returns, through the image of the bearskin, to the concept of the exorcist as part-man, part-beast of prey, a consuming, regenerative figure. The Han dynasty

---

[49] Idema and West 1982: 122.

commentator Zheng Xuan recorded that the effect of the bearskin worn by the Fangxiang was to stir fear in those who beheld him: 'The bearskin is to frighten and chase off evil spirits like today's *qitou*.'[50] The *qitou* or *qishou* was a figurine of a demon-eating, or demon-conquering, mythological spirit put inside the tomb next to the corpse in order to protect it from evil demons. The literal meaning of *qitou* is 'ugly head'. The Fangxiangshi in his bearskin was also from an 'other' world, he was part-man, part-beast.

The character for *qi* (ugly) is closely related to the character *gui* meaning spirit. It is formed out of the character *gui* (spirit) with the sound marker *qi* (see Diagram 14). Guo Moruo determines the *qi* phoneme as having the meaning 'eyes', 'face' and concludes that *qi* depicts a man wearing a mask.[51] Shen Chien-shih discusses the term *gui* (spirit) in relation to head and beast, suggesting that the top element of the *gui* character pictorially represents beast.[52] In this case, the character *gui*, meaning spirit, is composed of a beast's head and a limping foot. Combining the two ideas, the character *qitou* or ugly head conveys the idea of a beast head, limping foot and masked face. This confirms the importance of the relation between beast and man in the exorcism and death (regeneration) rituals. The bearskin of the Fangxiangshi, the beard of Zhong Kui both indicate the fact that these figures are part man, part beast. Furthermore, etymologically, there is a strong association between words such as *gui* (spirit), *qitou* or mask, in the sense of awesome, frightening: 'From the character *gui*, we have as derivatives: *wei* "fear", which has the head of a *gui* and the claws of a *hu* "tiger"; *kui* "huge", from which is derived *guai* "monstrous" and *kui* "large".'[53] A similar association between the concepts of *gui* (spirit) and *qitou* (ugly head, mask) is made by Sun Kaidi in his work on Chinese puppets when he derives the term for puppets *kuilei* out of the term *kui* meaning 'ugly, terrifying, huge'. Sun pursues the idea directly to the Fangxiangshi and proposes the thesis that the *qitou*, Fangxiangshi and

[50] Zheng Xuan, commentary to the *Zhou li*: 31/6b–71 Biot 2: 225.
[51] Guo Moruo, *Puci tongzuan kaoshi zhengfa*, plate 498.
[52] Shen Chien-shih 1936–7: 4.
[53] Ibid. Shen also relates the term *chou* (ugly) to *gui*. See chapter seven below for a consideration of the function of the grotesque in performance.

The character *gui* (spirit)   the sound marker *qi* (mask?)

= the character *qi* (used in *qitou*, ugly head)

Diagram 14   Constructing the character *qi* for *qitou* (ugly head)

kuilei marionettes are one and the same phenomenon.[54] Whether or not this is so, these three performing bodies share specific features associated with the exorcist: ugliness, huge size, beast-like, terrifying appearance.

In sum, these various performing and exorcist figures are etymologically related to the concept of 'otherness'. The character *gui* (spirit) can also be linked to another of the performing bodies discussed in this work in chapter five, the mortuary figure. Such a link further highlights the concept of the performing/exorcist body as 'other'. An etymological examination shows the close relation of three characters *gui* (spirit) *wei* (fearsome) and *yu* (anthropoid beast).

> These three characters originally stood for one and the same
> thing . . . *Yu* is explained as some animal that resembles the
> *gui*; *wei* is given as a hybrid character with a gui's head and
> a tiger's claw, whose monstrous appearance is calculated
> to inspire 'fear' and 'abhorrence', and *gui*, though a clear
> pictogram, is interpreted only in its derivative sense of
> 'ghost' or 'spirit'.[55]

[54] Sun Kaidi 1952.   [55] Shen Chien-shih 1936–7: 5.

Diagram 15 a   The character *yu*   b   The character *ou* (effigy)
(anthropoid)

The first term introduced here, *yu*, is then more closely examined:

> The inventors of characters were wont to assign to the genus or
> family *yu* all creatures of abnormal or singular appearance . . .
> Similarly, most of the animals mentioned in the *Erya* under
> *yu* are unusual and rare.
>
> The *Yu* looks like a *Mi* monkey but is larger. It has red eyes and a
> long tail . . .
>
> Guo Pu says the *Yu* looks like a *Mi*. It is clear that the *Yu* is not
> an ape. For *Yu* is a general term applicable to all anthropoid
> animals. As monkeys and apes have quasi-human
> characteristics, they may have been designated as *Yus*.[56]

The term *yu* is thus applied to strange-looking animals, ape-like creatures and then, by extension, to *any* anthropoid animal. The term *yu*
describes a beast which is part-man or man-like. This second aspect of
the term is confirmed in the similarly written character *ou* meaning
'counterpart, effigy' (see Diagram 15). Indeed, it appears the two terms
were interchangeable: 'A wooden idol or effigy *muou* may also be
called a *muyu* as, for instance in the Feng Shan section of the *Shiji*, the
wooden image of a dragon is called *muou long*.'[57] The correlation of the
two terms *yu* and *ou* is further suggested by the *Shuowen* dictionary
which gives the explanation of the term *yong* (mortuary figure) as 'an
effigy [*ou*] of a man'. Thus, the mortuary figure is conceived as an effigy,
or man-like artefact: 'The *Shiji suoyin* says "*ou* should be read *yu*, but
it may also be read *ou*". The *Shiji zhengyi* explains *ou* as a "mate or
counterpart, because it is a clay or wooden man which has taken its

---

[56] Ibid.: 6.   [57] Ibid.

form from a real man".[58] The term *ou* is used today to describe puppets, usually hand puppets (glove puppets) rather than mortuary figures,
but the example shows there is a strong identification between the
term *yu* (anthropoid) and *ou* (effigy, man-like) just as the other term
used to describe puppets, *kuilei*, is etymologically related to a group of
words meaning 'spirit', 'awesome', 'ugly head', 'dragged foot'.

The ugly head, or *qitou*, also belongs to the same group of related
terms. In his work on ancient burial artefacts, Luo Zhenyu defines the
qitou as a separate category of six kinds of mortuary figure including
armoured warriors, eunuchs, dwarfs, musicians and dancers.[59] However,
Luo's classification of burial figures actually presents closely related
variations of one phenomenon. The burial figure, whether dwarf, eunuch, entertainer/performer was something different, something other.
Even the 'armoured warrior' is strongly associated with the concept of
other body, in this case as part-man, part-beast. The Chinese armour
kao consists of scale-like pieces fitted together slightly overlapping
each other, like a fish or some kind of reptile. The 'armoured warrior'
burial figure is frequently presented with a beast's head.[60]

The close relation between anthropoid (part-man, part-beast)
and man-like in the form of an idol or statue is unmistakable and supports the supposition that the performative body is likewise either
part-man, part-beast (the Fangxiangshi with his bearskin covering) or
man-like (puppet) but absolutely *not* man pure. The raw material for (at
least exorcist) performance is thus not *any* body. Rather it is a special
kind of body – a body which is considered somehow to be *other* than
ordinary bodies.

The conclusion from the above evidence must be that the Fangxiang, the *qitou*, the marionettes (*wangzi*) and Zhong Kui share certain
elements such as part-human, part-beast, large-headed, animal-headed,
terrifying, lame or hopping, and that these elements are all part of a
shared performative code which defines the performer in each case as a
kind of *Grenzgänger* between two worlds – whether between the states

---

[58] Ibid.: 7. [59] Luo Zhenyu, 'Gu mingqi tulu' no date: 2413–555.
[60] There is also a strong relation between 'soldier' (as exorcist) and *xi*
(performance – the character includes the sign for 'lance') which,
however, can only be suggested here.

of life and death, health and infection, earth and heaven, real and not real (this world and the world of theatre), this and other.

The statement made by Zhang Chunhua concerning *jingju* costumes 'chuan po bu chuan cuo' (wear tattered, but never the wrong costume) could not be more serious in the light of such implications. Every item of the performer's appearance, whether deriving from the physique, dress, mask or make-up, signifies the role and the *content* of the piece the performer is about to play, because each item refers back to other identities (roles) in other times and spaces. The Fangxiangshi and the *nuo* performer adopt elements which refer to their ancestors – they perform with the presence of their (exorcist/creative) ancestors represented in their apparel. They literally embody their ancestors in their clothes. In the *jingju* example, the actors playing the concubine Yang Yuhuan or the exorcist Zhong Kui make choices as to the appearance of the role based on the ancestry of their teachers and the ancestry of the role. The sheer outward appearance of the performer manifests the presence of others, of those that went before, from the simple level of teacher to the more complex level of 'original' creator.

The example of the marionette has shown that the performing body adopts elements of various traditions into it in order to represent something. The human body and the artefact are identical in that both are the temporary embodiment of a set of identities (that may read empress, exorcist or ancestor, for example) rather than one simple, individual body which stands for itself, or for one unique interpretation of identity (the role). The Chinese performing body is one which is dislocated from its so-called 'own identity', and reformed as 'other'. It has a different body shape and size, it may be ugly or terrifying to behold, or it may be part-beast (hairy). It is the counterpart to the real (ordinary, earthly) man. The other body is reconstructed as a body from another world (of death, the spirit world, the fictive world of theatre). The reconstructed performing body, whether exorcist, empress or ancestor embodies a complex of identities which spans all time and all spaces. The events that are to happen (as they happened and as they will happen again and again *ad infinitum*) in the world of performance are contained in the performer's appearance from the very moment of his entry on stage.

3

Duan

(To sever)

Mei Lanfang has entered the stage as the concubine Yang Yuhuan. His appearance at this one moment embodies the content of the piece from the point of entry to the point of departure as empress/not-empress (concubine), dignified/not-dignified (drunk), beauty/not-beauty (chosen and rejected). The initiated spectator reads the diachronic scale of the play (what happens between moment A and moment B) vertically as well as horizontally: one moment encapsulates the whole. Moreover, the deliberate and carefully chosen signs Mei Lanfang adopts to appear as Yang Yuhuan invite the initiated spectator to penetrate the layers of meaning from the outside to within – right up to the perception of the male body of the performer Mei Lanfang. The body of Mei Lanfang, the actor and his heritage, is also open to the spectator. The spectator's gaze is directed towards the separate elements of articulation of Mei Lanfang's body underneath (and through) the costume: the movement of the hand, finger, eye or foot.

Although Mei Lanfang learnt the role of the concubine Yang Yuhuan from Lu Sanbao, he has made the role his own and now the only style of playing the role is the Mei style. None of the other three *dan* actors contemporary to Mei, the *si da mingdan* (four great *dan* actors), Cheng Yanqiu (1904–58), Xun Huisheng (1900–68) and Shang Xiaoyun (1900–76)[1] performed the role. The only traces of Mei's performance are those gathered from Mei's notes[2] and a rare film of Mei Lanfang playing the role in the 1950s. These materials shall serve to expose

---

[1] *Zhongguo xiqu quyi cidian* 1981: 336, 332 and 333 respectively. A rare photograph of all four without costume can be found in Mei Lanfang 1984: 125.

[2] Mei Lanfang and Xu Jichuan 1961.

the means of articulation of the performing body just as a Chinese spectator would perceive them in watching Mei Lanfang perform.

The dissected body

On her way through the palace gardens to the rendezvous with the emperor at the pavilion of a hundred flowers, Yang Yuhuan passes over the Jade Stone Bridge. She sees mandarin ducks on the water and goldfish swimming at the surface, and leans over the rail precariously to watch them play. The bridge sequence is broken by the sound of the *suona* (a reed-wind instrument) which imitates the call of geese. Then Eunuch Pei, accompanying his mistress, draws her attention to the approaching geese:

> Eunuch Pei:
> Mistress, the geese are flying![3]

Thus far, the 'geese' are in the distance, named and heard, but not yet present. Now Yang Yuhuan begins to dance with her fan and sings:

> Yang Yuhuan (*sings*):
> Geese in the vast sky, the geese are flying, ah, the geese, ah!

At this moment, the fan held by Yang Yuhuan imitates the movements of the geese. The geese are now present on stage. The fan is held horizontally and the cloth between the spokes made to shiver like the feathers of the bird. Mei Lanfang summarises the complex dance (the hand circles in a movement repeated on each side, while the feet move sideways) thus:

> As she sings, the right hand opens the fan level at eyebrow
> height, the left hand throws the water sleeve over the wrist
> in a downward movement; she turns, pauses, then continues
> the cloud step. Both feet must be exactly parallel, heel and toe
> working back and forth, slowly making progress on a flat plane
> in a semi-circle, singing all the while. The upper body must not
> shake, the feet must move smoothly if the movement is to
> appear beautiful. At the same time, the fan in her hand must

---

[3] The play text in this and all following chapters is taken from *Mei Lanfang yanchuben xuanji* 1959: 17–30. It is the revised *daomadan* version.

Duan *(To sever)*

make wave-like movements, which symbolise the movements
of the geese . . .[4]

The spectator sees Yang Yuhuan singing a description of the birds as
she sees them, and at the same time, the spectator sees the birds represented by her hand and fan. That is, the narrator of the situation, the
performer, plays both the role Yang Yuhuan observing the geese as well
as the object, the geese, being observed. The performance of this passage requires that the actor separate the parts of his body. The fan-hand
must present the geese flying while the feet make a movement known
as the *yunbu* (cloud step). In this step, first the toes of each foot touch
and then by lifting the heels slightly and rotating the ball of the foot,
the heels of each foot are made to touch. The toes then lift slightly,
the heels rotate and the toes are made to touch again, so that the feet
would make a continuous 'W' or waved line on the floor. In performing
the cloud step, the upper part of the body does not move and the feet
are hidden by the skirt so that the performer seems to be moving on
wheels. The movement is used most often to indicate the arrival of an
invoked goddess to indicate the fact that she is descending to earth on a
cloud, that she is immortal.

In the case of Yang Yuhuan, the moment when the hand becomes
the geese of which she sings, the body of Yang Yuhuan becomes as if
immortal – non-human. It allows the spectator to perceive only the
geese flying (the fan – the body of Yang Yuhuan merely provides the
base for the movement across the sky – as if Yang Yuhuan were a kind
of puppet master.

As she sings, Yang Yuhuan describes the geese flying free in the
wild, paired for eternity, as she sees, or wishes to see, herself and the
emperor. The geese projected by the performer's hand represent the desire of the role.

> Yang Yuhuan: *(sings)*
> Geese in the vast sky, the geese are flying. Ah, the geese, ah!
> The geese soar side by side . . .

The spectator reads the performance from the outside (the costume,
general appearance) to the inside (the individual articulate elements

---

[4] Mei Lanfang and Xu Jichuan 1961, vol. 2: 19–37.

of the physical body), both of which contain the whole content of the play and the role. In training for *jingju*, the student goes through the reverse process. He begins with a conception of his body as dissected into separate units of articulation, which he then learns to bring together to construct a whole. The student must master the five arts *shou-yan-zhi-fa-bu*: literally *fa* (the combined arts of), *shou* (hand), *yan* (eye), *zhi* (finger) and *bu* (step, foot). Each of these individual aspects of the body is trained and must work for itself first, and then be combined with all the others into a harmonious whole. Here, the system of five indicating the four outlying areas united by a central power, *fa*, refers to the performer rather than the role (as in the system of five in Yang Yuhuan's costume, for example). The term *fa* (doctrine, principle, way) suggests that the technique of uniting the individual parts is a technique or body of knowledge to which only the initiated have access. It is the same *fa* used in the term for the leader of *nuo* theatre, the *Fashi* (master of the way of doing things).

Sometimes the formula is altered slightly. There are at least two variations. The first is attributed to the *dan* actor Cheng Yanqiu: *kou-shou-yan-shen-bu* (mouth [voice], hand, eye, body, step). The second is the 'official' version propagated in the standard works on *jingju*: *shou-yan-shen-zhi-bu* (hand, eye, body, finger, step).[5] Both versions avoid the significance of the system of five united in *fa* (the method, the way), possibly for political reasons. The first omits it entirely, the second adds body and makes body or trunk displace *fa* as the most significant element.

In *jingju*, whatever the system of dissection for the purposes of training, each unit of articulation is accorded equal importance. The physical centre of the student's body, the abdomen/small of the back, the part which holds all the disparate units of the body together, is the literal centre of the performing body. All movements by the individual units of articulation stem from an initial impulse in the centre. The head, in particular, follows the line dictated by the position of the pelvis. Zhang Chunhua's warning 'only dogs and clowns wag their heads separately from the body' soared regularly over the training hall if students forgot this principle (Plate 7).

---

[5] *Zhongguo xiqu quyi cidian* 1981: 93.

Plate 7   'Only Dogs and Clowns Wag Their Heads': students learning the comic role at the China Theatre School

The *jingju* performers call their art *zonghe yishu* (a totalising art form), meaning that the separate performance techniques such as *chang, nian, da* and *zuo* (singing, recitation, movement and expression) are synthesised into one another. The term *zong* means 'to assemble', *he* means 'to unify'. The *jingju* body is trained, or prepared, in a disjointed way to exploit individual parts – hands, feet, eyes, voice – which are then put back together again to work as a whole (articulated) body.

The *jingju* student begins each morning at five a.m. with an hour's voice practice, *han sangzi* (calling). The student stands facing one of the outer walls of the school and runs through a series of calls to loosen the voice, and then rehearses arias or pieces of recitation from various plays. The voice training is not supervised. Each student must listen to his own resonance from the wall and correct himself.[6] Later, when the student learns a role, he first learns the spoken, then the sung text. The process of learning is line by line memorisation of the way in which the master has given it. Mei Lanfang's first teacher, Wu Lingxian

---

[6] For a comprehensive outline of *jingju* training, see Gissenwehrer 1983.

would make a pile of ten coins on the table next to him, and if Mei recited the piece correctly, he would move one coin to a new pile. When the new pile of coins was complete, Wu was satisfied and the lesson was over. If Mei made a mistake, however, Wu would return all the coins to their original pile and the process would start from the beginning again.[7]

The rest of the morning is filled with basic physical training. In the afternoon, the students divide to train for roles in their specific role category. Students are allocated a role category according to physical stature, voice and temperament. The student learns the role by rote from the master. Now that the text has been memorised, the student mimics the master as he sings or recites and demonstrates the movements that accompany the text, beat by beat (of the music) – the foot position, body position, tilt of the head, finger gesture. The master continuously impresses the rule of the five arts on his students: the performing units of the body each have separate movements to make – the eye, the hand, the head, the feet, the trunk – but they move in combination with one another, as if an invisible string were pulling them all. The eye moves only in combination with the hand, the trunk and the feet; the hand moves only in combination with the eye, the trunk and the feet and so on, and the whole is co-ordinated and initiated into movement by the centre of the body, the lower trunk.

The physical training session begins directly after breakfast and, even here, the body is treated as separate units. Each part of the body is stretched, flexed and prepared (see Plate 8). The morning exercises consist of *jiben wugong* (basic training, including stretches, leg exercises, jumps, camel spins, arm and hand positions), *tanzigong* (floor work, including tumbling, handstands, balances) and *bazigong* (weapon training).

The foundation of all *jingju* movements are the corporeal base, the legs – even merely standing on stage requires firm leg muscles. One of the first exercises of the day, *yatui*, stretches the leg muscles. The student stretches each leg for a period of up to thirty minutes at the side of his face in a side position, and against a bar in a front stretch. The foot is always flexed upwards. The leg stretch is considered a warm

[7] Mei Lanfang 1961, vol. I: 22.

Plate 8   Morning stretch at the China Theatre School

up – the extension of the powerful calf muscles helps circulation in the whole body. Such is the value of a leg stretch that performers do it back stage for at least ten minutes in the wings before going on stage.

After stretching, the student goes through a set of leg kicks (*titui*) to improve muscle condition. There are six styles of kick – *ti zhengtui* (straight front kick), *ti pangtui* (open side kick), *ti shizitui* (cross kick), *ti piantui* (outward rotation kick) which combines the first three (the leg kicks cross wise, follows through the straight front, and open side kicks), *ti houtui* (back kick) and *ti hetui* (inward rotation kick). The kicks are rehearsed with a step in between to ensure each leg is used. The sequence consists of step, kick, return the extended leg to the floor, step with the same foot, and kick the second leg. As the students execute these kicks, two or three to a row and in several rows directly behind each other, the teacher beats time with a stick. All the students must step and kick exactly on time.

As leg work is the basis of all movements on the *jingju* stage, it was decided to fill the morning timetable of Western students attempting to learn *jingju* in a workshop situation in Cardiff in 1986,[8] with similar exercises led by Ma Mingqun, deputy head of the China Theatre School. The first problem was that none of the students – including professional ballet dancers, actors, a fight-master and an opera singer – were able to step and kick in total synchronisation with the others without eventually bumping into each other (the sequence of kicks demands a drill-like attention to the size of step between kicks which itself affects the power of the kick from the standing foot. A bigger step is easier to execute after a powerful kick, but provides an infirm base for the next kick and so on). The second problem was more complex. Ma Mingqun had told the class not to worry about kicking the leg high. In the *jingju* schools, the students are expected to reach the height of their ears and eyebrows with their feet (and they do, see Plate 9). But, Ma insisted, it was more important to execute the correct movement than to achieve perfect height. He thus took the focus away from the kick. The Western class, however, threw all their energy into the kick – even if it was not high, it must be forceful, powerful, they thought. The

---

[8] The Cardiff Laboratory Theatre held two summer schools on *jingju* in 1986 and 1987.

Plate 9   Leg exercises at the China Theatre School

consequence was that once the timing was improved, a 'loud slap' was
heard as the students completed each kick. Ma had been beating, as is
the custom, on the up-kick of the foot. The slap was the down-beat
answer to his beat. Ma was horrified and it took some while to explain
to the Western students what he thought was wrong and how it was to
be corrected. The kick of the foot is light, not forced. The landing foot
springs on the floor only in order to prepare for the step and the kick of
the next foot. The students in his school make barely a sound as they go
through the routine of hour-long leg kicks. The only sound to be heard
is the teacher's beating – on the up-beat of the kicked leg.

This set of leg exercises is merely one aspect of the training of a
jingju student. Each part of the body – hand, arm, finger, head, eye, leg
and foot is first trained individually and then brought into a whole
articulated body by the method, or *fa*. The *jingju* performers have a saying, 'you jishu meiyou yishu' (there is technique but no art) to describe
a performer who has excellent physical skills but cannot combine them
into a harmonised (synchronised – articulate) whole.

The dissected and reassembled (articulated) body of the *jingju*
student is reflected in a more concrete way by performers in the *nuo*

4	9	2
3	5	7
8	1	6

Diagram 16   The Luo diagram

theatre. The underlying system of the *nuo* theatre relates the body to the Luo diagram of recreation, a matrix composed of nine individual cells arranged in three rows of three (see Diagram 16). Numerical values from 1 to 9 are accorded to each cell such that the sum of any straight line adds up to 15. While the *jingju* performer brings the individual articulate units of the body into congruence through training, the *nuo* performer brings the body into congruence through the act of performing in a space accorded the same values as the Luo diagram. According to mythology, the Luo diagram was given to Yu the Great to quell the flood. He used its pattern to stamp and hop across stones and divide the seas from the water in creating the world (see chapters two and seven). The Luo diagram was also used in early China for the purpose of divination and as a kind of fractal diagnostic physiognomy, whereby parts of the body were overlaid with the grid, as the example of the hand shows in Diagram 18. Alternatively, the body was divided into eight elements: the head, abdomen, foot, anus, ears, eyes, hands and mouth and these were plotted onto the eight outer cells of the Luo diagram (the ninth being the centre). In diagnostic terms, each cell of the Luo diagram is accorded a specific trigram from the *Yijing* (Book of Changes). Illness in some part of the body corresponded to the grid and help was sought from the oracle relating to that trigram.

A similar division of the whole body into nine parts was recorded in the ancient classics. Each part of the divided body was accorded the numerical values of the cells in the Luo diagram: '2 and 4 make the shoulders, 6 and 8 make the feet; 3 is at the left, 7 is at the right; 9 is

Duan *(To sever)*

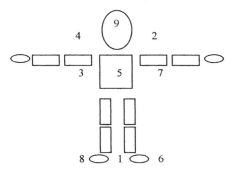

Diagram 17   The Luo body

worn on the head and 1 is underfoot [literally: trodden by the shoes]; while 5 dwells at the center'.[9] In this scheme, the *nuo* body, like the *jingju* body, is reconstructed by virtue of the physical centre of the body, the lower trunk (see Diagram 17). The description of the Luo matrix as it is applied to the human body suggests that it 'referred to an application of the magic square of three to a person, probably a man or god considered as a microcosm of the universe'.[10] This theory confirms the idea that the *nuo* performer and the Fangxiangshi, with his dance in the four corners, situate themselves as the (original) ancestor/exorcist/creator when they perform.

The way in which the microcosm, man – as the Luo diagram, might function can easily be shown by the example of its fractal application in the use of the hand in the *nuo* theatre. In the *nuo* theatre, the fingers of both hands contort, stretch, intertwine, hook and catch to make various signs known as *jue*, literally 'parting or dying words, an art, a mystery, a secret'.[11] Each sign has a specific meaning, for example, in the dance of the nine stations, or Yu step, each cell, or station of the Luo diagram trodden by the performer is accompanied by hand signs which represent that station. The performer who executes these signs is said to *huan jue*, which means to 'exchange', 'change', hand signs. This is the same character for 'change, exchange' as that used to describe the songs sung at funerals, *huan ge* (songs of parting,

[9] Cammann 1969: 42.   [10] Ibid.
[11] *Mathews* 1979: character no. 1700.

95

transition). Thus to make one hand sign after the other is to make changes to mark and make the transition from one station to another.

The hand sign vocabulary in the *nuo* theatre is veiled in secrecy and is seldom discussed by Chinese performers or scholars. However, some examples of hand signs have been published and it is possible to suggest how they are composed, and what they might indicate. The system of hand signs in the *nuo* depends upon the hand being conceived as divided into two grids of nine cells – two Luo diagrams.[12] In the Luo diagram, each cell is assigned a number from 1 to 9 such that the sum of any three numbers in a straight line, whether vertical, horizontal or diagonal adds up to 15, as shown in Diagram 16. However, the Luo diagram is not only composed of these digits; it is also assigned various cosmological values which rotate around a constant centre (exemplified by the middle digit 5 which is the mean of each opposite pair of digits), such as the *bagua* (eight trigrams) found in the *Yijing*, or Book of Changes, or the *wuxing* (five elements – earth, metal, wood, water, fire). The *jue* depends upon the projection of the Luo diagram with its trigram, elemental and numerical values, onto the palm and fingers of both hands (the left hand is illustrated below). The view of the hand as a Luo chart was and is a common device in palmistry. Quite simply, the relative positions or stations are imposed onto the flat of the hand,[13] as shown in Diagram 18, or onto the fingers,[14] as shown in Diagram 19.

The *jue* hand sign is made by combining the fingers and palm representing certain cosmological stations of one hand to other cosmological stations represented on the other hand (see, for example, Plate 10). Most of the hand signs are highly complex and require a great deal of manual dexterity (training) to execute. Both the *nuo* performer and marionette master, for example, can achieve a ninety degree angle between each finger and the next. The performer can use one handed signs where certain fingers and palm of the same hand interact, or he can extend the system to two hands. In most cases, the left hand is conceived as Yang (heavenly) and the right hand conceived as Yin (earthly) so that two planes of meaning are connected (two worlds) – earth on one hand and heaven on the other.

---

[12] See Berglund 1990; Cammann 1960, 1962 and 1969.
[13] Wang Hongqi 1989: 93.   [14] Huang Weiruo, note to the author.

Duan *(To sever)*

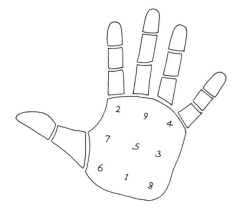

Diagram 18   The values of the Luo diagram imposed on the palm of the hand

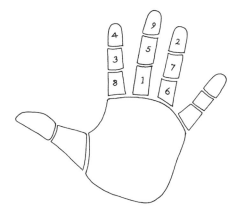

Diagram 19   The values of the Luo diagram imposed on the fingers

For example, the *jue* known as *riyue ergong* (the two palaces of the sun and moon)[15] represents the palace or residence of the gods. In this *jue* the tip of the middle finger of the left hand rests on the middle knuckle of the right hand (Diagram 20). The left hand represents the sun, the right hand represents the moon. The *jue* represents the brilliance of the sun and the radiance of the moon lighting up the four quarters – cleansing or exorcising them. In terms of Yin and Yang, the moon

[15] *Xiangxi nuowenhua zhi mi* 1991: 185.

97

Plate 10   *Tuipo jue* (breaking through) hand sign; performed by Tian Jingguang (82), *wu*-ist master in Fenghuang County, Hunan

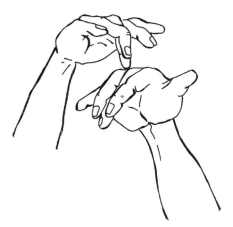

Diagram 20   Two palaces of the sun and moon

(Yin) and the sun (Yang) are brought together. According to the system of trigrams, the tip of the middle finger (*li* = fire, the south) rests on the back of the other hand in a position related to the centre top of the palm which also has the value of *li* – fire, the south. This hand sign is like a double *li*, or double Yang, indicating that the residence of the gods (heaven) is the radiant, all creative, male, Yang environment. The hand sign is used by the performer when he wants to show the residence of the gods (heaven) and open the gates so that the God may descend (Yang heaven may permeate the Yin earth). It is a hand sign which invokes. Moreover, the hand sign is not only a code which means 'the god from heaven shall descend'; it also figurally represents – corporeally – brightness, brilliance, Yang or the god descending. Expressed in terms of the radiation of light, it is not dissimilar to the process known as *kaiguang*, whereby artefacts are opened into life, discussed later in this chapter.

One Chinese author has maintained that all the spoken and sung text of *nuo* is translated into the language of the hands and fingers.[16] Zhou Bing cites a piece of text and lists some of the hand signs that accompany it.

> I ride a dragon car and chariot on the thunder,
> With cloud-banners fluttering upon the wind.[17]
> Riding upon tawny leopards, leading the striped lynxes;
> A car of lily-magnolia with banner of woven cassia;[18]
> I ride a water chariot with a canopy of lotus;
> Two dragons draw it, between two water serpents.[19]

The three couplets may derive from a cycle of songs known as the *Jiuge* or *Nine Songs*, a classical text which was possibly sung to accompany nine rounds of the nine stations dance. Zhou does not give any reference to how, or when these couplets are used in the *nuo* event. But from their content, they seem to accompany 'rounds' of the nine stations dance and represent stations which have to do with thunder

---

[16] Zhou Bing 1987: 174.

[17] These lines are identical to a passage in the poem *Dongjun* (*Lord of the East*) which comes from the *Jiuge* attributed to Qu Yuan (*c.* 339–278 BC). The relation of the ancient text to similar texts still used in *nuo* theatre promises sinologists a new approach to the *wu*-ist content of the ancient poem and presents some theatre scholars a challenge to the view that *nuo* is a 'primitive' form of theatre. I have used the translation by David Hawkes for this and the following couplets: Hawkes 1985: 113, 115 and 114 respectively.

[18] These two lines are identical to a passage in the poem *Shangui* (*The Mountain Spirit*) from *Jiuge*.

[19] These two lines are identical to a passage from the poem *Hebo* (*The River Earl*) from *Jiuge*.

(thunder chariot), mountain (chariot drawn by leopards and lynxes), and water (chariot drawn by dragons and water serpents). The chariot pulled by mythological creatures, or natural forces such as wind and thunder, is the vehicle used by gods when they descend to earth. In the light of this, the *jue* described by Zhou are a kind of standard formula for describing the journey of certain spirits or gods to the earthly plane. Zhou lists the hand signs which accompany these texts:

1 *huagai* (flower canopy), the imperial canopy
2 *mashi*, sign of the horse
3 *cheshi*, sign of the chariot
4 *leishi*, sign of thunder[20]

In his introduction to the *Nine Songs*, Hawkes acknowledges the theatricality of the poems and comments:

> the absence of stage directions, indicating who at any given point was supposed to be singing, or what they were doing while they sang, makes it impossible to be sure how they were performed.[21]

The hand signs named by Zhou suggest that as the performer sings the text of the god who has been called and is now descending, he also makes the hand sign which both *means* the kind of vehicle of descent and *is* the vehicle of descent. Thus the performer *narrates* the god descending as he *performs* the god descending in the same way that the concubine Yang Yuhuan narrates and performs the geese on the *jingju* stage.

The changes, or *huan jue*, of the hand actually reproduce (narrate and create) the object sung about by the performer (the god descending), yet the performer is also subject of his performance (the god descending). This depends upon the performer literally dissecting his body into different expressive units. When the performer gives the sign, for example, of the imperial canopy that covers the chariot, his hand represents the chariot. At the same time as he sings about the god descending on such a chariot he presents that god descending on his chariot. The performer 'travels' on his hand.

---

[20] Zhou Bing 1987: 174.   [21] Hawkes 1985: 95–6.

Duan *(To sever)*

Diagram 21   *jianjue* (sword sign)

A simple example can be seen in the case of the hand sign for sword, *jianjue* (Diagram 21). This hand sign is used principally in exorcisms. The first two fingers of either hand are extended together, while the thumb holds down the rest of the fingers against the palm in a pointing gesture. Here, the hand sign looks like a sword (long and pointed), and the hand is used as if it were a sword. That is, the hand is not conceived as holding a sword, but as the sword itself. The hand is an object. In an exorcism sequence, the hand sign for sword is directed at the four corners to slay any lurking demons.

In *jingju*, the same hand sign is used for two purposes: (1) in any movement sequence that uses the prop, sword (*jian*),[22] and (2) where the performer is showing anger. In the first instance, the hand sign is used, by the hand not holding the sword prop, as a kind of aesthetic balance. In sequences such as the sword dance by the concubine in the play *Bawang bieji* (*Bawang Takes Leave of His Concubine*) the concubine uses her free hand as a sword to make parallel movements to the hand that is holding the sword. In the second case, the meaning of the sword hand – as a real sword that can kill or cut – has been compressed

[22] Sword (*jian*) has a sharpened blade on both edges and is to be distinguished from knife (*dao*) which has one curved sharpened edge. The sword 'pierces', while the knife 'chops' or 'slashes'. Thus it is held and used differently.

to indicate anger. This use of the sword sign is called *fanu* (radiating anger) and its meaning depends upon the conception of the hand as an object which metaphorically wounds the opponent.

One of the most basic arm movements in *jingju* is the *yunshou* (cloud hand) movement. This movement varies in scale according to the role performing it. A female role may execute a smaller version (see Diagram 72 on p. 300), a male role a more extended version. It is a flowing movement where both arms work in parallel, split, intercross and end in a pose or *liangxiang*. The cloud hand movement generally accompanies a travelling movement – that is, the cloud hand movement is a connecting, travelling movement between segments of dance. The cloud hand can be directed from the right to the left, *zheng yunshou* (straight cloud hand), or from the left to the right, *fan yunshou* (reverse cloud hand). These movements are also known respectively as Yang cloud hand and Yin cloud hand. Ma Mingqun always taught that the cloud hand was a movement used to beautify the *guocheng* (passage) from one part of a movement sequence to the next. But, seen in relation to the way in which the *jue* hand works in *nuo* theatre, the cloud hand movement can be interpreted as the *literal* vehicle of movement from one point in time and space to another. The hands and arms make the sign of cloud, and the cloud, like thunder, is one of the main means of transport by which a *nuo* performer shows the movement of 'others' (deities) to the earth.

The *wusheng* (male warrior) in *jingju* also uses a hand sign which has exorcistic significance. This is a position known as *hukou* (tiger's mouth) (Diagram 22). In this position, the fingers are extended and held together but for the thumb which extends away from the hand as much as possible. Students are taught not to concentrate on keeping the fingers together but on stretching the thumb away – keeping the space between thumb and first finger as great as possible. This represents the tiger's mouth. The students are also taught that the reason for this position of the hand is that the greater the extension of the thumb, the firmer the outside edge of the hand along the smallest finger i.e. the better weapon the hand becomes in a fight. However, the name of the position focuses the real significance of the position not to the striking edge of the hand, but to the open side, for the tiger is one of the main creatures of exorcism. It destroys demons by eating them. Hence

Duan *(To sever)*

Diagram 22   *hukou* (tiger's mouth hand position)

the meaning of the position has to do with the non-fighting edge. He who makes the sign of the tiger's mouth has the power to exorcise, is the better warrior.

The *jingju* female hand positions are equally significant in a corporeal, physical sense. The most commonly used positions are built around the imagery of flowers.[23] The *lanhua zhi* (orchid hand) is the standard female hand position. Others include *luzi* (dewdrop fingers, literally drop of sap or nectar) when pointing to the cheek, *yunshuang* (frost falling) when holding the fan in reverse position, *yingfeng* (facing the wind) when forbidding something, *bingdi* (twin lotus buds on one stalk) for clapping the hands, *shene* (extended calyx) for holding the whip when representing riding on a horse, *turui* (the blossoming stamen) for picking up some tiny object.

Not only do these terms have to do with the imagery of flowers, their names also suggest the reproductive, sexual anatomy of flowers. Several of them are used in *nuo* theatre for similar purposes as those described above, but with extended meanings as, for example, the sword hand sign examined above. Another example is the hand position *nongzi* (ritual pose), used in *jingju* for carrying a tray, and in the

[23] Mei Shaowu 1984: facing page 1. Another forty-six hand illustrations from the same series are pictured in Qi Rushan 1979, vol. 2: 993–1006.

nuo theatre for holding the bowl from which water and salt are to be scattered, in a gesture of cleansing or exorcising. It is also used for holding a ritual water bowl filled with the ashes of burnt charms. It is regarded as more than simply a way or 'style' of holding a tray, or bowl-like object as in *jingju*, for the two extended fingers are accorded meaning through their values in terms of the Luo diagram. In the exorcism dance of Zhong Kui, one hand maintains this position while the other, raised above it, makes the sign of the god of thunder – it replicates the stone to which the thunder hand is the flint.

The example of the *Nine Songs* provided some insight to the way in which the *jue* used in *nuo* might work. Perhaps the strong floral/reproductive imagery of the names of the signs used in *jingju* by Mei Lanfang could also be linked to similar systems of allegory. The palace of the goddess of the water in the poem cycle, for example, is composed entirely of flowers (earth, female) as opposed to the heavenly palace which was represented in the *nuo* by the 'light' of the sun and moon (male). Thus, some of the hand signs used by the female role in *jingju* might represent the concept of the presence of deity, of the female beauty or goddess descending, particularly considering the imagery of the concubine Yang Yuhuan as flower, and as goddess (see chapter seven):

> I will build her [the goddess] a house within the water
> Roofed all over with lotus leaves;
> With walls of iris . . .
> Perfumed pepper shall make the hall.
> With beams of cassia, orchid rafters,
> Lilt-tree lintel, a bower of peonies,
> With woven fig-leaves for the hangings
> And melilotus to make a screen . . .[24]

Finally, hand signs are used extensively in the marionette theatre. Here, the hands of the marionette are carved in the shape of specific *jue* hand signs. Furthermore, these hand signs are reproduced, on occasion, by the marionette master's own hands as he manipulates the marionette. That is, the master pulls the strings of the marionette by using

---

[24] *The Lady of the Xiang [River]* in Hawkes 1985: 108.

Duan *(To sever)*

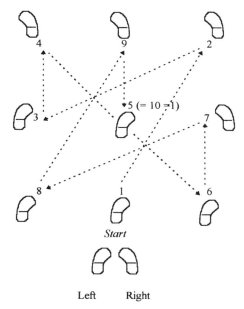

4   9   2

▼5 (= 10 ⇒1)

3   7

8   1   6

Start

Left   Right

Diagram 23   The Yu step

hand signs, so that the marionette and the marionette master simultaneously repeat the same hand sign, as if the hand sign were completely
separate from both artefact and mover. The effect is not unlike the sign
given by Mei Lanfang as Yang Yuhuan representing the geese independently of the body.

In the repertoire of movements belonging to the hand alone, it
can be seen that the hand is severed from the rest of the body and can
function independently of it. The hands, however, are merely one level
of meaning exploited by the Chinese performer; the feet and legs provide another.

The *nuo* performance is based on a step known as the Yu step,
which is a sequence of eight steps across the Luo diagram. In Diagram
23, the numbers refer to the stations of the Luo. The Yu step is made by
progressing numerically from 1 to 9. The central position 5 is equivalent to an unspoken 10 which is simultaneously position 1 of the next
sequence. Thus, each sequence circumscribes one step forward. In the
Yu step, the performer stamps once on each of the nine stations with
one foot and drags the second foot to join it in a movement highly

suggestive of the pattern of movement made by the *wangzi*, Chi You and *gui*, discussed in chapter two. Stamping on the earth in the Chinese model carries the meaning of suppressing evil spirits, so the simplest interpretation of the Yu step is that the performer ritually cleanses the stations of the grid by stamping his foot in each. These movements place the foot and the earth into strong relation with each other. Not only does the stamping foot literally press down the demon, it also calls forth a terrific force and an equally terrific sound.[25] The percussion orchestra in the *nuo* is a vital element of the performance – no performance takes place without it even, as I have witnessed, in Xia Yangchang in Guizhou, when the cymbal was dented and the drum skin torn.

The pattern of the feet on the earth in the Yu step, and other steps used in exorcism theatre and Daoist ritual have been recorded as early as the Song dynasty in a Daoist manual[26] from which Diagrams 24, 26 and 27 are taken. Each represents a different way of figuring or notating (with the feet) various cultural perceptions.

Diagram 24 shows a set of foot movements which reproduce the trigram for heaven (three unbroken lines) on top of the trigram for thunder (two broken lines above one unbroken line). Two trigrams on top of one another are known as a hexagram. All the eight trigrams can be combined with each other in this way to make a total of sixty-four hexagrams, each with its own meaning. The hexagram mapped by the feet of the performer above is the twenty-fifth hexagram, *wuwang* (nothing unexpected) (Diagram 25). The interpretation of this hexagram in divination warns the individual to undertake nothing rash, but to go along with whatever comes and to follow nature, or calamity will fall.[27] Thus, when manifested as a footstep, the hexagram ensures the mortal world follows its course without disaster. Diagram 26 reproduces with the feet the stellar constellation *Ursa Major*, symbol of cyclical change around the central (polar) constant. It manifests the idea of returning the world to original harmony; all things shall come round. Finally, Diagram 27 shows a double *Ursa Major* step, or two rotations of the constellation around the central northern star. One

---

[25] In the Japanese *no* theatre, huge ceramic jars are placed under the stage to enlarge the sound of stamping by resonation.

[26] *Daozang* 1986, vol. 32: 106.   [27] Wang Hongqi 1989: 227.

Duan *(To sever)*

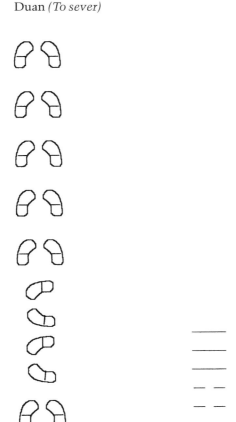

Diagram 24   The foot pattern *wuwang*   Diagram 25   The hexagram *wuwang*

rotation represents thunder and the other fire. It is also an invoking step, a step which recreates the powers of light and heat (Yang) to descend and intervene in the running of the cosmos.

Thunderous, percussive sound is one of the means by which a god is said to move to make changes (Yu hopped on sonorous stones, for example). It is also a sign of the god descending. Mythological gods are depicted riding on a thunder chariot, powered by wheels of cloud. (The *jingju* uses square-shaped flags to represent thunder and cloud at the entrance of various gods.) By association, the power of movement is 'cloud' power. Gods travel down to earth on magic clouds, on puffs of incense. Cloud, smoke and mist are all vehicles for the spirits to descend upon as well as vehicles for messages to be sent from earth to

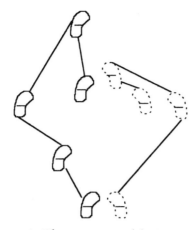

Diagram 26　The seven steps of the *Ursa Major*

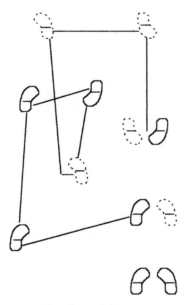

Diagram 27　Thunder and fire *Ursa Major* step

heaven and these images are repeated in the charm writing (*fu*) used to invoke spirits. The sign for thunder (*lei*) in charm writing (Diagram 28) is sometimes portrayed as four circles of thunder (drums) surrounding a double sign for cloud and this is taken to be the literal representation of a thunder chariot where the wheels provide the thunderous noise,

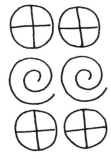

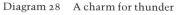

Diagram 28   A charm for thunder

Diagram 29   The character *lei*
(puppet)

the cloud the seat of the god. [28] This abstract sign for thunder/drum – a rounded square with a cross in the centre – is found again in the characters related to *gui* (spirit) examined on page 80 and tripled in the same-sounding character *lei* used to mean puppets, alongside the standing man radical (Diagram 29).

The images of thunder and cloud in performance, as well as the corollary sound of drum and burst of light, are equal, barely separable components which convey the idea of invocation to life. The classical term for thunder, used as a trigram in the *Yijing* (Book of Changes), is *zhen* whose second meaning is 'to quicken'. Both characters *lei* (thunder) and *zhen* (the rumble of thunder) are also composed of the element rain, which is considered the fertilising agent *per se*. The thunder/cloud image is one of direct and spontaneous creation.

Any percussive sound can also be described as invoking presence (see the significance of the percussion in *nuo* described in chapter seven). A performance which seeks to describe the moment of presence may use the device of stamping feet. Yu the Great, who gave his name to the Yu step used in *nuo*, originally created the world after the flood by stamping on special stones. Moreover, the percussive sound made by the dancing is linked to the idea of metamorphosis, of change into other forms/worlds. Thus, the stamping, drumming movement and sound of the performer's feet in each of the stations of the Yu dance not only puts down the spirits, it also first raises them up. In this sense, the

[28] Lin He 1990: 126.

stamping of the nine stations dance or the Yu step, may also be called a marking, mapping, naming or transforming dance. For, by stamping out each station, the performer actually calls it forth into being (calls the powers he believes represented in each station into being), marks it – by stamping an imprint on the earth, and cleanses it (by stamping) at the same time.

Moreover, after the performer has stamped or hopped in a cell with one foot, he drags the second foot to join the first, physically linking one station with another by his two feet at the seat of regeneration, the loins. Just as the fingers and palms of each hand interact with one another, so each foot of the performer makes contact with the value implied in each station of the Luo diagram that he treads, invoking and connecting them. The point of connection or unification/creation is, as in *jingju*, the lower part of the trunk, the loins.

The Yu step may consist of alternate or the same foot stamping in different stations. This requires the action of jumping, or hopping. Many other forms of *nuo* theatre are known in dialect as *tiaoshen* (hopping spirits). The mortuary figures were known as *yong* – a word which is etymologically linked to a phoneme *yong* meaning 'to leap, jump, dance' (see Diagram 30).[29] The hopping, jumping movement, which designates units of meaning and binds units of cosmological meaning to each other, relates the human performing figure in the *nuo* theatre world directly to the performance of artificial bodies in the tomb, or world of death.

The emptied body

In all kinds of performance thus far, the performing body is conceived as a composite of individual parts (hand or foot, for example) which are then brought together by a central force. The *nuo* performer sees the process of dissection as a literal one. In preparing to perform, he considers his body to be physically cut apart. This action is extremely dangerous. What if the performer cannot retrieve his individual parts after the performance and become 'himself' again? Thus, each *nuo* performance is preceded by a ceremony which first deposits the soul (essence) of the performer somewhere safe. Before he is entitled to do

---

[29] The Chinese character for *yong* is used in Japanese theatre as a term for dancing in a lively, hopping way, pronounced *odori*. See Ortolani 1990: 22.

Duan *(To sever)*

Diagram 30 a   The character *yong* (to leap)   b   The character *yong* (mortuary figure)

this, the body must be cleansed by fasting, abstaining from meat for a certain period of time, ritual washing, sexual abstention and so on.[30]

The process of putting the soul somewhere safe is known in different types of *nuo* performance as *zanghun*, which means, 'to store, to lay by, to deposit the soul'. At the start of the *zanghun* ceremony, the performer takes one or two sheets of paper money and, tearing them apart, he arranges them in the pattern of the Luo diagram with the eight trigrams. Then he takes seven whole grains of (husked) rice and puts them at the top and bottom of a Yin/Yang diagram, and wraps them up in paper money in a form which has a pointed top and wide bottom. This item is called the 'seven treasures soul flower'. This may refer to the seven-day period following death that the soul requires to sever itself from this world. Rice, as agnatic stuff used to include a member into the performing troupe, substitutes or represents the soul of the performer while his body is used for performance. The performer holds the flower pressed between the index and middle finger of the left hand and puts it into a large bowl in front of him. Kneeling in front of the bowl, at the altar to his master, he exhales three Yang (life) breaths and silently contemplates his master's voice and countenance. Finally, he sings the *zangshen zhou* (depositing the body charm).

> Deposit the body, deposit the body, truly shall deposit the body,
> At the Hall of the Three Great Ones,[31] come to deposit the body.
> The Hall of the Three Great Ones is not the place for the
>   disciple to deposit the body,

[30] Jiang Wuchang 1986: 44–92 lists some examples of preparatory rites before various kinds of performances.

[31] The Three Great Ones (*sanqing*) are Buddha, Laozi and Confucius. These three figures dominate the central altar in the *nuo* event.

Burn incense, transform water, my body is manifest (?)
Before Junwang's very eyes,[32] at Nianghuai's feet,[33] I deposit
　　three souls (*hun*),
In departing, three *hun* and seven *po* are given to you,
On returning, three *hun* shall be under Nianghuai's feet.
. . .

Three *hun* under the ancestor's feet,
Deposit the real body inside the stomach of an iron ox,
Three *hun* and seven *po* become the real body,
The human body shall become the Iron General.
When the mouth is thirsty it shall drink milk from the
　　iron oxen,
When the stomach is empty it shall be nourished by flesh from
　　the iron ox.
When the iron stick beats the ox, it shall not move,
When fire catches the mountain the ox shall not move.
On departing, deposit the seven *po* in one set of Yin trigrams,
On returning, release the three *hun* from one set of Yang
　　trigrams.[34]

Taking three sticks of incense in his right hand, he then makes the *jue*
of 'depositing the body' in the air over the bowl with them (thus triplic-
ating the signs). To see if the charm has worked, he throws the oracle
blocks. A Yin (dark, death) answer means that the soul has been safely
deposited. If this is the case, the bowl is placed in front of the images
of *nuogong* and *nuopo* ('father' and 'mother' of *nuo*). Finally, the performer must execute some hand signs for extra insurance. These are
the hand signs 'the heavenly seal', 'the earthly seal', 'yellow spotted
hungry tiger' and 'General One-Horn'; they are performed over the
bowl.

---

[32] The name can refer to the emperor, the ancestors, father, husband.

[33] The name means literally 'in the bosom of the mother' and probably is
meant as a generic term for all mothers. On this occasion, I take the
father and the mother referred to as being the *nuogong* and *nuopo* (father
and mother of *nuo*) possibly original ancestors, whose images are placed
on the central altar.

[34] *Zhongguo nuoxi diaocha baogao* 1992: 315–39.

Duan *(To sever)*

The preparation sequence continues with a rite to 'sweeten the gods', another to 'call up the soldiers', before the performer dances and sings the 'manifesting the substituted body' *(biaoda tishen)* declaring, 'Soldiers and cavalry from the five directions shall take care of my body. My body is substituted for a while.' This can be considered the conclusion of the depositing ceremony.

The process above is taken from *nuotangxi*. I observed a simpler version in the *dixi* theatre in Guizhou. Near the actual performance area, generally in a position directly related to the *nuo* altar, a tent is constructed out of straw matting. This is known as the *bamiaotang* (Hall of the Eight Temples)[35] and it is here that the performers put on the masks before proceeding through the audience, masked, to the performance area proper (Plate 11).[36] Some troupes set up their *bamiaotang* in the village temple and make a procession through the village to the performance area (Plate 12). Before putting on the mask, the performer dips his fingers into a special bowl of water and says the words:

> Substitute the body, come, substitute the body,
> Substitute the male body, replace it with a female one [in the case of performing a female role]
> Substitute the male body of P [name of performer]
> Replace it with the female body of F [the female role]
> Deposit the first soul in the body of P [name of the performer],
> Deposit the second soul in the nine clouds [heaven],
> Deposit the third soul in the king of heaven's water bowl.
> I give you three souls and seven souls,
> When I return, I shall ask the king of heaven for my three souls back.[37]

The deposited soul is placed in a special water bowl for safe-keeping. The performer is only host to the role he is to play for a temporary term – the duration of the performance. The body is emptied of its self, made passive host to the role. Now, any process of dissecting the body into

---

[35] Reference to the eight trigrams of the Luo diagram.

[36] Perhaps similar to the construction of the Japanese *no* stage with its 'bridge' or *hashigakari*, where the audience can observe the performer before he is actually involved in the action. See Ortolani 1990:184.

[37] Taken from author's field notes, Guizhou 1990.

Plate 11   Inside the *bamiaotang* (backstage tent)

Plate 12   Putting on masks in the temple courtyard after 'depositing the soul'

separate expressive units and reassembling them into the new body will not put the own body at risk.

Thus, in order to enter the process of dissecting the body into expressive units of meaning in the *nuo*, the performing body is first emptied of its personal or individual essence (soul). The soul is called out of the body and placed in a special bowl which itself is placed in the care of certain gods (ancestors). Hand signs are performed to ensure the soul remains in place and intact. The ceremony emphasises the temporary nature of the deposit. The performer repeats that he will go away for a while and then come back and ask for his soul back again.[38] The bowl is a temporary residence for the soul while the body of the performer is engaged in other activities (presenting a figure). The implication is that the body of the performer is prepared for performance in a way that makes him a pure artefact, an empty vessel. In *jingju* this phase may be compared to the first years of training, when the boys were put through a rigorous physical training and lifestyle that was based on the understanding that they were the purchased property of the master with no right to a sense of personal identity. One *jingju* school in Yingkou, Shenyang province, continues to practise a similarly severe (soul-less) routine. Despite temperatures well below zero, the children train seven days a week in an unheated hall from 5 a.m. to 7 p.m. under the school motto 'Strict instruction and learning through hard work (literally 'bitterness') is the only way to make the profession of *jingju* art flourish and promote the struggle.'[39] I visited in 1984 and asked one of the senior girls (age twelve) what she liked to do during her free hour every second Sunday afternoon. 'I like to help the younger students wash their clothes' was the reply.

A similar process of emptying the performing body before it can perform can be observed in mourning rites, where a *shi* (personator) is used as locus of worship for the mourning or death-anniversary ceremony. The personator is generally the male descendant of the deceased and provides the host body for the deceased in the same way that a

---

[38] If a person sleeps, or dies, his soul is said to have gone wandering and must be called back; thus it must be kept safely if the performer is to have it back after the performance. See De Groot 1982, vol. 1: 241–62, Erkes 1914 and Hawkes 1985: 219–37.

[39] Author's field notes. The 'struggle' is of course the communist one.

performer provides the host body for the role he is about to play. The grandson is preferred over the son, or someone from the generation of the grandson so that the direct descendant, the son, can show reverence to the deceased. Sometimes, the clothes of the deceased are laid out before the personator on the floor. The personator sits, is invited to drink and eat of the offerings that are donated to the deceased, as his representative. The personation ceremony is carried out under the direction of a Master of Ceremonies. All the personator is required to do is sit, and partake of the toasts and offerings as instructed. Some scholars have argued that the personator was directly active in the ceremony,[40] but the personator's main task was to provide the *locus* of worship, i.e. he was not required to *act as* the deceased might have done.[41]

The various actions and duties of the personator in ancient times are recorded in the Han volume, *Yili* (*Book of Etiquettes and Rites*). A brief passage in Chapter 35, for example, records a simple version of the personation ceremony and details the process of becoming a personator.

1   The Personator Enters.
  (a) The liturgist meets the personator outside the door.
  (b) The master of ceremonies descends and stands to the east of the east steps.

[40] In the *Shijing* classical collection of ancient odes, some verses suggest that the personation ceremony involved an 'abundance of sacrificial wine and food . . . shared by both the ancestral spirits (through the personator) and their descendants'. (Carr 1985: 22). From the same source, Carr concludes that the personators and participants were drunk: 'We are drunk with wine . . . the representative of the (dead) prince comes and feasts and is befumed (by the spirits); the good wine makes you merry.' Moreover, the personator may have 'spoken for' the ancestors to the descendants (Carr 1985: 22 n. 42).

[41] Perhaps this is similar to the situation in India where young boys are chosen to 'be' Krishna for the duration of certain performances. The Krishna sits in a special pose at the entrance to the performance area to receive the worship of the gathering spectators: 'For the *raslila* operates on a convention of incarnation, not possession – once the boy actor is wearing the special double crown, he is *en-theos*, but not by any shift of consciousness on his part. He can sit and chew gum or consult his quartz wristwatch. The onus of belief is not on him but on the audience.' George 1987: 129.

(c) The personator enters by the left of the door, stands facing the north while he washes his hands, the temple-keeper handing him the towel.

(d) When the personator reaches the steps the liturgist invites him to ascend, and he complies, and enters the chamber.[42]

Here the personator faces north, the side of death, of darkness, while 'washing his hands'. In the *zanghun* depositing ceremony detailed above, the soul of the performer was first put into a 'bowl' for safe-keeping before the process of substitution could begin. Does this passage suggest the personator, too, must deposit his soul in order to stand as substitute for the deceased ancestor?

The personator can (even should) be a member of the younger generation. Confucius suggested a babe in arms would also be appropriate.[43] If this is so, then the performative body may be considered to be somewhat passive. This fully complies with the idea, suggested above, that the performer empties his body of 'self' first. In both cases the performing body is pure material, artefact. In the case of the ancestor ceremony, the personator is perceived to be representing the deceased ancestor – that is, he is the temporary locus, abode, of the ancestor not by any virtue of *similarity* with the deceased (*imitatio*), though clearly it is of importance that the personator is the direct descendant – genetic reincarnation of, or mediator (*Grenzgänger*) between the deceased and those present, but by virtue of *being called so*.

The opened body

The process of taking the body apart in order to arrive at individual units of articulation for performance is simultaneous to the reassembly of the new body. As each part is dissected from the emptied body, it is placed in relation to the individual part of the role body. Part by part, the host body is cut up and replaced by the role body. The simultaneous process of dissection and reassembly is the technique by which a body becomes articulate(d). This process is an opening process known as *kaiguang*, which means 'opening to let the light shine out'.

The opening process as simultaneous dissection and substitution or reassembly into a new body is most simply observed in the use

---

[42] *Yili*, trans. Steele 1917: 135.   [43] *Liji*, trans. Legge 1885, vol. 1: 227–8.

of healing figures. These are figures made of straw, or bamboo sticks and paper. They can be obtained from funeral outfitters and are also used in the funeral ceremony to represent the deceased or servants to serve the deceased in the afterworld.

> In Amoy [Xiamen] the images used for the purpose are mostly very roughly made of two bamboo splinters fastened together crosswise, on one side of which is pasted some paper supposed to represent a human body. They are not larger than a hand, and those of men are distinguished from those of women by two shreds of paper, said to be boots. They are called *tishen*, 'substitutes or surrogates of a person', and may be had, for a cash or so apiece, in every shop where paper articles are sold for sacrifice to the dead and the gods, for they are also burnt as slaves for the dead in the other world.[44]

The figures are not specific: they are not made to represent any particular person. Nor are they made for a specific function, for they can be used in the healing process as well as in the mortuary ceremony. The only differentiation is that the male figure has boots on, the female does not. In the healing ceremony, however, the figure is accorded the identity of the sick patient – it takes on the *role* of the sick patient. This is achieved by two processes, naming and substitution.

The paper figure is first given the name of the sick patient in the form of writing – the figure is labelled with the name of the patient. The healing figure, the performing body, is not identified as the patient by reproducing the patient's characteristics, such as a large nose, small eyes or broad mouth. Rather, the performing body is declared to be, is called, the patient, by the written signs painted on it, which is a naming process. It is the patient because it has been called so.

The same principle of designation is used for burial figures in the world of the dead, as for example, the terracotta army in the tomb of Qinshi Huangdi. The exhibition on site declares the individual appearance of the soldiers, that each one is different from the next and that each statue was made as a substitute or representative of a real soldier. In fact, however, they are not:

---

[44] De Groot 1982, vol. 5: 920.

Hands, feet and heads were all made from moulds, often of several parts. Further, several different types of head, hand and foot were put together in different combinations to create soldiers both in different postures and with varying appearances.[45]

The burial figures, like the healing figures, are undifferentiated; they are not made in order to represent the individual characteristics of specific soldiers, but rather to represent the concept 'soldiers'.

The non-differentiation of human figures for the tomb is shown in the way the potter's apprentices may have amused themselves by deliberately mismatching figures in the Tang dynasty:

> By tilting a head to catch a shadow, by rearranging the arms or the legs, an entirely different expression could be achieved. Sometimes the apprentices were a bit careless, attaching a head to a torso not intended for it; an amusing example of this kind of mix-up is to be seen in . . . Toronto. The body is that of a man, usually called a falconer type . . . Various male heads have been fitted to this type of body, generally handsome, rather haughty ones, giving an impression of pride and elegance. The Toronto figure, however, has had a lady's head attached to the broad shouldered, slim waisted, unfeminine body . . .
>
> I have seen quite a few equestrian figures made in the same way; to male bodies, exactly like others with men's heads, female heads were added either in ignorance, fun, or a desire to include lady riders in a calvacade when there were no female torsos ready for the buyer . . .[46]

The buyer might not even have noticed for 'it is only when one sees hundreds of them together . . . that one can be sure that there were variations in joining heads, arms and legs to the standard torsos'.

Thus far, the figure is merely perceived as undifferentiated, it is passive in the same sense as the emptied body. The next step in the transitional process of dissection and reconstruction is a kind of equational one: the healing figure is held over certain parts of the patient's body and called upon to take the place of each part of the patient's body.

---

[45] Rawson 1992: 142.   [46] Mahler 1959: 124.

Substitute, be thou in place of the fore part of the body, that he
or she (here the name is mentioned) may live to a green old age
with greater strength than a dragon's.
Substitute, be thou in place of the back parts, that he may live a
long and happy life and live to a very old age.
Substitute, be thou in place of the left side, that health may be
ensured to him for year upon year; be thou in place of the right
side, that his years may be multiplied to him.
Once be thou in his stead that his days may be prolonged even to
one hundred and twenty years.
Twice be thou in his stead, so that no evil-omened or murderous
influences may dog his path.
Thrice be thou in his place, so that the full cycle of fourfold
seasons may ensure him peace.[47]

The first part of each line dissects the healing figure. Each separate part
of the patient's body will be replaced by each separate part of the healing figure. The figure is called the representative of the patient and, at
the end of this process, it is considered to have replaced the body of the
patient and adopted the sickness. The figure is not chosen for this task
because of any *material* likeness to the patient – it does not reproduce
personal characteristics of the patient – but because it has been dissected and recreated *as* a new (the patient's) body.

The same naming of parts as a simultaneous dissection and substitution (reassembly) is also seen in the *nuo* theatre. In the following
example, the master, or Fashi, is about to carry out a ritual to cut open
his forehead to use his blood to write various charms. The sequence is
known as *kai hongshan* (opening the red mountain). In preparation, the
master invites the help of his own master – he becomes his master's
representative. In this sequence, the body of the master is called upon
in four parts, the mouth, heart, hands and feet to reassemble itself in/as
the Fashi's own body.

FASHI: Master, I shall burn three incense candles to welcome . . .
CHORUS: To welcome the master.

[47] De Groot 1982, vol. 6: 1260.

Duan *(To sever)*

FASHI: Invite the master's father(s) in the green cloud valley[48] to transmit the charms, transmit the magic . . .
CHORUS: Illustrious, almighty spirit.
FASHI: Invite Laojun[49] to descend to this world, there is no other matter . . .
CHORUS: No other matter but . . .
FASHI: At the home of X, to substitute one body.
CHORUS: For a while.
FASHI: The words from the master's mouth . . .
CHORUS: Shall come from the mouth.
FASHI: The magic of the master's hands . . .
CHORUS: Shall come from the hands.
FASHI: The secret words from the master's heart . . .
CHORUS: Shall rise up from the heart.
FASHI: The [pattern of] the *Ursa Major* shall come from the master's feet . . .
CHORUS: Shall be [imprinted] underneath the feet.[50]

Two further examples from the masked and marionette theatre and one from the *nuo* shall serve to illuminate the process of transforming the artefact into the performative body by using the dissection-substitution-reassembly process *kaiguang*. The following text is used to open a marionette to a certain role before a performance:

> I open your left eye which shines, your right eye which lights up;
> Fine hearing to your left ear, fine hearing to your right ear;
> I open your forehead, like the sceptre of the Five Thunders;
> I open your tongue, river and stream of purity;
> I open your left hand which holds the gates to heaven in
>   your fist,
> Your right hand which blocks the demon's passage;
> I open your left foot which stamps [the impression of] the gates
>   of heaven,

---

[48] Green stands for the east. Both here and in the personation ceremony, the cutting up, substituting and recreation of the body occurs between the north (death) and the east (source of life, Yang).

[49] Another name for Laozi, the 'father' of Daoism.

[50] *Zhongguo nuoxi diaocha baogao* 1992: 317–18.

Your right foot which stamps [the impression of] the doors to
the earth.[51]

The purpose of the *kaiguang* ceremony is not to allow the presence of
the god or spirit represented by the marionette or mask *into* the artefact, but rather to allow the presence that the artefact holds *to shine
out of*, emanate from, the artefact. An example of a healing ceremony
among the Chuan Miao shows this aspect:

> I [the disciple] will in the future open up the god's (source of)
> light. When I have opened up the light of the head, the head is
> well. When I have opened up the light of the eyes, then the two
> eyes are bright. When I have opened up the ear light, the two
> ears will hear in all directions. When the nose light has been
> opened up, the bridge of the nose will give good light. When the
> light of the mouth has been opened up, the mouth will hold 16
> pairs. When the hand light has been opened up, then the hands
> can be doctors and go in all directions. When the stomach light
> is opened, there will be inside the abdomen several tens of
> intestines. When the foot light has been opened up, the feet can
> be doctors and go in all four directions . . .[52]

Here the process of dissection opens up the body to let light shine out.
The light shining out is the presence or power with which the body is
changed or healed. The dissection of limbs allows for gaps, breaks or
holes through which presence may radiate. This idea can be elucidated
by the concept of acupuncture meridians. In terms of this ancient
thought, *qi*, which can variously be translated as energy, the breath (of
life) or presence, flows around the body like blood:

> Nourishing *qi* follows routes which go hand in hand with the
> flow of blood. These channels are called *jingluo*. In popular
> translations they are called meridians, but their definition is
> 'a pathway, a channel'. Protective *qi* has no set abode; it is
> omnipresent in the body. At certain points *qi* wells up to
> the body surface, just as springs of water appear on earth.
> These points are called *xue* 'holes'. They occur at points

[51] Chu Kunliang 1991: 155 (author's translation from the French).
[52] Graham 1954: 40.

of discontinuity where muscle, tendon and bone make
depressions and gaps. These are the acupuncture holes.[53]

Thus the principle of dissection which underpins the transformation
process, taking the body apart in order to reconstruct it anew, may also
be seen in terms of holing or making cavities. It can be described as
pulling apart to open or rupture things that were once joined in a certain way to rejoin them in another, new way.

The moment of rupture is the moment when the 'light' or presence can emanate, is released. That is, the rupture *causes* the release of
energy (presence) or *qi*. In a text used to accompany the making of an
exorcistic straw figure for the *nuo* event in Dejiang county, not only
does the master dissect the body into holes or lesions as he makes the
figure, he simultaneously recreates the body into a whole, a united
(jointed) being. He is simultaneously destroyer and creator, just as the
myths of the Taotie and other exorcist figures have suggested in chapter two:

> From Heaven's wasteland the grasses grew in the first era,
> Each stem of grass came out of the earth and divided into a body.
> All over the earth the grass shall grow, all over the earth it shall
>   grow tall (or live long),
> Without a father, without a mother, with no parents.
> . . .
> I twist a head with seven orifices to be passages ('points of
>   penetration', *tong*)[54]
> I twist the hands so that they can do ten thousand things.
> I twist the feet that they may walk in the ten directions,
> From head to foot, the bones and the flesh are linked together.[55]

Finally, the *kaiguang* ceremony only allows that the opened body remain opened for a certain duration of time – the length of the performance event. In the *nuo* and marionette theatres this might last one day
or night, or it might last several days or weeks. Each performance event

---

[53] Wu Jingnuan 1991: 27.
[54] See Teiser 1988: 148–9 for a brief discussion of the use of the term *tong* as
'spiritual penetration' in a Buddhist context. The term is certainly
related to sexual penetration. See Hawkes 1985.
[55] *Zhongguo nuoxi diaocha baogao* 1992: 324–5.

Plate 13   Closing the masks ceremony

begins with an opening ceremony and ends with a closing ceremony
(see Plate 13) where the performer goes through the reverse process and
reclaims his own soul from the water bowl.

An unopened performing body, be it mask, marionette or human
body, is not considered changed, but everyday, normal. It is not filled
with another life, it is unable to emanate presence. Between performance occasions, the masks and marionettes are closed and put away in
special trunks. (There are similar trunks in *jingju* used for costumes,
headgear, shoes, props and weapons.) While there is a special order to
putting the artefacts away in the trunks,[56] the artefacts are not treated
as they were when they were opened. In the masked theatre of Guizhou, for example, I often witnessed rather rough, careless handling of
the masks when putting them into the trunk.[57]

[56] *Zhongguo xiqu quyi cidian* 1983: 143 lists the seven most commonly
used trunks in *jingju* and their contents. See also, Riley 1990: 9 n. 8.
[57] This treatment seems quite contrary to the handling of masks in
Japanese theatre, for example. In the *no* theatre, the actor perceives the
mask as permanently opened and treats it as the living ancestor/teacher.
The actor never touches the front or 'face' of the mask and the mask is
kept in a special pouch when not being used.

Duan *(To sever)*

In conclusion, the performing body is prepared (emptied), dissected and substituted, part for part, at the moment of reconstruction into a new whole. Each part operates and articulates on different levels of meaning – the parts may contradict each other, or repeat the meaning articulated by other parts. But all separate parts are united by the corporeal centre of the new body.

The head as body

The concept of the body as the sum of individual parts and related to the Luo matrix of creation is only one kind of performance model in China. Here, the lower trunk is the unifying power. If this is brought into relation to ancestor ritual, then it can be stated that the groin (seat of human reproduction) and the stomach (eating, consuming the ancestors) are the loci of representation/ recreation. This concept is based on the model of a mortal, human body. A second model of performance in China conceives of the whole body as contained in the head rather than the trunk, and this associates the performing body with the gods, who are perceived as 'men with over-large heads' (see the etymological examination of the character *gui* (spirit) in chapter two). In terms of the Luo diagram imposed on the human body, the head occupies the station corresponding to heaven. The head and heaven correspond to each other as spiritual regeneration, just as the loins (through the feet and legs) are placed in congruence with the earth, or mortal regeneration in the performance model described above.

The *qitou*, or ugly head mortuary figurine discussed in chapter two, is the prime example of the importance of 'head' in performance, for it was most probably used *in place* of the body of the (whole) Fangxiangshi in burial processions of lower status. The second element of the compound *qitou* means 'head' which is endowed with regenerative qualities for the character for head, *tou*, is closely associated with an etymologically related character *dou* meaning 'bean'.[58] The two characters for head (*tou*) and bean (*dou*) bear some similarities which suggest that the way in which the bean is planted in the earth and germinates into a plant, was seen to be related to the planting of human heads in the earth in the tomb and in the foundations of new temple or palace structures, in the belief that new life would spring up (see

[58] Hentze 1950: 800–20 and 1955.

125

Diagram 31 a   The character *tou* (head)   b   The character *dou* (bean)

Diagram 31). Human skulls, severed from the skeleton, were often put into the tomb as offerings to the deceased. Perhaps the Fangxiangshi did the beheading with his lance-axe.[59] This supposition would confirm the view of the Fangxiangshi as a regenerative figure – one who destroys in order to recreate anew.

The Fangxiangshi and the *qitou* led the funeral procession on its way to the grave. The funeral procession[60] itself can be mapped as five separate parts which largely correspond to the Luo diagram view of the body. In this scheme, the Fangxiangshi and *qitou* exorcists lead the procession in the position of 'head'. The mortuary gifts, which follow in pavilions in front of, and to the side of, the main pavilion where the deceased is carried, represent the shoulders and arms. The corpse itself is in the central position, the loins of the procession, followed directly by the eldest son, sons and grandsons down through the line of descendants. Each participant in the mortuary procession (re)forms one part of the deceased body. Ancient documents confirm that the exorcist Fangxiangshi headed the funeral procession:

> At royal funerals he [the Fangxiangshi] goes ahead of the coffin and, arriving at the grave, he leaps into the pit to beat the four corners with his lance in order to drive away the fang-liang spectres.[61]

> The Fangxiang, with four gold eyes, bearskin, black upper garment and red lower garment, brandishing lance-axe and shield rides on a [chariot borne by] four horses and exorcises in advance.[62]

---

[59] Hentze 1955: 33.   [60] De Groot 1982, vol. 1.
[61] *Zhouli*, trans. De Groot 1982, vol. 1: 162.
[62] *Houhanshu, Liyi zhi, Da sang pian.*

> . . . the procession, headed by the [Fangxiangshi] with standards
> and banners, and escorted by the highest officers in mourning
> dress . . .[63]

The degree of elaborateness allowed each rank was, however, controlled by fixed sumptuary laws.[64] Not only did the strictures try to
control the number, size and quality of gifts offered to the deceased,
they also controlled the employment of the Fangxiangshi. For, only
royal burials were granted the service of a Fangxiang in the Sui dynasty:
'Officers of the 4th rank to the highest may use a Fangxiangshi and
those of the three lowest degrees must use *qitou*.'[65]

And in the Tang: 'Behind the carriage in which the soul tablet
was conveyed came the carriage of the Fangxiangshi which, however,
was to be replaced with a *qitou* at funerals of any grade below the 5th.'[66]
And finally in the Song: 'The officers of the four highest degrees might
have a Fangxiangshi, and those below in rank to the seventh degree a
qitou.'[67] These documents show that there was a direct equation between the Fangxiangshi and the *qitou*. Lower ranking people had to
make do with a mere 'image' or 'bust' of the exorcist. The Fangxiangshi
exorcist was substituted by a 'head'.

Not only was the Fangxiangshi exorcist perceived as head, but
also the exorcist figure Zhong Kui. In ancient times, Zhong Kui was the
name given to a sceptre-like tablet which was used by the emperor in
carrying out ritual exorcism:

> 'The sovereign, while worshipping the sun in the morning (at
> the equinox of spring) wore in his girdle a large Gui, and had in
> his hands a Gui of dominion.' This large Gui, according to the
> Jianlong edition . . . was a piece of jade 'Three *chi* in length and
> it had a Zhong Kui head above the place where it tapered away.'
> It is to this head of that badge, which the most powerful man

---

[63] *Houhanshu*, ch. 16, trans. De Groot 1982, vol. 2: 401.
[64] Ibid.: 403; Mahler 1959: 130; *Rituals of Family Life*, trans. De Groot
1982, vol. 2: 710; *Mingshi*, trans. De Groot 1982, vol. 2: 699; *Tang huiyao*,
ch. 38.
[65] *Books of the Sui Dynasty*, trans. De Groot 1982, vol. 6: 1151.
[66] *Rituals of the Kaiyuan Period*, trans. De Groot 1982, vol. 6: 1152.
[67] *Songshi*, trans. De Groot 1982, vol. 6: 1152.

and exorcist of the State used to carry while worshipping the universal devil-destroying god of light on the actual equinox when this god defeats darkness and its powers that our Zhong Kui owes his origin.[68]

The image of the head of Zhong Kui, like the image of the head of the Fangxiangshi (the *qitou*), thus represented (substituted) the whole exorcist body.

Since 1980, archaeologists have been excavating a site at Sanxingdui in Guanghan county in Sichuan.[69] The site has revealed an ancient Shang city dating from the first half of the Anyang period (13–11 BC) and two extraordinary pits outside the city walls. Pit number 1 contained at least three hundred objects including a gold human 'face', one bronze human 'face' and a kneeling (masked?) figurine. The pit also contained some life-size 'heads' in bronze, filled with jade, cowry shells and animal bones. Pit number 2 revealed yet more of such heads, figures and sacrificial artefacts. There were forty-one bronze 'heads', and fifteen semi-circular 'faces' or 'masks' (see Plate 14). Moreover, a huge bronze figurine standing on a pedestal with a total height of 2.60 metres was also among the items found in the pit.

In both pits, the 'heads' were near life-size, and fitted with bronze necks which indicate that they might have been fixed to some kind of body, though the neck fitting is too small to allow a human to 'wear' the head. The masks ranged in size from life-size, to one which measures nearly 138 cms. across and 65 cms. in height. All the items found in the pits showed signs of having been burned before being put into the pits. The pits were identified as dating from two different generations. While other finds of bronze masks have been discovered in tombs, (the bronze masks at Xunxian,[70] discussed in chapter five, were fixed over the entrance to the inner chamber and functioned as exorcists like the heads of Chi You and Taotie described in the previous chapter) the Sanxingdui find is not a burial place. The official report of the findings at Sanxingdui concludes that the pits were the result of sacrificial offerings

---

[68] De Groot 1982, vol. 6: 1172–3.
[69] Rawson 1992, fig. 85, Guanghan sanxingdui . . . 1987: 1–18, Guanghan sanxingdui . . . 1989: 1–21, Bagley 1988: 78–86 and 1990: 52–67.
[70] Guo Baoqun 1936: 167–200, Sun Haipo 1938 and Meister 1938: 5–12.

Plate 14   Guanghan Sanxingdui sacrificial bronze head (13–11 BC)

to the god of heaven, since ancient documents suggest burning was a crucial element of the worship of this god.[71] However, it seems unlikely that a rite to the god of heaven, which was commonly celebrated on top of a high hill, would be executed in a pit, near a river bed. Instead, the

---

[71] Guanghan sanxingdui . . . 1987: 14.

event may have been similar to a contemporary exorcist event where the *wu* is required to walk barefoot over red hot coals in a pit containing metal blades, *xiahuochi*, in an act of propitiation still carried out in the Qianzhongjun area of Guizhou.[72]

Despite the lack of real proof for this or any other theory, a performative view of the heads must be based on the concept that the heads represented the bodies of various gods. Moreover, just as different units of articulation of the whole body were dissected and reassembled in the *kaiguang* ceremony, these heads represent the dissected body (beheaded) reunited (reassembled) into an over-large (god)head.

Large-sized heads and masks are used in performance in the *nuo* event. These head masks, like the Guanghan heads, represent deities. In the *nuo* theatre, they are manipulated by human performers. Most forms of *nuo* theatre, including the *nuo* in Dejiang county in Guizhou, are dedicated to two figures the *nuogong* and the *nuopo* (father and mother of *nuo*) whose images are placed in the centre of the main altar. These figures are generally to be interpreted as the 'original ancestors', sometimes related to the creators of the world and begetters of the first human beings, the brother and sister Fuxi and Nuwa. In construction, the images of the two *nuo* figures are similar to the bronze 'heads'. They are made of clay and are smaller (of varying sizes) but they also have a long neck extension which allows them to be fixed to a rod, or pole, as body, which itself is then clothed by wrapping a gown over it. In some cases, a pliant bamboo stick is bound cross-wise to the rod to make arms. At the invocation and escorting of the gods, *qingshen* and *songshen*, the *nuo* performer holds both rods with the heads of the two figures placed upon them, and executes a dance with them.[73] In this dance, the rod ends are rested upon the tops of the performer's feet, so that rather than move them with his hands, the hands appear only to steady the puppet, which moves from below, with the performer's feet, in a hopping, jumping style of movement (see Diagram 32).[74] The heads are thus seen to be active at the moment of calling them into presence and calling them out of presence. In the meantime, for the duration of

---

[72] Zeng Xiangjun 1991.

[73] *Zhongguo minzu minjian wudao jicheng. Dejiang xian ziliaozhuan* 1990: 91–4. See also Tuo Xiuming 1992: 167.

[74] *Zhongguo minzu minjian wudao jicheng. Dejiang xian . . .* 1990: 94.

Duan *(To sever)*

Diagram 32   *songshen* (escorting the gods in Dejiang *nuo*)

the performance, the heads *stand for* the whole presence (god-heads) and are placed, without the rod attachment, static on the altar.

Chinese rod puppets, the *zhangtou muou* (stick and head puppet) of the south, as for example, Cantonese rod puppets, are, like the bronze heads at Sanxingdui, very close to human proportions in size and, like the *nuogong* and *nuopo* of the *nuo* theatre, operated by a simple stick technique.[75] The heads are treated as separate units from the stick bodies which are interchangeable. The performer of the rod puppet is always visible, and seems to shadow movements which the puppet executes. A rod puppet of considerably smaller size (20 cms. high) is perceived, like the *nuogong* and *nuopo* principally as 'head' directed by the body of the human master:

> Before the performance started, the puppets were taken out of the trunk, a stick was attached to each hand, and the headless

[75] Kagan 1978: 106.

bodies were hung on a string . . . backstage . . . The puppeteer guides the right arm with his right hand, left hand and back-stick with his left hand . . . If a general has to show his strength by leg movements, the puppeteer transfers the three sticks into his left hand and moves the legs with a fourth stick.[76]

Here, the rod functions as the *device* by which the artefact is made to move when balanced on the puppeteer's own body. Or, to put it another way, the master's body becomes the rod/body of the puppet.

One form of *nuo* that exists in Sichuan province, and by chance also in Yunnan, known as *tiyangxi*, is based on the joint performance of marionette, masked performer, and performer without mask.[77] The event is divided into two main sections – the *tianshang 32 xi* (32 heavenly plays) and the *dixia 32 xi* (32 earthly plays). The heavenly plays are performed by the marionettes who represent various gods. The earthly plays are performed by masked performers before the altar on which the marionette-gods are now placed. The unmasked performers play at the end of the event when the masks have been replaced on the altar with the marionettes. The marionettes are god-like, they descend; once descended, they do not walk on the earth as man does, but seem like 'faces' (heads) moving independently of (as) bodies. A similar concept is described by Kleist: 'The puppets only need the ground to skim its surface in order to give the movement of their limbs new energy; we need the ground for resting, to recover from the effort of dancing . . .'[78] The performance mode is not unlike the goal of *jingju* students in training for the stage, exemplified in the leg exercises at the beginning of this chapter.

The head as body is, like the dissected body above, an opened body. The parts of the body have been dissected and recomposed as head, the unifying (heavenly) centre. The process of dissection and reassembly that defines the head as opened (presenced) performing body also forms part of the mortuary rite and concerns the ancestral tablet. During the

[76] Werle 1973: 75.

[77] Riley 1990a. The marionette gods of the *tianxi* and masks from the *dixi* are illustrated in Wang Chunwu 1992: 287–306, and in Hao Gang and Tao Guangpu 1993: 149–69.

[78] Kleist 1990: 559–60.

funeral procession from the home to the tomb, a wooden board, in-scribed with the name and rank of the deceased, is carried by the eldest son. At the tomb, he places it on the coffin lid. This board is known as the soul tablet or ancestral tablet. After the funeral, it is placed on the ancestral altar in the home along with all the others of generations of the same family or clan. In appearance, the ancestral altar is something like a model graveyard with various tombstones (soul tablets), each dedicated to a deceased member of the family. However, these tablets are also residences for the souls of the deceased. They are cared for by the living members of the family, offered food and invited to intercede with powers in heaven to direct fate kindly on the descendants. They are a kind of representational abode, or surrogate of the deceased person, whose body may have decayed but whose soul is present in the tablet and may be approached; who still deserves respect as the living body had done and who may even cause harm if left to roam uncared for. The process of substitution occurs when the ancestral board is carried to the grave and becomes the abode of the soul of the deceased.

At the graveside in Fujian in the late 1880s, the chief mourner (the eldest son) placed the tablet on the lid of the coffin and the mourners shouted to the deceased to rise up:

> These words have the effect of inducing the soul to enter the tablet. From this very moment the tablet is considered to be imbued with afflatus of the dead and to have become his perpetual duplicate, to serve as patron divinity in the domestic circle and there to receive the offspring's sacrifices and worship.[79]

The process of transformation is quite similar to that used in healing a patient. The figure (here the tablet) is labelled or inscribed with the name of the person it is to represent. It is then held over a part of the person's body and words are spoken to the effect that the surrogate shall now take place of the real body. From this moment, the surrogate is treated as the real body.

The comparison is even more striking when the concept of this wooden board and what it is supposed to represent is examined in

---

[79] De Groot 1982, vol. 1: 211–12.

detail. The Chinese term for soul tablet is *muzhu*. *Mu* means 'wood' and *zhu* is a term that can mean 'lord', 'master', 'owner' or it can also mean 'to lodge, to dwell'. It has been suggested that the origin of the wooden tablet was a life-like wooden statue of the deceased,[80] but since figural representation can be accorded identity by the opening process, this need not have been the case. However, the wooden tablet has an equivalent significance – it is treated as if it were the body of the deceased.

After having been laid over the coffin, the tablet is brought to a mandarin or scholar to perform the final inscription, to 'dot' the tablet. The dotting of red ink operates as a substitute for blood (sometimes the blood of a cock is used). By dotting blood on each separate part of the tablet body, the mandarin dissects (blood is spilled) and opens or recreates the new:

> First he dots the topmost part, which in most cases is engraved or painted with the image of a sun in the midst of clouds, saying: *Dian tian, tian qing* [I mark the heavens, may they radiate]. Then he marks the pedestal, pronouncing the words *Dian di, di ling* [I mark the earth, may the earth be vivified]. In this way, the natural influences of the Universe are summoned to work upon the tablet . . . Now the front side is dotted on the right and left at about the middle of its height, the words pronounced running *Dian er, er cong* [I dot the ears, may the ears be acute]; then come two points at about the same height but a little nearer the centre, with the words, *Dian mu, mu ming* [I dot the eyes, may

[80] The scholarly argument centres around a passage from the *Tianwen* 'When Wu set out to kill Yin, why was he grieved? He went into battle carrying his father's corpse: why was he in such a hurry?' (Hawkes 1985: 133, lines 161–2). The word 'corpse' is variously interpreted as meaning corpse, ancestral tablet or personator. Erkes (1928: 5–12) makes the case for ancestral tablet which was in the shape of the deceased, i.e. a statue of the deceased. Karlgren proposes the idea of ancestral tablet because: 'The wooden ancestral tablet was the resting place of the ancestor's spirit, once his body was dead and decomposed. In this sense it was a substitute for his body, his spiritual force had entered it, and therefore it was carried into battle, bringing this mental force of his into play on the side of the descendent.' (Karlgren 1930: 9). See also Schindler 1923: 320.

the eyes be bright]. Then follows a dot on the character for 'males' . . . indicating the male descendants who erect the tablet as an object of worship for the family, the accompanying words being *Dian nan, nan chang shou* [I dot the males, may the males live long] – and in the end a dot is placed on the character *zhu* 'tablet' . . . the words pronounced here are *Dian zhu, zhu xian ling* [I dot the tablet, may the tablet manifest the spirit].[81]

In the spoken text, the ancestral tablet is perceived *as if* it were carved or shaped in some way similar to the human body. This body consists principally of head and groin, as opposed to deity which is represented by head alone. However, it is *not* shaped like a real body. Like the healing figure, the performing body is undifferentiated until called into presence by identifying separate parts – ears, eyes, groin,[82] etc. – with that of the deceased.

The *nuo* masks, the bronze heads at Sanxingdui, the ancestral tablet, the marionette heads and the mortuary figure, the *qitou*, even the human skulls, were all marked with red paint, cinnabar, or blood, at the eyes, nose, mouth and ears. This shows that the process of *kaiguang* opening was carried out on them to recreate them as performing bodies. The head becomes the performing body (possibly deity) which is operated by another (human) body. The same process of opening can be seen as the *jingju* student cuts his body up into parts (*shou, yan, zhi, fa, bu*) and reunites them (*zonghe*) in a syncretic new whole (role) and as the *nuo* performer interprets his body according to the cells of the harmonising, unifying Luo diagram. In these latter examples, the performing body is a whole body, rather than 'head' or deity. Whether the performing body is an artefact, 'head' reassembled as deity, or a human performer reassembled as whole body into a theatrical or exorcist role, the treatment of both is the same. The performing body is pulled open, dissected into units of articulation to be reassembled as a *presenced*, articulate(d) body.

---

[81] De Groot 1982, vol. 1: 214–15. The square brackets are my translations.

[82] Implied in the dotting of the 'male' part is also the idea that future generations shall be fertile and bring forth yet more generations that the line be continued.

The spectator watching Mei Lanfang move as the concubine Yang Yuhuan, and as the geese that she describes, perceives the performance in a series of 'cuts'. He follows the montage of the events manifested in one brief moment of performance that might consist of the elements hand, fan, geese, eye movement, cloud footstep in any particular order or combination that he chooses to recreate them. The spectator confirms presence by reassembling the units of articulation in the mind's eye.

4 **Shenfen**
(Identity)

The performer Mei Lanfang presents the role of the concubine Yang Yuhuan at the same time as showing the 'geese' that Yang Yuhuan sees. Separate parts of the performer's body represent different things. Like a marionette master holding several puppets in his hands, Mei Lanfang manipulates the individual parts (puppets) of his body in articulating the role of Yang Yuhuan. Furthermore, the whole body gives out the syncretic sign of Yang Yuhuan in costume and make-up, so that Mei Lanfang is not only marionette master to various aspects of the story represented by bits of his body, and he is also inside the body, and he is also one of the marionettes held by (himself) the master. The Chinese term *shenfen* (identity) literally means 'body divided'. The Chinese performer is at once part of the presentation (inside), and the manipulator, or master of the presentation (outside). He exists at the intersection of proximity to the object being presented and at a distance from it. Such physical proximity and distance is closely echoed in the spoken dramatic text.

The shifting self
All the outward signs of Yang Yuhuan manifest the role *as* empress. However, the only occasions that Yang Yuhuan uses the first person pronoun are when she is the subject of the emperor's command.

> Yang Yuhuan (*recites*):
> Last night, the imperial edict was received, ordering *me* to come to the Pavilion of a Hundred Flowers today.

In this context, 'me' describes the unworthy, untitled, undeserving subject in relation to the great emperor. According to Chinese etiquette,

137

the speaker should always attempt to present himself in a more humble relationship than that which really exists. In the case of performance, it reveals a further depth to the role of Yang Yuhuan, for what is Yang Yuhuan without her role (identity) as concubine?

The personal pronoun appears only twice more, as she orders the eunuchs Gao and Pei to report when the emperor arrives:

> Yang Yuhuan (*speaks*):
> In a while, his majesty will be here. Inform *me* at once.

And later, when the emperor does not come, as she tells how she will persuade the emperor to promote the eunuchs if only they will go and fetch him to her:

> Yang Yuhuan (*sings*):
> *I'll* propose a memorandum to the emperor . . .
> To grant you promotion after promotion.

This 'I' is the defeated 'I'. Yang Yuhuan uses the personal pronoun in communicating with the eunuchs, which puts her automatically on their level, intimates her attempt to make them feel sorry for her – she is only an ordinary person, like them, trapped in her official position, but she will use that position to reward them if they do what she asks.

On every other occasion, Yang Yuhuan refers to herself as 'the mistress' or avoids a subject altogether by using the passive case. In part, this reflects the avoidance of pronouns in classical Chinese. The subject is generally either absent from the sentence altogether, or the sentence is expressed in a passive form. In speaking directly to the emperor, for example, Yang Yuhuan would use the term 'your slave' of herself – the relationship between speakers is thus established in the term used for the subject. However, there is a case for suggesting that the lack of subject in Yang Yuhuan's speech, and at times her objectification of herself (as the 'mistress', the 'concubine'), *distances* the role that is presented from the performer who presents it.

Yang Yuhuan's very first aria narrates the performer's own first entrance. The performer/narrator compares Yang Yuhuan to the mythological goddess of the moon, Chang E, and describes the entrance of Yang Yuhuan (as he presents her entering) as if she were the moon rising:

Shenfen *(Identity)*

> Yang Yuhuan: (*sings*)
> The wheel of ice[1] starts to rise over the island in the sea,
> See the Jade Hare, Jade Hare faces east and leaps,
> The wheel of ice departs from the island in the sea,
> Heaven and Earth shine brightly,
> Bright moon in mid-air,
> Like Chang E leaving the Moon Palace,
> Like Chang E leaving the Moon Palace.

The performer makes the pose *baoyueshi* (holding up the moon, see Diagram 59) as he sings these lines. The performer *is* the rising moon. Later, as Yang Yuhuan is on her way to the meeting place, the eunuch announces, 'Mistress, we've arrived at the Jade Stone bridge.' Yang Yuhuan sings of what she is doing, 'leaning' over the railings of the bridge. While she does so, the eunuchs tell her what she can see – that fish are in the water below, and that geese fly above them. Yang Yuhuan's reply is to use their statements almost as if they were prompts. She repeats their words exactly and then completes the rest of the line:

> Yang Yuhuan (*sings*):
> Leaning over the balustrade of the Jade Stone Bridge.

> Pei (*speaks*):
> The mandarin ducks playing on the water.

> Yang Yuhuan (*continues to sing*):
> The mandarin ducks playing on the water.

> Gao (*speaks*):
> Golden carp play at the surface of the water.

> Yang Yuhuan (*continues to sing*):
> Golden carp play at the surface of the water,
> Ah, at the surface of the water.

This device occurs again during the drinking scene:

> Yang Yuhuan (*sings*):
> Holding up the golden goblets,
> Palace maids and eunuchs attentively serve wine.

---

[1] Both this term and the Jade Hare of the second line represent the moon.

Pei (*speaks*):
Mistress, life on earth . . .

Yang Yuhuan (*continues to sing*):
Life on earth is like a short, spring dream . . .

Gao (*speaks*):
So, drink with abandon . . .

Yang Yuhuan (*continues to sing*):
So, drink with abandon, several cups.

The bridge scene is the first scene of intoxication – Yang Yuhuan sings, 'The scenery provokes a drunken desire in me.' The second scene of intoxication occurs when she has already had a good amount of wine and is quite drunk. When Yang Yuhuan is drunk, 'out' of her senses, she forgets her lines. But the performer, Mei Lanfang, is not drunk, he merely presents drunkenness.

Yang Yuhuan's final aria shows this aspect of distance to the role even more clearly. Here, the performer uses the second person singular 'you' when singing of Yang Yuhuan, as if the performer is already separate from the role, has left it for the dressing room:

Yang Yuhuan (*sings*):
Yang Yuhuan is as if in a dream tonight.
Remember the time *you* first entered the palace,
How kindly the emperor treated *you*,
How much he loved *you*;
But today, suddenly, is forsaking,
Can it be that from today, the two shall be forever parted!

Jingju is full of repetitions that concern the details of the plot. Even before Yang Yuhuan enters, the eunuchs discuss the rendezvous at the Pavilion of a Hundred Flowers and the planned banquet:

Pei (*speaks*):
Our mistress plans a banquet today in the Pavilion of a Hundred
    Flowers.
You and I must serve with care.

Shortly after entering, Yang Yuhuan repeats this information:

Shenfen *(Identity)*

Yang Yuhuan (*recites*):
This person, the concubine, [is] Yang Yuhuan. Last night, the
imperial edict was received, ordering me to come to the
Pavilion of a Hundred Flowers today and prepare a banquet.

She asks the two eunuchs if everything is ready, and then sings:

Yang Yuhuan (*sings*):
Let's go to the Pavilion of a Hundred Flowers!

Gao and Pei (*recite*):
To the Pavilion of a Hundred Flowers!

The company set out for the pavilion and after one circuit of the stage,
Gao and Pei announce they have arrived:

Gao and Pei (*speak*):
We've arrived at the Pavilion of a Hundred Flowers.

Yang Yuhuan (*sings*):
Already arrived at the Pavilion of a Hundred Flowers.

When the eunuchs inform her that the emperor has gone to the Western Palace to another concubine instead, Yang Yuhuan replies:

Yang Yuhuan (*recites*):
Ah! Last night, the imperial edict was received, ordering me to
come to the Pavilion of a Hundred Flowers and prepare a
banquet.

Thus the same information is repeated on five occasions almost verbatim, regardless of its somewhat minor importance to the play. One
practical explanation for this constant repetition of plot detail may be
the loose structure of theatre-going in China, for the spectators are free
to wander in and out as the mood takes them. In the tea-house performances, tea is served amidst much chatter, attention only being
directed to the stage when something exciting is about to happen. On
the other hand, the device also adds to the sense of 'narrative' that permeates Chinese theatre. The figures each narrate what they are doing
as they do it (leaning on the balustrade of the bridge, for example). This
technique is related to similar devices used by story tellers to slip in
and out of the figures they narrate:

A young beauty! twice eight years of age,
Too sad to comb her hair and wash her face.
Lying on the bed,
You'll be saying, this girl's depressed and worried . . .
Can't take tea, won't think of rice.
. . .

You'll be asking, what sickness does Yingying have?
Suddenly, look! She's thinking of,
Master Zhang.
All I can think of is young Zhang,
Does he think of me?
I eat less than half a bowl of rice a day,
Then I think of my young Zhang again,
And drink less than a bowl of soup in two days.
Soup! No! The soup is coming,
But what kind of food is that for a young girl?
You'll see, so starved from sorrow,
That my front presses my heart
Against the walls of my back.
Lo, who among you has ever seen
A grown girl of sixteen
Can't manage two steps . . .[2]

The performer (the story-tellers use the same verb as theatre performers, *biaoyan*, 'to manifest and display') slips in and out of the first and third person, at times narrating the situation, at times presenting it from inside the role. Thus the corporeal dissection of the body identified in the previous chapter applies to the dissection of the 'I' persona or self in the spoken text. The self of the performer is many selves, many others.

[2] From *Xixiangji* (*The Tale of the Western Wing*), in the form of *jingyun dagu* (Beijing Rhyme and Big Drum Story Telling). The piece was taught to me by Meng Zhaoyi of the China Art Broadcasting Company: Story Telling Company. I am not aware of a written text in this form. The Yuan *zaju* text of *Xixiangji* by Wang Shifu (*c.* 1250–1300) has been adapted into many different kinds of performance art. For a full translation of Wang's play cycle, see West and Idema 1991.

Counterpart

In the history of Chinese performance, there is a strong sense of the performer as someone who is other. The idea of family discussed in chapter one indicated that the performing body is not any ordinary body, but one who is given the right to perform by birth, initiation or training. Chinese *jingju* actors were technically élite, but in fact performers were generally regarded as social outcasts.

In performance, the actor represents something else, something other. In the case of Yang Yuhuan, above, the actor represents many others (concubine, slave, geese, moon, etc.). However, the sense of otherness that the performer embodies is not one of opposition. The performer is both distant from and close to the role, just as the manufactured performing artefact, the puppet, for example, etymologically represents the quality *otherness*, though the performance of the puppet rests on the quality of its *likeness* to real bodies.

The most striking aspect of Chinese performance is the analogy of theatre play to the afterworld, or world of the dead as world of 'other'. This can be traced to the etymological link between the words *kui* (puppet), *gui* (spirit) and *ou* (counterpart) as discussed in chapter three. The sense of otherness is embodied by the dead, or the spirits of the dead. The spirit of the deceased is considered to be *like* the living, but actually other, just as the performing body is considered to be *like* the living, but actually other. The Han scholar, Wang Chong, associates the concept of other with *gui* (spirit, ghost): 'Some say that *gui* have material existence like men. *Gui* exist and their abode is beyond the borders of China.'[3] Another early document, the *Yijing*, also conceives *gui* as something foreign, outside the regular borders of China proper. It records the fact that the enemy came from the *guifang* (land of the demons). Wu comments: '*Gui* is the ideogram for a ghost or demon. Are these demon regions located on a plane other than an earthly plane, or are they simply enemies in warfare? In military terms, any opponent is a demon.'[4] Other expeditions that were also led against this geographical

---

[3] *Lun Heng*, trans. Shen Chien-shih 1936–7: 2.
[4] Wu Jingnuan 1991: 215. Compare Wu's idea of spiritual leadership to the section describing ancestral tablets taken into battle in the previous chapter of this study.

or spiritual region *gui* are mentioned in the *Yijing*.[5] Moreover, the *Shijing* (*Book of Odes*), *Daya* section has, 'You have exasperated the Chinese within and the *guifang* regions abroad.'[6]

The Fangxiangshi exorcists embodied a similar concept of 'otherness'. They came from areas outside China proper and brought with them esoteric practices, unknown in the central government at the time, which were admired, despised and feared.

> Throughout archaic times, the word [*fang*] commonly occurs in the compound *sifang*, meaning four outlying areas, and hence refers to people, places and cultures removed from the central court . . . Fangshi were involved in exorcism, the practice of medicine and divination through heaven-man-earth parallels; they were virtually all from outlying areas and their practices were distinct in most areas from court orthodoxies.[7]

The full title of the Fangxiangshi in the light of this, may literally mean someone who belongs to the *shi* or 'guild of different people'. His function is to mediate between the worlds of spirits and the living. In his costume and appearance, he is part-man, part-not-man (part-beast, part ancestor/creator), he is 'other'.

Thus anything that derived from the outside, from beyond, was different, other, coming from another world. A common derogatory term for Westerners was the phrase *laogui* (old devil, one who comes from the other (demon) regions).

The two concepts – other/foreign, and the dead – were certainly conceived as being related, for not only were foreign prisoners valued as a political status symbol, they were also considered to have special powers because they originated from such *gui* (other worldly) places. Foreigners were almost exclusively employed in the stables to care for the most-prized sacrificial beast, the horse:

> As early as the third dynasty, grooms were chosen from among the prisoners taken in the wars on the borders of the empire. The *Zhouli*, speaking on the 'convicts of the south' (*manli*)

[5] Shen Chien-shih 1936–7: 14.   [6] Ibid.: 14.
[7] DeWoskin 1983: 2.

says that 'they shall serve the director of the stud and feed the horses'. The 'convicts of the east (*yili*) shall serve the herdsmen and feed the oxen and horses.'[8]

Furthermore, grooms (foreign prisoners of war) and other foreigners (often entertainers) were chosen to take part in royal sacrificial events: 'At the reception of a foreign visitor, or at a funeral service, they [the foreign grooms] led the horses to their appointed places on the meeting ground. They do the same when the consecrated horse is brought for the funeral service.'[9] Though this fact has obvious political implications – the captured prisoners are paraded before the foreign guest to impress him – it nonetheless confirms the association between foreigners and the powers conferred by the other world of (*gui*) spirits.

Foreigners, dwarfs and hunchbacks (people who were other) were also represented among mortuary figures from the Han dynasty and particularly during the Tang, when trade with the West opened up through the silk route.[10] It would seem that foreigners, being other, are appropriate images or representatives of, other worlds such as the world of death, or the world of spirits. So close was the association between the concept of death and foreign, that ancient script used the same character for both: 'Modern palaeographic studies have confirmed that the oracle graph for *shi* [personator/corpse] showed a prostrate body with arms and legs dangling limply; and that it was interchangeable with the oracle graph for *yi* "(eastern) barbarian".'[11]

The manufactured items in the tomb – mortuary goods including vessels, weapons, musical instruments and figures – are known by the Chinese term *mingqi*. This term has variously been translated as 'bright vessels', 'vessels to the eye of fancy', 'vessels in imagination' and 'spirit vessels'.[12] The second part of the compound, *qi*, is quite straightforward in meaning. It means 'a vessel, utensil, dish, implements, wares'. Thus *qi* describes something that has a use, it is a container of some kind.

The first term in the compound, *ming*, means 'light', 'bright', 'luminescence'. *Ming* is also used to mean 'illuminate', 'show up clearly'.

---

[8] Hentze 1928: 54.   [9] Ibid.: 54.
[10] Mahler 1959.   [11] Carr 1985: 4.
[12] Ibid.: 71.

The question, 'Do you understand?' uses the term *ming*, in the sense of 'see the light'. Something, or someone who is *ming* is therefore 'intelligenced', 'luminous'. The *kaiguang* (opening) ceremony derives from the idea that something which gives out light is presenced. In this sense, the mortuary figures must also be considered 'presenced figures'.

On one level, the term *mingqi* indicates items that are not the same as other *qi* or implements that might be used in ordinary daily life. The *Liji* sets the term *mingqi* opposite the term *jiqi* (sacrificial implements): 'Implements for the manes are implements fit for use among disembodied souls, just as sacrificial implements are fit for use among living men.'[13] The *mingqi* are only of use to the dead. The same work also records Confucius as saying:

> Those who make (valueless) implements for the manes of the dead show that they are acquainted with the proper method of celebrating obsequies, for, though such implements be ready at hand, they are unfit for real use.[14]

The *mingqi* are different from *real* artefacts in some way – they cannot be used as if real (hence the various translations of vessels of 'fancy', of 'imagination'), they should not be treated as real. The *qitou* head (a burial artefact, thus a *mingqi*) represented the presence of a (real) exorcist Fangxiangshi. Among the many burial goods are examples of *ge* axe made in jade which could not possibly have been used as real weapons, for they would have shattered on impact. Yet the presence of such lance-axes was possibly enough to suggest the presence of a Fangxiang or exorcist (who is particularly associated with this weapon) and, by extension, the performance of exorcism. The *Liji* recounts Confucius as saying:

> If we were to deal with our dead as if life were really extinct in them, we should be inhumane, and therefore we ought not to do so; but if we were to treat them as if they were quite alive, we should betray great ignorance, and therefore neither may we do so. For this reason, the bamboo instruments are not quite fit for use, those of stoneware cannot be well washed, nor can those

---

[13] *Liji*, trans. Carr 1985: 73.   [14] *Liji*, trans. De Groot 1982, vol. 2: 807.

of wood be carved. The cithems and lutes are strung, but not tuned; the mouth organs and Pandean pipes are in good order, but not attuned to the same key; there are also bells and sonorous stones, but no stands to suspend them from.[15]

Here, the musical instruments stand for real items but are not the same as the real items. The *mingqi* were clearly differentiated from articles of daily use: they were specially made and specially assigned to the tomb, but they were in some way imperfect – not fit for earthly use. This supports the view of death as a kind of life which is *similar* to this life, but not the same. The other world is not the negative or mirror copy of this world. Rather it is the same in outward appearance, shadows, or *seems* the same. This belief is current in contemporary Taiwan:

> According to the *tang-ki* [*wu*-ist priest], the underworld is organized into ten kingdoms or palaces, each ruled by one of the officials of the underworld. Each kingdom is a replica of the *iong* [this] world, containing the same cities, towns and villages in the same relationship to each other as in the *iong* world. After judgement, each person is sent to one of the kingdoms, depending on his date of birth and hence animal sign under which he was born. Most of the villagers have a simpler picture. For them, there is only one kingdom, which is a complete replica of the *iong* world. When people die they go to live in the area of the underworld that corresponds to the *iong*-world town or village they lived in.[16]

Visits to the underworld are made by some of the villagers, with the help of the priest, in search of contact with recently deceased members of their family. Their journey is prompted by onlookers who, on the basis of what the traveller relates as to his whereabouts, guide the traveller almost from house to house to find the person for whom he is looking.

The same fundamental belief permeates the whole historical and cultural spectrum of China. For example, the Han idea of the underworld shows the same basic premise: death is another kind of life. The dead person must be provided for in the same way as in life.

---

[15] Ibid.: 707.   [16] Ahern 1973: 232.

Burial practices . . . were intended to provide some form of guidance for the *hun* [spirit], so that it could safely be escorted on its journey to paradise, through the many dangers that were known to beset the path . . . At the same time, steps were taken to ensure that the *po* [spirit] would remain satisfied, appeased and benevolent for as long as possible . . . For this purpose large supplies of material goods were buried for its gratification and use, or attempts were made to preserve the body for eternity . . . it was also right and proper to provide for the further possibility that the soul should find itself in the grim and dour life of the Yellow Springs. For this reason . . . a retinue of servants that corresponded with the rank to which it could aspire [was provided].[17]

The dead in the other world cannot use real artefacts, as they would in real life. Instead, the artefacts must be other or transformed (made other) in some way. In its material form, the *mingqi* is useless. The *mingqi* artefacts in the tomb were *like* real objects but untuned, unglazed or unfit for use in this world. Paper houses, furniture, cars, refrigerators, and so on, are burned at the tomb site. Wooden or clay servants cannot really serve the deceased. However, once transformed (opened into presence) these items can be useful in the other world.

The representation of a human figure (*ou*) in wood, or other sculptured material is conceived as the mate, or counterpart to man. The most common wood for such wooden tomb figurines (as also masks and puppets) is the lightweight *dong* wood. The character for *dong* wood is made up of the radical meaning wood, and a sound marker *tong* which has the meaning 'like, similar'. Likewise, the masks and heads at Xunxian and Sanxingdui are made of bronze *tong*, which is made up of the radical meaning metal and the same sound marker *tong* meaning 'like, similar' (see Diagram 33). The articles for the other world are *gui* (foreign, other) but also similar or not-other.

The mortuary figures are transformed in some way in order that they can function in the other world. Often, the artefact was burned, or broken before it was put into the tomb (paper becomes ash, a pot becomes shards). In this case, the other or counterpart element of the

---

[17] Loewe 1979: 11.

Diagram 33   The related characters *tong* (similar), *dong* (paulownia wood) and *tong* (bronze)

item is transferred to the other world, rather than its materiality. Alternatively, the flames of the burning artefact and the dissection of body as the broken artefact transformed them into presenced bodies, as in the *kaiguang* ceremony. The counterpart image is like – takes the form of – the real but is actually 'other', is filled with presence. This suggests that the *mingqi* mortuary article, like the performing body, can be considered as a pre-formative body, a vessel (the emptied, performing body of chapter three – the outward form) to be filled through the process of *kaiguang* with another kind of presence (*qi*) – a presence related to and mediating with an other life.[18]

Such a theory is confirmed by the example of the *qitou* (ugly head) which is endowed with the power to hold or contain souls. The Chinese dictionary *Shuowen* (compiled AD 100) glosses the word *qi* as 'mask', in particular, a mask used in exorcism ceremonies. The same term, *qitou*, was also used to describe death masks. A record of customs in the Eastern Han, the *Taiping yulan*, explains the term *qitou* thus: 'Among the people, the belief is current that at death, the soul and energy of life float away. It is important to make a *qitou* to put over the corpse's face . . . to keep the soul in place and prevent it from rising and floating off.'[19] Thus the *qitou* is a representation of something man-like (head), it is also related to aspects or beings of another world (through its etymological association with the word *gui*), and it is

[18] The *Chinese-English Dictionary* 1981 does not even list the term *mingqi* under the character for 'bright', but under its homonym *ming* meaning 'dark, obscure, of the netherworld, or underworld'. This seems to deny (for political reasons?) any aspect of luminescence, or radiating of presence which is a key aspect of the mortuary items.

[19] *Taiping yulan*, ch. 552.

capable of holding down the soul or life-force of the deceased. It literally masks the orifices whence the soul would otherwise escape, it holds
presence in.

Automata

The man-made, or artificial performing body, the artefact, has been described as an item which is *like* the human body but actually *other*.
Both major terms in China for puppet and marionette are related to the
concept of otherness. The term *kuilei* belongs to the group of words
based on the character *gui* (spirit, other, foreign). *Ou* (puppet) belongs
to the same group through its relation to the character *yu* and means
'counterpart', 'opposite', 'mate'. The history of the Chinese theatre is
filled with examples of the performance of puppets or marionettes
(artefacts) which perform as if they were automata, independent of any
human mover or controller, though they may have had a human creator. That is, the actual mover/creator of the performing artefact is
visible but not *seen*. The perception of apparently autonomously motiv-
ated figures depends entirely on the spectator's gaze, just as the personation ceremony explored in chapter three depends on the attitude of the
participants towards the personator, or the geese presented by Yang
Yuhuan depend upon the spectator's view of Mei Lanfang.

The Chinese marionette players recite an event supposedly occurring in the Zhou dynasty at the court of King Mu (ruled 947–928 BC) as
the 'origin' of puppet performance. Since the work in which the tale is
narrated, the *Liezi*, purports to be contemporary but was written much
later, in the third century, its authenticity and value as historical source
has been doubted.[20] Nevertheless, if it is viewed from the performance
point of view, the tale supports the idea that the marionette is perceived
as something which is other, independent of its human creator.

> King Mu of the Zhou dynasty (ruled 947–928 BC) was making
> an inspection tour of the western frontier. On the way, the
> craftsman Yan Shi was presented to him. King Mu asked: 'What
> special skills have you?' Yan Shi replied: 'I can make whatever
> thing you ask. But I have already made something that I hope

---

[20] Dolby 1978: 97 and Stalberg 1984: 18.

you would like to see.' When Yan Shi next met the King, the
King said: 'Who have you brought with you?' Yan Shi answered:
'I have brought you a figure which can sing and dance and act.'
King Mu was amazed to see that the figure could walk forwards,
lift its head and bend at the waist; it seemed to move like a real
person. Ingenious! If one touched its face, it sang an appropriate
song. If one clapped hands, it began to dance rhythmically.
Whatever anyone could think up, it could perform – many
diverse things (literally a thousand transformations and ten
thousand changes).[21]

A point little regarded, is the beginning of the tale. The location of
the event is far away from the central court, when the king was on his
way to the *western* frontier. All that was situated outside or at the
edges of the state, to the west, was strange, barbarian, or foreign and
was termed *gui*.

The tale associates the performing figure with otherness (in
Chinese terms, death), echoed at a great distance in time and space by
Edward Gordon Craig:

> I think that my aim shall rather be to catch some far-off glimpse
> of that spirit which we call Death – to recall beautiful things
> from the imaginary world, they say they are cold, these dead
> things, I do not know – they often seem warmer and more living
> than that which parades as life. Shades, spirits seem to me to be
> more than beautiful and filled with more vitality than men and
> women . . .
>
> But from that mysterious, joyous and superbly complete life
> which is called Death – that life of shadows and unknown
> shapes, where all cannot be blackness and fog as is supposed,
> but vivid colour, vivid light, sharp-cut form; and which one
> finds peopled with strange, fierce and solemn figures, pretty
> figures impelled to some wondrous harmony of movement.[22]

The figure made by Yan Shi seemed to move of its own accord. The
account does not mention any controlling device used by the creator of

---

[21] *Liezi. Tangwen* 1965: 112.   [22] Craig 1914: 17.

the figure. The fascination of the figure lies in the fact that it seemed to be *like* a real human being but was actually totally other, like an alien being:

> King Mu thought it was not a mechanical figure, but a real person. Together with his retinue, he watched the figure perform. Just before the end of the performance, the figure began to tease a concubine standing close to King Mu. The king flew into a rage, and ordered Yan Shi to be executed. Yan Shi was very afraid, and began to tear the figure apart for the king to see. It was nothing but a wooden head, straw, glue and multi-coloured paint. King Mu was delighted and praised Yan Shi's skill.[23]

The term used in the Chinese text to describe the figure is *jiqiren*, which literally means 'mechanised man'. King Mu, like Don Quixote, perceived the figure as if it were real, yet when it was taken apart, it was only 'a wooden head, straw, glue and multi-coloured paint':

> 'Now I am fully convinced', said Don Quixote at this, 'of what I have very often believed: that these enchanters who persecute me are always placing before my eyes shapes like these, and then changing and transforming them to look like whatever they please'.[24]

Mechanical figures were known in China from about the second century onwards, and made for entertainment at court, as part of the *baixi* (hundred games) entertainments. One particular account of such mechanical figures describes an event on water *shuizhuan baixi*. It is typical of many which describe the performance of mechanised figures as if they had a life of their own, as if they were real. The dialectic between perceiving the mechanics of the moving figures and being fascinated by their apparent 'reality' is caught in the superlative, in over-exaggeration:

> [Ma Qun] carved a pavilion of wood in the shape of a wheel, set it out on flat ground, then immersed it, starting its operations by means of water. On it, he set forth dancing models of female

---

[23] *Liezi. Tangwen* 1965: 112.   [24] Cervantes 1950, Book 2, ch. 26: 643.

musicians, even making wooden people beat drums and blow pipes. He made a (model) mountain upon which he caused wooden people to stroll about freely, juggling, sword throwing, rope-climbing and doing handstands, and there were all kinds of officers performing their duties and people pounding grain and cock-fighting, with all manner of ingenuities.[25]

Closely associated with the hundred games on water, is the term *shui kuilei* (water puppets). In this record, the commentator concentrates on the performance of the figures only, as if the movers of and speakers for the figures (the marionette masters) were not even present:

There is another boat on the deck of which is constructed a small bunted loft, at the bottom of which are three small doors exactly like a puppet booth. It is moored directly across from the music boats. On the music boats the Adjutant presents the Congratulatory verse; music is played and the middle gate of the bunted loft is opened. Out come small wooden dolls on small boats. There is a man in white, fishing; behind him a small boy raises the oars to paddle the boat. They make several circles, talking. Music is played, they pull out a live fish. More music is played and the little boat goes back into the loft. Then, in consecutive order, there are other small dolls that play football, dance and whirl, and so forth. Each of them recites a Congratulatory verse then sings in harmony; music is played and it ends. It is called 'Water Puppets'.[26]

Another type of mechanised figure was represented in tomb frescoes depicting sequences of a tale or history in sculptured stone or wood panels. These panels are often laid out above each other on different levels like a cartoon to indicate fore- and background of the depicted event. Persuasive evidence has shown that such tomb frescoes depicted actual performances of wooden figures which were tipped, rocked or balanced against each other to move. One Han fresco depicting an audience with the Queen Mother of the West from the tomb of the family Wu,[27] is interpreted thus:

[25] *San guozhi*, trans. Dolby 1978: 100.   [26] Idema and West 1982: 38.
[27] See also Chavannes 1913, vol. 1, no. 110.

Left of the throne of Xi Wangmu kneel two men in long gowns
with wings attached to their backs . . . On their heads are
helmets in the shape of animal heads. That these two figures
represent costumed men, or actors, is obvious and often
remarked. However, these figures have always been separated
from the whole scene of which they are merely a part . . . The
four-footed men who approach the Queen from the right are
not merely artistic fancies, but depict figures used in a cult, or
performance, probably made of wood and brightly painted . . .
We see clearly that the heads [of the figures] are slotted into a
wide neck opening . . . the reason for this is that the heads were
movable and would swing to and fro like beads on a pagoda.
Technically, such movements could be achieved with weights
quite easily. The positions occupied by some of the little winged
men suggest that it was their task to tap the heads into
movement again if they stopped.[28]

The performance requires the co-operation of human and mechanical
figures, for the latter need some help in beginning a movement. The
human figures were 'often children, or at least young people'[29] who
were dressed in fabulous costumes for 'their legs are to be seen underneath the animals'.[30] Moreover acrobat or dancer's foot-stands, *pufu*,[31]
are represented on the back of the mythical animal for the human
figure which apparently dances there.[32] The human figures who act
contrast with other humans who manipulate the main (mechanical)
figures. Such frescoes seem to depict a performance involving mechanical figures, puppets and humans in costume. The position of such
frescoes in the tomb is evidence of the fact that figural performance
(*sangjia zhi yue* – 'mortuary entertainment' given as the meaning of
kuilei)[33] was part of the mortuary ceremony.[34] The mortuary figure

---

[28] Bulling 1956: 32.   [29] Ibid.: 34.

[30] Ibid.: 43.

[31] The *pufu* is in turn identified as a 'magical cushion' associated with the
dance of Yu the Great, see chapter two in this work.

[32] Bulling 1956: 32.   [33] *Houhanshu*. Wuxingzhi, Lingdi shuyou xiyu xiyuan.

[34] Bulling 1956: 43. Compare Bulling's description of the heads fitting to
wide necks with the example of mortuary figures from Dengxian county
described in chapter five.

(kuilei) was a figure of death – it was other, and yet it was a figure of life – it was *like* a real man. The fascination for the mechanical figure perceives the figure as if it were 'out of this world' – both in the world of death (other) and in the world of life (like).

The tale of Yan Shi and the mechanical figure states that the figure could perform all kinds of things: 'Whatever anyone could think up, it could perform.' It was versatile, changeable, a metamorphic figure. The Chinese term used here, *qianbian wanhua* (a thousand transformations and ten thousand changes) describes a performing figure that constantly shifts its identity. Despite the fact that the figure was later proven to be made of nothing but paper, straw, wood and paint (materials), it *appeared* to be something else. Moreover, even that something else was not constant, it kept changing, *moving*; it was many something elses all at once. This is the power of the performing body as defined by the costume of the Fashi performer in *nuo* theatre, for example. The power of *hua* (to transform) is symbolised by the flower (*hua*) and multi-patterned (*hua*) costume. The power to change or metamophose between identities is also expressed in the way the *jingju* performer and story teller slip in and out of the 'I' and narrated forms.

Proximity and distance

The Fangxiangshi, the family of *jingju* actors, the mortuary figure and the puppet are all conceived as performing bodies which are somehow other, from another world. In performance, they appear to move autonomously. At the same time, however, they are *like* bodies from this world and *attached* to bodies of this world. For the mechanical figures and marionettes have no life without the presence of their counterpart human life as creator or mover.

Mei Lanfang performs the geese with one hand and the body of Yang Yuhuan with the rest of his body. He is marionette (the role, Yang Yuhuan) and marionette master (his hand as geese is the puppet) at the same time. Nowhere is this relationship of artefact to mover more clearly shown than in contemporary marionette theatre. The division of one who plays the role (marionette) and one who merely controls, narrates the role (marionette master) thoroughly disappears. The marionette is perceived as *part of* the marionette master as much as Mei Lanfang's hand is part of him. The marionette master performs as exorcist, for example, with the marionette as if it were joined to his own body as part of his own corporeal expressive means. Marionette and master are one (jointed) performing body.

In October 1984, the Fulonggan Marionette Company from the Yilan region in Taiwan were hired by the director of a clothing company (Flourishing Cotton Interlock Clothing Company) to exorcise a 'fire star' that was held responsible for setting alight the factory in the village of Meicheng in Zhuangyuan county.[35]

The exorcism event consists of many smaller happenings which include marionette performance, religious ceremony and *wu*-ist ritual. It is an event which begins with a clear distinction between artefact (marionette, religious statue) and human. The middle section of the event rests on the total absorption of one into the other (a part-human, part-artefact performing body) and the closing section separates the artefact and human body once more.

The exorcism event contains three performance areas. Directly in front of the factory, a bamboo tent was set up which contained the marionette stage and an area for the performance of Daoist rites, with two main altars and offerings. A third event area was inside the Purple Cloud Temple, where the main deity worshipped was the god Jitian Dashengye.

The marionette stage was about one metre off the ground. There were two pillars at the front of the stage pasted with blue paper banners (representing the desired quality of water rather than the usual colour, red) bearing the words, 'Respectfully send the fire god of the south away' and 'Welcome in the water god of the north.' Across both banners at the top was a horizontal banner declaring the name of the troupe. The trunk of marionettes was put backstage at stage left, and the marionettes that were to be used in the performance taken out and hung above it. At the centre of backstage was a small table set up as an altar, with small 'statues' (marionettes) of the three patron gods of marionette theatre, Da Wangye, Er Wangye and San Wangye.[36] On this occasion, the marionette of Shuide Xingjun, the Daoist Minister of

---

[35] The record of the event is taken from Song Jinxiu 1985: 89–111.

[36] Schipper 1966 explores the identity of these gods. Note, however, they are addressed in familial terms of respect with the postfix *ye*, a term meaning 'uncle' (of the ancestral family).

Water Control, was also put on the altar. By this action, the marionette, *kuilei*, is associated with the idea of deity – it is placed on the altar in the position of deity with other deities. Moreover, since marionette bodies are interchangeable and undifferentiated, it is the *head* of the marionette which represents the deified body. As in chapter three, at this point in the ceremony, it is 'god-head'. It is offered raw food of a nature (untransformed) which reflects the distance between the human and the deity.

Whilst the marionette troupe prepared the marionettes (fitting heads to bodies), villagers gathered in the Daoist ritual area to offer incense and paper money to the various Daoist, Buddhist and local gods whose statues were set up on the central altar: Tianshang Shengmu, Shennong Dadi, Guansheng Dijun, Sanguan Dadi, Guanyin Fozu, Zhongtan Yuanshuai, Fude Zhengshen and Dongyue Dadi. The altar to the right of this was piled up with paper money and incense sticks, and the altar to the left bore the various food offerings: tangerines, oranges, pears, cake, biscuits, three pieces of raw, dried soya bean curd, a large piece of raw pork and a live cockerel. Behind this altar was a bucket[37] made of papier mâché, painted blue and filled to the top with rice. Stuck into the rice were two branches of willow (symbols of Yang) to the left and right, and a banana leaf (*shan* 'fan' puns with 'fortune') with the words, 'Shuide Xingjun shall exorcise the fire and bring harmony' written in an ash and water ink (the ink is made up of the burnt ashes of a written charm mixed into water). On top of the rice were laid three rows of duck eggs (*yadan* 'duck egg' puns with 'repress disease') also with writing on them. Reading from right to left, the twelve characters on each egg signified: 'metal-wood-water-fire-earth', 'exorcise-disperse-evil', 'this-exorcism-to the- [four] quarters'. Each egg was also marked with the date (26th October). At each side of the bucket were candles and incense sticks. Underneath the same table was a straw mat to be used later in the exorcism.

The first part of the event begins with a general propitiation, or cleansing ceremony (*pudu*) in the ritual area. This event is led by a

---

[37] Song uses the term *tong*, meaning 'bucket' rather than *dou* which is almost certainly the correct term. See chapter one in this work for the significance of the rice bucket in ancestor offerings and initiation rites.

(Daoist-Buddhist) priest, Fashi, who 'mystically increase(s) the food available for the ghosts to ensure sufficiency, so that they will no longer be hungry [troublesome to the living]'.[38] The ceremony effectively disperses any lurking troublesome ghostly presences: and it 'satiate(s) the hungry ghosts who would otherwise thieve the food offerings earmarked for the deceased' (in this case, the star god).[39] The *pudu* ceremony is also a kind of salvation ceremony, for at the conclusion of it, some souls who have been condemned to hell will be released and sent to heaven. During the ceremony, villagers from Meicheng and surrounding areas approached with their offerings and laid them out on the altars before retiring to pray. After the ceremony was over, the Fashi cleansed the area by beating it with the straw mat. At this point the marionette Shuide Xingjun is still deity – distanced from the humans. He, like the other statues on the altar is to intercede for humans in the world of spirits, because he is, like the world of spirits, other.

At the same time as the *pudu* ceremony is going on in the area for Daoist rituals, the neighbouring Purple Cloud Temple is engaged in its own propitiation rite. This involves moving the statue of the temple's patron god, Jitian Dashengye, and begins inside the courtyard directly in front of the temple, within the temple grounds. It is the beginning of the section in the exorcism event when the human body and the artefact are joined. An altar is set up here with incense and written charms. Two members of the temple shift the statue of the god onto a litter which they then shoulder. Stepping the Yu step or similar patterns of creation, or 'quickening', they move all around the temple courtyard before, surrounded by many members of the temple, they arrive in front of the temporary altar. One man then takes up a silver rod in his hand and with it moves the statue's hand to take a brush soaked in sweat to write a charm on a piece of black paper. After this, the statue is made to hold the charm, and it is shouldered again and carried through the village from house to house to take the message of the charm of peace and harmony to each household.[40]

---

[38] Thompson 1988: 74.   [39] Cohen 1988: 193.

[40] A small household altar was probably set up outside each home. At certain points, the procession stops and members of the temple carry out individual libations on behalf of the god.

Thus far the actions in the exorcism event have been concentrated on the Daoist statues and performance area outside the marionette tent. The same sequence witnessed here – deity alone – joint performance of human and deity, is repeated in the marionette tent at the heart of the event. In the marionette tent, another rice bucket with a banana leaf and two twigs of willow was placed on the right hand of the stage. At the left of the stage, a whole raw cockerel and several pieces of raw pork had been placed as an offering to the head of Daoism, Laozi. A live cockerel and a live duck were also prepared backstage. The marionette master, Xu Jiansun, took a written charm and burnt it in a special bowl known as the 'water charm bowl'. Then he took the banana leaf and the twigs of willow, soaked them in the ash and water mix and, holding the bowl and twigs with *jue* hand signs, sprinkled the four corners of the stage with the ash–water mixture. This process cleanses the stage.

Xu Jiansun then took the food offering to the altar of the patron deities of the marionette theatre where, on this occasion, the marionette Shuide Xingjun was also positioned. This offering is to guarantee that the marionettes perform with the spiritual help, power or permission of the gods required. To be sure that the deities concerned agree to the performance taking place, the marionette master tosses the oracle blocks until he achieves one positive, one negative answer. He then takes blood from the cockerel's comb to write a series of charms, including charms to suppress evil, which are put in the four corners of the stage, water charms to exorcise the fire and protective charms which protect the performers from harm in their contact with the evil forces during the exorcism.

The writing of charms is a special skill passed only from father to son, or master to disciple. It is generally performed by Fashi priests, though marionette masters have their own repertoire of charms. Although Xu was also a member of the Zheng school of Daoists, he used the style of charm writing from the repertoire of marionette theatre on this occasion.

The marionette players covered the decorative name banners over the stage with another blue banner. This is because the exorcism is not an event for spectators – the advertisement banners must be hidden. The marionette of Shuide Xingjun was moved from the altar to the props table directly in the front of the stage. This marks the moment of transition from deity (*distanced* from man, on the altar) and performing body (*part of* man, in the performance). The props table was also laid out with offerings of food and drink, paintings of various deities and various written charms. Then Xu handed out the protective charms to all the marionette performers, and they attached them to their sleeves.[41] The charms read 'Respectfully command the Chief General of Paradise to send off all evil and protect this body and bring peace.'

Xu recited a charm, took a knife moistened with water and, at the right front side of the tent, beat the tent board three times with the knife. Backstage, the sounds of gong, *suona* and flute began and Xu made the signs of the eight trigrams with his hands while stamping the dance of the 'seven stars' (the *Ursa Major*, see chapter seven). When this was finished, he took a water bowl with salt and water in it and scattered the contents over the right front of the theatre tent. The grains of salt and drops of water represent soldiers and generals coming down from heaven to assist in the exorcism.

If the marionette has thus far been conceived as head (the deity – literally god-head), placed on the altar and distanced from the master or performer, when the marionette (or statue) is made to move by the performer, it is part of a joint performing body. The marionette master provides the (hosting?) body, the *device* of movement.

During the central part of the event, the exorcism proper, the marionette master Xu Jiansun has carried out certain actions and recited certain texts which are now repeated verbatim by the marionette which he manipulates, for whom he speaks and sings. The exorcism is first indicated by the master alone once, and then by the master a second time through the extension of his body into the marionette (deity) – or the extension of the deity through the marionette into his body. The marionette master thus performs the exorcism with the marionette as if it were one of his own limbs, like the separated hand of Mei Lanfang in performing the geese. It is joined to his body. The master provides the body for the god-head.

---

[41] Prior to the procession of Wang Gong in Guizhou, I was also given a protective charm with my name written on. I was told, however, to wear it in my hat or anywhere near my head.

Xu brought out the marionette Shuide Xingjun holding a twig of willow in its hand, and it struck the pose *liangxiang* from the *chou* or comic role type. At intervals of music, Xu called upon the marionette to exorcise the fire star. Then the marionette was moved to the right front of the marionette stage and, holding a banana leaf fan in one hand and the willow twig in the other, it dipped these into the burnt charm water bowl and shook the drops off onto the stage in order to release yet more heavenly soldiers, in a replica movement to that done earlier by the master alone.

The marionette was then made to take the live cockerel and, holding it by the cockscomb, circle the front stage, drawing a charm in the air with the blood dripping from it. It then took the duck and repeated the same movements, exactly as the master had done before.

Finally, the marionette was moved to the site of the factory. Only one percussionist with a gong followed the marionette master and the marionette Shuide Xingjun. Xu called out charms and painted other charms in the air with his hand as the marionette also executed various charms with its hands, and the exorcism proper, which took only three minutes, was complete. At the very moment of exorcism Xu, the master, speaks charms and performs *jue* with the hands that control his extended body, the marionette, which also makes *jue* and calls charms. The two bodies are for the brief moments of the actual exorcism (the mediation between two worlds to put the microcosm back to rights) *indivisible*.

The marionette performers now covered the original couplets concerning the exorcism event with new banners bearing the couplets 'Heavenly peace, earthly peace, peace of the three Yangs (the three Daoist deities)' and other good wish couplets. These were written on a background of red paper. The spectators gathered and the marionette troupe performed the play *Powuguan (Crossing Wuguan Pass)* from the Histories of the Sui and Tang dynasties. The marionette master Xu Jiansun and his colleagues are no longer 'visible' to the audience. The focus of the attention of the spectators is entirely on the marionettes and the 'play' they perform. In the closing section of the exorcism event, thus, the marionette master and the marionette are divided, separate again.

Such 'performances' after the exorcism are interpreted as entertainment to break the tension of the exorcism event and celebrate the effective exorcism. However, on several levels, the piece is actually the tail part of the exorcism proper. On a simple level, the end plays are nearly always battle pieces representing the victory of the good over the bad – a clear repetition of the aims of the exorcism event. On another level, it is supposed to entertain the deities called down into the marionettes who performed the exorcism as a kind of thanksgiving. However, the title of the play, *Powuguan* (*Crossing Wuguan Pass*) can also be considered a pun, *powuguan* meaning 'piercing the five senses' (eyes, ears, nose, mouth and heart), which suggests the piece actually escorts the deities used in the exorcism back to heaven – it 'closes' the marionettes after the exorcism, just as they had been opened (*kaiguang*) before it.[42] Thus, though it may seem as though this is 'play' pure, it actually circumscribes the process of separation of the marionette master from the marionette-deity as one performing, mediating (*articulated*) body.

The last piece of this day (the troupe were hired for one day of two sessions) was the reunification play or *tuanyuanxi* depicting a marionette husband and wife greeting each other and greeting the spectators. The significance of this play at the end of the exorcism is similar to that of the 'happy monk' (or big-head, see chapter seven) who gathers any remaining demons and disposes of them. For the term *tuanyuan* means 'reunification'. The worlds of heaven and earth, other and like are confirmed and 'settled' in peaceful Yinyang like harmony. The marionette company was then dined inside the Purple Cloud Temple with the various village heads and dignitaries, food (cooked and transformed) was offered in celebration of the sense of one family (the marionette master is seen as the embodiment of the clan ancestors).

The master's voice

In the exorcism event, the marionette master and the marionette were separate and then joined into one performing body. They executed certain actions one after the other in repetition, as well as simultaneously. The distance and proximity between the artefact and the human performing body is reflected, not only in the actions of the body, but also

---

[42] See chapter five for a similar example in the play *Mengjiangnu* (*Wife Meng*).

in the spoken and sung text. The voice is used to shift the persona or identity of the performing body(ies) in the same way as the concubine Yang Yuhuan shifts the position of the 'I' persona in the *jingju* piece. In the cleansing rite to clean the stage before the exorcism can begin, i.e. at a point where the marionette Shuide Xingjun is in the position of deity on the altar, the marionette master recites:

> Call upon *(zao)* the Third *(san)* Water Master's Third *(san)* Son,
> Call upon *(zao)* the Water Spirit Lad,
> To make *(zao)* the water flood into vast seas,
> The water drain, ooze and seep away *(san)*.
> The hand is holding water of the eight compass points,
> Poplar and willow are soaked in the water.
> Sprinkle *(sa)* them once, and the sky becomes clear *(qing)*,
> Sprinkle *(sa)* twice for the earth spirits *(ling)*,
> Sprinkle *(sa)* three times that all shall be pure and clean *(jing)*,
> Pure and clean *(jing)*.
> The nine dragons shall destroy evil,
> Let the command be obeyed as law, with speed.[43]

The key to the piece lies in the numeral, *san* (three), which puns with 'to disperse'.[44] The first three lines begin with the same character, *zao* (to report to), which puns with 'to create', so that the word is repeated in succession three times directly under one another. The character *shui* (water), is also repeated in the same position in the three opening lines and twice in the following two lines, making the numeral five which represents the centre of the compass in line five. Lines seven, eight and nine repeat the verb *sa* (sprinkle), which puns with 'scatter' three times in the same position in the line, and the verbs *qing* (to become clear), *ling* (spirit) and *jing* (to be cleansed) form a group of three. Since the whole piece is constructed as three sets of three lines, echoed in the concluding lines with the 'nine' dragons (the Luo diagram), it is possible to reconstruct the whole piece on a grid similar to the Luo

---

[43] Qiu Kunliang 1983: 13.

[44] Backstage in *jingju*, the word *san* is avoided as superstition dictates that mention of the word before the performance will break up the troupe and cause bad luck.

diagram. In such a case, the four outer cells may be filled with the four terms *san* (disperse), *zao* (create anew), *sa* (to scatter) *qing* (cleanse) and the central cell may be filled with *shui* (water). Thus water is seen to have the effect (because it unites) of all the outlying principles – it exorcises, is placed in the central, exorcising position.

The speaker of the above text is not persona, but voice. It is the voice of the marionette master who, like a Fashi, is in a position to mediate between worlds, who is initiated into the techniques of speaking charms. Thus the charm depends on the right words being spoken in the right order (to replicate the figure of the Luo diagram) by the right person (the professional) in order to be effective.

Although Chinese verbs do not show conjugations, the position of the verbs at the beginning of the lines suggests that the text follows the imperative tone. The last line, which repeats the formula of an earthly 'imperial edict', reflects the conception of the spirit world as a replica of the earthly world, so that hierarchical structures on earth are repeated in heaven. Thus the formula used by imperial commands on earth will be as effective in heaven. Since, however, the speaker is not the imperial commander in heaven, the charm must be seen as simply prescriptive in form, like a recipe, or formula (pattern), the reading of which will be effective for itself. Such an interpretation suggests that words spoken as text in performance are independent (cut off from) the individual personality of the speaker.

The following text is recited by the marionette master in front of the three images of the patron deities of marionette theatre as he brings the various cooked (transformed – close to the human world) offerings to their altar. It shows how close the two worlds of master and marionette (deity) become in the performance:

Marionette Master:
Solemnly invite Pu An,
Come to these million homes,
Scatter clean water to subdue and send off disaster,
With Jinganglang Shijun.
Feet stamp the heavenly rotation, and the earthly rotation,
Fire return to its proper place.
Ten thousand heavenly troops, ah!

164

Each soldier protect Pu An and assist in carrying out the
   command.
One male (name of speaker) stands before the incense burner,
   prays and invites
Pu An to come down.
The heavenly soldiers shall obey the command promptly as
   law.[45]

Immediately after this, he takes a set of uncooked (untransformed)
offerings to the left front of the stage:

Now is an auspicious time for spirits,
Heaven and earth do business together.
As the smoke of incense rises,
The spirits travel ten thousand *li*.
As the smoke falls,
The spirits descend.[46]

In the first section of the text, the marionette master names or calls up
specific deities to assist in the exorcism. Apart from the generally prescribed 'heavenly soldiers', the gods Pu An and Jinganglang Shijun are
called upon. Pu An was a Zen Buddhist monk known to be particularly
gifted at exorcism – a series of Pu An spells form the basic repertoire
of exorcism. Such spells make no literal sense at all in Chinese or Sanskrit,
but they are read first vertically and then horizontally, which has been
described as a celebration of sounds.[47] In the light of the analysis of the
text above, however, perhaps even these spells, considering their vertical and horizontal (diagonal?) reading have meaning when projected
onto the Luo diagram. The second god called upon is a Buddhist exorcism god with special visual skills for tracking down the demons.

   The naming of these exorcist deities is recited in front of the
three marionette deities and balanced against the naming of the speaker
(marionette master) who calls them. Thus two parties are named in
the one event – the gods and the mortal. This text uses naming to reinforce the sense of the two worlds coming together – as it later states
'heaven and earth shall do business together'.

---

[45] Qiu Kunliang 1983: 13–14.   [46] Ibid.: 14.
[47] Picard 1991: 32–8.

Not only does the speaker name himself, he also is obliged to imply the first person when he describes the movements he will enact, '[My] feet will stamp the heavenly rotation and the earthly rotation.' The movements of his feet on the right stations of meaning will cause the echo response in heaven so that heaven shall 'put fire back in its proper place'. In this text, the lack of pronoun allows the proximity of the two actors – the marionette master and the emperor of heaven (perceived in the marionette?).

Introducing the self

In Chinese theatre, the performance of the marionette master with the marionette as one body is generally prefaced by a few lines of introduction. These lines describe the role played by the marionette, but in the light of the concept of the united (jointed) performing body, such lines may also be termed 'self-introduction'. The concubine Yang Yuhuan does not rely on performing the geese with her hand alone. She also sings a description of them as she sees them. She introduces them, though they are part of her/Mei Lanfang, her/his hands. The following passage is taken from an exorcism by a marionette representing the exorcist figure Zhong Kui. It is preceded and accompanied by a sequence of movements known as *tiaotai* (jumping [on] the stage). As the puppet is suspended by strings, the marionette master also stamps his feet simultaneously to the marionette in a series of hopping, jumping, stamping movements to provide the sound effect. Thus, the marionette master also performs the *tiaotai* as he manipulates the marionette to perform the same movements, just as he makes the same *jue* hand signs as the marionette he controls. The marionette master and the marionette are one.

This aspect is emphasised in the constant reminder of the identity of the 'I' (the corporate body of marionette and master). In the following text, the master introduces the marionette, Zhong Kui, by qualifying the 'I' persona (*wu*) with the title, 'deity' or 'god' (*shen*). This is consistent with most performance styles. The 'I' persona is always qualified by status, title or role in the introductory. In the case of *jingju*, Yang Yuhuan, for example, first speaks of herself as *bengong*, 'I, the concubine'. In both cases, the term used for 'I' is indicative. It is depersonalised, like the royal 'we' rather than the private 'I' (*wo*) used in general conversation of oneself.

> Zhong Kui (*sings*):
> The best scholar in all the land,
> But that vexed the Tang king a good deal.
> So the Jade Emperor awarded me a green sword,
> And ordered [me] to the mortal world to destroy demons.
> (*speaks*)
> I, the god, come from Zhongnan mountain, am Zhong Kui,
> Received the Jade Emperor's decree
> To go on a tour of inspection in the mortal world.
> Travelling on an auspicious cloud. (*music*)
> (*speaks*)
> Ah, look, I, the god, have arrived,
> And scrutinise X place (*substitutes the name of the location*),
>   casting the gaze about.
> (*looks down*)
> Many disciples, pure and clean of heart,
> A tall makeshift stage with acting and singing of old plays
> Concerning the business in hand today.
> Above replies with heaven's meaning,
> Below prays for health and peace.
> Unfortunately evil spirits have upset this place,
> Troubled ten thousand people.
> I, the god, shall take his gold cockerel as edict
> And the precious sword as command.
> Able to see and hear the demons clearly, I, the god, shall give the
>   orders.
> (*A cockerel is put into the marionette's hands. The marionette*
>   *throws it down in the right hand corner of the stage. The*
>   *marionette is given a duck, which it tosses in the left hand*
>   *corner of the stage.*)
> (*speaks*)
> Ah, look, my, the god's, command has been obeyed.
> Let me, the god, pronounce some good wishes here.

I, the god, command fortune and prosperity.
Good fortune fill the hall.[48]
At one door, nine successful candidates in the exam,
And Gong and Sun, the two Prime Ministers.
Ah, I, the god, see that in X place (*substitutes the name of the
    location*),
The host of disciples and their homes are peaceful now.
There's nothing for it, but to return to the heavenly palace,
And hand back the edict.[49]

The first four lines of the marionette Zhong Kui form two couplets of self-introduction known in Chinese theatre as the *yinzi*. The *yinzi* is usually performed by the main figure on entering the stage for the first time. The content of the *yinzi*, according to most scholars, serves 'to establish the general atmosphere of the scenes that follow'.[50]

In the *nuo* theatre, a similar kind of introduction is used when the performer first puts on the mask of a certain figure. Instead of *yinzi*, the term used to describe the introduction, or self-introduction is *shuo gensheng* (telling the roots of birth, biography). The *nuo* piece *Mengjiangnu* (*Wife Meng*), from Taoyuan in Hunan, begins with the figure Xu Baiwan, the father of the heroine:

> Xu Baiwan:
> I've grown old without children to depend on,
> And hate the heavens for such injustice.
> (*sits*)
> An old fellow like me, my life is incomplete,
> Sitting in the ancestral hall without a child is futile.
> Even if I accumulate piles of gold and silver,
> I lack a child to mourn the parents' death.[51]

Zhong Kui's introductory speech also follows this pattern closely. In four lines, the marionette recounts the history of the figure: Zhong Kui

---

[48] Zhong Kui politely glorifies the matshed tent to ancestral hall. However, the matshed is, for the duration of the performance, entirely equivalent to an ancestral hall – two worlds are one.
[49] Qiu Kunliang 1983: 15.   [50] Wichmann 1991: 48.
[51] *Hunan xiqu chuantong juben* 1982.

was deprived of his rightful place as the best scholar in the land because his ugly appearance displeased the emperor Wu De (reigned 618–627 AD). He committed suicide and, through the pleading of his friend Du Ping, was granted a posthumous honour by the emperor. In the underworld, the jade emperor awarded him a magic jade sword and charged him with destroying any evil demons that troubled the mortal world.[52]

Zhong Kui and Xu Baiwan are well-known figures in Chinese mythology and it is certain that everyone knows at least the rudiments of the myths that surround them. Does the summary repetition of their past histories simply remind the spectator of the identity or history of the figure before him? In the Zhong Kui piece, not only does the *yinzi* sum up this myth, it is followed by the same summary two lines later. The purpose of the *yinzi* as it is used here is surely something more than merely to provide atmosphere, or biographical details.

> Zhong Kui (*sings*):
> The best scholar in all the land (*ke*),
> But that vexed the Tang king a good deal (*duo*).
> So the Jade Emperor awarded me a green sword (*jian*),
> And ordered [me] to the mortal world to destroy demons (*mo*).

In Zhong Kui's self-introduction is a subtext formed of the last character of each line which reads *ke* (academy), *duo* (a good deal), *jian* (sword), *mo* (demons). These words are homonyms for '*ke* (judge), *duo* (seize), and *jian* (trample on), *mo* (demons)'. The *yinzi* contains the *content* of the play to come in concentrated form. It *is* the play just as the costume and outward appearance of Mei Lanfang as the concubine Yang Yuhuan contains the content of the piece to come. The point of entry (appearance, textual introduction) embodies the point of departure. Once again, the spectator reads the diachronic scale of the performance vertically as well as horizontally.

In the art of story telling, this aspect of the *yinzi* is well developed. The story teller begins each saga with a *yinzi* couplet which may be in the form of a saying or phrase encapsulating the theme or main content of the story to come. This is followed by a single episode

---

[52] The story of Zhong Kui is recounted in Doré 1936: 171ff., Warner 1984: 106 and De Groot 1982, vol. 6: 1174ff.

or story known as the *ruhua* (getting into the speech of things) which takes the theme of the *yinzi* and gives a different example of a similar theme. Only then does the story teller finally begin the first episode of the saga to be presented (over days, weeks or sometimes months).

In *jingju*, the *yinzi* is sometimes followed by a second set the scene poem or speech called the *dingchang shi*, or *dingchang bai*. Zhong Kui's set the scene speech slips immediately into the first person pronoun, 'I, the god, come from Zhongnan, am Zhong Kui.' This reflects the story teller's move from narration to the inside of the main character (see the example at the beginning of this chapter). Thus the same pattern of proximity and distance is repeated across many different types of Chinese performance. The *yinzi* functions as a condensed statement of the themes that will follow – in Zhong Kui's case, a pure homonym of what is to follow – and, as a consequence, though the statement may be made *by* the figure, is not necessarily *of* the figure. The *yinzi* is remarkable for its lack of the first person pronoun and contrasts with the setting the scene pieces that follow.

In some forms of *nuo*, this aspect of narration and first person pronoun (distance and proximity between role and performer) is even more extreme. In Guizhou *dixi*, for example, many of the texts used for the performance are actually story telling texts. A narrator, or voice, carries the plot of the story, including the actions of the protagonists as well as their appearance, reactions and so on. In the course of story telling, at particularly intense moments, the narrator also speaks the figures of his story in the first person. In rehearsals for *dixi*, the troupe leader often reads the story as it stands in the text, if there is one, while the other performers listen. From the play *Yezhen baibiguan* (*Scouting the White Jade Pass at Night*), the hero Li Shimin sings,

Li Shimin (*sings*):
The king of Qin (Li Shimin) listens to these words, prepares to
    go out in advance and scout the pass,
Let us first put on the golden helmets, fixing two pheasant
    feathers at the top,
Let us put on the apricot coloured robes and tie the jade belt at
    our waists,
Taking the insignia in the left hand, sword in the right,

Shenfen *(Identity)*

Chorus *(sings)*:
Sword in the right.

Li Shimin *(sings)*:
Fight for the Tang court with knife raised on high,

Chorus *(sings)*:
Knife raised on high.

Li Shimin *(sings)*:
I leap in the air on my swift horse,

Chorus *(sings)*:
On my swift horse.[53]

In this piece, the hero moves from the third person singular to the first person plural to the imperative, to the first person singular. The chorus also slip in and out of narrative and direct speech. In performance, the *dixi* actors are always present in the performing area to function as chorus. When a certain individual figure is required to perform, the actor moves into the centre of the performance area from the ranks of chorus who encircle it. He will retire there again when the role is done. Thus, the actor moves from undifferentiated chorus figure, to persona and back to chorus, many times in the performance.

In another passage from *dixi*, from the saga of the hero Xue Ding-shan titled *San tuofang* (*Three Times Captured and Three Times Released*), the heroine, Fan Lihua sings:

Fan Lihua *(sings)*:
The night's discussions have now ceased,
Today, at five bells, daylight has dawned.
The old general awakes under the soldier's canopy.
Lihua comes forward to see her father.
When she is before the altar, she kneels down on both knees,
Father why are you in such sad spirits?
And the old general replies, Ah, child, today, you do not know,
The soldiers of the Tang prince have come down the pass.
Yesterday there was a great battle on the river,

---

[53] Author's field notes, Guizhou 1990.

Many were killed and a retreat was called.
What clever strategy does my daughter have
To chase away the Tang soldiers?
Lihua said, Father! Let your daughter lead the troops,
She can certainly capture the Tang soldiers.
She and second brother will steal revenge.
The old general was happy when he heard this, and said,
My daughter must be careful when she goes out to fight.
The Fan family dragon and tiger shall startle the enemy troops.[54]

Both these passages from *dixi* show how the story telling texts are used in their pure form. No attempt has been made to 'dramatise' them by assigning parts, and while this may be derived from a purely practical decision (ease of learning the part) it shows a fundamental lack of concern with the concept of persona, the 'I' of a role. Fan Lihua narrates her own actions, Bottom-like, and even speaks her father's speech to herself in the form of the first person.

The same technique can be observed in the Zhong Kui marionette performance. The part begins with a narrative of the figure Zhong Kui. The middle section starting 'I, the god, from Zhongnan mountain, am Zhong Kui' and ending 'I give the command' is largely *self*-narrative: 'Ah, look, I, the god, have arrived, / And scrutinise X place, casting the gaze about.'[55]

The next passage that follows is the actual exorcism with the blood of the cockerel and the duck and takes the form of active imperative:

I, the god, shall take his gold cockerel as edict
And the precious sword as command
Able to see and hear the demons clearly, I, the god, shall give
the orders.

The final section returns to the narrative form, 'Ah, I, the god, see that in X place / The host of disciples and their homes are peaceful now',

---

[54] Author's field notes, Guizhou 1990.
[55] Qiu Kunliang 1983a: 15. Subsequent references are to the same edition and page.

and ends with a note of regret that the action is over. Now the figure Zhong Kui is returning to a position of non-action: 'There's nothing for it, but to return to the heavenly palace, / And hand in the edict.'

This piece has striking similarities with the last aria of Yang Yuhuan, where the performer seems to be hanging up the role even while still on stage – performer and role separate themselves:

> Yang Yuhuan (*sings*):
> Yang Yuhuan is as if in a dream tonight.
> Remember the time *you* first entered the palace,
> How kindly the emperor treated *you*,
> How much he loved *you*;
> But today, suddenly, is forsaking,
> Can it be that from today, the two shall be forever parted!
> . . .
>
> There's nothing else to do but return to the solitude of the cold
>   and lonely palace.

The articulated body is a divided body (*shenfen*). Not only is the Chinese performing body dissected into different corporeal elements of articulation, and reassembled into a new body for the duration of the performance, the articulate(d) body continually redissects and reassembles itself in different ways throughout *one* performance. The concubine Yang Yuhuan metamorphoses into the geese that she sees as well as the moon, the empress, the slave. The role is made up of many separate 'I's or personas which the actor Mei Lanfang represents at different moments with different parts of his body. The same process of continual change is reflected in the different parts of speech used by the Chinese performer. The performer separates his body into narrator, subject and even inanimate object.

The constant creation and recreation of the articulate(d) body as different kinds of presence has repercussions on the relationship between the actor and his own body, as well as between the actor and an artificial body, such as a marionette. In one performance the relationship between the performer and the performed may vacillate at any point along the line which stretches from total absorption – parts of the same performing body, to total distance – narration, third personal pronoun and imperative in speech, for example. The concept of changing proximity and distance between the performer and the thing performed can be identified clearly in puppet theatre and mortuary rite. However, it is also a fundamental aspect of the human theatres such as *nuo* and *jingju*. Mei Lanfang dissects his body in order to articulate the role Yang Yuhuan, the story of what happens to her, the things she sees, and the situation around her, with the different performative units of his body and voice.

5

Yang
(Life)

Mei Lanfang writes of the entrance of the concubine Yang Yuhuan:

> As soon as the favourite concubine enters the stage, there is a
> *liang douxiu* 'shaking out alternate sleeves' movement. The
> body leans down slightly; the attitude must be dignified and
> poised. The following two arias in *siping* mode require the
> most voice technique in the whole play.[1]

Shaking out the sleeves is one of the most basic techniques in the
repertoire of sleeve movements in *jingju*. It is generally used to signal
to the orchestra that the actor is ready to sing, or talk, or execute some
movement that requires a change in the accompaniment. Shaking out
the sleeve is also used as the first moment of an entrance to allow the
audience to register the appearance of the role (see chapter two) and to
interpret the structure of the body in pose.

> Start with the right hand, palm inward, a little below the chest.
> Move downward and towards the right in a curve. On reaching
> the front of the slightly bent knee, make a quick turn at the
> wrist, and throw the sleeve backward and a little to the right.
> The eyes should follow the motion of the sleeve and the body
> should lean forward in harmony with the hand movement. The
> left hand may go through the same movements, but in the
> opposite direction . . . either alternately . . . (*liang douxiu*) or
> together (*shuang douxiu*).[2]

The shaking out the sleeve movement is slow, graceful and is punctuated by two 'stops' at either side on the completion of the movement

---

[1] Mei Lanfang and Xu Jichuan 1961, vol. 2: 21.   [2] Zung 1937: 79.

with the sleeve, where the performer pauses a moment and holds a pose (hence its use for entrances to allow the spectator to appreciate the presentation). The role of Yang Yuhuan is made up almost entirely of similar *zaoxing* (poses): as she turns to look over the balustrade of the bridge, as she follows the movements of the fish, as she watches the geese and as she takes the wine cups. Yang Yuhuan's movements are fluid, there are no sudden *liangxiang* (radiant poses) punctuated by the percussion. Even when she learns that the emperor is not coming and cries out in an ascending tone, as if she were building up to the classic *liangxiang* situation expressing shock, for example, she dissolves the moment into a regretful sigh.

The term *zao* literally means 'to build, to make'; *xing* means 'form'.[3] Yang Yuhuan's presence on stage is composed of a series of poses or *zaoxing*. One pose of the concubine Yang Yuhuan articulates a whole realm of meanings visible to the spectator. The *liang douxiu* movement at the opening of the play indicates sex (*dan* role – Mei Lanfang adopts the female body shape and finger positions as he manipulates the sleeves), rank (the curtsey is slight) and attitude (the *qingyi* makes slow, graceful movements). Yang Yuhuan shows a smile of youthful anticipation. The head tilts and shakes provocatively during the poses, so that the 'tails' of the phoenix head-dress shudder, articulating the excitement Yang Yuhuan feels. The time line of Chinese performance is not horizontal or sequential, but vertical, driving down into the inner layer. Thus, this one pose of Yang Yuhuan, as she shakes out the sleeves, manifests lack of dignity (the head shakes, the mouth is formed in a smile) to a degree near intoxicated. The point of departure (the *drunken* concubine) is embodied in the point of entry in terms of bodily shape or position, as much as it is contained in mere appearance, that is, both without and within the performing body.

Barely has the body come to rest from the movement towards such a pose, when it shifts out of it again towards the next. But the spectator first acknowledges the significance of one pose before committing himself to the sequence of movements and poses through the play, and fitting these both on a horizontal, sequential pattern and a (multi-layered) vertically connective one.

[3] The same character is used in Japanese theatre for the various movement patterns or sequences, *kata*.

Body as pattern (*hao*)

The term *hao* (expend) is used in *jingju* training in the sense of 'hold a position for a long length of time'. The first leg exercises of the morning consist of three kinds of leg-hold *haotui* – holding the leg in front, across the body and to the side against a bar.[4] The *hao* exercise is followed by proper stretches, *yatui*, where the body bends down towards the leg to stretch the muscles. There is a significant difference between holding the leg in a position, *haotui*, and stretching the leg, *yatui*. *Hao* (holding a position) is also used when teaching the student all the basic arm, hand and body poses that are needed in *jingju*. The *yunshou* (cloud hand) and the *shanbang* (mountain arm) positions are all taught by requiring the student to hold the correct position for up to thirty minutes without rest. In the past, students were encouraged to hold such positions by balancing cups of water on each thigh for a plié pose, for example. If the water spilled, the length of time the student must hold the pose was increased. Alternatively, a burning incense stick was placed in each hand, and the student would have to hold the pose until the incense had burned to the end.

Hao, or holding a position, say the Chinese masters, provides the performer with a repertoire of 'patterns' (poses) which are so drilled into the performer's body, that he can execute them on stage without even having to think. The body automatically falls into the correct position. In the case of a *liangxiang* pose, the position on stage is held for several seconds, and the effect is sharpened by the percussive orchestra. The poses made by Yang Yuhuan are held for considerably shorter lengths of time but are, in principle, the same. The training of positions through the technique of *hao* can be more easily observed in the more accentuated, slower *liangxiang*. But, as in the role of Yang Yuhuan, nearly all *jingju* movement sequences are composed of many such poses (whether held for a longer or shorter time) tied together by connecting movements of passage, called *guocheng*. It is not the pose alone which makes a performance.

Each pose, like each cell of meaning in the Luo matrix when it is bound to the *nuo* performer's body, is connected to another pose (cell of meaning), both at surface levels (sheer outward appearance) and across

---

[4] Wan Fengmei 1982: 88–9.

the vertical levels of depth as far as the inner body. In sum, a *jingju* movement sequence is composed of the passage (*guocheng*) between such poses (*liangxiang, zaoxing*) and the poses themselves. It can be read horizontally, vertically, through one layer of meaning or through several simultaneously, like the Pu An charm that can be read both ways, or like the numerical values of the Luo creative matrix which always give the same answer no matter which route is taken.

If a frame by frame analysis of a *jingju* sequence were made, it would be apparent that nearly every frame contains such a pre-defined pose ('form'). The passage movements are themselves built up from such patterns or poses; they could technically be 'stopped' at any moment and they would manifest one or other pose, fractally. The term *liangxiang* means 'radiant, glowing appearance' (*Er-scheinung*). The body in a *liangxiang* pose (or briefer *zaoxing* pose, pattern or form) is the body which has been through the process of opening (*kaiguang*, 'opening to let the light shine out'). It is a body which manifests or radiates presence.

These poses or pre-determined patterns (*zaoxing*), represent the reconstructed body. The student is taught to separate the individual parts of his body in training, and then to reassemble them (*zonghe*) in certain fixed patterns (*hao*) of meaning. The *shanbang* (mountain arm) position is a pose which indicates size and strength, or the *fanshou* (reverse hand) position by a martial female role may signify victory, for example.

The Chinese performing body is like a puzzle, made of different pieces, which fit together in different ways and which can be read in different ways – on the surface or in depth, or by alternating surface and depth meanings. It is thus a body which is always *held apart*, or held in suspension as puzzle, for it can only be reconstructed by the individual gaze of the spectator at the moment of watching. This means that the body (puzzle) is always viewed as a construct of separate parts, as a dissected or 'opened' body which emanates presence (*liangxiang*) by virtue of its articulation.

The concept of body as pattern, and the reading of the body on more than a surface level, is exposed clearly in the example of Zhong Kui. The tableaux of bodies made by Zhong Kui and his spirits form linguistic puns which all have very specific exorcist meanings, explained in detail in chapter seven. Even the typical stance of Zhong Kui, as he stands on the stage, is a pose which corporeally represents the linguistic sign, the character *gui* (spirit). Zhong Kui stands with raised sword in one hand, one foot lifted at the knee, with the fist of the other hand resting on it. In this pose, a demon (not visible to mortals) is imagined cowering under the raised leg.[5] The example of Zhong Kui shows that the body can *literally* be conceived in the essential form of a linguistic sign (character).

Zhong Kui is often represented as a guardian or door god, protecting households from demons. Thus he is a god of the *threshold*, the liminal state between two worlds. The *jingju* actor He Guishan belonged to the painted-face role category and specialised in *jiazi hualian* roles (the stance painted face). He Guishan was especially famous for his presentation of the *ershisi shi menshen jiazi* (twenty-four door god poses). As Zhong Kui makes each pose to represent the twenty-four guardian gods, the actor He Guishan transforms the surface body of Zhong Kui into the body of another door god. Each reconstructed door god stands for one of the twenty-four solar terms that determine the yearly cycle. Thus, one performance calls the twenty-four guardian gods into presence and guarantees protection against the entry of evil demons for the whole year round. The performance time is perceived to be more than the movement from position A to position B. The cyclical flow implied by the twenty-four door gods means that the point of entry (A) is neither point of entry nor point of closure; these are both contained in the infinite balance of the circle. The performance contracts the annual cycle of harmony and order into twenty-four poses, fractally.

Blooded bodies

The *jingju* training is a dissection of the body into individual parts which are then reassembled into fixed patterns (*hao*) which form the basis of all movements on stage. Such patterns or poses, whether *liangxiang* or *zaoxing*, represent specific meanings and are the expression of

---

[5] Also illustrated in De Groot 1982, vol. 6: plate 14. Note this Zhong Kui is also devouring another demon. Or, is he spitting it out, as figure of regeneration?

a body which is *presenced*. The poses manifest or radiate presence by virtue of the articulation of the body.

In the *nuo* theatre, the performing body is prepared (made articulate) in a general way, by training and through the initiation process, for the performing group. But the performing body is also specifically articulated for each performance (dissected) by the opening ceremony *kaiguang*. The opening ceremony metaphorically pulls apart the individual units of the body and reorganises the separate parts into a new, jointed body. This process is not without its threatening aspect, for tearing a body apart implies the spilling of a quantity of blood. The idea of spilling blood is, however, a desired thing, an integral part of the process of reconstruction (not only because the blood is collected for the writing of charms).

A piece from the *nuo* repertoire, *Mengjiangnu* (*Wife Meng*), which recounts the legend of Wife Meng, shows the regenerative power of blood. The modern version of the play, when performed in the *jingju* theatre, where it is known as *Ku changcheng* (*Crying at the Great Wall*), narrates how Mengjiang's husband has been seconded by the Emperor Qinshi Huangdi to slave labour at the Great Wall. After many years have passed, Mengjiang decides to search for him. When she finally arrives at the Great Wall, she learns that her husband is dead. She cries so bitterly that the gods in heaven bring him back to life. In the *jingju* version this *qingyi* role is renowned for its difficult singing part, the *kuqiang*, or crying melody.

In the *nuo* version of the play, however, blood plays a more direct role in bringing the dead back to life. On her journey, Mengjiang is directed to her husband by a black raven. It leads her on a circuit of the four city walls – east, south and west which are connected by the Great Wall (and again in the passage of her feet), and finally comes to rest at the north gate (the north is associated with death). Realising that her husband must be dead, she decides to collect his bones and give them a proper burial in his homeland. But she cannot determine which bones are his among the many skeletons buried within the Wall. She bites her finger, and allows the blood to fall over them all. Immediately the bones of her husband rise up:

> Mengjiang (*sings*):
> One stamp of the feet, one crying voice,

10,000 miles of the Great Wall collapse.
As it crumbles, the bodies and bones of millions of men come to
    light.
How shall I know those of my husband?
Husband and wife are one flesh and bone.
. . .
The tooth shall bite the finger.
. . .
And watch the blood spilling onto the earth.
I'll sprinkle the bones with this blood.
Drip, drip, drop, drop, soak the body,
Searching again, sprinkling other bones,
But none drips on husband's body.
Seeing the corpses and bones tears at the heart,
Mengjiang's tears are drenching.[6]

This aria comes from Scene 12 which is sub-titled, 'Circling the four
gates – Blood from a cut identifies the bones – Reunion'. The scene
reproduces the sequence of events required by the Fashi in exorcism
– the ritual circuit of the nine stations (related to the four directions),
the dissection of the performing body, and its reassembly in a new,
articulated body (the unification of the body is equal to the unification
on the earthly and heavenly planes, see chapter seven). The process of
exorcism undertaken by the Fashi is thus *repeated* or *summarised* in a
theatrical play.

In this scene, human secretions such as tears and blood are the
transforming fluids which bring to life dead matter. The power of
Mengjiang's stamping feet to crumble the Great Wall is the power of
naming, or definition – it exposes the skeletons not otherwise visible
to the human eye. Blood is perceived as a 'vital life fluid', it has the
power to give life. In the taxonomy of Yin and Yang, blood is considered
to be ultra Yang. The colour of blood is a Yang colour, the colour of the
south, of light, of heat – all of which are associated with the idea of
'life'. Moreover, as examined in chapter two, in the context of death
and marriage rites, red is the colour of transition between states of
being.

---

[6] *Hunan xiqu chuantong juben* 1982: 135–44.

The example of the play *Mengjiangnu* has shown how life is brought into the fictive figure in the world of theatre through the regenerative power of blood. The power of blood to transform, to regenerate life in the world of death can also be observed in ancient mortuary ceremonies. In this sense, the two worlds of theatre and death as worlds of an 'other' kind of life are comparable. The mortuary rite provides the literal example of regeneration through the flow of blood. Just as the *jingju* student metaphorically dissects his body in training to reconstruct it on stage and bring life to the fictive world of theatre, the moment of real dissection in the mortuary ceremony is the promise of new life for the deceased in the underworld.

In a royal tomb situated in Wuguancun, near the ancient Shang city of Anyang, in Henan province and dating to approximately 1300–1050 BC,[7] one hundred and thirty-one human and animal victims were unearthed. Among them were fifty-two birds and animals, forty-five complete human skeletons and thirty-four human skulls:

> . . . On the platforms on both sides of the chamber there are two rows of human burials, seventeen on the east and twenty four on the west, each with a certain amount of mortuary articles, including . . . many other animal and human victims. One of the human victims was placed in the *yaokeng* under the coffin in the prone position together with a *ge* axe.[8]

The entire Shang royal cemetery at Anyang has yielded about 1,500 human skeletons of bodies slaughtered on the occasion of royal funerals.[9] The cutting of flesh releases quantities of blood, which is the colour of Yang. The colour red is vital in its exorcist function during the dangerous passage of transition between states – unmarried and married, alive and dead. The bride wears red to keep bad influences away from the ceremony, as she is in transition towards what she calls the world of death, the married state; the Fangxiangshi wears a red coat during the exorcism; the mythological exorcist figure Zhong Kui wears the red gown of an official scholar and has a red face; most exorcist masks placed in tombs are made of reddish bronze, and so on. In all

---

[7] Cheng Te K'un 1960: 73–4 and Hu Houxuan 1974: 74–83.
[8] Cheng Te K'un 1960: 73–4.   [9] Bagley 1990: 61.

cases, the colour red has a strong exorcist, liminal signification. The tomb must be filled with as much blood as possible to guarantee life in the underworld.

The Fangxiangshi leaps into the pit, before the coffin is deposed, in order to cleanse it of any lurking demons by pointing his lance in the four corners of the grave. Although the most detailed description of the Fangxiangshi's actions in the exorcism concerns a seasonal exorcism in the palace, the event at the grave site may well have been similar:

> The Exorcist grasps a halberd . . . A youthful troupe . . . shoot in all directions. Their flying missiles scatter like rain . . . their torches surge forward like flames . . . driving out the pestilential demons to the four extremities of the world . . . They batter the Qimei and chop to pieces the Qukuang. They decapitate the Wei serpents and brain the Fangliang.[10]

> May all these twelve spirits drive away the evil and the baneful. Let them roast your bodies, break your spines and joints, tear off your flesh, pull out your lungs and entrails. If you do not leave at once, those who stay behind will become their food.[11]

In both Han citations, the exorcism seems to depend on physical dismemberment – the spilling of blood and chopping up of bodies, whether actual or only 'presented'. The exorcism can thus be described as a process of regeneration.

Not only were skulls and skeletons found scattered in ancient tombs, indicating mass slaughter, man-made mortuary artefacts were also smeared with blood, red chalk or cinnabar powder, as in the case of the tomb of Marquis of Cai, a Zhou burial in Shouxian county, Anhui province:

> Most of the woodwork of the burial had disintegrated. In the southern section of the pit there remained two large patches of lacquered fragments with red cloud scroll and geometric designs, piled to a thickness of about two centimetres . . . In the centre of this section fragments of the lacquered coffin were also found in a layer of red cinnabar about two centimetres thick.[12]

[10] Bodde 1975: 84.   [11] Ibid.: 82.
[12] Cheng T'e-Kun 1963: 155.

Many bronze exorcist masks, including the heads at the Guanghan Sanxingdui find, were also daubed, 'in some cases their eyes and mouths were painted with vermilion',[13] and in a Zhou tomb at Puducun village near Xian, fragments of a jade tiger,[14] covered in cinnabar, were found in the mouth of a skeleton[15] and a late Zhou mortuary figure in wood from Changsha (c. 5–3 BC) had traces of vermilion around the mouth and at the edges of the collar.[16]

Not only was blood spilled at the graveside and articles smeared with vermilion powder. In some cases, the slaughtered carcasses themselves were smeared with red stuff: 'A few pots were placed at the bottom; seven corpses, ten severed heads and parts of two more victims were added, then a layer of earth followed by nine more heads and twenty bodies, many apparently smeared with vermilion.'[17] This smearing of blood, or 'blooding', is an integral part of the process of substitution. Blood is smeared over straw figures, ancestral tablets and masks as part of the *kaiguang* or 'opening ceremony' – it is the process by which the body is metaphorically dissected and the life-giving force of Yang is transferred in the artefact. Here, the physical *dismemberment* of real people releases the life-giving force.

Ritual blood spilling was a major process of all building construction in ancient China and demonstrates the regenerative, creative power of blood. Royal palaces and tomb structures were literally built upon the flesh and blood of the people. A typical building of a royal palace at Anyang in the Yin (1324–1066 BC) cost many lives:

1 Laying the Foundations.
A small pit is dug at the bottom of the pit prepared for the foundations. A dog or small child is buried there. Seven such pits were found at Xiaotun's site B, and among the thirteen pits unearthed, fifteen dogs and four small children were found.
2 Setting the Plinth.
After the foundations have been laid, but before the columns or

---

[13] Bagley 1990: 62.
[14] See Hentze 1941: 171ff. for a discussion of the significance of the tiger in exorcism and in the process of recreation.
[15] Cheng T'e-Kun 1963: 55.   [16] Trubner 1968: 14, fig. 7.
[17] Hu Houxuan 1974: 78; illus. 3 on page 83.

plinths are erected, a hole is dug and a dog, ox or sheep laid inside. Two such pits had used human sacrifice.

3   Securing the Gateway.

At the site where the front entrance to the palace is to be built, a human or animal offering is buried. Site B showed five such places to have executed this ceremony and, in thirty pits, four dogs and fifty humans were found.

4   Completion Ceremony.

At the completion ceremony, chariots, humans and animals are buried in pits. At site B, 127 such pits were found containing five chariots, fifteen horses, twelve sheep, ten dogs and five hundred and eighty-five humans.[18]

The total sum of human victims slaughtered in the process of building one royal palace on the Anyang site amounts to nine hundred. As for killing for the tomb, the philosopher Mozi (lived in the period between 720–221 BC) suggests there were strict rules about how many human victims were to be killed for whom:

> . . . in the case of a son of Heaven, the maximum number to be killed and buried should vary between several hundreds and several times ten, and that of a Prince or a great officer, between several times ten and a certain minimum.[19]

The exorcist function of blood – keeping off the evil influences – is always simultaneous to the recreation, growth or inspiration of new life. For blood is the vital force of life *per se*. Thus, the tombs were filled with as much blood as possible to provide the deceased (pronounced lifeless) with as much creative influences as possible that he may survive in the other world.

Two very early clay figures, dating from the late Shang (1300–1050 BC), have been found at the Xiaodun site near Anyang, in Henan province,[20] which show the hands tied together (one figure's hands are tied together in front, the other's hands are tied at the back). The heads

---

[18]   Ibid.: 79.   [19]   De Groot 1982, vol. 2: 669 and 728.
[20]   Cheng Te-Kun 1960: 289, plate 29, b and c.

of the figures are raised up and their mouths gape open. These figures are said to be representations of prisoners of war, or slaves who were slaughtered on completion of building the tomb complex. Skeletons with traces of rope have been found in tomb no. 1 (of Yin date) at the Yidu Subudun site in Shandong province,[21] suggesting that victims may have been tied together and led to the tomb ramps before being beheaded on the site, and thrown into the pits.

Beheading was a common form of slaughter for the tomb. Perhaps the Fangxiang and his *ge*, or lance-axe, acted as executioner. In two cases, the tomb at Wuguancun cited above, and tomb no. 1001 at Anyang,[22] the tombs contained a human skeleton in a special pit directly under the coffin. The human skeleton was accompanied by a *ge* axe, suggesting that the Fangxiangshi was ultimately himself a victim, killed and buried in the tomb in order to continue to exorcise on behalf of the deceased in the underworld.

Frozen bodies

The human victims found in the tombs divide into two groups. In the case of those of lower rank – prisoners and slaves who had helped in the construction of the tomb site – known as *renji* (men who are sacrificed), the bodies simply lay exposed in the tomb or tomb pit. Those of high rank, however, killed to 'accompany the dead' in the after-life (*renxun* or *xunzang*, those who 'accompany' or 'follow' into the grave) were provided with a proper coffin, mortuary goods, and often their own slaughtered servants. This suggests that those of high rank were not necessarily present in the tomb for the sake of providing Yang through the sacrifice of their blood. They were not brutally slaughtered, nor blooded, nor were their skeletons severed or buried in pieces. Thus, blood is not the only regenerative material used in the mortuary ceremony. If other materials also provided 'life' in a situation of death, what are they, and are they, like the figurative use of blood in performance, also used to provide 'life' in a situation of theatre?

The classical collection *Shijing* (*Book of Odes*) describes three brothers of the Ziju family, ministers, and all in their youth, who were buried in 619 BC to accompany King Mu of the Qin state into the after-

---

[21] Hu Houxuan 1974: 80.   [22] See ibid.: 76.

world.[23] The scene of the killing of the three brothers is written in the form of an ode, entitled *The Yellow Bird(s)*:

> Crosswise fly the yellow birds,
> They settle on the jujube trees;
> Who follows prince Mu?
> Ziju Yansi;
> Now this Yansi, he is the champion among a hundred men;
> When he approaches the pit (grave) terrified is his trembling;
> That blue Heaven, it destroys our good men;
> If we could redeem him, his life would be worth that of a
>   hundred men.
>
> Crosswise fly the yellow birds,
> They settle on the mulberry trees;
> Who follows prince Mu?
> Ziju Zhonghang;
> Now this Zhonghang, he is a match for a hundred men;
> When he approaches the pit, terrified is his trembling;
> That blue Heaven, it destroys our good men;
> If we could redeem him, his life would be worth that of a
>   hundred men.
>
> Crosswise fly the yellow birds,
> They settle on the thorn trees;
> Who follows prince Mu?
> Ziju Zhenhu;
> Now this Zhenhu, he is a match for a hundred men;
> When he approaches the pit, terrified is his trembling;
> That blue Heaven, it destroys our good men;
> If we could redeem him, his life would be worth that of a
>   hundred men.[24]

---

[23] Although no archaeological evidence has yet supported the details of the ode, the *Liji* does mention their case. See De Groot 1982, vol. 2: 722. For alternative renderings of the ode, see De Groot 1982, vol. 2: 222, Jennings 1969: 142, and Pound 1955: 63.

[24] Karlgren 1950: 131.

Historical records of the Qin dynasty, describing another royal burial, suggest that ritual washing was an important preparation for the tomb, just as the *nuo* and marionette performers undergo cleansing rituals of abstention from sex, fasting and washing before carrying out the *kaiguang* (opening/severing) ceremony:

> This sepulchre measured several miles in circumference . . .
> and Xi said: 'The men who have done this work so cleverly, We
> shall send along with the Empress into this grave hill.' Those
> who knew this regarded those men as sons of misfortune. Wei
> Kui, the Imperial Charioteer of the Right Hand, and some
> others, fearing they too would have to follow the defunct into
> the tomb, washed their hair and bathed their bodies, and
> awaited their death.[25]

Like Wei Kui, the three Ziju brothers were probably ritually prepared for death, but not blooded before their bodies were placed in the tomb for, as high ranking nobles, they would have been accorded coffins and their own mortuary gifts. The reason for their deaths must lie elsewhere than in the spilling of blood as a source of the life-giving Yang force.

The ode to the brothers must be read on another plane than its literal one. The jujube and mulberry trees, mentioned at the beginning of each stanza, are symbols of reproduction, and life. The word for mulberry, *sang*, is a pun on 'mourning' or 'funeral', but the mulberry tree itself is the tree of the east (the rising sun) and the tree of light (*fusang*).[26] The jujube is a species of date, the written form of which reproduces the character *lai* 'to come' twice.[27] The jujube was also used to mark a ritual area. Ministers of justice in the Zhou and Han would hear cases under a jujube tree and the same plant marked the boundaries of places where scholars sat their literary exams. The wood is red to the core, the image of an honest heart.[28] The imagery of the ode serves to associate the brothers with the quality of Yang and regeneration through linguistic and symbolic pun.

The three Ziju brothers were all young. According to the

---

[25] De Groot 1982, vol. 2: 731–2.   [26] Granet 1959: 434, n. 2 and 435, n. 1.
[27] De Groot 1982, vol. 1: 75.   [28] Van Gulik 46–7.

Chinese, a young body is composed of Yang principles. Among the skeletons found in tombs, the majority of child victims were found to be intact, while the adult victims were usually headless. This would seem to imply that the young bodies were intrinsically Yang, and did not need to be put through the process of dismemberment in order to provide Yang.

That the young (immature) body is perceived to be full of Yang is confirmed in many kinds of Chinese performance examined in this study. The Fangxiangshi was accompanied by 120 young boys in carrying out the seasonal exorcism: 'In this ceremony, one hundred and twenty lads from among the Palace Attendants of the Yellow gates, aged ten to twelve, are selected to form a youthful troupe.'[29] The Palace Attendants of the Yellow gates were eunuchs (in the Chinese view, equivalent to non-mature males). The boy assistants were most probably apprentice eunuchs and thus 'doubly' filled with Yang (young male) qualities. Young boys are also considered the best mediums in communicating with the other side, and this again, is due to the fact that they are thought to be full of Yang. Wang Chong (lived *c.* first century) comments: 'Popular opinion pretends that boys are *yang*, and on this account spiritual revelations come forth from the mouths of boys. Lads and *wu* contain *yang*.'[30] Moreover, many priests and exorcists at the turn of this century were also young boys:

> They are called *shentong* i.e. 'godly youths' or 'youths who have *shen* or divinity in themselves' or 'youths who belong to a god'. More popularly, they are known as *jitong* 'divining youths' [mad youths], or *tongji* 'youthful diviners,' even simply *tongzi* or youths.[31]

Similarly, the *shi* personator of the deceased was preferably a child: ' "A superior man may carry his grandson in his arms, but not his son." This tells us that a grandson may be the personator of his deceased grandfather but a son cannot be so of his father.'[32] As a body filled with the Yang, or life-giving principle, the young body is likely to be able to act as 'host' to another life. A small boy was well equipped to communicate

---

[29] Bodde 1975: 81.   [30] De Groot 1982, Vol. 6: 1209.
[31] Ibid.   [32] *Liji*, trans. Legge 1885, Book I: 87.

with the gods: '. . . at a sacrificial festival, a child came out of his specially constructed soul tent[33] at the time of the offering; and then the child grew into the shape of the deceased and talked with the person making the sacrifice.'[34] Thus the youth of the nobles offered to the tomb may have provided a source of Yang, just as the dismembered bodies of others did in the form of their blood. The Ziju brothers were bodies literally 'cut off in their youth'. Perhaps a similar concept of the youthful body as a Yang body, able to 'give life' or presence to another, underpins the use of young boys in many kinds of Chinese performance (see Plate 15). In *jingju*, for example, in the past, a *dan* role actor began his studies at the age of seven or eight; if his voice survived puberty, his stage life was, nonetheless, finished by the age of full manhood (thirty).

The Ziju brothers were probably given their own coffins and mortuary goods. To the east of the tomb provided for Qinshi Huangdi (where the terracotta army is to be found) are located the graves of two hundred and fifty-six nobles, who were buried with their own mortuary goods.[35] As noble burials, these, like the Ziju brothers, were neither blooded nor dismembered. Pits to the west of Qinshi Huangdi's tomb, however, were filled with the remains of those who had helped to construct the tomb and who were apparently 'trapped' there. These latter burials were neither noble, providing exorcist, regenerative qualities through scholarship or youth, nor were they blooded. This model suggests a third method of providing life in the world of death:

> When the coffin had been deposed in the grave, some one
> suggested that, whereas the workmen and mechanicians who
> had made the machines and concealed the valuables knew
> all about the same, the buried treasures might forthwith be
> scattered in all directions. So, when the great ceremony (i.e. the
> burial) was finished and the valuables had been stored away,
> the interior gate of the road leading to the tomb was closed, and
> the lower and exterior gates of that road were both shut too, so

---

[33] Could this be similar to the matted tent, the *bamiaotang*, used by the players of *nuo* to deposit their souls and put on their masks in preparation to the performance?

[34] Eberhard 1968: 338.   [35] Ledderrose and Schlombs 1990.

Plate 15   Apprentice boys take red mask roles to represent Yang exorcist qualities in contemporary *dixi*

that none of the workmen, artisans or men who had been employed in storing away the treasures ever came out again.[36]

Literary evidence suggests the capture of such victims was somewhat random and sudden (though bloodless). This is an account of the tomb built for He Lu's daughter in 510 AD after she had committed suicide:

> She was buried outside the Chang gate, to the west of this capital. Tanks were dug and the earth piled up (for a tumulus); a crypt of veined stone was built . . . Thereupon they played with white cranes in the shop-streets of Wu, so that the crowd followed to look at them; and then receding, they caused men and women to pass with the cranes[37] through the gate which opened upon the road which led unto the crypt. Engines, now suddenly set at work, shut the gate upon them. This slaughter of living persons to make them accompany the deceased was disapproved by the denizens.[38]

The sudden and brutal capture of hundreds of victims suggests that these bodies served in the tomb as 'frozen' figures. They represent the idea of life stopped in motion, just as the tableaux made by the figure Zhong Kui represent 'exorcism', and the *zaoxing* poses made by Yang Yuhuan punctuate and give meaning to Mei Lanfang's performance.

Grave graces – the mortuary figure

The mortuary figures (grave graces[39]) in the examples below originate from different historical and geographical contexts. They are made of

---

[36] *Shiji*, trans. De Groot 1982, vol. 2: 400–1.

[37] The white cranes actually 'dance' as if, Pied Piper-like, they entice the population to the tomb. The cranes are possibly literary invention, or perhaps suggest the importance of dance in the funeral procession (dancing white cranes form a part of the masked exorcism event in Korea).

[38] De Groot 1982, vol. 2: 419 and 726.

[39] Craig 1914: 83: 'The Marionette . . . appears to me to be the last echo of some noble civilization. But as with all art which has passed into fat or vulgar hands, the Puppet has become a reproach . . . They imitate the comedians . . . Their bodies have lost their grave grace, they have become stiff . . .'

different materials – wood, bronze and paper – but they are all made specifically for the grave. Such figures are generally thought to be substitutes for real slaves, warriors, who were sacrificed at the tomb edge to continue to serve their lord in the underworld:[40] '[At] all such burials, be they of real servants or of models . . . the ancient rulers of China sought to perpetuate the world as they knew it both within their tombs and in the parks which surrounded their tombs above ground.'[41] The idea that statues of humans replaced real human victims ignores the fact that many tomb complexes contain both figures and human victims (as at the terracotta army tomb of Qinshi Huangdi) and obscures the function of both human slaughter for the tomb and the mortuary figure: they are put into the tomb for the purpose of *regenerating* the deceased in the after-life. In one case, the blood of slaughtered humans provides Yang, the vital life-giving force, or Yang is contained in the youth, or in the rank (scholars and officials are natural exorcists, full of Yang) of the victim, or Yang is held frozen in eternity by the brutal 'stopping' of life in the tomb by suddenly letting down trap doors and closing gates.

The idea of a 'frozen' life (still life) is repeated in the man-made mortuary figure. It is a figure made of materials which are specially chosen to fill the tomb with the same quality of Yang. However, unlike the still life of real bodies stopped in motion, the mortuary figures not only moved before being put into the grave; they also were believed to move after the deceased was put in the tomb – eternally. Real blood, real youth and real frozen life have been shown to provide Yang in the world of death. The human figure in a pose, like the man-made mortuary figure, also manifests the quality Yang, which guarantees life after death. How does this compare to the function of the reconstructed, man-remade, human figure in a pose (*zaoxing*), in the situation of theatre? To what extent can the mortuary model of frozen life provide clues as to the recreative act(s) of the performer in the fictive world of theatre?

The following study of mortuary figures provides a handbook of Yang – life in the world of death (Yin). The mortuary figure in the world

---

[40] See, for example De Groot 1982, vol. 2: 721–94 and 800–6.
[41] Rawson 1992: 139.

of death, its construction, its materiality, its movement and its regenerative function, parallels almost exactly those of the performer in the
world of theatre.

From a tomb of about 168 BC in Mawangdui, near Changsha,[42]
comes one female figure of approximately 50 cms. tall, cut from a single
block of wood, and then doused in a white base before the details of
her face and dress are painted in black and crimson. The robe reaches
from the neck to the ground and is decorated with cloud patterns. The
inner robe can just be seen at the neck underneath it. The hands are
held in front, in a gesture of respect, or suggesting the figure were holding something. The hair is carved, as if gathered in a bun at the top and
back of the head. The feet are hidden underneath the robe. In profile,
the whole figure measures only 13 cms. The facial features and body
are flattened, curving away from a straight profile only at the proffered
hands, the nose and the gathered hair at the back of the head. A piece of
bamboo sticks out of the head about 5 cms. It bears a solemn expression. One male figure of similar height, carved and treated in the same
way, was also found in the same tomb. It has an almost identical profile.
The gown is similarly decorated with cloud patterns in black and crimson. The position of the hands is also alike. It, too, has a bamboo stick
of about 5 cms. attached to the top and is equally solemn (see Plate 16).

One hundred and one such figures (ninety-two female, nine male)
were found along with sixty-one others, apparently musicians. These
are also carved from a single block of wood and bear similar expressions. Some are depicted kneeling, as if before a musical instrument,
and others stand. Some have no arms or hands and probably such limbs
would have been made of bamboo, or straw, and inserted into the main
trunk of the body, or fixed to a costume. Others have an added hairpiece
attached to the carved hair to form a long, loose queue, and some were
clothed in silk garments as well. Many, not all, also have the small
bamboo stick on their heads.

Finally, a bundle of thirty-six sticks, flattened at the top and bottom and carved to form three sides with roughly painted faces were
also deposited in the tomb. Thirty-three were made of peach wood.

---

[42] See *Changsha Mawangdui yihao hanmu* 1973, *Changsha Mawangdui
yihao hanmu fajue jianbao* 1972, Loewe 1979 and Rawson 1992: 195
and 315.

Plate 16   Changsha Mawangdui wooden mortuary figures

Twenty-two were tied together with string just as the separate strips of bamboo of a manuscript are tied together. Three were dressed in hemp underclothes and silk robes.

The two sets of figures were discovered in tomb no. 1 at Mawangdui just forty kilometres from Changsha in Hunan. The tomb dates to approximately 168 BC (early Han), and is one of three attributed to the family of Li Cang, a prime minister of Changsha, his wife and son. Tomb No. 1 belonged to his wife, Countess Dai, who died at about fifty years of age and whose well preserved corpse was found intact.

The tomb is typical of Han tombs of the area. It is a rectangular pit, aligned to the four points of the compass, wider at the surface than at the bottom and graduating in four steps downwards before sloping sharply. At the surface, the tomb was covered with a small funerary mound. The depth from the bottom of the pit to the top of the mound was 20 metres.

The coffin was placed at the bottom of the pit, which had been lined with white clay and charcoal for added protection against the damp.[43] The body lay within four coffins, each inside the other in the centre of the tomb, and the wooden figures and other accessories such as food, silks, vessels and so on, were placed in four side chambers dug into the walls. The tomb contained a total of one hundred and sixty-two figures. The hundred and one figures which can be classed as one group, following the description above, were placed differently: fifty-nine were found in the eastern chamber; thirty-nine in the southern chamber and three in the northern chamber.

The group of thirty-three mannikins were tied together and placed on top of the inner coffin lid underneath a silk painted banner. The three clothed figures were placed in the crevices between the inner (fourth) coffin which was made of silk and richly embroidered and the third coffin, lacquered and decorated, in the three quarters: east, west and south.[44]

The main figures are dressed in court robes indicating that they represent servants and officials of court life (see Plate 17). The cloud pattern on their dress, however, also links them to the heavenly other world, for clouds indicate the transport of gods or spirits from another world. 'Through much of Han poetry rushes a cosmic wind on which spirits are borne aloft to a world of immortal spirits and mystery. Designs based on cloud scrolling are attuned to the same mood.'[45] The

---

[43] Loewe 1979: 22.

[44] *Changsha Mawangdui yihao hanmu fajue jianbao* 1972: 100, figure 93 (1), (2) and (3).

[45] Watson 1974: 96.

Plate 17   Changsha Mawangdui wooden mortuary figures

colours of the gown are red and black, which follow the same system of meaning explored in the context of exorcism. Red is a Yang colour, of light, heat and the south. Black is a Yin colour, of darkness, cold and the north. Both colours indicate a sense of the figure, like the Fangxiangshi exorcist, as one who can 'go either side' into the world of light and life or equally into the world of darkness and death, as *Grenzgänger*.

The Mawangdui figures are generally described as 'southern', deriving from an area covering Hunan and Hubei provinces known as the State of Chu which flourished during the Eastern Zhou period (770–221 BC).

The particular wood chosen to carve these and the Mawangdui figures has not yet been identified. However, the ancient *Shuowen* dictionary comments, 'A *yong* (mortuary figure) is a man made of *dong* (paulownia) wood.' *Dong* wood is distinguished by being very lightweight – one of the reasons for its continued use today, along with poplar (*yang* which puns directly with Yang), in carving masks for the *nuo* theatre. The *dong* wood is also believed to have life-giving properties because it is classified as a Yang wood, hence the other reason for its use in making masks for the *nuo*. Furthermore, *dong* is also used to make coffins. The material chosen to represent the human figures in the underworld is intrinsically Yang. The very material ('genetic stuff' – compare Mei Lanfang and the sense of family in chapter one) of the figure 'gives life'.

The character *dong* is made up of the radical for 'wood' and the sound signifier *tong* which alone has the meaning 'together with, conjoined with, jointed' (see Diagram 33 above). *Dong* could be interpreted as meaning 'counterpart in wood'. This definition of *dong* wood confirms a physical proximity between man's body and the *dong* wood:

> The *dong*, more commonly called *Wu-dong*. This is probably the Sterculia Platanifolea, a stately, large-leaved tree growing in the central and southern provinces of the empire, at least down to the latitude of Amoy [Xiamen]. It produces an excellent light timber, much used for fine carpentry of all kinds, for musical instruments and the like. 'The *Erya* calls it *jian* because it is suitable for the manufacture of coffins'; in point of fact we find in the oldest Chinese documents the word *jian* very frequently used to denote an inner coffin. 'This word denotes the coffin nearest the body, and the wood got the name *jian* from the fact that it was placed *next to* the body.'[46]

The source makes a pun on the word *jian*, for it is composed of the element 'wood' as radical and the element meaning 'relation, kin'. The association of the *dong* wood to the human body is again apparent in another explanation of the word *yong* (mortuary figure). For the *Shiji zhengyi* declares, '*ou* is a mate or counterpart, because it is a clay or wooden (*dong*) man which has taken its form from a real man' and the *Shuowen* explains, '*Yong* is an effigy (*ou*) of a man.'[47]

Dong wood was also used to make percussive instruments, coffins, ancestral tablets and portal gates:

> M. Bonifacy notes that nowadays, among the Lolo, the dead are represented by wooden figures of 10 cms. in height . . . the Laqua use a domestic altar in the shape of steps supported by urns which contain, they say, the souls of their ancestors. The rites which operate the transferral of souls into urns of figurines

[46] De Groot 1982, vol. 1: 302.   [47] Shen Chien-shih 1936–7: 7.

among the Laqua and Lolo are not unlike the [Han] Chinese rites
which prepare the link between *huan* (summoning the soul)
and the ancestral tablet . . . In the winter season, the season of
death, the Chinese use masks in order to fix the wandering soul
(*huan* the soul of the ancestors) . . . The fact that the sacred
trees (doors used in portal gates) serve in the making of
instruments (*caisses sonores*) and coffins is somewhat
curious.[48]

The *dong* wood is not only used for musical instruments and coffins as
a wood of transition, it is also used to literally 'support' the doorway; it
is the wood of the threshold (liminal wood). The quality that unites all
these uses of *dong* wood is the fact that it is used to signify Yang in a
situation of change, or transformation.

While most mourners at a contemporary Chinese funeral avoid
all possible contact with the coffin, some women directly seek it. Once
the corpse is settled in the coffin: 'The young women of the deceased's
family (daughters-in-law and married daughters) kneel in the centre of
the circle and sing funeral laments while rubbing their unbraided hair
against the coffin.'[49] The women, whose hair after marriage is always
bound, do not wash their hair after this polluting action until the
seven-day period of mourning is over. 'By exposing themselves to this
aspect of pollution daughters-in-law may, in fact, be taking on the fertility of the deceased, embodied in the flesh.'[50] The wood of the coffin is
filled with Yang, has regenerative qualities, just as a mortuary figure
made of *dong* wood is directly regenerative.

Peach wood was used for the thirty-six mannikins at the Changsha Mawangdui grave and it is also considered to have exorcist and life-
preserving properties. It is a 'cleansing' or exorcist wood, a branch of
which was placed above the doorways by officials after the court exorcism of the Fangxiangshi as a guarantee that no demons will return.
Moreover, at funerals, the peach wood protected the living from the
evil influences of the grave-site: 'When a ruler goes to the funeral rites
of a minister, he has with him a *wu* and a *zhu* holding respectively a
piece of peach wood and reeds.'[51] The blossoms and twigs of the peach

---

[48] Granet 1926: 441, n. 1, and Eberhard 1968: 333.   [49] Watson 1982: 162.
[50] Ibid.: 74.   [51] De Groot 1982, vol. 1: 41.

tree are medicinal; the fruit confers longevity, even immortality.[52] This
has the consequence that old coffins (along with peach-wood) are often
part of the remedy prescribed for a range of illnesses:

> Old coffin boards. These are not poisonous; they conquer the
> influences of spectres, dissolve obstinate inner evils and pains
> in the heart and belly, and counteract asthmatic affections,
> as also perturbations caused by bad dreams. Those who are
> constantly under the influence of spectres and spirits should
> make a decoction of the wood in water and wine, adding a
> branch of a peach tree growing on the east side of the trunk, and
> they will vomit them out . . . When babies cry at night, kindle
> some old coffin wood and let the flames shine over them and
> then they will be quiet immediately.[53]

Thus the various woods chosen to make mortuary figures are imbued
with the life-bringing quality of Yang. They fill the tomb with regenerative power.

A second model of mortuary goods imbued with Yang, is a collection of bronze masks, early Zhou in date, situated in Xincun in
Xunxian county, Henan province.[54] In tomb no. 1, twelve bronze masks
hung on the east and west walls. Tomb no. 2 yielded two large animal
masks. Tomb no. 8 contained seven 'Fangxiang'[55] masks and a halberd
with an inscription. Tomb no. 28 contained the broken pieces of
another mask. Tomb no. 42 contained twelve lance-axes (ge), two hal-
berds (ji), various shields and swords and three masks. In sum, a collection of masks and weapons was found that can be associated with the
Fangxiang in his role as exorcist. The masks and weapons were scattered in east–west positions, that is, in relation to the rising (Yang) and
setting (Yin) sun.

Eight of the Xunxian masks were constructed of separate pieces
– the eyes, nose, mouth and ears, possibly suggesting the pieces were
sewn or affixed to some other item, perhaps a piece of leather (and

---

[52] See, for example, Doré 1936: 717–21.   [53] De Groot 1982, vol. 1: 328.
[54] Guo Baoqun 1936: 167–200, Sun Haipo 1938 and Meister 1938: 5–12.
[55] Guo calls them this in his article, see note above, though there is no
direct proof for his theory.

worn?). Furthermore, separate ear pieces and head-dresses, clearly belonging to these masks, were also found.

The separate construction of the ear piece can be compared with the masks used in Anshun *dixi*. Here, the face of the mask is made of one piece of wood. The two 'ear' pieces are made separately and drilled so that strings can pass through the mask and be tied round the performer's head. When the mask is not being worn, the two ear pieces are tucked under the face. This structure makes the masks very fragile. Handling the masks, it often happens that the ear pieces become chipped and snap off and have to be replaced. None of the performers could (or would) say why the ear pieces were made separately, but the ear pieces are actually more like 'wings'. Perhaps it is intended to represent the idea of the god, presented by the mask, travelling down to earth on these special 'wings'.

Two kinds of mask were identified at Xunxian: a human face, which consisted of six separate parts (two eyes, two ears, nose and mouth), and other, 'animal' masks in one piece. Of the first (human) kind, eight masks were found intact and twelve masks in broken pieces. Of the second (Taotie? demon?-style) six masks were found whole, and four masks were discovered in broken pieces. The different styles in the animal masks can be classified according to the shape of the ear – hooked at both ends like a reverse C, curled at the top end only, like a reverse P, or leaf-shaped. The eyes were either round or almond; the eyebrow either full half moon, gridded half moon or sliced half moon. The horns were either single ram horn, double ram horn, ram horn with three prongs (antler?); the mouth – open half moon, half moon with teeth top and bottom, half moon with top teeth and nose – bulb, anchor and inverted anchor-bulb-root combination).

The character for bronze, *tong*, is made up of the elements 'metal/gold' and 'similar' (see Diagram 33 on p. 149). It is the same construction as the character *dong* which has the element 'wood' and 'similar'. Thus the bronze artefacts are, like the wooden ones, *counterparts* in metal. Moreover, the colour of bronze associates it with the principles of exorcism and Yang. The *Shuowen* dictionary explains, 'bronze is *red* gold'. The term for red, *chi*, is used in all exorcism vocabularies as a pun for 'to expel, exorcise'. Furthermore, gold is considered to have life-preserving qualities: 'He who swallows gold will exist as long as gold.'[56] 'If there be gold and jade in its nine openings, the result is that the corpse does not putrefy.'[57] Thus the red/gold, bronze masks are seen to be the epitome of exorcist qualities. They destroy *and* preserve, or give life. The Fangxiangshi wears over his head a bearskin with four gold eyes. The term *pi* could mean fur, or skin, as in leather. If leather was used in combination with the Xunxian tomb masks, then perhaps bearskin – for the bear represents regeneration from the dark and cold (the tomb) because it hibernates over winter in a cave and only emerges on the coming of spring (light, life).

The final mortuary model of regeneration is a mortuary house made of paper over bamboo splints for 'a woman in the Li lineage' in contemporary Taiwan:

> Outside of her large, three-room house stood representatives of two armed door-guards. Inside the front gate, in the open courtyard, were replicas of an electric fan, two television sets, an electric rice pot, a washing machine, a car with tail fins, a radio, lawn furniture, and a refrigerator, along with several servants wielding mops and brooms. The entire display was arranged in the Li ancestral hall; on an adjacent table stood a paper figure representing the deceased woman.[58]

The paper house, and other items, are laid out in the ancestral hall of the deceased's home while the participants of the funeral procession gather. They are then carried to the grave site, and burned. They are made of tissue paper, stretched and glued over a framework of bamboo splints. These materials are specially chosen that they burn well; they are not designed to be durable. The burnt items are changed into a form that the deceased person can use in the world of the dead.

The wooden and bronze mortuary goods examined in the study have confirmed the concept that the figures are designed as 'frozen life', to provide Yang or 'life spirit' in the tomb. They are considered, to an extent, to be eternal figures – figures that do not deteriorate with time, figures that continue to provide Yang-life in the underworld. However, in the case of paper goods, the figures are designed to be destroyed.

---

[56] De Groot 1982, vol. I: 273. [57] Ibid.
[58] Ahern 1973: 226.

This apparent paradox is easily explained, for the fire that consumes the figures provides huge quantities of the desired Yang in the form of light and heat. Moreover, the goods are 'transformed' (*kaiguang*) by fire for use in the underworld.

Such mortuary items for burning have been in use in China since at least the Han, for in the *Houhanshu*, one record dictates that among the items buried along with a high-ranking official were, 'Nine carriages and thirty-six straw images of men and horses.'[59] One eighth century document tries to suggest that the straw figures were a model for later wooden figures:

> Houses and sheds, cars and horses, male and female slaves, horned cattle and so forth are made of wood. Before the dynasty of Zhou ruled the empire, cars of clay and souls of straw were in vogue; after that dynasty wooden puppets (*yong*) were used.[60]

However, it is more likely that both wood and straw were used contemporaneously. Confucius (lived fifth century BC) opened a debate about the difference between the use of straw and wooden figures, so that it seems unlikely that either temporal or cultural–geographical distance separated the use of the different materials:

> Those who make valueless implements for the manes of the dead show that they are acquainted with the proper method of celebrating obsequies for, though such implements be ready at hand, they are unfit for real use. Why, if implements of the living were used for fitting out the dead, would there not be a risk of this leading to the burying of human beings with the dead? . . . Vehicles of clay and souls of straw have been in vogue since olden times and their use is based upon the same principle as the use of implements for the manes . . . Confucius declared that those who made straw souls were virtuous, but those who made wooden puppets (*yong*) were inhumane, for was there not a danger of their leading to the use of human victims?[61]

This passage seems to confirm the idea that straw and paper mortuary goods were intended for burning, whereas the wooden and clay items

[59] De Groot 1982, vol. 2: 403.   [60] Ibid.: 808.
[61] Ibid.: 807.

were not. Confucius bases his argument on the opposition of 'real' and 'not real', commending the 'not real' as the correct form for mortuary goods. Another passage, also attributed to Confucius, goes further: 'Confucius also said, the first maker of wooden mortuary figures (*yong*), did he not remain childless because he made these images of man and used them?'[62] In this passage, the term for the wooden mortuary figure is *yong* and thus clearly indicates the kind of figure that 'hopped'. The term for straw figure, as it is used in these ancient documents, is *chuling*. De Groot translates *chuling* as 'straw souls'. The term *chu* means 'scrap' or 'fire' wood – the kind of highly flammable lightweight twigs that are used to start a fire. It is also sometimes used for the grass given to cattle as fodder (as food for the beast, which is itself food for the next in the chain – regenerative?). *Ling* means 'spirit' or 'soul'. The straw figure used in the mortuary ceremony seems to have been quite similar to the figures now found in various *nuo* and healing events (described in chapter three). In the *nuo* theatre, such figures are also burnt after use. The passage attributed to Confucius, however, seems to object to the fact that the wooden figures were made to move, and criticises the 'maker' – the 'mover' – perhaps as one who dares to assume power over 'life' – a recurring vilification of the actor in the theatre in many cultures.

Whether human flesh, wood, bronze or paper, the *purpose* of all mortuary bodies in the tomb was to provide Yang. The artefacts were made of materials that were considered to be Yang – if dressed, then in the colours of Yang; if positioned, then placed in positions related to the south and east, the Yang orientations, or they were put near (to contact, infect) the corpse with Yang. The function of so much Yang inside the tomb was one of revitalisation and regeneration in a situation of end and decease. Yang dominated the Yin qualities of darkness and death and kept away evil influences for Yang is exorcistic. Yang also provides a suitable live 'host' to the revived spirit of the deceased for:

> . . . if a body is properly circumvested by objects and wood
> imbued with Yang matter, or in other words, with the same
> *shen* afflatus of which the soul is composed, it will be a seat for

[62] *The Works of Mengzi*, 'Liang hui wang' 1: 4.

the manes even after death, a support to which the manes may firmly adhere and thus prevent their nebulous, shadowy being from evaporating and suffering annihilation.[63]

The body of the *jingju* performer, like the mortuary figure, is a body filled with Yang. The training method, which enforces the metaphorical bodily dissection of the various limbs, creates the possibility of recreation in a new body, a new pattern or arrangement of limbs (*hao*). In the performance, the actor moves from pattern to pattern, rearranging the parts of his body in ever new forms. The *jingju* performer brings together (*zonghe*), and holds (*hao*) essentially severed parts together in a system of five (hand-eye-finger-foot-harmony) plus a system of four (singing-recitation-acrobatics-action) making his body physically congruent with the creative matrix of the Luo diagram – an articulate(d) body. In the *liangxiang* and *zaoxing* poses, the performer radiates presence (life, Yang) by virtue of such articulation. The mortuary figures provide life in a situation of death through the spilling of blood (actual dismemberment), through the concepts of youth and 'frozen' life. The performer provides life in a situation of theatre by the metaphoric spilling of blood (training in parts), and the constant reconstruction of the body into specific forms (poses – still lifes) of meaning.

---

[63] De Groot 1982, vol. 1: 348.

6   **Qi**
(Presence)

Mei Lanfang has been on stage in the performance of the concubine Yang Yuhuan for nearly three minutes. He is still upstage left, at the point of shaking out each sleeve, signalling to the orchestra that he is ready to sing. The *zaoxing* poses he makes during this movement must impress the spectator. He must convey all the aspects of appearance, poise, school or style of presentation of the role as well as his own version of it, in this first encounter. The Chinese performers say, he must *faqi* (radiate presence).

Qi is what makes a performer a good performer – without it, the performance is considered worthless, a waste of effort. The worst criticism a *jingju* performer can receive is that he is *meiyou qi* (has no presence). Literally, the word *qi* means 'air', 'spirit', 'energy' or 'breath'. In performance terms it can mean, quite simply, 'breath control'. In singing and moving, the performer must ensure he has the right quantity of breath at all times. Thus, the shaking the sleeve movement at the entrance of Yang Yuhuan, in practical terms, serves as the moment when the performer can gather his breath for the singing section to come.

However, *qi* means much more than mere breath control. A performer who has *qi* is considered to be 'in-spired', moved by a special kind of energy or filled with presence. During training, the master will often point to the student's abdomen and demand that the student draw up his *qi*. This is the heart or residence of *qi*, the undefined and indefinable centre of the human body from which presence (force) flows.

On the *jingju* stage, the basic pose positions of performers of all role categories depend upon the roundedness of arms never being fully extended but always describing a curve. When holding the arms out

Diagram 34   *fanshou* (upturned hands)

Diagram 35   *shanbang* (mountain arm)

from the body, the backs of the hands face the chest (see Diagrams 34 and 35). When the leg is raised, the toes are turned back towards the ankle, or the sole is hooked inwards (see Diagrams 36 and 37). These positions reinforce the sense of holding or containing *qi* presence in the body, closing or embracing it to the body – the body is replenished,

Diagram 36   *goujiao* (upturned foot)   Diagram 37   *kuaijiao* (hooked sole)

is always refilled with presence. The *jingju* master teaches his students that *qi* not only refers to the effort, strength or energy required to hold these difficult positions, it is also the power of presence contained by them. Thus, when the student needs to rest after rehearsing a long sequence, it is forbidden to lie or sprawl exhausted on the floor, for this would dissipate the *qi*. Instead, the student takes up a crouching position, with heels raised off the floor and hands resting over the thighs, in order to encourage the flow of *qi* energy which has been expended in the movement to return to the solar plexus, seat of *qi*, and there be replenished, *shouqi* (gathering in the *qi*, see Plate 18). The importance of holding in *qi* in order to radiate presence is so vital to the performer, that Zhang Chunhua, as many *jingju* performers, criticises classical ballet. In his view, the ballet dancer does nothing but throw the *qi* away – hands, feet and even the position of the head, are fully extended – worse, they 'droop', they throw the *qi* (life) away from the body.

Movement is life

In the *kaiguang* opening ceremony, the artefact was dissected by being named part by part. The body was severed and, at the dislocation of each part, regenerative blood flowed. Alternatively, the artefact was simply daubed with blood, red ink or cinnabar powder to indicate the metaphorical process of dissection (Yang). The *kaiguang* ceremony is the process by which bodies are cut up in order to radiate presence. Literally, the term *kai* means 'to open', 'to cut', *guang* means 'lustre', 'to radiate'. The *jingju* body, like the artefact, is conceived as being cut up into individual parts (in training), which are then reassembled in

Plate 18   'Gathering the *qi*' – students resting between exercises at the *jingju* School in Yingkou, Liaoning Province

order that the body can radiate presence (*qi*). Thus the concepts Yang, *ming* (light, the *presenced* burial artefact) and *qi* in performance terms are related. The performing body, be it marionette, mask, mortuary figure, mask or human body, is prepared for performance in the same way. The process of dissection causes, or happens simultaneously to, the regenerative process of reassembly into a new body.

However, this is not the end of the process. The transformed, or prepared body must express or *manifest* its presence. The manifestation of presence in Chinese performance is through movement. The body must move, be seen to move, or be moved in order to show presence. The Chinese term for perform *biaoyan* (manifest *and display*) reflects this idea.

It is generally supposed that movement is the method or technique by which a spirit or presence is called into the body. That is, the body executes movement *in order* to become presenced. Steady rhythmical percussion and circling, stamping movements are thought to mesmerise the performer and transport him into another kind of state, or trance.[1] This is a misleading Western interpretation of the Asian ('primitive') model, as if a Chinese scholar were to maintain that Westerners drive themselves into trance when dancing the waltz – a circular, regular, repetitious dance. Close examination of the Chinese model shows that the process of calling the spirit to be present (*kaiguang*) takes place *before* movement begins. Movement does not *induce* the spirit to be present. It is the *manifestation* of the spirit's presence.

Furthermore, the specific kinds of movement identified as 'trance-inducing' – circling and leaping, have fixed meanings in the context of Chinese performance. Such movements are not aimlessly repeated until such time as the performer transcends some kind of 'state'. Each movement is carefully programmed in the context of performance, controlled and executed with clear intention.

In the *nuo* theatre, the performer makes a circuit of the nine stations of the Luo diagram. In doing so, he stamps at each station and pauses there, briefly, to make a pose consisting of hand signs and elements of text which correspond to that station. For example, at the station *qian* (heaven), he sings of the powers of that station, makes the *jue* (hand sign) of heaven, and stamps with his left foot. For, when the Luo diagram is brought into congruence with his own body, the left foot has the value of heaven. Several means of expression contained in the human body (hand, foot, voice) articulate the concept 'heaven' simultaneously. They represent, embody or bring to life (in different corporeal, physical media) the term 'heaven'.

The example of the play *Mengjiangnu* showed that the effect of Mengjiang's stamping was to call up the bones of all the skeletons buried underneath the Great Wall. It was an act of designation. Mengjiang's stamping foot pierced the thick walls of the Great Wall and revealed the bones of the bodies buried under it. Her stamping foot reproduced the bones from another level or plane of being. Similarly, in

---

[1] In his work on the Japanese theatre, Ortolani repeats this tired equation once more: 'Primitive shamanistic rituals were seminal for the origin of dance in Japan, and provide the source of the two oldest terms for dance: *mai* and *odori. Mai* is derived from the custom of the shamaness of circling around and around to reach a state of trance . . . *Odori* is traced back to the fact that male shamans would leap repeatedly up and down to induce the deity to possess them.' Ortolani 1990: 23.

Enter   Exit

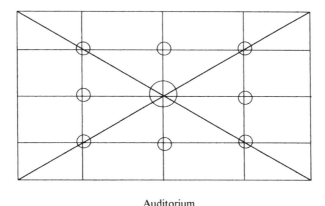

Auditorium

Diagram 38   The *jingju* stage

the nine stations dance, the stamping feet of the performer *designate*,
name and reproduce each station with the body. The body articulates
the concept of heaven (normally invisible to the mortal eye), corporeally reproduces it, embodies it, in order to do business with it.

Like the *nuo* performance space, the acting area of the *jingju* is
perceived as if it were divided into nine areas (see Diagram 38). During
training, the master will sometimes mark the grid on the floor to help
the student orientate himself.[2] All sequences of movement in *jingju*
performance are dedicated to the exploitation of this scheme. The student must be able to repeat his movement sequence exactly in any size
of space in any orientation. That is, he moves according to the nine-
point grid, and not according to a fixed number of steps between movements. The matrix is like a fractal, nine point system that can expand
or contract into infinity, that is, any unit of space is any unit of space.
Such a concept radically challenges the Western concept of space as
fixed or determined. In the Chinese model, the performing body is not
constrained by the restrictions of shape or size of the body and space.

---

[2] In the Japanese *no* theatre, the stage space is actually divided into the
  nine squares, each of which has a special name. See programme notes to
  the Kanze Company (Zeami-za) in Munich 1982: 12.

211

The performer *can* move in a fictive (other) world/space. In training, the student is forbidden to orient himself towards the auditorium. He must learn to rotate his movement sequence in any direction, taking due north, due east, south-west or north-north-east, for example, as his axis.

Thus the *relations* the performer makes with his body as he moves between each cell or area of the stage space are more important than the *perspective* of the spectator. That is, the performance is not directed towards the spectator. It is aimed at making connections of meaning through the space of the stage that correspond to the creation of the other world. The initiated spectator can follow these connections, will not need to place himself opposite the stage (as in the auditorium) because, technically speaking, there is no auditorium.[3]

The performer moves on the stage curving around one point, and moving directly to another, like a chess piece on a board. As he does so, he is involved in a process of continual expending and gathering of *qi*. The *liangxiang* pose, which is held for several seconds, is the moment of expressing presence and the moment when the performer catches his breath – expends the old and takes in new. The *liangxiang* is always made at one of the nine points. The term *liangxiang* means 'radiant, luminous appearance' – it is the moment when the performer must glow, send out the quality of presence termed *qi*. The *liangxiang* is a point of transition – the expression of *qi* (force) which captivates the spectator's gaze happens at same point at which *qi* is returned or gathered. The movements between *liangxiang* points (points of presence), i.e. movements outside the nine points or cells, are *connecting* movements of passage, or *guocheng*, between moments of presence.

In terms of the Luo diagram, the *liangxiang* is the moment when presence is especially manifest, for in *jingju*, the nine cells made by the imposition of a Luo diagram plan, are considered to be the only effective points on the stage at which to halt and execute a *liangxiang* pose. The deputy head of the China Theatre School, Ma Mingqun, explained,

---

[3] Ancient Chinese stages were open on all four sides; the *nuo* theatre is generally performed on an open piece of ground. The move to the proscenium arch, Western style theatre, has profoundly restricted the structure of perception in forms such as *jingju*.

'these points are aesthetically the most pleasing to the spectator, so they are best suited to perform the *liangxiang* pose'. In the *nuo* theatre the performers orientate themselves around each station in order to name, designate or articulate the presence that fills each station. By analogy, the *jingju* performer does the same. The nine points on the stage are the positions best suited to articulate presence *faqi* (giving off presence).

The action of stamping was examined in chapter three as a defining, or naming movement. When such movements are put together in a sequence, the stamping feet (whether alternating between the left and right foot, or depending on one foot only) actually link named (reproduced) stations of meaning. The stamping feet *connect* – make grammatical sentences of – the nouns contained in each station. Thus stamping, hopping movements, so-called trance-inducing, are actually the process by which meaning (units of grammatical sense) is created.[4] *Yong* (leap, hop, skip) is closely related to another character, *yong*, meaning 'burial figure' (see Diagram 30 on p. 111). Both characters have the same sound signifier. The character meaning to skip or hop bears the 'foot' radical, the character meaning burial figure has the radical 'man'. At best closely related, they are brought into direct context with each other by a Tang dynasty rhyme book, the *Guangyun*. The *Guangyun* introduces the character *yong* (burial figure) thus: 'A *yong* is a man made of wood. When putting the coffin in the grave, the mechanism inside its body is manipulated to make it do dancing, leaping, hopping movements (*yong*), so its ancient name is *yong* (burial figure)'. Here, the author understands the term *yong* (burial figure) to have derived from the fact that it hopped and skipped (*yong*). A similar explanation is found in the earlier commentary of Zheng Xuan (in the late Han) on a passage in the *Liji*. Zheng explains the character *yong*: 'A *yong* is an image of a man, having facial features and a control mechanism that allows the figure to move just like a real man.' Both records show that

---

[4] One of the two movements identified by Ortolani in the Japanese theatre as 'trance inducing' is *odori* which means to leap, or hop. The Japanese script is made up of a large number of Chinese characters which were borrowed by the Japanese to express their own language in written form. The written form *odori* is spoken as *yong* in the Chinese language. In both languages, this character means 'to hop', 'to skip', or 'to jump'.

the burial figures moved in some way. The way that they moved (hopping, skipping, dancing – *yong*) was associated with the name for burial figures *yong*. Moreover, both statements maintain that the figures had some kind of mechanism, were controlled in some way, or made to move. The way that they moved was a sequence of leaps and hops from one foot to the other, or on one foot – a connective series of stamping, or designative, recreative steps, not unlike the movements made by the *nuo* or *jingju* performer over the nine point Luo matrix of creation in the world(s) of exorcism and theatre. The action of leaping is *not* an act of invocation or inducement into trance. It is the sum of a series of actions of creation (stamping) which manifest presence. Only if the performer is first presenced (*kaiguang*), does he have the power to create/*move*.

Life in the other world

In chapter five, it was shown that the purpose of putting mortuary figures and humans in the tomb was to provide a source of Yang in the afterworld for the deceased. The mortuary figures were made of Yang materials and placed in Yang positions, or 'cut off', frozen in the flow of life. Some were even daubed with red paint suggesting the opening (*kaiguang*) ceremony had been carried out on them. Thus the figures were almost certainly conceived as presenced figures, figures *with life* in a situation of death. The mortuary figures were known by the term *yong*, which is related to the concept of leaping, and hopping. The mortuary figure was almost certainly moved, or was made to move, to manifest that presence. This concept parallels the same pattern in human performance. The performer is dissected, reassembled into an articulate(d) body which leaps and hops (*moves*) over the nine point creative matrix to manifest life in the fictive world of theatre.

The figures of female servants and musicians from the tomb at Mawangdui in Changsha have a piece of bamboo attached to the head, which is between five and seven centimetres long, suggesting they were perhaps suspended from some kind of framework, or stand, in the procession towards the tomb site. Alternatively, they may have been dangled over the tomb pit before being placed in their positions. Several of the male figures are carved without arms and these limbs would have been provided by a robe, wrapped around them with some form of stick device to make the arms inside the sleeves. This would have meant that as the whole figure was moved, the arms automatically followed in a swinging, waving movement, depending on the severity of the movement. Such figures may have been attached to a framework, which itself may have been placed on one of the gift-bearing palanquins in the procession to the tomb.

A second kind of figure, from a tomb dating to *c.* 107 BC, in the county of Laixi, in Shandong province,[5] is made of wood and is approximately 1.82 metres tall. It is constructed out of thirteen separate pieces: the head and neck, three pieces for the shoulders (a central piece to hold the head, and two joining pieces either side), a piece each for the arms, two pieces running from the shoulders to the hips, joined at hip level by one cross-wise piece, a piece each for the upper legs, and a piece each for the lower legs. The legs are shaped, becoming narrower towards the ankle, and the facial features are carved. The figure is thought to have been clothed but no garments survived. However, the piece of wood joining the body at the hips and the legs had been drilled with many holes, possibly to assist in the tying, or fixing of the garments.

Next to the figure, a silver rod 1.15 metres long, and four iron weights in the shape of tiger tallies, were found. Considering the fact that the figure could certainly be made to sit, kneel or stand, the arms could be made to move, and possibly the head made to turn, it seems likely that this figure moved either by the device of strings and weights, or by manipulation with the rod, or a combination of both. The size of the figure indicates that it may have taken either one man and a supporting framework to control it – in which case the figure would be affixed somehow and made to make simple movements from that fixed position – or several men. Perhaps it was moved like the temple statue figures, such as Wang Gong, in the litter procession preceding the *nuo* event in Guizhou described below. Alternatively, it may have been moved by a system like that used in the Anhui Zhong Kui dance, where the performer ties the feet of the figure to his own feet and carries the body by a framework attached to his shoulders. Such a device leaves the performer's hands free to manipulate the arms of the figure. False

---

[5] Stalberg 1984: 18, Liao Ben 1989: 74 and Wang Mingfang 1979: 4.

arms are attached to the performer to add to the deception that the two bodies are separate (see Diagram 39a, b and c).

A third kind of moving mortuary figure is represented by a set of figures dating from between 633 and 688 AD, which were found in the tomb of Zhang Xiong and his wife in Asitana, in Turfan county, in Xinjiang Uygur Autonomous Region (on the Silk Road).[6] Among them, are seventeen male wooden figures and two female of approximately 22 cms. in height, a set of figures riding horses, 33 cms. in height, seven figures of civil officials, five pottery soldiers, two horse grooms, 55 cms. in height and various warrior and dancing figures. The seven civil officials are made with wooden heads fixed on a squared off wooden stick. Twisted paper is used for arms, and the whole figure is dressed in silk.

The tomb belonged to a Chinese general, Zhang Xiong, who died in 633 AD, and his wife Qu Shi, who died fifty-five years later in 688 AD. It is one of a total of sixty-five discovered in the area, which was controlled by a small community of Chinese. No information is available concerning the position of the figures in the tomb. However, a series of wooden beams, winding corridors, columns of wood and brackets were found which suggest some kind of architectural model – possibly a small stage. The seven figures wear the hats of Chinese civil officials. They wear yellow silk gowns with white trousers and a black belt with leather boots.

The heads of these figures are quite distinctive. The faces of the men are carved and painted with thick, upturned lips, a large protruding nose and narrow, close-set eyes. The official archaeological report comments that these figures are simply officials, indicating the fact that Zhang Xiong was awarded an honorary prefecture title (*Yongan taijunjun*), and was thus entitled to own such civil officials in his tomb. Zhang Xiong's wife, Qu Shi, came from the ruling clan of Turfan and was equally qualified to have such figures in her tomb.[7] However, it has been argued that the figures are too lively in expression to represent civil officials. The alternative explanation for the yellow costume

---

[6] See Yijiuqisan nian Tulufan . . . 1975: 8–27, Jin Weinuo and Li Yuchun 1981: 149–60, *Xinjiang chutu wenwu* 1975, and *Xinjiang lishi wenwu* 1978.

[7] Yijiuqisan nian Tulufan . . . 1975: 17.

Diagram 39a, b and c   Anhui human-puppet performing figure

of the figures is one which derives from the costume used in a theatrical performance, or jester skit:

> In the age of Zhao Shile (approximately 335 AD) the adjutant played Zhou Yan, who was the governor of Guantao who appropriated several hundreds of bolts of silk and was punished. Afterwards, at every banquet, one of the jesters would put on a head cloth, and an unlined yellow silk robe. One jester would ask him 'What official are you, mixing it with the likes of us?' And he would answer, 'I was the governor of Guantao.' Then he would shake his robe and say, 'I was punished by the government and got this, so I ended up amongst you lot', and everyone would laugh.[8]

This episode is recorded in the standard histories of Chinese theatre as one of the earliest examples of theatre. It is taken to be an example of a real-life situation which was later turned into a theatrical, comic piece.[9] The Turfan mortuary figures are thought to be puppets representing the jester skit described above, largely because of the yellow costume and the presence of the wooden 'stage'. Whether or not this is so, the mortuary figures were certainly moved in the same kind of way. Perhaps the figures are representations of puppets, in the same way that many mortuary figures represent entertainers, rather than *actual* puppets. Here, the borders between moving figures that manifest presence in the world of death and moving figures that manifest presence in the world of theatre seem to disappear entirely.

A fourth kind of mortuary figure may have been designed to move when it was jolted. Fifty-five pottery male and female figures, including some musicians, and one drummer (whose portrait is identical to one of the tomb's wall paintings), were found in a tomb dating to approximately the North and Southern dynasties (420–581 AD) and situated in the south-west of Henan, near the city of Dengxian, in Xuezhuang village.[10]

The figures are made in three parts, the body, the head and the

---

[8] *Taiping Yulan*, ch. 569: 2702, 'Zhao shu'.

[9] See, for example, Zhou Yibai 1980, vol. 1: 24 and Dolby 1976: 7.

[10] *Henan Dengxian xuezhuang caise huaxiang . . .* 1958.

hands. The head and the hands were fitted separately into the body. The figures are between 19 cms. and 30 cms. high. The female figures wear long gowns, while the male figures wear short gowns and trousers. Some figures wear an overcoat of red colour.

The pottery heads are made in one piece with a tapering neck extension which is not painted. The rim of the bottom of the neck stands out from the neck extension so that, when the head is fixed to the body, the head rests lightly in place. The same device was used for the construction of the hands which are fitted similarly into the openings at the sleeves. Many of the figures found were broken and the heads and hands were disarrayed. Not only the excavations, but also movements of earth may well have caused these figures to fracture – they are clearly more fragile in construction than figures fired in one piece. Herein lies the possible purpose of their design: the heads and hands may have shivered, or shaken, as the whole figure was moved – in the funeral procession, or in placing them in the tomb.

Even paper mortuary figures manifest the presence within them by movement. The images burnt at the grave site flare up and burn quickly, often in bursts, as each part of a piece suddenly catches fire, making the whole construction collapse within itself and be consumed by flames. Sometimes, pieces of blackened, crisp tissue paper fly up out of the flames and are carried by the wind.

Man and the model

Life in the underworld is represented through the movement of the mortuary figures just as life in the theatre world is articulated through movement of the performing body. The examples above have shown, however, that the figures (even the pottery ones) do not move by themselves. They need the help of man to set them in motion and in most cases to keep them in motion. Who moved the mortuary figures, and what is the relationship between mover and moved in the context of *presence*? This question once again seems to close the gap between the idea of figural performer in the world of death and human performer in the world of theatre. The sense of performer in each case is identical and interchangeable.

The Fangxiangshi exorcised the grave by leaping into the pit and thrusting his lance-axe into each of the four corners. A similar event was recorded in Fujian at the turn of the century and hints that the exorcist at the tomb side moved in a wild, uncontrolled way:

> At Amoy [Xiamen] it is still fresh in the memory of the
> people how at the burial of a gentleman, who had been the
> prefect of a department in Jiangxi province, four men, clad
> in fanciful spectral attire, walked in front of a Kailushen of
> colossal size, dancing and screaming all the way. At the grave,
> they worked themselves into a fit of raving which resembled a
> demoniacal possession; they cast themselves by turns into the
> pit, frantically yelling and brandishing their swords, and thus
> brought about a general *sauve qui peut* in the unseen world
> of spirits.[11]

The description of this event seems to echo the concept that moving in a wild, uncontrolled way is trance-inducing. They 'worked themselves' into a 'fit' which caused 'demoniacal possession'. The Fangxiangshi is thought to have 'leapt' into the pit and 'brandished' his lance in the four corners. In both examples, the commentator interprets the dance of the exorcist as wild and raving – a lack of control which derives from the fact that the dancer uses movement to work himself into a different state than that which is 'normal'. The ancient record was written at a time when the Fangxiangshi was despised and mistrusted at court; De Groot is a Western theologist writing at the turn of the century. In the light of the meaning of stamping as a designative, recreative act which links units to express or manifest presence, the interpretations above are clearly false. The exorcist, like the *nuo* performer, may seem to the *uninitiated* eye to be wild, uncontrolled or raving in his movements. What both the Fangxiangshi exorcist and the *nuo* performer actually do, is manifest the presence already within (through the *kaiguang* ceremony) by specific, controlled, expressive movements of meaning (the Yu step across a Luo diagram grid, for example). The Fangxiangshi exorcist dresses as ancestor/creator and manifests the presence of that ancestor in his movements.

The relation of the opening ceremony (*kaiguang*) to the articulation of presence through movement is clearly seen in the example of

---

[11] De Groot 1982, vol. 1: 163.

the spirit medium. Here, as the intensity of the *kaiguang* ceremony is increased, and more charms are burned, so the presence called into the body of the medium becomes increasingly articulate – active.

> The medium . . . is sitting at the altar-table . . . quietly chatting with his club-brethren, while two of these on either side repeatedly utter an incantation in a chanting voice, in order to 'invite or bid the spirit' *qingshen*; meanwhile they burn incense and 'eye-opening papers' [*kaiguang* charms] . . . The symptoms of the descent of the spirit into the medium shortly appear, that is to say, effects the *guantong*, or 'communication with the medium'. Drowsily staring, he shivers and yawns, resting his arms on the table, and his head on his arms as if falling asleep; but as the incantation proceeds with increasing velocity and loudness, with the accompaniment of one or more drums, and as the 'eye-opening papers' are being burned in a quicker succession, he suddenly jumps up to frisk and skip about. Thus the spirit 'sets the medium to hopping or dancing', *toutong* or *tiaotong* [hopping boy, dancing boy].[12]

The movements of the medium are similar to those of the mortuary figure, the Fangxiang and the exorcists. He hops, or dances to manifest presence.

This would seem to confirm the thesis that both artefact and human body are treated in the same way in the *kaiguang* process as suggested in chapter three. This, in turn, seems to imply that in the case where artefact and human perform together (masked human, human and figure), the two apparently different bodies (different materials) are actually conceived as one thing. The human is opened and the artefact is opened, and both move in a leaping, hopping way together to express the *same* presence.

A similar process can be seen most clearly in the example of the Fangxiangshi. In the burial procession, the Fangxiangshi goes ahead to exorcise. He is followed by the mortuary gifts (including the figures), which are followed by the corpse. Last of all come the mourners. In one citation, the Fangxiangshi is described as riding a chariot pulled by four

---

[12] Ibid., vol. 6: 1273–4.

horses at the head of the procession: 'The Fangxiang, with four gold eyes, bearskin, black upper garment and red lower garment, brandishing lance-axe and shield rides on a [chariot borne by] four horses and exorcises in advance.'[13] Another Han document adds: 'When Yang Hou of the Han died, the Fangxiang chariot and the Phoenix chariot escorted the coffin to the tomb at the head of the procession.'[14] Thus the Fangxiangshi seems to have been accompanied by a phoenix chariot. The only other record of such a chariot comes from the *Zhouli* where the author states: 'At internments, the Officer of the Grave Mounds addresses the human images which are placed upon the cars adorned with phoenixes'.[15]

The phoenix is a bird attributed with Yang, and associated with the creative principle – fire, heat, light, the south (see chapter two). It only alights on the equally Yang-filled *dong* tree,[16] resides in the 'Vermilion Hills', eats nothing but the seeds of bamboo (symbol of youth and long-life) and sweet spring water (symbol of immortality). On this chariot, placed in direct relation to the Fangxiangshi, at the head of the procession in the exorcising position, are placed the 'human images' on a cart which is thoroughly associated with the idea of regeneration. Moreover, these human images are 'addressed'.

The Fangxiangshi, in his mask of bearskin and four gold eyes was a presenced performer. The mortuary figures were presenced figures. Both are set in relation to the other as if the Fangxiangshi were responsible for setting the figures in motion, for making them manifest the presence within them as well as himself. Thus, the artefact is actually *a part* of the performer – an extension of his physical expressive means.

The Fangxiangshi may have moved the mortuary figures in the procession to the grave. Both human and figure were filled with the same kind of presence. The quality of Yang that the exorcist seeks to substitute for the Yin surrounding death was contained in his own presence as ancestor/exorcist/creator and in the materials and beings

[13] *Houhanshu, Liyi zhi*, 'Da sang pian'.
[14] *Taiping yulan*, ch. 552, 'Han guanyi'.   [15] De Groot 1982, vol. 2: 807.
[16] The same species that provides the wood for masks, coffins and mortuary figures.

of the mortuary figures. Moreover, not only was the Fangxiangshi set in relation to the artefact, the mortuary figure. The Fangxiangshi was himself masked, was bound to an artefact – dressed, or appeared as ancestor.

The bronze human-looking masks at Xunxian have been identified by Chinese scholars as Fangxiang masks. One mask in tomb no. 8 bears the inscription of a character which seems to show a man, depicted frontally, with an extra large round head with a line through it. According to the theory that supernatural beings or divinities, *gui*, were portrayed in this way,[17] the mask seems to have been intended as the representation of a deity. Several more masks were shown to be animal masks. The combination of human and animal masks seems to imply some kind of action expressing the relation between two *dramatis personae*. This might suggest a similar scenario in the tomb to that enacted at annual exorcisms:

> The Exorcist (Fangxiangshi), [his head] covered with a bear skin having four eyes of gold, and clad in a black upper garment and red lower garment, grasps a lance and brandishes a shield. Palace Attendants of the Yellow Gates act as twelve 'animals' wearing fur, feathers and horns, and the Supervisor of the Retinue leads them to expel evil demons from the Palace . . . As this takes place, the Exorcist (Fangxiangshi) and the twelve 'animals' dance and shout, going everywhere through the front and rear palace apartments. They make three rounds, holding torches, with which they send the pestilences forth out of the Meridional Gate.[18]

In this exorcism sequence, the Fangxiangshi and his helpers 'dance and shout' and make three 'rounds' of the palace – a combination of leaping

---

[17] Schindler 1923: 298–366, Hentze 1943: 35–41 and Shen Chien-shih 1936–7.

[18] Bodde 1975: 81–2. In this citation, the centre (meridional) is the exorcising force. The Chinese term for the Meridional Gate is *duanmen*, the same *duan* as that used in the Dragon Boat festival where pestilences are gathered and sent off to sea on a boat. The term as it is used here directly refers to the gateway of the true south (influence of light, heat, Yang, life).

and circuitous movements which are associated with the manifestation of presence.

The mask of the Fangxiangshi was even filled with enough presence in some cases to dispense with the human body of the Fangxiangshi altogether. This was the *qitou*, or ugly head, that was made in the likeness of a Fangxiangshi and used at burials where the deceased was of too low a rank to afford the presence of a real Fangxiangshi. The *Shijing* provides an account of the *qitou* at the grave-side:

> *Qitou* serve to protect the spirit of the deceased. They are called *suyi beisu*, in which term *su* means 'likeness', and they are called *kuangzu* (?ravening obstacles), or also *chukuang* 'grave assailers'. If they have four eyes, they are called Fangxiang, if they have two, they are named *qi* or 'dancers'.[19]

The *qitou* mask is equivalent to the body of the Fangxiangshi. Like the Fangxiangshi, it is moved around the four corners to 'assail' (brandish) in a raving way – it expresses the presence 'exorcism'. The term *qi*, translated as 'dancers', is used to describe both the *qitou* artefact, the Fangxiangshi (a man with four eyes, i.e. masked), and the exorcist (a man with two eyes, i.e. not masked). The same term is found in the *Shijing* to mean, 'a repetitious dance, the *qiqi*'.[20] Furthermore, a later commentary on this text adds, '*qiqi* is a dance that cannot be controlled by the dancer'.[21] The term *kuang* means 'wild', 'raving'. The same word was also used to describe the helpers of the Fangxiang who leapt into the grave to help carry out the exorcism. Thus, the *qitou*, the masked Fangxiangshi and his four unmasked helpers were also considered to be presenced and hopped, leapt, stamped (moved in an 'uncontrolled' way) to manifest the presence within them. In this sense, the three kinds of performing body are alike, undifferentiated. The Fangxiangshi treats his mask as a part of his own presenced being. He physically moves the mask (provides the body) not in a separate, distanced way, but as part of that same (reassembled) body.

The same principle has been observed in marionette theatre described in chapter four. In the marionette exorcism, the marionette

---

[19] De Groot 1982, vol. 6: 1152, Granet 1959: 324   [20] *Cihai* 1979: 598.
[21] Ibid.

master executes movement sequences alone which he then makes the marionette repeat verbatim. The marionette master could carry out the exorcism by himself, but instead he supports his exorcism through the extension of his own body into a figural body, the marionette. In controlling the marionette, the master uses exorcist hand signs. He also stamps, and makes the footfall sounds for the marionette, as the marionette dances. Both figure and human are performing as one presenced being. The master can increase the effectivity of his movements by extending his own body into an apparently separate figure, which is actually part of him. In this sense, the human and the figure operate no differently from the human alone, who cuts his body up into separate expressive units.

The close physical union between artefact and human body is well demonstrated in the marriage between a living person and a dead person represented by an ancestral tablet. Such a posthumous marriage is arranged for the spirits of children who died at an immature age, or unmarried people. After a death, the ancestral tablet of the deceased is placed on the clan altar and tended by the descendants. If someone has died without descendants, there are no provisions for that soul or spirit to be cared for, and it is feared that the dissatisfied spirit will trouble the rest of the family. The purpose of the posthumous marriage is to provide the deceased with a family who are obliged to care for the soul tablet. In practical terms, it means that the ancestral tablet of an unmarried person, or child, is given a place on someone's ancestral altar, for otherwise such souls have no automatic right to a place there. Sometimes the tablets of such people are kept hidden for years in cupboards before a suitable partner can be found.

The *process* of a posthumous marriage, however, treats the ancestral tablet as a real body (since it has been opened to the presence of the deceased at the burial site, see chapter three). It is dressed in clothes, spoken to and attended as if it were the deceased:

> The first step in the marriage procedure was to prepare a contract which identified the groom and stipulated that his two living children would become the bride's children. This document was then submitted to the bride for her approval. 'Had she refused, that would have been an end of the matter',

but she agreed.[22] The two families then exchanged a series of gifts, the groom's side sending to the bride's wedding cakes and NT $120 as a bride-price, receiving in turn a dowry consisting of a gold ring, a gold necklace, several pairs of shoes and six dresses all fitted for the use of the groom's living wife. On the morning of the wedding day the dead bride's family held a feast for her benefit 'feeding her the same as if she were alive'. The bride's mother and the go-between then placed the girl's tablet in a taxicab and conveyed it to the groom's home . . . On leaving their own home, the bride's brother invited her to get into the cab, and on arriving at the groom's home informed her of their arrival and invited her to descend. The bride was always treated as if she were alive and participating in the proceedings. During the feast, her tablet sat on a chair next to the groom, and after the feast it was put in his bedroom . . . The next day, the tablet is put on the ancestral altar.[23]

The treatment of the ancestral tablet suggests it is conceived of as a body. However, this body does not *really* require food and clothing. These things are part of the earthly contract between the two families and oblige the groom's side to care for the tablet on his altar. However, the tablet-body is treated as the *manifestation* of the presence of the deceased. The actions that the ancestral tablet is put through – being invited in the cab, offered food, even put in the bedroom of the groom – are the same as if the tablet were alive. The written contract between the families is supported by a series of actions and processes (a wedding – a piece of representation, or theatricality) in order to be considered binding – the tablet is made to move. In each case it is moved by the family member responsible for that part of the ceremony. The bride's mother and brother escort her to the new home and then she becomes the responsibility of the groom. First, the tablet is addressed as the presence 'daughter', and later as 'wife'. One night later, it is addressed as

---

[22] The questioning of the deceased bride takes the form of throwing oracle blocks. When the two blocks fall convex side up or flat side up they are said to indicate a negative and a positive answer respectively. The blocks are thrown until the (desired) answer is achieved.

[23] Wolf 1974: 151.

'mother' – the children of the husband will pay their respects to her tablet as to that of their own mother. In all cases, the tablet as presence depends upon its relation to the living presences around it (who move it).

Even in a situation where the figure is of great size (larger than the human performer), and has to be operated by several men, the same principle holds. The performing body is composed of parts which may be human and which may be artefact, but which both depend upon the idea of movement as the articulation, or manifestation of a shared, or the same presence. The following examples derive from the procession of temple deities. These deities are opened (*kaiguang*) and then paraded around the entire clan territory to 'touch' each household and pronounce health and prosperity on the clan members. The statues are carried or supported by village elders (temporary *wu*). Thus, both the artefact and the humans are presenced bodies which operate together as one whole being. This situation replicates almost exactly the *nuo* performance event. Instead of using a human as the ancestral/creator (the Fashi), the statue of the ancestor is positioned as the central, unifying figure. He, in turn, is literally supported by (borne by) the 'next in line', initiated males of the same clan or family. In both situations (and the sequence of participants is repeated in the burial procession where the corpse is followed by his descendants, in order of proximity to the deceased) the lack of differentiation between bodies of different materials and different times (different worlds) in one space and time, strengthens the concept of 'family', of participation in the regenerative cycle of life and death.

The patron saint of Anshun *dixi*, in Guizhou, is a god named Wang Gong (Prince Wang). In the village of Jichang, Anshun county, it is said that Wang Gong was a real man who was born in Huizhou, Anhui province (more than 1,000 kms. to the north-east of Guizhou) in 605 AD. Other villages set the date anywhere between 581 and 618 AD. With the help of his troops he put down a rebellion and saved the people from starvation. He helped found the Tang dynasty, and was honoured at court. He died and was buried in Xi county in Anhui where a temple now dedicates the spot.

Many of the villages in the Anshun area have names which include the suffix 'garrison', 'pass', 'fortified defence', 'camp'. The people who live in Anshun believe that their ancestors came from the Jiangnan area (Jiangsu, Jiangxi and Anhui provinces) in the course of various punitive and controlling expeditions to the south, particularly Yunnan, in the early Ming dynasty. These villages were set up as strongholds on the way. In Jiuxi village, for example, the Gu family records state,

> The ancestors of this clan came to the Guizhou area in the second year of Emperor Hong Wu's reign (1370) on a punitive expedition to control the border to Yunnan. It was our duty to come under the orders of the commander-in-chief Gong Ying, and after the situation was calm, and great service was rendered by us, we settled in the garrison. Thereupon our sons and daughters were born here.[24]

In Jichang village, the village elders recount that when their ancestors travelled to the south west from the Jiangnan area, they brought with them the statue of Wang Gong as a protective spirit. In the same way that a family clan will take the ancestral tablets with them if they are forced to move away from the ancestral village, so the statue of Wang Gong, as a kind of ancestor to whom offerings and prayers are made to protect the clan, is also transferred. Thus, Wang Gong is seen as a kind of original ancestor. He is thought to have been a real man who was made a god because of his good deeds, and all the clans in this area claim to be directly descended from him.

On the anniversary of Wang Gong, which falls either on the 16th, 17th, or 18th of the first lunar month of the year (the villages have different opinions as to the exact date), the statue of Wang Gong is taken out from the local temple and paraded round the village. The statue is made to halt at every household. Each householder sets up a temporary altar with various offerings of wine, pork, rice and sweets. The retinue that in turns carries the statue on its litter, and in turns accompanies it, is made up almost entirely of village elders. One of them accepts the offerings in the name of Wang Gong, spills the wine on the ground in front of the household and pronounces health, good fortune and long life to the inhabitants. In Jichang village this

---

[24] Author's field notes 1990.

anniversary is only celebrated every five years, due to the enormous expense and complex logistics involved, as many smaller villages also take part.[25]

In 1990, I witnessed the procession of Wang Gong in Jichang village (a garrison town surrounded by the ruins of ancient fortifications). On the morning of the event, at the temple where the image of Wang Gong is kept, yellow 'protection' charms were painted with the name of each sponsor/participant and handed out. These should be worn inside a hat, or anywhere near the head. At the altar, a cock's blood was scattered and opening *(kaiguang)* charms were written with it, and burned before the statue (see the cock feathers stuck to the altar in Plate 19). The statue was then carefully raised onto the litter (Plate 20) which was borne by at least twenty men at a time, different teams taking the burden in turn – it appeared to be extremely heavy. The litter was preceded by the three *dixi* troupes from Jichang[26] in mask and full costume, and a team of percussionists from the temple with gongs and drums. Firecrackers were lit in front of the litter at almost every step to cleanse the path – the noise, smoke and colour of the costumes, flags etc., of the whole retinue served to exorcise, or cleanse the road it trod. Watched from a roof top, the old men carrying the litter seemed to stumble with the weight of it, charging suddenly forwards into the crowd at times, so that both the lives of the bearers and the spectators *seemed* at risk.

De Groot cites an occasion of a similar litter being used in obtaining oracular writings. The image of the god in the litter is opened *(kaiguang)*, and placed in the litter. The litter is borne aloft and the shafts of the litter are seen to inscribe the dust with oracular signs:

> The medium and three of his club-brethren having shouldered
> the shafts, the spirit is brought into the litter and the medium in

---

[25] That is, since 1985, the first time the anniversary was celebrated openly after the Cultural Revolution.

[26] The three troupes represent three branches of the original clan. Performers from each troupe kept apart from each other and did not attend each other's performances, although on this occasion, all three performed simultaneously alongside each other. The spectators moved back and forth between performance areas, or in some cases, simply turned their heads and watched parts of all three.

Plate 19   Opening the statue of Wang Gong at the altar

Plate 20   Placing Wang Gong on the litter

the usual way by means of incantations 'eye-opening papers',
and incense; from that moment it becomes heavy and impels
the bearers to queer and unsteady careering . . . the litter is
regularly carried to private dwellings where medical or
geomantic advice is wanted. On the way thither, the four
bearers move most unsteadily, lurching about, running or
stopping irregularly; and at times the holy load weighs so
heavily upon their shoulders, that one or two of them, even
all, must sink on their knees.[27]

Similarly, in the marionette exorcism in Meichang village, in Taiwan,
the statue of Jitian Dashengye from the Purple Cloud Temple was
shouldered by two members of the temple, and carried out into the
square courtyard, 'with stumbling steps and impressive momentum'.[28]

In all of these examples, where the litter is used for different
occasions, in different parts of China, the spirit or god represented by
the statue is called upon to be present through the *kaiguang* or opening
ceremony. This presence is then expressed by an uncontrolled careering, lurching, stumbling of those carrying the litter – as if the bearers
are powerless against the forceful (moving) presence of the spirit. However, as the examples of the Fangxiangshi and the marionette master
have shown, the *mover* of the artefact in each case is also presenced.
The litter only appears heavy with presence because the bearers seem
to stumble and lurch from side to side. It seems unlikely, however, that
twenty or more men bearing a litter would stumble and lurch in perfect synchrony as they do, if the burden were really as heavy as the spectators imagine. The movements only appear wild and uncontrolled to
the uninitiated spectator. The examples of the Fangxiangshi and exorcist have shown the travesty of all too hasty suppositions by the outside observer. Even contemporary Chinese scholars fall into the trap
and declare the movements of the *nuo* performer 'primitive' and 'free'.

The side to side 'lurching' of the litter bearers seems to indicate
the fact that they, like the *nuo* performer, are dancing the Yu step. They
are articulating specific cultural perceptions with their feet through
the Luo matrix, as one body with the statue of Wang Gong. The Yu step
is made up of eight steps plus one linking step which is the end of one

---

[27] De Groot 1982, vol. 6: 1316, 1317.   [28] Song Jinxiu 1983: 97.

sequence and the beginning of the next. The eight steps move from side to side and back and forth in the diagonal plane at an angle of less than 45° that actually circumscribes one full step forward (see Diagram 23 on p. 105). The Yu step is named after Yu the Great, the ur-creator, who danced this sequence of steps across the Luo diagram to recreate the world.

If indeed the litter bearers do execute the Yu step, or some derivative, or relative of it, it suggests that not only the statue is opened or presenced, but also the bearers. In this sense, the bearers, as male descendants of the line are adopting, or repeating the 'pattern' of the clan ancestor, both in the statue and the invisible Yu, or original creator. The presence within the statue (and within the bearers – they are one body) is manifested through the precise, controlled, intentional movement – back and forth, side to side across the Luo diagram in an act of direct recreation.

Presence in time
The examples in this chapter have shown the lack of definition between different kinds of presenced bodies. All are considered as parts of the one body – a whole, unifying, central body which embodies the ancestral presence(s). In this, all times are one – all generations are contained in the here and now.

The reassembled body of the *jingju* performer articulates presence by gathering up and expressing *qi*. *Qi* radiates from the points of juncture in the body as the body moves and communicates presence, particularly in the moment of caesura or *liangxiang*. The *jingju* performer conceives the *liangxiang* pose as stops in the performance, moments which function, as in any language, in the literal sense of breaking words into grammatical phrases – units of meaning. The stops function as punctuation. A *liangxiang* pose is a moment when the spectator has the chance to perceive presence in summary, in a pose. However, the moments of *liangxiang* also dictate the *rhythm* of the performance. Time is marked. In the *jingju* and *nuo* performances, time is marked at the spatial stations of the Luo grid. Units of meaning begin and end at these stations.

In a contemporary performance of the role Yang Yuhuan, the actor stops to pose four times more often than Mei Lanfang in the

1960s. The performance is so full of poses, that the spectator quickly loses interest. Zhang Chunhua compared it to watching an hour of football when the only action is the scoring of goals, there is no build up, no let down. There is no *time* to contemplate the role, or what is happening on stage because the audience's attention is forced towards the technically perfect, but empty stancing.

The statue of the god in the litter, the mortuary figures, ancestral tablet and masks of this chapter were seen to move to articulate presence. Moreover, such items moved in conjunction with/as part of a mover of some kind. Kleist termed such a body *Gliedermann*, man made of limbs, or parts of a body, from *Glieder* (limbs) and *gliedern* (to assemble, put together):

> Each motion . . . has its own centre of gravity; it is enough to agitate this, in the very heart of the figure, and the limbs, which are nothing more than pendula will follow without more ado, in a mechanical way, of themselves.
> . . . This movement was very simple . . . whenever the centre was moved in a straight line, the other parts of the body followed in a curve, and sometimes when the figure is accidentally shaken, the whole falls into a rhythmical dancing movement . . .
> I asked him if he thought that the machinist controlling the figure had to be a dancer himself . . .
> The line described by the centre of gravity . . . is mostly straight . . . and there is something mysterious about it. For it is nothing less than the path of the dancer's soul, and he doubted if such a line could be found except by adopting the centre of gravity in the marionette as his own, i.e. that he dances too.[29]

The Chinese mortuary figures and their various constructions closely reflect this concept of the 'mysterious' (other, ugly, deformed, giant) life presence which is articulated, made to articulate *through* the performance or movement of a human figure.

---

[29] Kleist 1990: 556–7.

*

The different parts of the performing body have been shown to be reunited in a certain pattern or rhythm. This can be expressed fractally in time – the chain of ancestors through history. Or it can be expressed in terms of space, and the proportional relations identified in the Luo diagram. The typical percussive pattern accompanying *nuo* theatre is based on the structure 3 – 5 – 7, the middle line of the Luo diagram and coincidentally the mathematical formulaic proportions of the Golden Section.

The actor Mei Lanfang, as any *jingju* actor, severs his body into several units of expressivity which come together in the performance to express presence. How he puts these individual parts together depends upon his ability to interpret (manifest) these relationships. All movement sequences are punctuated by moments of extra *qi* (presence) in the *liangxiang*, or pose, which is executed at special points on the stage. It is the performer who decides when these moments shall be. Although a sequence will always include a *liangxiang* at such and such a place at such and such a time (downstage right, between movement A and movement B, for example), the exact timing of it depends upon the performer's personal *qi* (rhythm, breath). The *liangxiang* fails if the actor misses the moment – his presence is dissipated. Thus a star performer in the past would always bring his own drummer to ensure the best partnership of percussion and movement in time. Zhang would often describe the fall of an unpopular actor through deliberate bad drumming.

Although Chinese performance is based on percussive patterns which are fixed (as in the *nuo* example above), the performer (in all forms of performance, from story-telling, to marionette theatre) does not follow a regular musical beat dictated to him by the orchestra. The performer interprets the prescribed rhythm in his own way, and the orchestra follow. The *jingju* orchestra sits stage right – the *sigu* (main drummer) never takes his eyes off the performer, drumming the rhythm that he sees. The drummer's own rhythm is then punctuated by the gongs. It can be stretched by the performer, quickened, broken or made regular. Zhang Chunhua calls it *houpi jinr* (monkey sinews) – elastic. It expresses life – *qi* is breath, something living.

A *jingju* performer without *qi* is like a dead performer (in the *nuo* example, he embodies no ancestors, he is mortal, an ordinary body, empty), but perhaps he has enough technique to get by. A *jingju* performer with no *jiezougan* (feeling for rhythm) can find another profession. For if the performer is not able to punctuate his own performance, the moments when he attempts a *liangxiang* pose will be out of place. It is not enough to learn the movements, and breathe in and out at the right points on the stage. *Qi* is bound to the concept of rhythm – presence articulated as *movement* in space in time.

7

He
(To unify)

Mei Lanfang constructs the role of Yang Yuhuan through a complex of systems including every aspect of performance – costume, music, text, movement in space and voice. Each performative unit is visible to the spectator at every moment – he can interpret the role according to the linear progression from moment A to B; or he can interpret it by uncovering layers of meaning within one moment, A, or he can alternate between these methods. In whichever way he chooses to perceive the role, the physical body of the actor Mei Lanfang is the centre, the unifying element. In chapter five, it was shown that the quality of Yang provides 'life' or presence in the other worlds of death and theatre. The world of death and the imagination are Yin worlds, which must be infused with Yang if they are to be brought to life. The actor in the Chinese theatre similarly brings opposing elements of Yang and Yin together to interact and provoke presence, or *qi*. That is to say, it is the *interaction* between the opposing qualities Yin and Yang, female and male, dark and light, death and life which is the cause of presence. The *nuo* performer physically situates himself at the centre of the Luo diagram in order to unify the outlying eight cells of cosmological meaning and recreate the world space through presence. The *jingju* actor playing Yang Yuhuan not only exploits the abstract concept of Yin and Yang represented by the Luo diagram on the stage space; he also brings his body into congruence with the aesthetic idea of Yin and Yang through pose, movement and text.

The Yin/Yang figure is a circle divided into two halves which generate each other in a constant process of ebb and flow. The role Yang Yuhuan embodies this symbol through textual imagery and actions which directly refer to her as either Yin or Yang, as well as in a complex of dichotomies and oppositions which are held so intensely together in the body of Yang Yuhuan/Mei Lanfang they almost seem to be oppositions no longer, and merge into one another, into presence (*qi*).

The body as Yin and Yang

Even before the entrance of the figure Yang Yuhuan on stage, the two eunuchs enter and recite four lines of introductory poem which set the scene as the imperial palace, and introduce the idea that Yang Yuhuan is filled with the quality of Yang:

> Eunuch Pei:
> Many's the year lived in the imperial palace,
>
> Eunuch Gao:
> Surrounded by flowers of the four seasons.
>
> Eunuch Pei:
> Eunuch of the palace inner chambers,
>
> Eunuch Gao:
> Until death, [serve] the emperor.

On one level, in this shared poem, the eunuchs are merely narrating their position in the imperial household as responsible for the inner chambers – where the concubines of the emperor live. On another level, the eunuchs compare the many imperial concubines among whom they live to flowers of the different seasons, each has her own particular beauty, each has her own season – the time when she is most attractive (and a time when that season is past). This is the introduction to Yang Yuhuan – she is the favourite concubine who nonetheless is going to be overlooked in preference for another. Yang Yuhuan is about to enter as one of the flowers who has been picked, though in the spectator's mind she has already been discarded.

The eunuchs' four lines are followed by another six in ordinary speech with the same content. The eunuchs introduce themselves, and their purpose in waiting for Yang Yuhuan on her way to rendezvous with the emperor. Thus, the opening lines are placed directly prior to the entrance of Yang Yuhuan. She is a flower.

Mid-way through the piece, Yang Yuhuan has drunk some wine

and feels unwell, so she retires to remove her outer coat. The two eunuchs remain on stage and sweep and tidy – a practical device to give the actor playing Yang Yuhuan time to change costume. But the scene also expands the view of Yang Yuhuan as flower. The eunuchs re-arrange 'pots of flowers' (there are none on stage, the lifting of the pots is mimed), commenting on them, moving them, just before Yang Yuhuan re-enters.

> Gao:
> What flower is in this pot?
>
> Pei:
> This pot is peony, or another name for it is 'flower of luck and wealth'.
>
> Gao:
> Not bad, 'flower of luck and wealth'. And what flower is in this pot?
>
> Pei:
> This pot is yulan magnolia . . .
>
> Gao:
> . . . And what's this one?
>
> Pei:
> This is the flowering wild crab-apple.
>
> Gao:
> Is it the golden flowering crab-apple?
>
> Pei:
> Yes, it's also called 'luck and wealth'.
>
> Gao:
> . . . Here's another pot. It's very heavy, what is it?
>
> Pei:
> It's an orchid. Smell it, see if it's fragrant.
>
> Gao:
> It's very fragrant.

The peony is the 'queen of flowers'. In colloquial speech, the peony refers to any attractive young woman. More specifically, it refers to the female genitalia, 'When the dew drops, the peony opens.'[1] It is considered to be a spring flower (Yang). The yulan magnolia was originally reserved only for the emperor who would bestow a magnolia root on someone who had won imperial favour. The magnolia also symbolises a beautiful woman – and is sometimes known as the 'flower that welcomes spring' because it blossoms before the leaves appear (Yang). The wild crab-apple, or cherry-apple, is often used to symbolise 'hall' (pun on the word *tang*) and implies the phrase, 'may your house be rich and honoured', a phrase which implies Yang qualities.[2] Moreover, Yang Yuhuan was known by the nickname *haitangnu*, 'the cherry-apple girl' (youthful, or Yang). The term *lanhua* is used to describe a range of flowers including lily, orchid and iris. The scent of the orchid is like a woman's breath, the orchid room belongs to a young girl (Yang) and the orchid also flowers in the spring (Yang).

All four flowers brought into association with Yang Yuhuan are spring blossoms, implying the youth (Yang) and fresh beauty (Yang) of Yang Yuhuan. The flowers are also associated with sexual imagery and are symbols of luck and wealth (Yang) suggesting that Yang Yuhuan has both because she has been specially chosen by the emperor. Immediately the pots are in place, Yang Yuhuan re-enters the stage and the two eunuchs hurry away 'to prepare more wine'. She approaches the flowers, bends down to pick one from the 'pot' on the left side of the stage, raises it to her face, and smells it. She repeats the same movement to the right, then turns back to her wine. But the performer must show she is too drunk to focus on the flowers – she spins as she picks each one, as the flowers in the pots on the ground spin for her. Yang Yuhuan and the flowers are indivisible.

On another level, however, the references are ironic: all the flowers are cultivated in pots, they cannot grow freely. The spring flower must fade in favour of the summer flower, Yang Yuhuan is unlucky, the emperor has chosen another concubine after all.

Both of Yang Yuhuan's entrances in the play are preceded by 'flower' scenes, leaving the impression 'flower' firmly in the spectator's

---

[1] Eberhard 1986: 231.   [2] Ibid.: 21.

mind as Yang Yuhuan enters the scene, so that the idea of beauty/fav-our, and fading beauty/disfavour is closely associated with her from the very start. In the imagery of Yang is also the imagery of Yin (death, fad-ing beauty, bad luck).

Zhang Chunhua heavily criticised the recent rewriting of parts of the play. Now, for example, the flower-arranging scene is followed by a long dialogue between the two eunuchs, during which they assess the drunken state of the concubine and warn each other to be careful. Zhang explained that the flower scene, which relates so directly to Yang Yuhuan, should not have been displaced. The flower scene and the entrance of Yang Yuhuan belong together. It is a small example of the subtle ways *jingju* is being reformed. What seems to be super-ficial, dramaturgical editing actually affects the meaning of the play very deeply.

Whereas Yang represents youth, beauty, warmth, light, Yin rep-resents age, fading beauty, cold and dark. The quality of Yin is present in the figure of Yang Yuhuan from the very opening of the piece. Yang Yuhuan's entrance is preceded by eight handmaidens bearing lanterns which indicate the time of the action as evening, or night (Yin). In her first aria, Yang Yuhuan compares herself to the moon goddess, Chang E:

> Yang Yuhuan *(sings)*:
> The wheel of ice starts to rise over the island in the sea,
> See the Jade Hare, Jade Hare faces east and leaps,
> The wheel of ice departs from the island in the sea,
> Heaven and Earth shine brightly,
> Bright moon in mid-air,
> Like Chang E leaving the Moon Palace,
> Like Chang E leaving the Moon Palace.

The first line of the aria introduces the words, 'sea', 'island', 'ice', 'wheel'. The first images of which Yang Yuhuan sings are cold (the moon), water, ice, isolation (the island) and roundness. She is describing the moon rising and for her, the moon is like a wheel of ice. The reference to the Jade Hare belongs to the tale of Chang E set out below and again refers to the moon and cold – jade always remains cool to the touch. The aria describes the moon rising out of its icy desolation towards the sky, where it will meet the sun and unite heaven and earth in the brightest of lights. Even before she has sung the name of the goddess associated with the moon travelling towards the sun (Yang), the imagery already refers to Chang E, and positions Yang Yuhuan *as* the moon goddess (goddess of Yin), *as* the moon rising in the sky.

The legend of the moon goddess Chang E recounts that she was married to the archer Shen Yi. One day, during his absence, she found the pill of immortality he had been given and ate it. When Shen Yi returned, he demanded to know where the pill was, and in fear, Chang E opened the window and flew away. She reached a desolate, luminous sphere, where the only vegetation was cinnamon trees (cinnamon symbolises longevity). She spat out the covering of the pill of immortality and this was changed into a hare as white as jade. The jade hare is considered to be the ancestor of the Yin (dark, female, cold) principle. As punishment, Chang E was forced to live all alone on the moon. The God of Immortals then prepared Chang E's husband to take up immortal residence in the sun palace. He was permitted to visit the moon on the fifteenth day of the moon cycle, and this is believed to be the reason for the moon's particular brightness at these times – the meeting not only of both sun and moon, but also the principles Yang and Yin. While Shen Yi is permitted movement from the centre to unify the outlying areas, Chang E was forbidden to travel to the centre, to his palace, because the moon can only be bright through the presence of the sun. She was forced to live in a palace on the moon named *Guanghangong* (Palace of Great Cold).

Yang Yuhuan enters the stage at night like the moon rising in the darkness (however, the actual light is transposed to the handmaidens who bear the lanterns, which are not lit, they only indicate the fact that it is dark). She is like Chang E waiting outside the winter palace for the rendezvous with her husband. She is like Chang E in that she cannot visit her husband but must wait for him to visit her. She is like Chang E in that she feels isolated, alone, cold and deserted in the times when she is not chosen.

Furthermore, in the saga of Yang Yuhuan outside the episode portrayed in this play, she will be forced to commit suicide to save the emperor from defeat. The gods, pitying her plight, make her an immortal goddess and she is reunited with the emperor eternally in heaven. This aspect is already hinted at when the eunuch Gao says, just before she arrives, 'See the incense smoke rise up in curls; our mistress's phoenix chariot has arrived.' Incense smoke is often a sign of the movement of gods, as is the phoenix chariot (though in this case the phoenix also directly represents the concubine). The line is echoed in many such entrance lines in the *nuo* theatre before various immortals appear. Thus, Yang Yuhuan is like Chang E in that she is immortal (in the minds of the spectators there is no time – past, present and future are all present in the role Yang Yuhuan). The point of departure is present in the point of entry. Time, like the written Chinese language, is vertical.

Just as the Yang imagery of the flowers portended the negative aspect of Yin, the imagery of Chang E is also filled with irony. Yang Yuhuan's first words are of coldness, isolation in a vast expanse. Though it seems as though it is this she is leaving, for the centre, for warmth and light, in fact she is leaving only to return to it again, for the emperor has gone to see someone else. In the imagery of Yin runs the hope of Yang (the sun, the emperor) and in the imagery of Yang, the return to Yin.

If Yang Yuhuan embodies the symbol of Yin/Yang in the imagery associated with her, she also embodies the concept of Yin/Yang by the fact that she is both male and female. Yang Yuhuan is a *dan* role traditionally played by men. During the piece, this simple male–female dichotomy becomes so multi-layered that the differentiation between the sexes becomes invisible. Mei Lanfang, as Yang Yuhuan, embodies both male and the female elements indivisibly in one.

The male actor of the concubine Yang Yuhuan even 'plays' at being a male. For, towards the end of the play, after Yang Yuhuan has drunk a great quantity of wine and has been unable to persuade either of the eunuchs to go and fetch the emperor, she slaps eunuch Gao three times around the face in anger. She warns him with gestures that if he does not obey, she will demote him, and she signifies this by knocking off his hat, for the hat is the sign of rank at court. She teases him with it, offering it back to him and then withdrawing it, trying to put it on him herself and missing in her drunkenness. Finally, she puts it on top of her own head-dress. The scene is narrated by Gao:

> Gao:
> Mistress, that's my hat! You're going to wear it? All right, hat
> on top of hat! Give me back my hat.

Wearing the eunuch's hat, Yang Yuhuan imitates the walk of a *sheng* or male role, taking large strides with swinging arms. More than merely a joke in a state of drunkenness, the implication is that Yang Yuhuan would almost rather 'be' a eunuch than a concubine, rather 'be' a male than a female. The image of Yang Yuhuan as a male role – moreover a role that is actually neither male nor female (eunuch) – is set in contrast to the conception of her as Chang E and as a flower – thoroughly female images. Yang Yuhuan finally tosses the hat back to the eunuch (in the traditional version, not before she has vomited into it) and he puts it on.

Mei Lanfang is a male actor. The *dan* role type was traditionally played by men and boys until after the communists came to power in 1949, when boys were officially no longer trained for the role. Women did perform publicly, and indeed several of the Hangzhou troupes of the late eighteenth century gained a considerable reputation,[3] though the female actors in such early companies were also prostitutes, and socially ostracised.

The *dan* role was, however, of chief importance in the rise of *jingju*. The actor who brought the Anhui style to Beijing and is considered the 'father' of *jingju*, Wei Zhangsheng, was a *dan* actor (see chapter one). Indeed, most of the records of theatre performances, companies and individual actors of the period around the late 1700s, concern *dan* actors.[4]

The *dan* actor had a limited stage-life, being considered old at thirty (Mei Lanfang continued to perform in his sixties though this may have been for political reasons). Young apprentice *dan*, known as *xianggong*, were available for hire at private parties and much of the literature concerning the theatre of this early period suggests that the *dan* role actors were viewed as embodying both male and female qualities and were strongly associated with the homosexual scene: 'Homosexuality is now widespread enough that it is considered in bad taste not to keep elegant servants on one's household staff, and undesirable not to have singing boys around when inviting guests for dinner.'[5] Part of the admiration of the spectator for the performance stems from the

---

[3] Mackerras 1972: 71–4.　　[4] Ibid.: 106.

[5] Ibid.: 45.

knowledge that a man is performing. The *dan* actor sings, recites and speaks the entire role in a falsetto voice (a tradition which the female actors of *dan* roles continue today). The skill of the actor is perceived underneath the role. The male is perceived through the female, as part of the indivisible male–female body.

The skill of a performer of female roles is not the performer's ability to *act like* a woman. Rather, the *jingju* actors stress, the skill lies in being 'correct'. The qualities which make a good *qingyi* actor are 'neatness, cleanliness and correctness of dress', which are 'more important than looking beautiful'.[6] This sentiment seems to be echoed in the comments concerning some of the great *dan* actors such as Mei Qiaoling, Lu Sanbao and Wang Yaoqing, that they were unattractive ('fat', 'stern') in costume, i.e. beauty or any such quality was not necessarily a prerequisite for becoming a *dan* actor. The clothes – the outward appearance – suffice to make the role.[7] If the correct moves are made (patterns), accompanying the correct style of singing, the female role is well presented. Zhang Chunhua once criticised male *dan* actors who dared to execute *dan* movements out of costume (as in a demonstration, for example). He found the idea profoundly shocking, he used the word 'obscene': clothes maketh the woman. Mei Lanfang as Yang Yuhuan is neither just female nor just male. The Yin, or female quality is present in the Yang, male quality, and vice-versa.

Yang Yuhuan not only embraces two apparently opposite sexes,

---

[6] Scott 1971: 35.

[7] A similar aesthetic is recorded by Zeami regarding the portrayal of women on the Japanese *no* stage: 'If the actor's style of dress is unseemly, there will be nothing worth watching in the performance. When it comes to impersonating high-ranking women of the court . . . The actor must make a proper investigation concerning what is correct . . . if the actor dresses in an appropriate *kinu* or *kosode* that will doubtless suffice. When performing *kusemai, shirabyoshi* or mad women's roles, the actor should hold a fan or a sprig of flowers, for example, loosely in his hand, in order to represent female gentleness. The *kinu* and the *hakama* as well should be long enough to conceal his steps, his hips and knees should be straight and his bodily posture pliable . . . he should certainly wear a robe with long enough sleeves and should avoid showing the tips of his hands . . . in the case of a woman's role, proper dressing is essential.' Trans. Rimer and Masakazu, 1984: 10–11.

Yin and Yang, she also embodies two contrasting worlds of consciousness – a drunken, intoxicated state (Yin), and a sober state (Yang). Mei
Lanfang recorded that after performing the role in the Soviet Union, 'a
foreigner' summarised the role into three phases of intoxication: 'The
first phase is when the concubine drinks behind her sleeve. The second
phase is when she drinks without hiding her mouth behind her sleeve
and the third phase is when she drinks with abandon.'[8] However, close
analysis of the text shows that the quality of drunkenness is present
from the very moment of her journey towards the place of rendezvous.
First she slips on the bridge, and then, inviting the geese to land, she sings:

> Yang Yuhuan (*sings*):
> . . .
> Hear your servant's voice and land in the shade of the flowers,
> The scene provokes the desire to be intoxicated.

The moonlit bridge, with its golden carp, mandarin ducks, geese and
flowers, is a garden paradise, rich with symbols of good fortune and
eternal love. The Chinese name for the carp is *li*, a pun on 'advantage,
profit'. The word for fish, *yu*, is a homophone for 'wealth', and the combination gold-fish means 'plenty of gold'. The mandarin duck is a symbol of marital bliss and faithfulness, for the mandarin duck keeps its
mate for life. The wild goose is similarly a bird that mates for life and
is also a harbinger of good news. As she sings these lines, Yang Yuhuan
fills her own ears with good omens, she becomes drunk on the scene
and slips on the bridge.

The prompting done by the two eunuchs, calling her attention
to the fish, ducks and geese is repeated later when she has had something to drink. Both scenes reveal the state of her intoxication is so
great that she has forgotten her lines, or does not see properly what is
around her. Moreover, the last few lines of the bridge scene show her
to be sensually as well as sexually excited – an aspect perhaps more
openly exploited in the *huabu*, unrevised version of the text?

Thus the state of intoxication, of being out of consciousness, or
in transition between two kinds of consciousness begins at the opening
of the play, before any wine has been drunk. The first round of actual

---

[8] Mei Lanfang and Xu Jichuan 1961, vol. 1: 37.

He *(To unify)*

Diagram 40   *woyu* (coiling fish)

drinking follows the Soviet spectator's assessment of 'drinking behind the sleeve' – the convention which maintains the dignity of a *qingyi* when she shows drinking on stage. Most critics are keen to see the drunkenness of the concubine as a representation of the fallen beauty – she is not just drunk, she is tragically drunk. She does not merely tease and joke, but her smiles are filled with tears – *kuxiao* (sad smiles): 'After the Favourite Concubine learns that the Emperor has gone to visit another concubine instead, the certainty that she originally felt in her position evaporates, and she becomes angry, jealous, and hurt . . . As she becomes intoxicated . . . she abandons herself to her pain . . .'.[9] Elizabeth Wichmann interprets the role in a Western way entirely according to the 'feelings' of Yang Yuhuan, and not her actions (a Chinese way).

In the middle of the play, Yang Yuhuan makes three low turns as she smells the flowers in each of the three pots put out for her by the eunuchs. At the end of the turn, she has wound her body like a cork screw in a position known as *woyu* or 'coiling fish (fish out of water?)', spiralling to a point where the body cannot turn any further (Diagram 40). She has almost literally 'turned herself into' the flowers in her drunken state. At the last stage of drinking, later in the play, Yang Yuhuan makes a slow turn towards the tray with the goblet proffered by Gao, Pei and the handmaids, and taking the goblet between her teeth, drinks it by rotating from the hips through a full 180°. This movement is known as *man fanshen* or 'slow body turn' (see Diagram 77).

[9] Wichmann 1991: 133.

The movement is particularly difficult to execute at a slow pace as it should be here. The back bend should be deep and the arms should rotate on one plane, like a windmill, and not dragged off course by the body as it spins. Yang Yuhuan makes these spins as she sniffs the flowers and as she takes her last three cups of wine to show that for her, everything around her is spinning because she has had too much to drink. Just as the fan became the geese, now the performer spins on behalf of the surroundings which Yang Yuhuan perceives as spinning.

In this movement, Yang Yuhuan is *physically* on another plane. Instead of moving in the second dimension, parallel to her body, the upper part of her body and arms shift to the third dimension, at ninety degrees from the rest of the body. If one projects the principle of the Luo diagram onto the stage beneath her feet, then Yang Yuhuan is physically connecting with points on a similar diagram in a different plane with the upper part of her body. Her body is the axis which mediates between the planes.

The body as axis in space

The concept of the body moving in different planes of meaning to connect or contrast them in *jingju*, is more concretely explicit in the *nuo* theatre. In this section, one sequence from the *nuo* theatre of Dejiang County in Guizhou province,[10] shall be examined. The movement is an integral part of most kinds of *nuo*. The movement sequence is known as *Yubu* (step of Yu), and consists of eight steps in a diagonal pattern across the nine stations of the Luo diagram, shown previously in Diagram 23 (see above, p. 105). Each cell of the Luo diagram is accorded a digit from 1–9 such that the total of any three numbers in a straight line adds up to fifteen (see Diagram 16 on p. 94). The performer makes the Yu step by stamping out the sequence of digits: 1-2-3-4-5-6-7-8-9. Thus the Yu step consist of eight steps. The performer takes a ninth step forward to begin the next sequence, moving the diagram with him one step. Thus, although he appears to be starting the next sequence from position 5 (the centre), in terms of steps, he is repeating the se-

[10] *Zhongguo minzu minjian wudao jicheng: Dejiang xian ziliao juan* 1990: 46–52.

xun (wind)	*li* (fire)	*kun* (earth)
zhen (thunder)	0	*dui* (vapours)
gen (mountain)	*kan* (water)	*qian* (heaven)

Diagram 41　The Luo diagram as a cosmological scheme

quence from position 5 and treating it as if it were 1. The eighth step brings the performer to the same-but-new starting point – the point of departure is contained in the point of entry. The ninth step is a linking step, an end-but-first step which begins the next pattern. The Yu step is always consistent, regardless of what values are placed on the Luo diagram. Various dance movements which use the Yu step, however, may be named differently. The following sequence is called *cai jiu-zhou* (stamping out the nine provinces) but the Dejiang theatre claims seventy-two other names for similar dances including, for example, *guaziwu*, or *tiao bagua* (dance of the trigrams) where the trigram system is laid over the Luo diagram.[11]

The mathematical basis of the Luo diagram (a 'magic square of three') means that it is an equalising diagram – all routes of three digits in a straight line add up to the same sum. The matrix represents the philosophical (Daoist) idea of life as change in constancy. The cyclical pattern of the Yu step across the Luo matrix creates changes (connections of things that were not connected before) which, however, interminably repeat themselves.

When other, cosmological, values are placed on the diagram, they too are seen in an equalising position. The Luo diagram as a cosmological scheme is represented in Diagram 41. The various values

[11] Ibid.: 25–6.

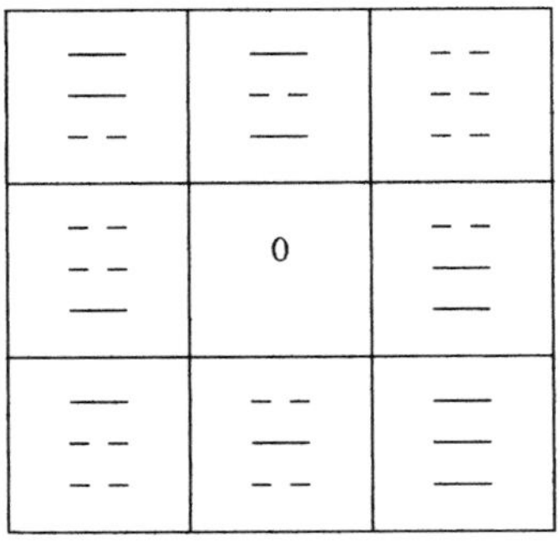

Diagram 42   Trigram values imposed on the Luo diagram

such as wind, mountain, thunder and vapours represent the *bagua*
(eight trigrams) or system of 'changes' recorded in the *Yijing* (*Book of
Changes*). The cyclical pattern between opposite pairs around the central axis replicates the cycle of life and death. The trigrams for these
are shown in Diagram 42. In this diagram, the oppositional positions
of the cosmological values represented by the trigrams are clearly
marked. The trigram for earth, top right (three broken lines – perme-
able, earth, female), and the trigram for heaven, bottom right (three
unbroken lines – impermeable/penetrative, heaven, male) are directly
opposite each other. The system of trigrams is an ancient system of
divination and philosophy recorded in the *Yijing*. The trigrams represent all possible phenomena in the world, and their changing domin-
ances represent the cycle of creation and destruction, which is the
pattern of all life:

> All things endowed with life have their origin in *zhen* (thunder)
> as *zhen* corresponds to the east. They are in harmonious
> existence with *xun* (wind) because *xun* corresponds with the
> east and the south. *Li* is brightness and renders all things visible
> to one another . . . *kun* is the earth, from which all things
> endowed with life receive food. *Dui* corresponds to the middle
> of autumn. *Qian* is the *gua* [trigram] of the north-west. *Kan*
> is water and the *gua* of the exact north and distress, unto

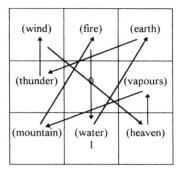

Diagram 43   The Yu step and its cosmological values

which everything endowed with life reverts. *Gen* is the *gua*
of the north-east in which living things terminate and also
originate.[12]

The circuit of the eight trigrams in the Yu step reproduces the cycle of
life described above, because no matter what station is chosen as position 1, all opposites are balanced, all sums equalled by the performer's
body as he moves across the diagram. If the steps of the performer
mapped in Diagram 23 are interpreted according to the trigram, or cosmological values suggested above, then the performer begins at *kan*
(water) and moves to *kun* (earth), *zhen* (thunder), *xun* (wind), *qian*
(heaven), *dui* (vapours), *gen* (mountain), *li* (fire) and ends at the centre
(see Diagram 43). The sign thunder *zhen* (to quicken) is accorded importance as a principle creative force: 'In the month of mid-spring, when
day and night are of equal length, thunder utters its voice and it begins
to lighten.'[13] Moreover that creative force depends on equal balance.
Life springs when Yin and Yang are equal to each other, just as Yin and
Yang in the *jingju* role Yang Yuhuan provides presence. In the case of
the concubine, the theatrical or fictive 'life' of Yang Yuhuan is engen-
dered by the combination of Yin in Yang and Yang in Yin.

In the *nuo* theatre, not only is the cosmos brought into congruence with the Luo matrix of creation but elements of the human body

[12] De Groot 1982, vol. 3: 961.   [13] Ibid.: 962.

251

wood	fire	earth
metal	0	wood
earth	water	metal

Diagram 44   The Luo matrix and the five elements

as, for example, the palm of the hand, the fingers or elements of the human body as a whole (as demonstrated in chapter three) are interpreted according to its scheme.

The description of the Luo diagram in terms of the human body may 'have referred to an application of the magic square of three to a person, probably a man or god considered as a microcosm of the universe'.[14] Perhaps an exorcist in the world of spirits and death? Perhaps an actor in the fictive world of theatre?

The Luo matrix was also early associated with a third plane of cosmic philosophy. If the trigram grid represents the heavens, and the human grid represents man, then the third grid represents earth. The earthly system applied to the Luo diagram is known as *wuxing* (five elements). These are earth, metal, water, wood and fire. The sequence of the elements, like the sequential rotation of the heavenly, trigram values, was thought to represent the sequence of creation, death and regeneration: earth generates metal, metal generates water, water generates wood, wood generates fire, fire generates earth; earth destroys water, water destroys fire, fire destroys metal, metal destroys wood, wood destroys earth and so on. The grid for this system is shown in Diagram 44. The grid of the five elements is also expanded by many other earthly phenomena such as the five seasons, for example,[15] spring,

[14] Cammann 1969: 42.
[15] The Five Elements were also correlated to the Five Animals, the Five Creatures, Five Grains, Five Organs, Five Colours, Five Tastes and Five Smells, see Bodde 1975: 38.

spring	summer	Indian summer
autumn	0	spring
Indian summer	winter	autumn

Diagram 45   The Luo matrix and the five seasons

South-east	South	South-west
East	Centre	West
North-east	North	North-west

Diagram 46   The Luo matrix and the five orientations

summer, Indian summer, autumn and winter (see Diagram 45). Further-more, it was logically extended to include the five orientations on earth (including the centre as the fifth orientation), as shown in Diagram 46. In Chinese maps, the south is always at the top.

Thus, the function of the Luo matrix is to connect opposing values around a central, unifying power. It is a temporal/spatial diagram which maps the changing patterns of life and death within the concept of constancy (the centre). At a temple feast in Guangde county, in the south-east of Anhui province, a dance is performed known as the *tiao wufang* (dance of the five orientations). In this dance, not only are the values of the orientations, seasons and colours applied to the diagram, but also specific deities: Pan Guan, judge of hell, stands at autumn (execution), Tudi, the lord of the soil, stands at summer (crops), the Daoist stands at spring (creation) and Heshang, the laughing monk (see later this chapter), stands in the centre, the position of unification.[16]

The title of the *nuo* dance in Dejiang, *cai jiuzhou*, refers to the nine provinces. These are the nine provinces created by Yu the Great when he vanquished the flood and created the world (China). It also expresses the concepts of centrality and the peripheral. The Chinese believed their kingdom to be at the centre of the world (hence *Zhong-guo*, the 'middle kingdom'). All peoples outside the centre were barbarians, other, which is equivalent to *gui* demons, or the other world. Thus the Luo diagram represented the political, geographical and philosophical power of the centre to unite and control.

In performance, the Luo diagram is projected onto three different planes – the heavens, the body and the earth. These stand in relation to one another such that the touch of any one point on any one plane has the same effect on the opposite or equal point in the other planes. The performer of *nuo* uses his body as the middle plane, to connect, or mediate between the cosmological systems:

> Assuming that the [Luo diagram], as a celestial diagram, was considered as situated in the sky, directly above its opposite on earth, with the cycles of progression following the same direction in each, then, the Yang cycle would start in the upper, primarily Yang square, taking every second number in succession from the complementary numbers in the lower square. Meanwhile the Yin cycle would start in the lower, basically Yin square, taking its alternate numbers from the complements in the corners of the upper square.[17]

In the performance, the body of the performer intercedes between the earthly and the heavenly cycles. Moreover, the performer's body also offers its own numerical/cosmological values, for the feet have the value of 6 and 8, the head 9, shoulders 2 and 4, the arms 3 and 7, torso 5 and loins 1. What this means is that the performance takes place not on a flat piece of ground, an empty space, but within a three dimensional cuboid space which is very carefully defined as not empty (in the sense of Peter Brook) but full of meaning (see Diagram 47). The Chinese

---

[16] Fan Jingru 1991: 3.   [17] Cammann 1969: 55.

He *(To unify)*

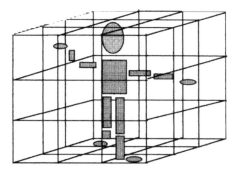

Diagram 47   The Luo body in space

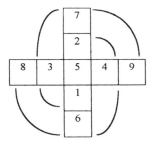

Diagram 48   The Hetu (River Chart)

model of the *nuo*, or *jingju* performer in space is not unlike the image of the performer within a globe perceived by Laban,[18] with the difference that the Chinese space is designated cosmological meaning. The planes heaven, earth and the body are brought into congruence by the Luo matrix, they are temporarily one unity, in the presence (and movements) of the performer.

The power of movement created by a journey across the cells of the Luo diagram is best explored in the example of its complement diagram, the *Hetu* (River Chart; Diagram 48). The River Chart plots the numbers 1 to 9 in a cross, such that both pairs of arms, 8 plus 7, and 6 plus 9, add up to 15. The route which travels the inner numbers, 1-2-3-4 + 5 also equals 15.

Although the River Chart does not *look* like the Luo diagram, it

---

[18] Laban 1991: 142–3.

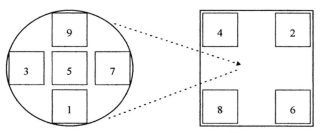

Diagram 49   Heaven (circle) and earth (square) in one

nonetheless represents the cyclical state of flux between stations topo-graphically. Following the odd numbers 1-3-7-9 gives a circle, and the even numbers 2-4-6-8 do the same. The two circles seem to drive each other forward endlessly, like a windmill. That is, the mutual interac-tion of Yang (odd) and Yin (numbers) creates movement. Such move-ment is at once newly created and at the same time cyclical, never changing. The River Chart also proposes an alternative way of reading the standard Luo diagram, which is, to focus on the even and odd num-bers as separate groups. In the Luo diagram, the even (Yin) numbers form a square, which is a symbol of earth. The odd (Yang) numbers of the Luo diagram create a (dissected) circle, which represents heaven. This read-ing of the Luo diagram replicates in visual form the concept of earth (square) and heaven (circle) *in one*, as shown in Diagram 49. Thus, in nego-tiating the diagram in performance, both worlds are brought together by the physical body of the performer. Furthermore, the Luo diagram can also be rotated, reflected or inverted to suit various seasonal or lunar changes.[19] The ancient Daoist manual, *Daozang*, gives the patterns of foot steps to be taken across the cosmological (trigram) matrix to reflect the changing seasons, as illustrated in Diagram 50.[20] In each circuit, the pattern of the agricultural season is mapped, from spring and birth, to autumn and harvest. Because it is a circuit, the repetition, or pattern of the cosmos is always implied. Moreover, each pattern motivates the next by numerical balance, as shown in the River Chart.

Thus the Luo matrix can be applied in many different ways to

[19] Explained at length in Cammann 1960, 1962, 1969.
[20] *Daozang* 1986, vol. 29: 427.

He *(To unify)*

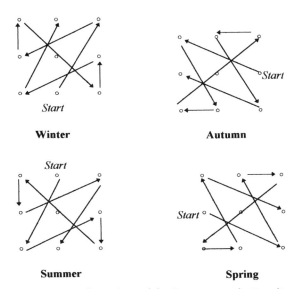

Diagram 50   Seasonal rotations of the Yu step over the Luo diagram

reproduce certain cultural perceptions – the rotation of seasons, lunar and solar phases, the pattern of life and death and so on. The matrix can bring the macrocosm and the microcosm together, and negotiation of these two systems by the human body can regulate or change either. Temporarily, the performer has the power to reorder the cosmos. In the Dejiang *nuo* theatre model, the Luo diagram is accorded different oppositional values to those used in the standard diagram (Diagram 51).

1	6	4
8	5	7
3	2	9

Diagram 51   The Dejiang Luo matrix

Yang	Yin	Yin
Yin	Yang	Yang
Yang	Yin	Yang

Diagram 52   The Dejiang Luo matrix in terms of Yin and Yang

In this diagram, the route of three numbers neither provides one multiple, nor do the even (Yin) numbers and the odd (Yang) numbers reproduce the image of square and circle (earth and heaven) as elucidated through the example of the *Hetu* above.

However, there is logic to the Dejiang version of the Luo matrix, since certain correlations can be perceived. The odd (Yang) and even (Yin) numbers in each line reproduce a typical triadic pattern as shown in Diagram 52. If a Yin line in the trigram system is a broken line, a Yang line unbroken, read vertically, this diagram yields the trigrams for *li* (fire), *kan* (water) and *dui* (vapours, air). This is only one possible way of interpreting the matrix. Another is to chart the frequency of each station visited in the nine rounds of the Dejiang *nuo* performance onto the diagram (the performer visits the top left cell three times in the dance, the middle cell twice, and so on; see Diagram 53). In this case, the resulting pattern yields a similar mathematical or formulaic pattern of balance and equality. The same pattern, 3 – 2 – 1, is also echoed in another performance medium: music. It is recreated in the percussion section by the large gong (see Diagram 54[21]).

The *cai jiuzhou* dance consists of nine rounds or circuits of the Luo diagram which, in this case, equates the map of the nine earthly provinces with the heavenly cosmological stations represented in the

[21] *Zhongguo minzu minjian wudao jicheng: Dejiang xian ziliao juan* 1990: 51, transcribed by Hein Drop, Leiden.

258

He *(To unify)*

3	2	1
2	2	2
1	2	3

Diagram 53   Frequency of cells visited in the Dejiang dance

Diagram 54   Percussion section of the Nine Provinces dance

trigrams. The diagram is not marked in any physical way on the performance area. The performance takes place in front of the *nuo* altar which
is set up either in the temple or in a villager's home in the ancestral, or
main hall and the performer faces the altar, i.e. *away* from the spectators towards the statues of various gods, including *nuogong* and *nuopo*
(father and mother of *nuo*). The singing part, shown in Diagram 55, is
sometimes accompanied by the *huqin* spike fiddle. The long 'rests'
marked in the score are filled by the percussion sequence alone.

Each movement of the *nuo* performer in each bar of the score has
been recorded, so that it is possible to reconstruct what the Dejiang
performer does (how long he takes between movements, if he rests at a
particular station, etc.) by comparing the score to the movements, and
plotting them on the Dejiang version of the Luo matrix (see Diagram
56). The chanted text that accompanies the first circuit of the Dejiang

259

Diagram 55   Melody sung to the Nine Provinces dance

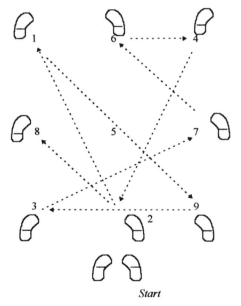

Start

Diagram 56   Steps taken in the Nine Provinces dance

dance can be found below (p. 266). Altogether the nine rounds of the performer's dance are accompanied by seven repeats of the musical score. The stations are numbered according to the Dejiang matrix in Diagram 51.

> 1st Round of the Nine Provinces Dance:
> Bars 1–5: The performer begins at position 2.
>> 6–7: Left foot moves to position 1, right foot follows.
>> 8–10: Right foot moves to position 9, left foot follows.
>> 11–15: Performer remains still at position 9.
>> 16–17: Left foot moves to position 3, right foot follows.
>> 18–19: Right foot moves to position 7, left foot follows.
>> 20–21: Right foot moves to position 6, left foot follows.
>> 22–23: Left foot moves to position 4, right foot follows.
>> 24–25: Left foot moves to position 2, right foot follows.
>> 26–27: Left foot moves to position 8, right foot follows.[22]

The title of the movement *cai* (stamp) *jiuzhou* (nine provinces) indicates that the first foot to land in a certain section is the stamping foot, while the second foot follows by dragging behind. Here, the combination of designation (stamping) and connecting (dragging) is the process of recreation in the (by the) physical body of the *nuo* performer.

In the first round of the dance, the performer visits each position once. He starts in the middle station of the bottom row which, in the Dejiang model, has the cosmological value 'earth'. The final step to the left-hand station of the middle row, which has the value of mountain in the Dejiang model ('in which living things terminate and also originate'),[23] links the end of round one to the beginning of round two. In this sense, one round is equal to one circuit, one complete journey (all stations are visited), but it is also the beginning of the next journey. The steps in the first round actually circumscribe a journey from the bottom row middle, to the middle row left – the beginning of a circle around the Luo matrix. The whole pattern of steps in the dance, including all nine rounds, replicates a circuitous sequence – each last step forming the beginning of the next, till the end (there is no end). Time, as cycle, is

---

[22] Ibid.: 50–1.   [23] De Groot 1982, vol. 3: 961.

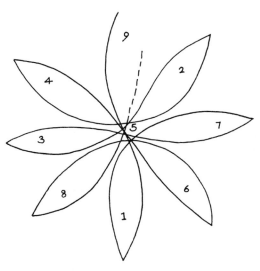

Diagram 57   Manifesting the mathematical/magical Luo as a flower of transformation

simultaneously vertical and horizontal. All times are one in the moment of the performance.

Yet another form of *nuo* theatre, *shangu nuo*, shows how the performer relies on the digital values of the Luo matrix to make his journey one of re-creation.[24] The performing area of *shangu nuo* is marked out by eight altars in a circle, each accorded its relative name from the trigram and numerical system accorded the standard Luo diagram. Thus, the topography of the performance area can be considered to be identical to the Dejiang model examined above. The performers move in line from one altar to the next, circling one and passing to another altar *via* the central performing area. When the movements of the performers are mapped on a chart (Diagram 57), the numerical values of stations linked by the performers always add up to fifteen, i.e. the performers manifest the mathematical/magical properties of the Luo diagram. The performers enter the area at 9. Passing the centre 5, they

[24] Ren Deze 1990. See also Wang Fucai 1991 for a series of foot patterns dedicated to the principles of the Luo diagram.

circle 1, mapping the first total of 15. The next steps take them from 7, through 5, to 3, which yields 15 and the following steps connect 4 and 6 through the centre, also giving 15.

The circuit of the performers around the altars/Luo diagram linking opposing pairs through the central position, creates a mathematical balance or equality for, 'The middle number of the Luo diagram is not only the physical mean between every opposing pair of other numbers, by reason of its central position; it is also their mathematical mean, since it is equal to half the sum of every opposing pair, all of which equal ten.'[25] The central station is vital to the balance of the diagram, it is in effect, the meaning, the axis:

> In this square, the respective pairs made up of large and small odd (Yang) numbers, and those composed of large and small even (Yin) numbers, were all equal to each other. Thus all differences were levelled, and all contrasts erased, in a realm of no distinction, and the harmonious balance of the Luo . . . square could effectively symbolise the world in balanced harmony around a powerful central axis.[26]

Moreover, in the *shangu nuo* example, the pattern made by the feet of the performers represents a flower, *hua*, which puns on another word *hua* (to change, to transform). The movements around the nine stations made by the performer's feet cause *change* in the cosmos – sickness, death, demons are dispelled and the earthly world is *put back together again.*

In the standard Luo diagram, the five earthly elements are so arranged that: 'The wood of 3 and 8 conquered the earth of 5 and 10 (in the center); the earth conquered the water of 2 and 6 and so on.'[27] If the system of earthly elements is applied to the *shangu nuo* example, the sequence mapped by the performer reads:

> Fire seeks Water to combine and give birth to the myriad things;
> Metal looks for Wood for the promise of a good harvest;

---

[25] Cammann 1969: 48.   [26] Ibid.: 48.
[27] Smith 1991: 61.

Water and Metal are equal to the opening of the Heavenly Gate
and Earth's Door.[28]

The phrase of earthly sequence mapped by the feet of the *shangu nuo*
performers in their circuit of the altars achieves the same result as
the Dejiang *nuo* performer in the dance of the nine provinces. For the
duration of the performance, the earthly and heavenly worlds are one
(entered and exited through one opening which is both Heavenly Gate
and Earth Door). The open Gate/Door is the point of transition between
worlds, the moment of invocation.

The Luo matrix of cyclical change expressed as constancy is the
underlying pattern in most *nuo* theatres. Although the sequence of
steps has been well recorded by Chinese scholars, it is only when they
are interpreted according to the mathematical properties inherent in
the matrix that the pattern of steps renders coherence. If, for example,
each pair of steps (connecting two stations of meaning) passes the central station, the route made by the performer's feet always replicates
the magical, creative power of 15, the *physical mean* (as shown by the
examples in Diagram 58). The world is physically reconstructed in
its correct order by the footwork of the Fashi, or *nuo* performer. The
stamping foot designates, the dragging foot connects, and the sequence
of steps recreate, rebalance or harmonise the new form of the cosmos
(again).

All these various systems lead, through the circuitry of the Luo
diagram, to a sense of balance, of making all things equal, all things
come round. The progression of waxing and waning describes a process
of change and constancy. Its use in the *nuo* performance suggests a formula which might read:

Presence (life) = movement = change = presence (life) . . .

That is to say, the power of life is manifested through eternal, or cyclical movement. Movement causes change, change causes new constel-
lations and new life. The formula circumscribes the Yin/Yang theory of
ebb and flow, from which all things proceed: 'From the One there came
the Two, from the Two came the Myriad Things.'

---

[28] Ren Deze 1990: 7.

He *(To unify)*

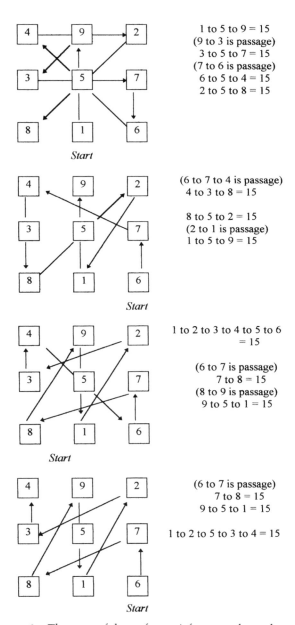

1 to 5 to 9 = 15
(9 to 3 is passage)
3 to 5 to 7 = 15
(7 to 6 is passage)
6 to 5 to 4 = 15
2 to 5 to 8 = 15

(6 to 7 to 4 is passage)
4 to 3 to 8 = 15

8 to 5 to 2 = 15
(2 to 1 is passage)
1 to 5 to 9 = 15

1 to 2 to 3 to 4 to 5 to 6
= 15

(6 to 7 is passage)
7 to 8 = 15
(8 to 9 is passage)
9 to 5 to 1 = 15

(6 to 7 is passage)
7 to 8 = 15
9 to 5 to 1 = 15

1 to 2 to 5 to 3 to 4 = 15

Diagram 58   The route of the performer's feet reproduces the creative mean

The body as axis in time

The *jingju* performers call their theatre the art of the four skills *chang*, *nian*, *da*, *zuo* (singing, recitation, martial skills and acting) which are all embodied in one performer. On stage, a performer must be able to show and sing surprise while making a somersault backwards in the air, if so required, to repeat the linguistic text in the media of the body. The co-ordination of the different media in presenting aspects of a role is actually repetition. That which is expressed by the voice is picked up in movement. The human body is the unifying central power.

In the *nuo* theatre, the performer also uses his voice (and, for example, his feet) to express the same meaning. When stamping on one station, he calls its name and makes the sign of the same station with his hand. The *nuo* performer exploits the different meaning potential of the different units of articulation to pull together different worlds. The chant which is sung to the dance of the nine stations has nine verses to accompany the nine circuits of the nine stations. At each station, the performer sings the name of the station in one or other of the different cosmological systems mapped onto the Luo diagram. In the first round, the performer sings the name of a trigram (heavenly) station and pairs it to the name of one of the nine (earthly) provinces. Thus the body of the performer simultaneously divides and unites voice (heaven) and feet (earth). In the following example of text from the Dejiang *nuo*, the heavenly system is marked by italics, the earthly by bold print. Each line is sung at a different station, the numbers mark each step.

(1)   In the first circuit of the nine provinces, the first [station] is *kan*,

(2)   Then to **Lizhou** passing southern seas,

(3)   The left foot rests on *zhen*, **Qingzhou**,

(4)   The right foot stands on *dui*, **Xijing**,

(5)   *Qian* enters **Yong**, the centre,

(6)   *Xun* enters **Xuzhou** country,

(7)   *Kun* sends forth to **Jingzhou** camp,

(8)   *Gen* protects **Youzhou**.

(9)   Soldiers from the 8 directions return to *kan*,

(10) From *kan* the soldiers shall enter the **central palace**.

He *(To unify)*

> One round of the nine provinces has been stamped out clearly,
> Hand the successful trigrams to the ancestors.
> One round of the nine provinces is complete and fulfilled,
> Let the second round of the nine provinces begin.[29]

The following eight verses of the chant all constitute their cosmologies differently to different effects. The first round is a straightforward naming of the systems accorded to each of the stations: a defining round. The performance area is mapped out and accorded meaning. It is described as being sent up to the ancestors, that is, the performance area is equated with the world of the ancestors in heaven.

Once brought together (the gates of heaven and earth are open and passable) the second round of steps begins with the first visitation of a spirit from the other world, 'When the Buddha appears in the central palace, *qian* (heaven) is perceived . . .' Rounds two to eight can be considered to be the calling up of heavenly soldiers in the different stations to arise and travel and cleanse the corresponding earthly stations of demons. Constant cross-reference between cosmological systems acts as a reminder of the temporary proximity of the two worlds. Thus, in round six, for example, the elements represented by the heavenly trigram system affect the earthly, provincial system directly:

> **Lizhou** sends out heavenly fire (*huo*),
> In a while the city of **Dui** [lake] **zhou** shall burn,
> And then calm the battalions at **Li** [fire] **zhou** . . .

In this verse, the positions have become so synonymous that they are marked as both heavenly and earthly names (bold and italics together).

Finally, round nine seems to position elements of the heavens in relation to this world (if the first round can be described as putting the world in relation to the heavens, now the reverse is apparent). That is, the descendants shall rise to the heavens when it is time (rather than having the ancestors descend); the living are now the major subjects in the cosmological system:

(1) One son shall sit at *kan*,
(2) The second son, at **Lizhou** camp with ten thousand others,

---

[29] *Zhongguo minzu mingjian wudao: Dejiang xian ziliao juan* 1990: 48–9.

(3)   The third son [child] at **Qingzhou** shall be the *mother*,[30]
(4)   The fourth at **Xuzhou** shall release the soldiers off to march,
(5)   The fifth at **Jingzhou** be recruiter of the horses,
(6)   The sixth shall go to ***Duizhou*** city,
(7)   The seventh to **Jingzhou** city,
(8)   The eighth to **Yongzhou** city.
(9)   Only the ninth is too young,
      He shall follow the grandfather's generation and sit at the city of
      the nine provinces.
(10) *Qian* [heaven] and *kun* [earth] shall remain unchanged for ten
      thousand generations.

In this round, the eight generations are sent out to heavenly posts to help control and direct the various stations which correspond to those on earth. The ninth child, the present (living) generation will thus benefit from the influence of his ancestors and, in effect, the whole nine provinces (the world), at the heart (city) of which the performer/ descendant/child has positioned himself through the actions of the nine provinces dance, shall be peaceful and fruitful.

Crosswor(l)ds

The body as physical mediator between different worlds (*Grenzgänger*), the body as the central, unifying power, is the body as exorcist/recreator. Even Zhong Kui's performance, which does not depend so physically on the concept of the Luo diagram, exposes two simultaneous systems of meaning which refer to this world and the world of spirits. Under the surface of what Zhong Kui does on stage is a whole vocabulary of meaning that is barely noted – whether out of ignorance or design. Nearly everything associated with Zhong Kui is a linguistic pun for some function of exorcism. Like the *nuo* performer who jumps systems to bring two worlds together, Zhong Kui is articulated in two linguistic systems.

Zhong Kui's make-up includes the image of the bat, a common sign of good luck in opera make-up, since the word *fu* (bat) is a homophone for the word *fu* (fortune). The bat is especially associated with

---

[30]   The Queen Mother of the Western Heavens *Xi wangmu* is implied in this station.

He *(To unify)*

the exorcist Zhong Kui, however, because of a tradition which identifies Zhong Kui with the phrase 'zhi jian fu lai' meaning 'hold the sword and the bat/fortune will come – the warrior shall exorcise evil'. It is a homophone of the phrase 'zhi jian fu lai' meaning 'nothing but good fortune is seen coming this way'.

The play *Zhong Kui jiamei* (*Zhong Kui Marries Off His Little Sister*) consists of Zhong Kui's visit from the heavens to his sister on earth. The play relates Zhong Kui's journey to earth to marry his friend Du Ping to his sister and to help in the wedding preparations. On the very simplest of levels, the play positions Zhong Kui as spirit unifier, or mediator – he brings man and woman together. However, on a deeper level, the play has a more direct, exorcist meaning. In the journey sequence to earth, each of the spirits which accompany him carry special props. One spirit carries a vase with three lances in it, *ping sheng san ji*, symbolising peaceful (*ping*, 'vase' puns with 'peace') promotion (*sheng* the 'capacity of the vase' puns with 'promotion') to the rank of three grades (*san ji* 'three lances' puns with 'three grades'). Moreover, like the Pu An charm used in exorcisms, it can be read backwards,[31] *ji san sheng ping* meaning 'scatter the crowd [of demons] and bring peace'. Another of the spirits carries a *posan* (broken parasol), a pun on words meaning 'destroy all the bad luck'. The third spirit carries a *gudeng* (single lantern), which is a homophone meaning 'bind, tie up and trample on [the evil spirits]'. The fourth spirit carries a shoulder pole bearing a box of books at each end, a lute at the front and a sword at the back, signifying Zhong Kui's double identity as scholar and exorcist and the fifth spirit carries a whip, the key instrument of exorcisms, as groom to Zhong Kui's horse.

This latter role deserves further explanation, for the figure of groom represents the concept 'exorcism' *pars pro toto*. Zhang Chunhua, a *wuchou*, martial comic role, once demonstrated a lengthy sequence he titled *xima* (washing the horse). The sequence used to be performed before any main heroic character (including Zhong Kui) mounted his

[31] Or in the Chinese classroom, when the writing on the blackboard may continue in any direction, like a crossword: from right to left or vice-versa, from top to bottom or vice-versa, wherever there is space. Copying from the blackboard is a question of unpuzzling the maze of characters into sensible phrases.

horse. Here, the pun revolves around *xi* meaning 'to wash, bathe' and *xi* meaning 'the sacrificial beast'. The *matong* (horse groom) always played by a *wuchou*, enters the stage leading the horse, i.e. he holds a silk whip in his hand. As suggested in chapter two, the historical groom was associated with the idea of 'other' or 'foreigner'. Here, the *wuchou* or comic martial role plays at being the 'other'. This seems to suggest a relationship between the physically active (*wu*, martial) and the comic (*chou*) to the exorcism ritual, an issue which shall be explored in more detail below.

The initial entrance of the groom is generally about as acrobatic as the skills of the particular *wuchou* allow – somersaulting, tumbling, cartwheels and camel spins make up the sequence which covers all four diagonal lengths of the stage. Since the action of washing which follows is exorcist in nature, the incredible feats of jumping and leaping must be related to the function of leaping in the *nuo*. Even in *jingju*, the *chou* role was nicknamed the *kai kou tiao* which means 'the one who opens by leaping'. The groom finishes his leaping and scatters water over the stage three times in an act of cleansing before miming sprinkling (an imagined) horse for the same purpose. He then shows brushing down the horse and saddling it. These movements require good technical leg skills. He must hook the horse's tail with his foot in a high sweeping movement, brush it and toss it back; he must balance the horse blanket over one raised knee, beat it and throw it over the horse's back by kicking his leg out in a wide swing.

The horse has highly powerful connotations in Chinese mythology. It was one of the chief animals of sacrifice at tombs of the Shang dynasty, and is said to embody the male, Yang principle, so that this sequence brings the exorcist cleansing power directly onto the stage. The *dixi* troupe from Anshun's Jiuxi village perform a play taken from the Tang and Sui Histories called *Xima jiujia* 'Washing the Horse Saved His Highness' as an act of direct exorcism.[32] The actors show how the Tang king, Li Shimin, is in the process of capturing the city of Luoyang when the festival of Duan Gong (see p. 278) causes him to pause for a day of rest. He rides out to the Imperial Gardens with his minister Xu

---

[32] The following material is taken from the author's field notes.

Maogong, dismounts at an artificial hillside and looks out over the city. By chance, he is seen by the enemy, Dan Xiongxin, who sends out forces to capture the king. The king's minister manages to escape and, on the way to find help, comes across the great general Yuchi Gong who is stripped to the waist (a metaphor for spiritual cleanliness prior to executing a rite) at the riverside washing down his horse. Without waiting to put on his armour, the brave general rides off at once and defeats the enemy and saves the king. Thus it is said that washing the horse saved the emperor. In performing this play, the role of Li Shimin is played by the troupe leader, Gu Zhiyuan and the more energetic role of the general by deputy troupe leader, his son, Gu Guangxing. The Ming name for the village was Gu Cheng – the same Gu represented by the Gu family. The hierarchy of the roles played is exactly reflected in the hierarchy of those playing the roles – the world of ancestor-play and the real world of family and clan are precisely equated.

The movement sequence *xima* (washing the horse) has been banned from *jingju* since the 1950s, since it was believed to be superstitious in content.[33] In the performance of Zhong Kui, the horse is also shown being prepared and saddled – not only a metaphor for ritual cleansing, but also a metaphor for the desire to obtain a higher official post, since scholars did the same before leaving for the capital city to take the imperial exams. Once again, one apparently simple element – the horse – is actually a complex of symbols, in this case reflecting the two important qualities of the figure Zhong Kui as exorcist and scholar.

This, perhaps is the true reason behind the reluctance to perform it as a regular element of the repertoire – its sub-text is a *direct* or *actual* act of exorcism.

The grotesque body as unifier

The *nuo* and *jingju* performers position their bodies in the central station of the three dimensional stage space – the corporeal body is the unifying power of recreation. Just as a distinction was identified in

---

[33] Yet another example of the effect of apparently insignificant reforms to *jingju*. The groom role is now played as acrobatically as possible for the sole purpose of winning admiration from the audience, like a circus trick, without the cleansing ritual.

chapter three between the idea of the dissected body being reassembled as either body, or as over-large (god)head, the focus of unification as the process of recreation is either expressed by the loins, the physical centre of the body (as in the examples above), or as head. In the latter model, the idea of recreation or regeneration is articulated by the *mouth* which consumes the old and spits out the new.

The *qitou* ugly head, the Taotie and the Fangxiangshi, are depicted with large, gaping mouths or are described as consuming demons in the process of exorcism. Serrated teeth, fangs in the top and bottom jaw are common features of depictions of Chi You as bear in the tomb, and the exorcist bronze masks and heads found at Xunxian and Sichuan. More-over, many wooden exorcist masks in the *nuo* are similarly fanged and toothed with gaping mouths.[34]

The term *qitou* was examined in chapter two from the point of view of its etymological relation to words meaning 'big', 'terrifying' and 'ugly'. However, the wide gaping mouth can also be seen as a smil-ing, laughing mouth. The comic role type in *jingju* is known as *chou*, a term that etymologically means 'ugly'. As in many forms of theatre around the world, that which is funny (clown) is associated with that which is distorted from the norm, that which is also ugly.

At the marionette exorcism event in Taiwan, the first *liang-xiang* pose that the marionette figure of the Daoist Water Minister, the god Shuide Xingjun, makes on entering the stage is taken directly from the *chou* or clown repertoire.[35] Given the serious nature of this part of the exorcism event, this fact is remarkable. Moreover, the three patron gods of the marionette theatre *per se*, the three Wang brothers, are con-sidered to be 'divine jesters'.

> Music being the great unifier, the Three Brothers are divine musicians . . . their music is in such perfect harmony with the order of the universe that a single note is sufficient to stir the entire nation. They become the music masters of Emperor Ming-huang the most famous theatrical amateur in Chinese history, and instruct the beautiful actresses of the Peach Garden.[36]

---

[34] *Guizhou nuo mianju yishu* 1989.   [35] Song Jinxiu 1985: 101.
[36] Schipper 1966: 85. 'Peach' in the last line is a mistranslation for 'Pear'.

Further exploration of the myth of the three brothers reveals that they carried out exorcisms by performing in a comic way:

> The Three Brothers lure the agents of pestilence by their fun-making, in which they are assisted by numbers of 'Demon lads'. It is generally assumed that the *nuo* processions . . . are in themselves sufficient to expel the demons of pestilence. Our case here is somewhat different. The drumming and playing of the jesters and their lads is done for the purpose of 'gathering' or 'unifying'; the playing *kuilang* attract the demons, and these can thus be captured.[37]

The exorcism in Taiwan began with the marionette Shuide Xingjun being placed on the altar *next to* the Wang gods of exorcism. Though the marionette is not a *chou* role, it is brought into relation with the role type. Thus the first *zaoxing* pose (form, shape, pattern) articulates the duality grotesque and funny. The marionette figure 'posing as' the clown role-type the moment before it enacts the process of exorcism gives the sign that the exorcism is to be carried out: it reminds the spectator of the relation of the marionette to its patron gods, the divine jesters, and even adopts their *form* (their power as exorcists *per se*?).

The presence of the element 'funny' in exorcism depends upon a pun on the words *he*, meaning 'unification', and *he* as the Chinese onomatopoeia for laughter: 'This is called the "uniting" of the pestilences, and the jesters in this case act as gods of "Union", *hehe shen*.'[38] The *chou* role (Zhong Kui and his groom are both *wuchou* martial-comic roles) unites by being funny/grotesque in order to dispel the demons and restore order (recreate) the world. Thus the generally held (official) view in China that comic sequences are included in the exorcism event to entertain, or 'sweeten' the gods which have been invited to attend, as well as to provide a kind of catharsis after the exorcism, is severely challenged:

> Le théâtre, lui aussi, possède cette caractéristique d'écarter le néfaste. Même si ce n'est que pour fournir une tension dramatique, puisqu'une fin heureuse plaît d'autant plus qu'on

---

[37] Ibid.   [38] Ibid.: 87.

aura montré d'une façon convaincante les dangers et désastres qui doivent être surmontés. Cependant, la catharsis procurée par le théâtre chinois est beaucoup plus profonde.[39]

Instead of this Western interpretation of the phenomenon of comedy in the exorcism event examples from exorcism performance and even *jingju*, suggest that comedy is actually one of the *tools* of exorcism, rather than mere entertainment or diversion.

In the model of the reassembled body as head, the performing body is perceived on two levels. Ugliness can frighten away evil spirits, and a gaping mouth can consume evil spirits. But ugliness is also considered amusing, funny – a gaping mouth can be a smiling, laughing mouth. Both these qualities in turn, through etymological relations, have the power to unify, to bring together (in order to be rid of) evil spirits. The act of unification is the sub-text of the act of laughing. The statement from the Han dynasty declaring the puppets to be *sangjia zhi yue* (*entertainment* for funerals)[40] can be seen in a new light. The marionette or puppet performance at the tomb edge served an explicitly unificatory (exorcist and regenerative) function. It provided the unifying power of recreation in a situation of dissolution (death).

By the same token, what appear to be pure theatrical elements of the *nuo* which are considered mere 'entertainment', 'real plays', the *xiaoxi*, *daxi* or *zhengxi* (as opposed to 'magical' sequences directed by the Fashi) must be interpreted as having *direct* influence on the exorcism in hand. Thus the *zhengxi* performance of *Mengjiangnu*, said to provide light relief after the exorcism sequence carried out by the Fashi, is as exorcist in *function* as the performance of *Zhong Kui Marries Off His Little Sister*.

The laughing head with a gaping mouth, as a symbol of the power of exorcism, is a common feature of nearly every festive event in rural China – the dance of the Big Head. Performers wear large papier-mâché heads and dance through the streets. The heads depict laughing monks, or children. An early record from AD 502–57 states, 'In the twelfth [lunar] month on the eighth day, the villagers bear small drums at their

---

[39] Van der Loon 1977: 158.
[40] *Houhanshu. Wu xing zhi*, 'Lingdi shu you xi yu xiyuan'.

waists, and wearing [over their heads][41] a Hugong or Jingang Lishi 'head', they carry out the exorcism.'[42] The Hugong head is related to the idea of *qitou*, for the term *hu* means non-Chinese, principally Western or *gui* (foreign). Three significant elements of the Hugong head associate it with exorcist powers:

  1   The Hugong head is 'other' because it is said to be the representation of a Buddha. Since many early Buddhist images bore the sign of their *hu* (western – for the Chinese) origins,[43] the Hugong head is deemed 'foreign', different, an outsider.

  2   The Hugong figure is possibly a kind of ancestral god in the same way that Wanggong is of clans in the Anshun area of Guizhou, described in chapter six. Both are said to be real men who have been deified. Hugong was possibly Hu Ze, who lived in Zhejiang and served under the Song emperor Ren Zong. Through his upright and honest character, he saved the people of Wuzhou from having to pay exorbitant and corrupt taxes. After his death he was worshipped as a protective and peace-bringing god.[44]

  3   Yet a further interpretation, and one that is not necessarily opposed to either of the two theories above, is that the name of the figure derived from the fact that it was heavily bearded, or hairy, since the term *hu* means 'hairy'. This interpretation links the figure to the concept of part-man, part-beast of prey as the exorcist power of consummation and regeneration, explored in chapter two in relation to Zhong Kui and the Fangxiangshi.

The second figure in the citation, Jingang Lishi, is a Buddhist warrior attendant who is so sharp-eyed that he can see and destroy any evil demon.[45] In both cases, whether the Hu figure is interpreted as a Buddhist or simply mythological god, the people are 'dressing up as gods'

---

[41] The Chinese word is *dai* which generally indicates that the item is worn on or over the head and face.

[42] *Jingchu sui shiji*.   [43] Huang Weiruo in a personal note to the author.

[44] *Zhongguo fengsu cidian*, 1990: 737.

[45] Some Chinese scholars have tried to associate the Buddhist exorcism rite, which includes Jingang Lishi, directly to the *nuo* exorcism conducted by the Fangxiangshi. See Granet 1959: 334.

by putting on an extra large 'head'. Moreover, their performance is directed towards exorcism.

In ancient China, on specific lunar anniversaries, the Buddhist monks themselves also performed wearing large heads to represent certain Buddhist gods. Such performances, whether story-telling, feats of magic, or masked theatre, were a crucial part of early Buddhist methods of teaching in China.[46] The performance of Buddhist monks wearing large 'heads' was known as *wupusa*, or the 'dancing Buddha'. As early as the Tang dynasty, a musical piece known as the *Pusaman*, (the wild, raving? Buddha) most probably accompanied such performances. The exorcist subtext of apparently wild or uncontrolled movements exposed in the previous chapter might be relevant here.

A similar kind of dance, not performed by Buddhist monks, but including the wearing of a similarly large 'false' head, is known today as *wubolao*, *wubaolao*, or *wubaoluo*. These names may well be a simple corruption of the term *wupusa*, since, for example, along the lower reaches of the Changjiang (Yangtze) River, the people pronounce *pusa* (Buddha) as *baolao*.[47] The *wubaoluo* dance is still an integral part of many annual processions and even in Anhui province, Guichi, an important element of the *nuo* event.

In the Song dynasty, the dance with the large head was one of the many performances offered in the entertainment quarters:

> At the time of the pronouncement of the pardons after each grand ceremony [of New Years'], they . . . steal the pheasant [from on top of the pole]. They do pole-climbing, tumbling, stilts, striking with criss-cross rollers, escaping from ropes, costuming as ghosts and spirits, *carrying the gong*, the dancing judge of hell, dancing with hacking knives . . .[48]

Here, *baoluo* is translated in its literal sense, 'carrying the gong'. From its position next to the costuming of ghosts and spirits and dancing the judge of hell, the correct translation should be 'dancing the Big Head', and it probably refers to similar figures as those of Hu and Jingang Lishi, i.e. exorcist figures.

[46] Ch'en 1964 and Mair 1989.
[47] Personal note to the author by Huang Weiruo.
[48] Idema/West, 1982: 78. *Nansong guji kao* 1983: 88.

He *(To unify)*

A poem from the same dynasty describes the dance of the Big Head in association with the performance of *kuilei* puppets, here specifically marionettes, with a marionette figure known as Guolang (Young Guo):

> In the performance area, *Baolao* pokes fun at Guolang.
> Guolang's clothes and style of dancing are disordered and wild.
> But if *Baolao* should enter the performance area and begin to dance,
> His own dance is even more silly and unconventional,
> His own costume yet more dishevelled and his sleeves too long.[49]

Guolang was a figure in the marionette repertoire with rotund body and balding hair. The marionette theatre in general came to be known as Guolang, Guogong, or Tugong after this figure who was said to have been a real man, a joker, who became ill and lost his hair:

> People ask, why are marionettes known by the name 'Baldy Guo'? In the ancient volume, *Fengsutong*, it is written that people with the surname Guo are nicknamed 'baldy'. This certainly derives from a real man named Guo. Because he fell ill, he lost his hair and his head was round and shiny. Moreover, this Guo loved making jokes and teasing. So people began to call puppets by the name of Guo because puppets would perform the figure of Guo making jokes.[50]

The piece described in the poem could, in the light of this information, be interpreted as an exorcist piece. If Baldy Guo 'had been ill', perhaps the figure Baolao (Big Head) was enacting the exorcism of the illness through his own 'wild, chaotic movements'. Alternatively, the two figures present a balance of oppositions – *Young* Guo and *Old* Bao. Moreover, the piece is described as being humorous as the Big Head laughs to create laughter and Guolang 'loved making jokes' – the sub-text of exorcism.

Several descriptions of Song entertainment mention the *kuilei* puppet in association with the figure Big Head. In the Song dynasty

---

[49] Yang Danian *Kuileishi* in Chen Shidao's *Houshan shihua*.
[50] Yan Zhitui, *Yanshi jiaxun*.

nanxi play text, *Zhang Xie zhuangyuan* (*Top Graduate Zhang Xie*) the indecisive Zhang Xie says, 'It looks as though Baolao is performing in front of the *kuilei* tent.'[51] And in the record of the celebration events held at court for the Song emperor's birthday, 'At the thirteenth toast, the clappers beat solo while the *kuilei* dances Baolao.'[52] Indeed, from about the tenth century AD, the Baolao performance was an important and regular feature of celebrations and entertainments sometimes reaching huge proportions. On the night of the fifteenth day of the first lunar month (*yuanxiao*), or lantern festival (celebrating the first full moon of the first month), it was reported that among the seventy odd troupes performing were also the Baolao.[53] Another work records that at a performance in the Southern Song capital, Linan, there were '300 or more people from Fujian as Baolao, and 100 or so Baolao from Sichuan'.[54]

In the citations above, the Big Head figure was deemed to be a kind of puppet, yet from the historical evidence, it would appear that the Baolao was in fact a man with a large false 'head'. The connection between puppet and Big Head is a controversial one. Huang Weiruo, a teacher at the Central Academy of Drama in Beijing, believes that the Baolao, or Big Head figure is possibly a kind of puppet termed *rou kuilei* (flesh puppet) in documents of the southern Song,[55] a category about which there has been much discussion among scholars.[56] The Big Head performer is certainly seen to be at least *like* a puppet – he performs in the performance area designated to the puppets and he even performed *with* the puppet Baldy Guo.

The Baolao type of Big Head dance is often performed today during the great Duanwu festival – the Dragon Boat festival on the fifth day of the fifth lunar month. At this festival, evil demons, pestilences and harmful things are rounded up and sent off to sea on paper boats which are then burned. The Big Heads which take part in the celebrative processions are known as *da wawatou* (big baby heads), for the masks look like the oversized heads of young children, placed over the

---

[51] *Yongle dadian xiwen sanzhong* [no date]: 54 and Dolby 1976: 27–33.
[52] *Dongjing menghualu* 1982, ch. 1.   [53] Ibid., ch. 2.
[54] *Xihu laoren fansheng lu.*
[55] Huang Weiruo, in an unpublished work on the history of *kuilei.*
[56] Sun Kaidi 1952. Sun believes *rou kuilei* was the term given to the performance of children on adults' shoulders.

head of an adult. In some areas of China the dragon boat festival is known as the *wawajie* (baby festival) from another exorcist event which uses the Big Head in an annual ritual cleansing of all children in the village for the sake of their protection from evil spirits.

The Big Head performer is also present in various types of *nuo* theatre[57] – whether directly in the form of *Baolao* as in the Guichi *nuo*, or indirectly in the form of the *heshang* (laughing monk) – the figure who closes the *nuo* event with a laughing, cleansing, sweeping ritual (see Plate 21).[58] The monk in the *nuo* has a shaved head, huge smile and sometimes a spotty face – echoes of Baldy Guo?[59]

The terms Baolao, or Baoluo for Big Head, as corruptions of Pusa (meaning Buddha) may, however, not be a result of a purely linguistic change dictated by geographical differences in dialect. One written form of the character *bao* means the abalone, a shellfish with a flat, snail-like shell lined with mother of pearl known for its ear-shape. *Lao* means 'old man', a term of respect often used in titles of gods' names.

The alternative written form of *baoluo* has a different character for *bao*, meaning 'carry'. The second character *luo* means 'gong' – hence the mistranslation of the term as 'one who carries the gong'. However, both terms Baolao and Baoluo seem to imply a sense of something large, round and shiny – the abalone shell, the gong. This suggests one aspect of the mask/head covering was a round, metal plate, perhaps related to the mask of the Fangxiangshi with his 'four gold eyes'. 'When in 1053 the Chinese general Di Qing went to fight Nong Zhigao, the Thai, he wore a copper mask probably in order to appear himself as a deity.'[60] The concept of (ancestral/exorcist) deity represented by a metal disc as face is perhaps also echoed in the Dejiang *nuo* where the main instrument to replicate the Luo matrix in a pattern of 3-2-1 is the large gong (the dominant instrument of *nuo* as opposed to the drum as is often supposed).

---

[57] See, for example, an illustration of one such Big Head from Anhui *nuo* in Zhu Jianming 1993: 213.

[58] Riley 1990: 11–17.

[59] Van der Loon associates the history of the laughing monk (*xiaomian*) with New Year's festivals and a similar figure in Japanese theatre, the dance of the *okina*. Van der Loon 1977: 157.

[60] Eberhard 1968: 330.

Plate 21   Four *nuo* masks – *heshang* (the Laughing Monk)

The dance of the Baolao in Guichi's *nuo* event takes up the idea of metal disc as god or spirit face in a dance known as the Baolao 'coin' dance. Two performers, both wearing Big Head masks of children's faces, carry a large Taiping coin in each hand. During the dance, the performers mask and unmask their 'faces' with these coins. The coins are made to look as if they were made of bronze, i.e. they are red-gold in colour and shiny. Each coin is engraved with a short phrase such as, 'May there be favourable weather for the crops, may the land be prosperous and the people be at peace.' The dancers perform to the percussion of the gong (*luo*) and another performer recites a long eulogy. The performance sets up associations between the round coins ('fortune'), the gong and the Big Head, which seem to suggest a metal (bronze) 'face' as the unifying force – in other words: the exorcist (see chapters two and five for the exorcist signification of the colour yellow, and the metals gold and bronze).

The *jingju* is not without its own laughing monk figures such as Lu Zhishen, for example, or the monk in the *kunqu* piece *Xiashan* (*Descending the Mountain*). In both pieces, the monk merrily leaves the temple for a worldly life – a metaphor for the descent of all non-mortal beings (gods) to the earth. The humorous monk is a laughing, cleansing, unifying monk.[61]

The unifying, creative power – the power of the performer, derives from a body which has been severed and reassembled to embody sets of oppositions in harmony. In the first model examined in this chapter, the performer places himself in the central spatial position in order to unify or mediate two different cosmological systems – heaven and earth. Fractally, the performer's own body also embodies the unifying principle through the congruence of his corporeal centre (the regenerative loins) with the central power of the Luo matrix of creation. In the second model examined in this chapter, the power of unification is represented by the dichotomy of extremes grotesque and funny, represented by the gaping mouth. Here, the body is reconstructed as (god)head. The reconstruction of the body as head also changes the material of head to manipulate the exorcist power of the metals gold and bronze. The

[61] Kagan 1978.

Plate 22   Bronze Taotie exorcist mask from the tomb entrance

god(head) is made of rare and exorcist (Yang) materials and provided with an ugly–funny appearance and gaping (laughing–consuming) mouth as the locus of the regenerative principle (see Plate 22).

The reconstructed performing body literally (corporeally) holds together different worlds – in the case of Yang Yuhuan, the dichotomy of Yin and Yang, in the case of the *nuo* performer, the balance of heaven and earth, in the case of the marionettes and Big Head, the grotesque and the funny. In more abstract terms, the reconstructed performing body also contains different times and different spaces – he embodies all times (all ancestors) and all spaces (heaven and earth). The unified (articulated) body is able, in its turn, to unify, to equalise, harmonise and control the cosmos – put the world back to rights.

8

Yuan
(Round)

Yang Yuhuan (sings):
The wheel of ice starts to rise over the island in the sea,
See the Jade Hare, Jade Hare faces east and leaps,
The wheel of ice departs from the island in the sea,
Heaven and Earth shine brightly,
Bright moon in mid-air,
Like Chang E leaving the Moon Palace,
Like Chang E leaving the Moon Palace.

Yang Yuhuan is like the moon rising in the sky towards its zenith – the rendezvous with the emperor. But he does not come and she returns to her palace, 'There's nothing else to do but return to the solitude of the cold and lonely palace.' The moon rises only to sink again, in a cyclical pattern of waxing and waning, in a pattern of eternal recreation.

The cyclical path of Yang Yuhuan as moon can be divided into four separate sequences.

1   Before the concubine enters the stage, Mei Lanfang sings from off, 'bai jia!' which means, 'The court is moving!', 'Let the retinue set out!', or 'Off we go!' The phrase not only introduces the role about to come on stage, it also indicates the movement of the body of the court, led by Yang Yuhuan. After the introductory sequence, the eunuchs declare it is time to move to the Pavilion of a Hundred Flowers and call again, 'bai jia!'

2   The concubine rises from her seat, echoes the 'bai jia!' and the eight handmaidens and two eunuchs make one whole circuit of the stage (*pao yuanchang*) while Yang Yuhuan walks three steps forward to indicate her journey, and arrives at the Jade Stone bridge.

3   There follows the arrival at the Pavilion of a Hundred Flowers and the drinking scenes.

4   At the end of the play, when Yang Yuhuan is quite drunk and realises that the emperor certainly will not come, she sings for the last time, 'bai jia!' and the retinue gather around her and escort her back to her palace. The wheel has come full circle.

Yang Yuhuan's circuitous journey can also be interpreted through the Luo diagram. She leaves the Palace of Great Cold, comparing herself to Chang E, who lived in the palace of that name and who travelled the *jiuzhong* (nine celestial divisions of heaven). The Palace of Great Cold signifies the north, the dark, cold Yin principle. She is travelling towards the Pavilion of a Hundred Flowers in the centre, where the emperor, who *is* the centre will be waiting:

> Yang Yuhuan (*sings*):
> Like Chang E travelling the nine celestial spheres of heaven,
> The clear cold falls on the Palace of Great Cold, ah, Palace of
>   Great Cold.

However, the emperor has vacated his position, and gone to the Western Palace. Yang Yuhuan leaves the north, the winter and the cold, the trigram *kan* associated with 'pit', or 'hole' on her way to the centre. But the centre is empty, the emperor is in the west – the position of the setting sun, the trigram *dui* associated with 'lake' and 'pleasure'. Yang Yuhuan comes from depths and darkness, but the emperor has chosen sun, and pleasure. Moreover, the (eastern) spring flower imagery that is linked to Yang Yuhuan contrasts with the choice of the emperor for a (western) 'setting' sun, a more mature woman. The empty centre unbalances the harmony of things, things are not right with the world. Yang Yuhuan is forced to return to her cold, northern palace once more.

In the dance of the nine stations in the *nuo* theatre, the performer makes a circuitous journey which links opposite pairs in the nine stations diagram. In doing so, he harmonises the cosmos and pulls everything into balance, exorcising sickness and demons. Yang Yuhuan's journey is based on the same intent. In the opening aria, she sings 'Heaven and Earth shine brightly', but the words she uses for heaven and earth are the trigram names for these worlds, *qian* and *kun*. Thus she is relating her journey to the cosmic one of Chang E, where the sun and moon meet on the fifteenth of every month. Her goal could be compared to the hand sign *jue* named *riyue ergong*, the two palaces of the sun and moon, discussed in chapter four, which opens up the heavenly gates to let the light shine out (call the heavenly emperor's presence to her). The journey is one from two extreme oppositional units towards connubial union (invocation – the mutual intercourse of two worlds, heaven and earth).[1] However, the journey she makes cannot succeed if the emperor has vacated the centre, she must return to her position, nothing has changed, she is condemned to suffer loneliness and neglect in an unbalanced, inharmonious situation.

In her search for union, Yang Yuhuan passes through many different bodily states, or shapes. The play shows her shifting from shape to shape in a metamorphic process of constant *regeneration*. Yang Yuhuan begins as the moon, then becomes a flower, and then the geese. Her next transformation is during the intoxicated sequence where she spins into the *woyu* (coiling fish – fish out of water?) pose. Yang Yuhuan is like the wriggling fish struggling for breath and she is spinning for the earth that spins for her.

This is followed by the last shape when she plays a man. First, she takes the part of the eunuch, dressing as him by taking his hat. Then she signifies that he should go and fetch the emperor by miming the characteristics of the emperor. She points to the Western Palace (where the emperor has gone), she indicates a long beard (of the emperor), she brings the index finger of each hand together (signifying the coming together of man and woman), and finally she points to the seat of honour (where the emperor ought to sit). The eunuch misreads the signs:

> Gao (speaks):
> Ah, you want me to call some more people to move the table
> and chair to that hillside to drink wine, is that it?

Yang Yuhuan is transformed from lunar sphere to flower (like a mythological goddess descending to the mortal world), to geese, to fish

---

[1] Desired sexual intercourse between the shaman and the invoked deity is also implied throughout the ancient cycle of shaman songs, *Jiu ge.*

(struggling for breath), to eunuch, to emperor, to a producer of signs that are misunderstood. Powerless, *role-less*, she returns to her original starting point – void, emptiness, lack of signification.

> Yang Yuhuan (*sings*):
> All that is left is icy cold and clear, the desolate one returns to the palace!

The proxemics of Yang Yuhuan's movements on stage support the concept of circuitous journey. If they are mapped on the stage floor, a cyclical, whorling pattern emerges (see Diagram 61). The first line of the opening aria – 'The wheel of ice starts to rise over the island in the sea', is sung as she turns a complete circle on the spot to the left (1). During the second line, 'See the Jade Hare, Jade Hare faces east and leaps', she makes two full circles, one to the right (2), and one to the left (3). In the third line, 'The wheel of ice departs from the island in the sea', she stands downstage and gestures looking at the moon (Diagram 60). This *zaoxing* pose is a half curtsey with the fan held open in the right hand which is raised above the head. The left arm gestures parallel to it. The pattern of the body corporeally reproduces the Yin/Yang diagram (4). The fourth line, 'Heaven and Earth shine brightly', is the reverse pose (5).[2] The fifth line, 'Bright moon in mid-air', opens the *zaoxing* pose into a half curtsey with both arms raised in a curved shape over the head in a complete circle (Diagram 59). The fingers make the *bazi* (number eight) pose – stretched like the Chinese character for the number eight – to indicate the roundness of the moon (6).[3] The last two lines of the aria, 'Like Chang E leaving the Moon Palace, like Chang E leaving the Moon Palace' are sung to two more complete turns (7) and (8), after which Yang Yuhuan turns to face the table and chair centre stage to address the eunuchs (9), 'She has arrived.' This is her first truly static position. The entrance movements of Yang Yuhuan, when charted on the floor, reproduce the curling movement of a cloud, or incense smoke, of increasing density. From one whorl at the beginning, upstage left, the cloud patterns increase in size and expand on a diagonal path to the full circles presented downstage centre, before Yang Yuhuan turns to sit centre stage (Diagram 61). The descent of immortals to the earth on

[2] Wan Fengmei 1982: 15.   [3] Ibid.: 16.

Yuan *(Round)*

Diagram 59 *baoyueshi* (holding up the moon)

Diagram 60 *tuoyueshi* (embracing the moon)

Enter

Exit

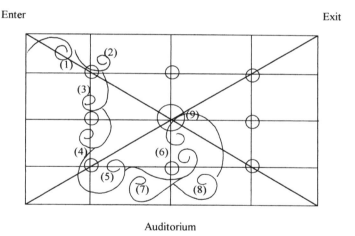

Auditorium

Diagram 61   Yang Yuhuan's entrance sequence

clouds or bursts of incense smoke has been discussed in chapter four, though a *jingju* performer would simply declare the movement aesthetically pleasing.

The whole company moves off towards the Pavilion of a Hundred Flowers *pao yuanchang* (running round the stage once to indicate

287

the passage of time or space). But Yang Yuhuan is not a part of this company. She takes three slow steps on the spot so that the first handmaids to complete the circle 'catch her up'. Yang Yuhuan does not move forward. She remains in the same position before the journey and after it, so that the technical device by which space is presented on the Chinese stage, *pao yuanchang* (running the circle), defeats Yang Yuhuan. Her desire to move, to meet, to join, is frustrated by her own proxemics, which move in continuous never-ending circles as in her entrance sequence, or remain static (on the way to meet the emperor).

The journey across the Jade Stone bridge, the first state of intoxication, is presented by constant turning. The concubine spins to show that the earth spins for her. Yang Yuhuan spins when she sees the ducks, she spins back and forth when she sees the fish, she spins again in larger circles as her eyes follow the geese represented by the fan in her hand. The scene literally makes her dizzy or intoxicated.

On her second entrance, after removing her outer gown, she has another set of three low body spins, *man fanshen*, as she admires the flowers put out for her by the eunuchs. This intoxication scene echoes her first. Drunkenness is equated with the spinning world. The impression of dizziness during the final drinking scene increases when she makes a mid-level body turn with the cup in her mouth three times (once to stage right, once to stage left and once to the centre).

While the intoxicated sequences are marked by Yang Yuhuan's body spins and circling movements, the static phases of the play are marked by the changing position of the table and chairs on the stage. It is well known that *jingju* depends upon no set, but uses a table and chairs to represent any item (such as mountain, bridge, bed, etc.) that is required. But it is less well known that the position of the table and chairs on the stage also builds a language itself. The initiated spectator can interpret much of the play by interpreting the relationships between the positions of the table and chairs and the figures who use them.

After the entrance sequence, Yang Yuhuan sits in front of the table to ask the eunuchs if the banquet is ready. The table is placed centre stage, and the chair in front of it. The stage is divided exactly in half and the downstage area of the stage is known as the *waichang* (outer stage). When the chair is placed in this area, the constellation is known as *xiaozuo* (minor seating position). It is used for any role as a resting

Yuan *(Round)*

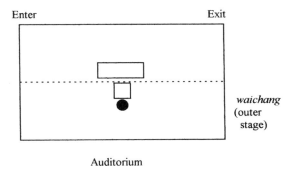

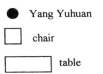

Diagram 62   *xiaozuo* (exterior setting)

place from which to sing the introductory aria, and generally indicates an exterior setting (Diagram 62).

The same position, *xiaozuo*, is used when she arrives at the Pavilion of a Hundred Flowers, in expectation of the emperor's arrival. On learning that he has gone to another concubine, Yang Yuhuan orders the eunuchs and handmaids to bring her wine. The chair is now set behind the table, and Yang sits there to drink her first cups. This position is known as *dazuo* (major seating position). The chair is placed in the upstage position known as *neichang* (inner stage), indicating an interior (Diagram 63). This position also represents the position of command – Yang Yuhuan seeks to take over the central role herself since the emperor has neglected her.

A third phase is reflected in the final constellation of table and chairs after her second entrance, having changed her robes. Now the two chairs are placed to each side of the table in a position known as *bazikuayi* (figure of eight chairs at the side).[4] This is the standard arrangement of table and chairs for a celebration or banquet event

[4] The Chinese figure of eight is formed of two strokes / \ .

Enter   Exit

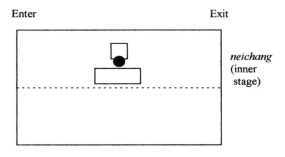

neichang
(inner
  stage)

Auditorium

Diagram 63   *dazuo* (interior setting)

Enter   Exit

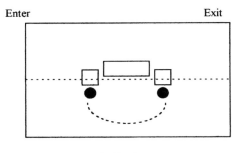

Auditorium

Diagram 64   *bazikuayi* (banquet setting)

(Diagram 64). Yang Yuhuan would usually take up the position at stage left and the emperor the chair at stage right. However, the emperor does not come. During the drinking sequence that follows until the end of the play, Yang Yuhuan wavers between both chairs. She sits on one, then the other, back and forth at least six times before she is finally so drunk she falls to her knees.

Thus the play alternates between the phases of intoxication (spinning) and static moments (based around the positions of the table and chair) which reflect Yang Yuhuan's attempt to occupy control of the centre and her defeat. Yang Yuhuan spins in circles, yet she is also obliged to occupy the place determined by the position of the table centre stage. She moves only to return to the starting position.

This aspect is taken up in the final section of the play and repro-

Enter   Exit

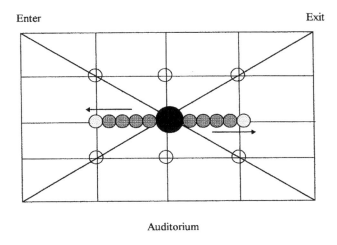

Auditorium

 Yang Yuhuan

Handmaid

Eunuch

Diagram 65   Yang Yuhuan wavers at the centre

duced in one sequence. The eunuchs, desperate to encourage her to stop drinking and return to the palace, announce that the emperor is coming after all. Yang Yuhuan rises, and is supported by two hand-maids, who in turn are supported on each side by two more, until Yang Yuhuan is at the centre of a 'chorus' line of handmaids and the two eunuchs. She lurches to one side, then the other, then back again several times, before falling, with the whole line, onto her knees to greet the emperor she thinks is coming. From this position, she wavers between leaning stage left and leaning stage right and this is echoed along the line, before the whole line collapses with her when she hears that the eunuchs have tricked her after all (Diagram 65). The line of handmaids with Yang Yuhuan at the centre make an unusual constella-tion on the *jingju* stage, where such blocking is usually rounded into a semi-circle. However, it presents the idea that Yang Yuhuan is seeking to restore harmony by placing herself at the centre of a line which phys-ically links the eastern and western positions. Yang Yuhuan believes

291

the emperor will come. But Yang Yuhuan is only a concubine, not an empress as her costume implies. She does not have the power to take over the central position and change the course of events. Her play is ended (until it is played again).

The moving centre

In the *jingju* performance, the performer adopts the unifying, central position in space and time to create the theatrical (fictive) world. Yang Yuhuan tries to manipulate the constellation in the fictive world so that she is the centre, so that she takes control, but she is defeated. The role is displaced, dismissed by the actor even while still on stage (see chapter four), returned to the dressing room to be 'hung up' until the next performance, like the marionette bodies and heads at the side of the stage in marionette theatre.

In the *nuo* theatre, the Fashi must adopt the central position in order to reconstruct the worlds of heaven and earth as one and manipulate and control (recreate) them so that disease, death or demons are expelled. The model of Yang Yuhuan has shown how important control of the *central* position is in controlling the theatre world, but what value does the central station hold for the *nuo* performer?

The *nuo* sequence *cai jiuzhou* (stamping out the nine provinces) depends upon a topographical reproduction of each province to be stamped on, or designated. The performer stamps and hops between sections in a prescribed order, singing them and reproducing their names with certain hand signs. The nine provinces marked by the performer represent the geographical division of China into nine 'provinces' or areas by the mythological figure Yu the Great who divided the waters of the great flood and marked land from water in an act of original creation. According to the *Shiji*, these were Ruo, Hei, He, Yang, Jiang, Yan, Huai, Wei and Luo.[5] Other sources identify the nine provinces as Ji, Yu, Xu, Jing, Yong, Yan, Qing, Yang and Liang.[6] However the land was divided, the central cell of the nine provinces represented the central, imperial power. The division of the (known) world (China) into nine areas or provinces is repeated fractally in the division of all private lands into units (fields) based on the nine-cell

[5] *Cihai* 1979: 143. [6] Mathews 1979: 171.

Diagram 66   The character for *jing*   Diagram 67   The structure of a well
(well)

system,[7] which themselves are further divided into nine by the *jingtian*
well-field irrigation system. The character for well, *jing*, represents the
nine cells of the Luo diagram (Diagram 66). After the pit has been dug, a
structure is made of several layers of four beams laid over one another
to form a square. The pattern of the beams, which overlap at each
corner, repeats the pattern of the Luo diagram (Diagram 67). The structure is then lowered into the bottom of the well to fortify the walls, and
contain the source water.[8] Here, water, the very source of life, springs
from the centre of an architectural structure which replicates the Luo
diagram. The well can also be described as a square beamed structure
within a circle dug from the earth (it brings the two worlds of heaven
and earth together). Not only is the system of nine used to define the
known world above ground, the Luo diagram is also used underground.
The same Luo structure is used in the tomb to fortify the walls around
the central pit where the coffin is placed. The source water, and the
body of the deceased, are placed in the central position of the Luo diagram: the unifying, controlling, regenerative force.

In the heavens, the system of nine is applied to the nine palaces
(*jiugong*), a term which refers to the creation myth associated with Tai
Yi or The Great Unity. This god is often represented as the Pole Star,
the axis of the universe, which remains constant while the whole
constellation *Ursa Major* (the dipper) moves through the cycle of eight
different (compass) orientations. Tai Yi represents the Original One,
whence flowed the Two (Yin and Yang) whence came the Myriad

---

[7] The character for field can be written with three rows of three cells, see
Gao Mingbian 1980.
[8] Berglund 1990: 71–2.

Things. Tai Yi is represented as an original creator in a similar way to Yu the Great. Tai Yi held his world together (created and kept it) by making a journey to palaces in each of the eight outlying areas, returning each time to the centre, reaffirming his position as the centre. In this model of the cycle of life, the ladle or scoop of the stellar pattern fills and empties like the paddles on a water wheel. Movement is self-perpetuating, creates itself infinitely around the central (fixed) axis.

On the surface of the earth, between the heavens and the earth, stands man, whose body is also dissected into the nine values of the Luo diagram. The human body occupies the central position of a three or four dimensional cosmos, the human body is the unifying, controlling, creating force.

The two creation myths concerning Yu the Great and Tai Yi equate the creation of the world (China) with the movement of a body. The body moves from one station to the next in a simultaneous mapping (defining), linking (unifying) gesture. In performance, the human body 'touches' different cells of different planes of meaning (earthly, heavenly, that of the underworld). The journey is circuitous, cyclical, for the traveller returns to the point of departure, or refers back to the centre between stations, marking the axis of the movement.[9]

> The idea that a ritual journey, usually a ritual circuit, could be a means of acquiring or affirming power proved an extraordinarily persistent one, recurring in different forms of art, literature, even in political theory. Along with it, there developed the idea of a synthetical, mandala-like cosmos whose various parts were presided over by various powers. These powers could be induced to give either their submission or their support to the traveller who approached them with the correct ritual. A complete circuit of the cosmos would make him lord of the universe, able to command any of its powers at will.[10]

Movement on and in the Luo diagram presents the possibility of a cyclical sequence that constantly repeats itself, the moment of completion

[9] Compare Puck in Shakespeare's *A Midsummer Night's Dream*: 'I'll put a girdle round about the earth', Act 2, Scene I, line 175.
[10] Hawkes 1985: 47.

is the moment of the new beginning. The act of creation is repeated as an act of exorcism, reforming the chaos of sickness, death, or drought into a new, whole, order. The exorcism is an act of recreation, and by analogy, each role created by the actor in the theatre world is an act of recreation in the real world.

Theatrum mundi

The term used in *jingju* to describe the principle of circuit, or round-ness, is *yuan*. Everything that the performer does *must* be rounded. No *jingju* performer would think of perceiving his body, or the stage arena as directly related to the Luo diagram, but they are. A performer may have no knowledge of the Luo diagram, though he may be aware of the trigrams through their use in fortune-telling, just as any Chinese cit-izen. However, the body is dissected into expressive units: the four arts, *chang* (singing), *nian* (recitation), *da* (movement) and *zuo* (acting) – and the five skills *shou* (hand), *yan* (eye), *zhi* (finger), *fa* (method), *bu* (step). Both are systems of four (united in the one body, five); and both systems together in the one body also make nine. The stage space of *jingju* is divided into the nine cells of the Luo diagram as the best points on the stage at which to pause and hold a *liangxiang* pose (presence).

The *jingju* performer mostly enters upstage left. He moves be-tween the nine points on the stage, circling them, circumscribing them and then suddenly arrives at one, and makes a pose. The sequence of movements may last five, ten or twenty minutes and his presence on stage may develop into a situation of speech without movement. But it is concluded by the performer's exit which is mostly from upstage right, indicating that the performer's movements on stage are a *passage* through the time/space box called stage. The diagrams below illustrate three typical movement sequences over the stage of nine cells. The first represents the broad scheme of movements executed by *qingyi* Yang Yuhuan in the whole play. The second maps the first few *liang-xiang* points typical of the *zoubian* entrance movement of the *wudan* (female martial role). The third represents the same moments of a *qiba* entrance movement of the (*hualian*) painted face.

Yang Yuhuan, principally a *qingyi* (singing role) with some ele-ments of the *daomadan* (light martial role) moves sedately between moments of stasis and circularity. The proxemics of Yang Yuhuan on

Enter   Exit

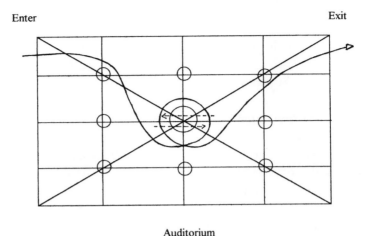

Auditorium

Diagram 68   Yang Yuhuan's movement sequence

stage corporeally reproduce the *content* of the role. Yang Yuhuan is elected to the centre, called to the emperor, only to be ousted from it by him. The loop of circularity stretches off stage from the moment of her exit to the moment of her re-entry the next time the role is played.

The term *zoubian* literally means 'walking by the side'. The movement is used by martial roles (*wusheng, wuchou* and *wudan*) to demonstrate speed, lightness of foot and stealth. It is frequently used for a night-time sequence where the performer indicates the preparation for a secret or surprise attack. The cautious stealth of the movement is captured by the strict avoidance of, and sudden contact with, the nine points of *liangxiang* pose (Diagram 69).

The term *qiba* literally means 'the overlord rises up'. The *qiba* is used by the painted face to demonstrate his strength and power. Instead of circumventing the nine points in a fluid, circling movement, the *hualian* moves like a chess piece along the main diagonal line. Rather than using curves to unify oppositional values, the painted face travels in straight lines intersecting the nine points to actively sever (hold apart) the stage space (Diagram 70). This increases the impression of force, of determination, and power.

Passage from one state to another in a flow of movement is, as demonstrated in chapter seven, an act of creation. The *jingju* performer recreates himself in the fictitious world of the theatre, the *theatrum*

296

Yuan *(Round)*

Enter   Exit

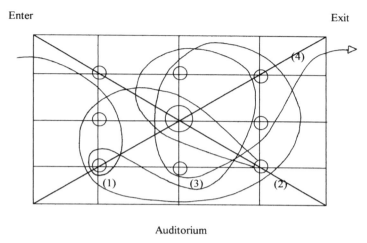

Auditorium

Diagram 69   *zoubian* (female martial role entrance sequence)

Enter   Exit

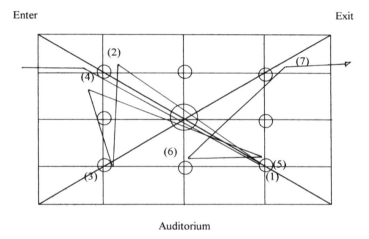

Auditorium

Diagram 70   *qiba* (painted face role entrance sequence)

mundi, by placing his body and the stage space into congruence with the Luo matrix.

All the positions of the performer's body, both in a *liangxiang* pose and in the connective moments in between, his arms, hands, legs, tilt of the head, tilt of the waist, bend to the principle of *roundness*. The performer literally *embodies* opposites values in order to unify and recreate harmony. Each pose to the left is countered by one to the right, each movement forwards by another backwards. The *jingju* performer seldom moves in a straight line between stations and this is explained by the *jingju* masters as the need to exploit the aesthetic value of opposition. According to this principle the performer, when intending to move to the right, will first move or gesture to the left. The performer thus makes a negative (left) movement before the positive one (to the right). The completed movement or gesture consists of a whole movement which actually connects opposing directions. This, say the performers, has the direct benefit of catching the full attention of the spectator to the desired movement. For, the spectator first perceives the forewarning (shadow) of the movement to come and can follow the movement from its very beginning to completion.

In one sense, this means that the performer actually *shows* the spectator what he is about to do as well as doing it – as well as narrating it, as in chapter four. It also means that nearly every action on the *jingju* stage shows a rounded movement embracing the negative or shadow and the positive. The arms physically *re*present roundness (the image of harmony, equality, balance) by sweeping the full half circle from left to right in order to gesture to the right, for example (rather than merely pointing directly – in a straight line – to the right). The principle of the rounded body also reflects the concern of the *jingju* performer to hold presence, or *qi*. The performer is a vessel 'holding' oppositional forces through which presence, *qi* is articulated. The performer moves on the stage in a process which constantly empties and replenishes the source of life, *qi*.

In terms of the Luo diagram, the *jingju* performer is a mediator (*Grenzgänger*) between opposites, an equaliser, a bringer of harmony. This is certainly a viewpoint held by *jingju* performers themselves, although it is perceived in the sense of achieving aesthetic harmony – something that is rounded and complete is far more pleasing to the observer than something rough edged and incomplete. The *jingju* performer strives to achieve *mei* (beauty) through the aesthetic of roundedness.

The *jingju* performer, using his body like the *nuo* performer, manipulates the central, creative, or axial position. The character *zhong* (for 'China', for example, the Middle Kingdom) is a square box (the earth) with one vertical stroke cutting through it as axis (Diagram 71).

Yuan *(Round)*

Diagram 71   The character *zhong* (the centre)

The human body stands in this position on stage, he is the physical mean between movements to the left and right to the front and to the back. Not only is the stage floor the arena for a ritual journey by the performing body as it creates itself in the theatre world. The stage space is also conceived and touched by the performer in its third dimension. The same system of nine points is projected into space around the performing body so that while his feet make a ritual journey of points or stations on the floor, the other limbs (hands, finger, arms, head, legs, trunk) make a similar journey around the stations in space. The *jingju* performer, like the *nuo* performer in Diagram 47, stands between planes of meaning. While the *nuo* performer physically links the three worlds of earth, man and heaven, the *jingju* performer stands between the real (earthly) world and theatrical (role) world.

Each role may move around the Luo matrix and its centre differently. Yang Yuhuan merely circles it, never accessing the central cell. Others, like the *hualian*, dissect the matrix with their movements and others, like the *wudan*, circumscribe it. In simple terms, for example, a victorious warrior stands at the centre; a defeated one stands at the edge. Thus, the performer and his manipulation of the body space around him in *jingju* is directly related to the articulation of presence in, on and over the nine point matrix – to the creation of the *theatrum mundi*.

The movement *yunshou* (cloud-hands, Diagram 72) used between movements as the means of *guocheng* (passage between states) is one of the most basic elements of *jingju* performance. A close analysis of this movement demonstrates the awareness and manipulation of three dimensional space by the performer. The cloud-hand movement touches every plane of meaning (fractally in flux), because it flows as it passes from plane to plane, embracing the space towards the body

299

Diagram 72   The female role *yunshou* (cloud-hand movement)

which stands as axis. (1) The arms begin in a parallel position at the side of the body. (2) They then pass to the front of the body and cross. (3) One arm moves over the head, the other arm extends from the front of the body to the side. (4) Both arms sweep a half circle from one side of the body to the other. (5) One arm remains still, the other sweeps a half circle from one side of the body to the other. (6) Both arms extend slightly forward of the body. (7) The extended palm flicks inwards as the eyes and head jolt to the front in a *liangxiang* pose.

The *yunshou* movement is used by all role categories. Each role category has its own interpretation of the basic moves, so that a female role keeps the arms closer to the body, never fully extending them, while the male role may open the movement more away from the body. But the movement always begins with the arms of the performer in a position which describes the form of the Yin/Yang diagram (1). It concentrates these two opposing planes into the centre of the body (2), unifies the centre with the outlying space by transversing all planes of a globe which take the body as centre (3, 4, 5), and reaffirms the whole human body as axis to the surrounding space, as director of it (6).

The performer need not remain still when performing the *yunshou* movement. Indeed this is seldom the case in performance. The *yunshou* accompanies the movement of the legs and feet across the floor. The cloud hand, the travelling hand (of the gods) can be described as a kind of propeller which moves the body. It is not the feet which are perceived to be moving the body from position A to position B, but the flow of the arm movements. The feet simply follow. The *yunshou* is extremely difficult to execute in a way that satisfies the master. It demands precise *cognisance* of the size (which must remain constant) and position of the globe described by the arms in relation to the rest of the body, and awareness of the centre of the body as axis to a movement. It demands interpretative *feeling* for rhythm and tempo, both in its flow of movement (articulation of changes, presences) and the concluding *liangxiang* (radiating one presence – constancy), for the movement is learnt in seven phases, but can be condensed to three beats of the drum, 'ba, da, cang'[11] (one beat of the left stick, one beat of the right, and then a beat of the large cymbal). In condensing the *yunshou*, certain elements are given more emphasis, others less. The *yunshou* may be used as the prelude to a *liangxiang* pose, or it may simply function as passage to another movement. In each case, and according to the role category using it, the *yunshou* is as elastic (Zhang's 'monkey sinews') as each performer wants it to be. The performer defines and controls the space around him by performing it in his own way.

---

[11] Each beat of each percussive instrument is given a phonetic name. For example, 'ba' always means the left stick beating the drum, 'da' the right, and so on. The students memorise the percussion patterns according to this phonetic system, and say they are *nian* 'reading aloud' the percussion. See Wu Chunli 1983 and *Zenmo da luogu* 1982.

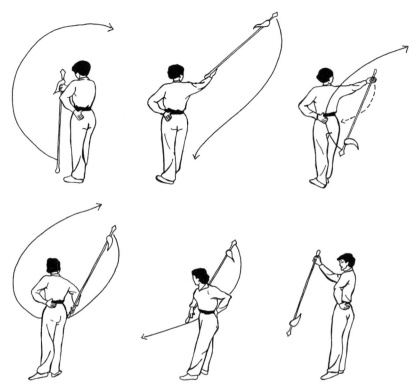

Diagram 73   *yehua* (challenging spin)

The principle of roundness dominates all movements on the Chinese stage. In the play *Changbanpo* (*The Battle of Changban Hill*), for example, Li Huiliang (the Zhong Kui actor described in chapter two) plays the role of the military hero Zhao Yun and exploits his skills with the single lance to demonstrate axial centrality and presage the role's inevitable victory. The lance serves to extend the line made by the arm, so that the tip of the weapon paints the space in arcs around him. Li Huiliang literally cuts the space around his body (several Chinese terms such as *pan* and *duan* meaning 'to distinguish', 'to determine' bear a cutting knife or axe radical. The act of cutting is one of demarcation, definition).

In a demonstration of power, Li Huiliang executes a movement known as *yehua* (challenging spin, Diagram 73). The lance is held at

Diagram 74   *beigon ghua* (back bow spin)

seven-eighths along the staff and rotated in front of the body and
behind the body in a continuous, flowing movement. The lance paints
a double wheel either side of the performer's body where the pivot
of the wheels are the point made by the extended arm, i.e. outside the
centre of the body. The movement places the performer's body at the
rim of the two wheels. The two wheels are painted by the lance in a
continual forward S shaped movement, as if they were rolling forward.
Because the body is placed on the rim of these it seems as if the performer is also moving, rolling forwards in a threatening way. The four
banners attached to his back shudder as the movement ends one cycle
and begins the next (between movements 5 and 6) in an almost animal-
istic, threatening way, like a bird ruffling its tail feathers, or a rattle-
snake preparing to strike.

The challenging spin is followed by another demonstration of
axial power – this time, one which exploits the horizontal plane around
the actor, known as *beigong hua* (back bow spin, Diagram 74). Li Huiliang makes the lance spin over the shoulder blades and back banners

Diagram 75   *tai niezi* (loose tuck somersault from a platform)

in a shape like a bow from which to shoot arrows. In doing so, he makes
his back the central pivot of power. The back is a significant expressive
unit of the *jingju* body. Many movements (including some entrances,
such as the *qiba*) are performed with the back towards the audience.
There is a repertoire of movements for expressing through the back, as
for example, the flag shudder, when the four flags shiver while the rest
of the body remains static to indicate strength. The power of the back is
a shadow or negative of the power of the front part of the body – a pre-
vision of the real fighting power (the positive or opposite side) which is
the more fearful for having to be reconstructed in the *imagination* of
the spectator. Li Huiliang finishes this movement by tossing the lance
up into the air in a spin in front of him and catching it again behind his
back. He seems to have eyes in his back, like a god.

At the climax to the play, the hero Zhao Yun tries to persuade
the wounded empress to take his horse and escape the enemy territory.
She, however, tricks him and leaves her child in his care as she jumps
into a nearby well, killing herself. The well is represented by a table
with a cloth over it. Li Huiliang leaps onto the rim of the well as he
sings his distress and just catches the neck of her coat before making a
sideways somersault from the well to the floor in a movement fully
expressing his horror as he realises he has failed her, and stands, by the
well, holding the lifeless robe. The loose tuck side somersault from
the table top or *tai niezi* is a leap which requires immense lightness of
the foot (*nie* means to tiptoe, be light-footed, Diagram 75). It contrasts

with the tightly bound strength of a tucked somersault, where the energy of the tumble carries over to the landing. Here, the performer lands in an open, almost unfinished pose, before making a *liangxiang* as he gazes at the lifeless robe. The sideways tumble, a recoil of shock, is nonetheless so perfectly executed (pulling the energy back out of the landing to make it silent) that the spectator knows that Zhao Yun will take the imperial child after all and rescue the imperial house. These movements and many others that make up the role of Zhao Yun convince the spectator that the hero is truly in command of the total stage space and will inevitably conquer the enemy by the end of the play.

After Zhao Yun's various battles, Li Huiliang leaves the stage for a quick change and returns as the role of the God of War, Guan Yu. Zhao Yun is a *zunlian* (plain face) *wusheng* (military male) role, but Guan Yu is a *hualian* (painted face) military/deity role. The quick change is effected by smearing the face with red and painting the features in black over the top of the old make-up. Jin Zongnai a former *wusheng* delighted in recounting the tale of an actor who, as he played the role of Zhao Yun, drank more and more spirits in the wings so that by the time he should play Guan Yu, his face was naturally red, and he needed only paint in the features. Li Huiliang's change from mortal Zhao Yun to the dragon war god Guan Yu, however, is marked by the entrance of the *matong* (horse groom) as detailed in chapter seven. The movements of the *matong* contrast greatly to the strong, powerful displays of Zhao Yun and Guan Yu, and consist of lengthy tumbling, leaping, acrobatic sequences.

Though the *matong* provides the context of deity and exorcist which preface the entry of Guan Yu, his own movements also demarcate and fill the total stage space. One element of such a sequence, a movement known as *feijiao xuanzi* (flying feet and rotation leap or camel spin, Diagram 76) shows how the *matong* rotates his body in different planes in the air, in contrast to the grounded, axial movements of Zhao Yun/Guan Yu.

The same control and manipulation of the stage space around the body to demonstrate presence shown by these military roles is also evident in the gentle, feminine movements of Yang Yuhuan. The *man fanshen* (slow spins, Diagram 77) that Mei Lanfang makes as he smells the flowers and takes Yang Yuhuan's last drunken sips of wine provide

Diagram 76   *feijiao xuanzi* (flying feet and camel spin)

Diagram 77   *man fanshen* (slow turn)

a good example of the way in which the whole *jingju* body moves through various planes of the globe-space. Here, the head, arms, hands, trunk, legs and feet contact with all possible planes of the theatre space in one single movement which carries the *content* of the whole of the play. Yang Yuhuan is drunk on the scenery and later on the wine. She enters another world of consciousness and spins because for her, the world is spinning. Yang Yuhuan reproduces the spinning world with her body in the *woyu* (coiling fish) pose. The spins contain the temporal scale of the play – the point of departure in the very title of the play (the *intoxicated* concubine) – and the spatial scale (the performer gives temporary life to Yang Yuhuan through her attempt to grasp control of the centre, like a ritual journey of creation).

    Even in apparent dis-harmony and lack of co-ordination, there is

306

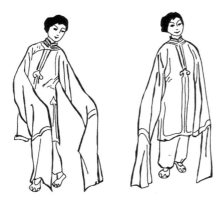

Diagram 78   *zuibu* (drunken step)

symmetry and roundedness on the *jingju* stage. Mei Lanfang must execute a step known as *zuibu* (drunken step, Diagram 78) to portray the
intoxicated concubine. The actor begins the step facing the auditorium, with both arms hanging at the side, naturally. As the left foot
rises to take a step, it crosses in front of the right foot. At the same
time, both arms swing to the left. Following the impetus of the movement, the right foot takes a small step to the right and both arms swing
to the right across the body. The left foot makes a step forward to reach
the level of the right foot, and the whole process begins again in reverse
starting with the right foot. There should be no pause in the step, but
rather the impetus of the swinging body propels each step to be made.
Unlike all other *jingju* movements, the actor's eyes in the drunken step
show no *shen* (spirit, life) or focus. The Chinese actors often criticise
the Western performer for not focusing with the eyes enough, making
the performance lifeless. The eyes are trained by staring at light bulbs
and incense sticks to widen them and increase the impression of focus.
Such exercises are known as *fei yanzi* (making the eyeballs fly). Furthermore, the upper body must be relaxed and, most importantly, follow the impetus of the feet. The chest must be upright, as if trying to
regain balance. The drunken step deliberately contravenes most of the
basic rules of stepping on stage. The pit of the stomach and loins, the
seat of *qi*, is denied and the centre of the body moved to the feet which
are, apparently, moving of their own accord. The stiff upper chest seems
to attempt to balance the lack of control in the feet – in sum, a body

Diagram 79   *tiao tiemen kan* (jumping the iron pit)

totally at odds. Yet, the actor who performs the drunken step also adheres to the basic principle of roundedness in that each element of the step is balanced by its opposite; left and right, unstable feet, stiffened chest. The movements forwards are balanced by those to the side; the intoxicated concubine almost rolls on the stage in small circles, going nowhere, just as her entrance dance was filled with spiralling circles of hope and desire.

Not only does the *jingju* body claim the central position for himself through rounded, embracing movements in space, he can also achieve the sense of axiality within one body or pose. In chapter one, the actor Zhang Chunhua was accepted as apprentice to his master because he could perform more leaps than the master. The same leap, *tiao tiemen kan* (jumping over the iron-gated, or grilled, pit, Diagram 79) is performed by the spirits who accompany Zhong Kui. In this movement, the spirit almost seems to jump through his own centre as the foot negotiates the hole made by his other leg and arm. The moment of centrality is in the air – typical of the nature of the spirit role as one who comes from the other world.

The general who enters with such aggressively diagonal steps in the *qiba,* such as Zhong Kui, for example, also makes poses during the

Yuan *(Round)*

Diagram 80   *zaichui chengzhangshi* (letting fall and pushing up pose)

sequence which repeat the message of axiality in the one body. Like Yang Yuhuan in the coiled fish position, twisting her body around the axis of her loins, the general indicates all four directions with the arms, legs, head and trunk, linking them together at the same abdominal point of *qi*. In the pose, *zaichui chengzhang shi* (letting fall and pushing up pose, Diagram 80), Zhong Kui first stands with his legs expressing one diagonal, while his feet express the other on a horizontal plane. Meanwhile, the arms balance the position of the legs in a vertical, or third dimension. One hand is open, the other is clenched. The head and upper body lean away from the extended leg (1). In the second part of the movement, which completes the moment of *liangxiang*, the upper body shifts minutely to make a cross diagonal to the legs and the raised arm pushes up while the lowered hand presses down. The head flicks to the diagonal (2). The movement seems to embrace the idea of centrality in Zhong Kui, the exorcist, by describing diagonal, opposition, 'torque' in one body, rather than simple roundedness.

The *da hualian* (great painted face) role is very closely related to the comic role, *chou*, also known as *xiao hualian* (small painted face). It is the same relation as that explored between the consuming exorcist (over-size, grotesque) and the comic exorcist (laughing). The *chou* role is used in many types of Chinese theatre to cleanse the stage before the main (usually deity) roles appear, as for example, the *matong* groom who prefaces the arrival of Guan Yu or the spirits who accompany

309

Zhong Kui. However, the painted face general also functions as exorcist on the Chinese stage. His standard military entrance, the *qiba*, is a cleansing dance which allows the weapons he actually or metaphorically carries (he is always dressed in *kao* armour) to touch and exorcise all four corners of the stage before the main action begins. Most *nuo* theatre begins, for example, with a fighting routine known as *xia sijiang* (enter four generals). Two pairs of generals enter the performing area and work a complicated, turning routine with the lance, changing partners and directions until all four corners of the performing area have been thoroughly 'touched' or cleansed. Only after this sequence, which may be lengthy or short, according to the skills of each troupe, can the advertised play begin. The generals are direct relations of the terrifying Fangxiang exorcist of the Zhou dynasty, who cleansed the tomb in a similar way before the corpse could be lowered into it. The fighting routines of the *nuo* performers are often highly skilled, breathtaking displays of martial skill. In Anshun, several villages, such as Yan Qi and Xia Yangchang, perform with real, rather than theatrical, *dao* (knives) which seems to fuse the exorcist ritual with the theatrical element of this event even more closely. Wu Chungui, from the village of Qilin Dun told me that the fighting routines performed by his troupe are derived from the real military training given to the village ancestors – soldiers of the Ming dynasty who were stationed in the area and finally settled there (the suffix *dun* means garrison). Wu's claim is not so unlikely, since the area in front of the village temple (also used for theatre) was commonly the largest available space in which to practise military drill. It also echoes the comments made by Qi Rushan, cited in chapter one, that village boys were automatically trained in martial arts and admired the theatre for its use of similar patterns. The Chinese character for theatre includes the element *ge* (axe), the same weapon associated with the Fangxiang exorcist – reinforcing the close relation between exorcist ritual, acting and martial skill in a space specially designated as place of worship, place of performance.

All fight routines used in Chinese theatre express total exploitation of the concept of roundedness. Whether two opponents are involved, or four or six, against each other in pairs, or against a single defender, each block or cut to one side is balanced by one to the other; each forward attack is balanced by the reverse until final victory for one side (which in the light of such balance can seem arbitrary). The proxemics of such fight routines also always work along the four diagonals of the stage and include an embrace of the whole stage by *pao yuanchang* (running the circle) between sequences as the opponents size each other up. The four generals cleansing the *dixi* stage similarly balance their sequences with mirror patternings and repetitions, leaving the stage area before any victory can be declared. The plot of the movements in the sequence acted by the Xia Yangchang village are strikingly similar to a description of a ritual display of battle recorded in the ancient work, *Liji*. Here, it states that state banquets in the Western Zhou dynasty (1066–771 BC) included the performance of a *dawu* (great battle). The battle consisted of six movements:

1 A group of fighters enter from the south.
2 They divide into two groups and face each other at east and west.
3 The soldiers fight, then turn to the south and perform fighting techniques.
4 They turn to the north (where the king sits) and kneel.
5 The soldiers stand and bow to the north.
6 The soldiers retire.

The performance is said to enact the victory of the Western Zhou, who came from the south to conquer the reigning dynasty, and who then conquered the southern area of China around Anhui, before returning again to the capital. Whether or not this is so, the ritual centre is once again clarified by *demarcating* the four outlying areas, north, south, east and west. The display not only reconfirms the dynasty in its control of the centre, it also cleanses and exorcises the centre of that world, the royal palace.

A similar choral movement of confirmation of centrality, or creative power (the theatre world in this case) is also apparent in contemporary *jingju* in the role of the chorus, or *longtao* (*long* means dragon, *tao* can mean suite, set, links, 'those who follow'). The *longtao* can represent handmaids, guards, soldiers or a whole army. It is 'body' or *corpus*, rather than a group of individuals. The *longtao* may preface the entrance or exit of a major character and it is usually composed of four, six or eight actors who should be the same height and same general appearance, so as to emphasise the sense of generalised body. The *longtao* moves across the stage in complicated intertwining patterns which largely reflect the *taiji* symbol of Yin/Yang and circularity.[12] The *longtao* initiate and complete the events on the stage by literally 'rounding them off' – the aesthetic and ritual end harmony is confirmed by its movements in the same way that the Zhou dynasty was recon-firmed in the re-enactment of its assumption of central power.

Thus, the *jingju* performer moves according to the circular pattern dictated to him on the floor of the stage as he navigates the points of the nine point matrix and replicates the global lines in the various planes with his body. The body shifts the centre of the globe towards his own centre and away from it, sometimes standing at the nucleus of the globe in his own bodily axiality, sometimes at the rim threatening attack or diverting from the centre according to the particular expres-sion required by the situation of the role. The body shifts in and out of positions in relation to the space/time of the stage – the body con-stantly creates and recreates itself within the theatre world.

In the *nuo* theatre the exorcist performer manipulates his body in the Luo matrix between centre and periphery to unify the two worlds of heaven and earth and regenerate order. Just as the *nuo* performer positions his body at the centre to recreate earthly and heavenly worlds, the *jingju* performer perceives his body as axis to the *theatrum mundi*. His corporeality is dissected (trained) and reassembled (formed) anew in the same moment as he is dissected (at the rim) and unified (at the centre) – within one movement sequence. The performer defines the individual stations of meaning by his touch (whether leg, foot, arm, hand, head, trunk or voice, etc.) and connects them, in so doing, to one another in a repetition of the ritual journey of recreation attributed to Yu and various other ancestral–creative figures. By analogy, the action on the *jingju* stage does not rely on the reproduction of this world, *im-itatio*, but on the constant, ritual, regenerative process of recreation of an-other world.

The literal application of the Luo matrix and its cosmological values onto the *nuo* performing body was shown, in the previous chap-ter, to recreate and unify two worlds (heaven and earth, life and death,

---

[12] Ye Yangxi 1983.

sickness and health). In the *jingju*, the nine point matrix is used metaphorically to unify all times and all spaces in the theatre world. In *jingju* the fictive world, the *theatrum mundi*, is created by the performer's body and his manipulation and connection of the centre and the periphery. The real body does not disappear into the theatre (other) world it creates, but deliberately manipulates proximity to and distance from it in order to constantly give it (new) *presence*.

Conclusion

The Chinese performing body, whether human (Mei Lanfang in *jingju*, the Fangxiangshi, Fashi, or Zhong Kui in exorcist events), or human and artefact (marionette master and marionette, exorcist and mask), represents one composite body which has been *metaphorically* dissected and reassembled anew. In *jingju* the de(re)formation of the performing body is achieved in training; in the exorcist and marionette theatres it is the outcome of initiation rites and the use of charms. The same process of regeneration can be observed in mortuary rites where the dissection of bodies prepared for the afterworld is *literal*. Huge quantities of life-giving force, or Yang, are provided by the spilling of human blood as the bodies are physically dismembered.

In both cases, whether metaphorical or literal, the process of dissection is simultaneous to the process of reassembly, the creation of a new body. This process is known as *kaiguang* – letting the light shine out. The newly created, reassembled body holds itself apart – articulates – in order to emanate, or *manifest* presence. It *moves*. The movements made by the Chinese performer actively designate and connect – *create* – the temporal–spatial world of theatre performance.

Because the Chinese performer is shadowed by the many presences of his family ancestors as well as the inheritance of his teachers, the performer does not stand alone on the stage as an individual representing a role. Rather he is shadowed by the presences of the past which are *visible* to the Chinese spectator. This means that the body of the Chinese performer provides the mediation between all past times and the present. He *embodies* all the ancestors.

The Chinese term *biaoyan* (to manifest and display) invites the spectator to begin his perception of the performance with the outside

314

appearance of the actor – the costume and mask, or make-up. From this moment, the spectator's gaze penetrates the actor's presentation to the inside, to the bodily posture and attitude inside the outer apparel. All aspects of the play to be performed are present in the various items of appearance from the very moment of entry. The Chinese spectator reads vertically at each moment of the play, connecting layers of meaning with each other in both directions.

The performer is trained (prepared) to dissect parts of his corporeal body in performance as separate units of articulation – hand, eye, finger, foot. The Chinese performative body recomposes itself as marionette and marionette master. The hand may portray an aspect of the play outside the role, such as the geese that Yang Yuhuan sees, while the rest of the body presents the role seeing the geese. The feet designate and connect, transporting the performing body across the stage in time.

Two kinds of performance model have been identified in the Chinese theatre. The first is where the performing body is dissected and reassembled into a new (articulated) *body*, such as in the *jingju* or *nuo* theatres. The second kind is where the performing body is dissected and reassembled as (god)*head*, or deity, which is then united and detached from the human performing body in the performance situation. In the *nuo* masked theatre and marionette exorcism, both models are used within one performance, at different moments of the event.

The articulation of the Chinese body is not only corporeal, dependent on the actor's bodily means. The performance text also maintains and dissolves distance and proximity between the performer and that which is being performed. The performance event is composed of a constant shift of persona between third person and narrative, imperative and designative.

The production of great amounts of Yang in the mortuary situation – the killing of human life, the stopping of human life in its youth and figurines made of special materials, placed in positions related to orientations which are Yang – *guarantees* life in the world of death. The concept of regeneration expressed in the mortuary situation as Yang and *ming*, is perceived in the theatre world as *qi*. Here, the performing body is also shaped into forms (poses) which articulate *qi* or presence – through roundness, opposition and symmetry. The performer expresses (and gathers) *qi* at precisely determined aesthetic or cosmological stations of meaning around the stage. The *liangxiang* pose (body form) held at each station, and connected to others by movements of passage, guarantees life in the fictive world of theatre.

Not only the pose alone, as pattern or form of life, creates the theatre world. The Chinese performer *moves* to manifest the presence of life within. Moreover, the movements of passage that the Chinese performer makes across the stage designate and connect – *articulate* – or create the theatre world in the present, real world. The performing body connects planes of meaning with his corporeal body; positioning himself as the axis of time and space, he mediates the other world of theatre in this world. All times and all spaces are brought together by the articulate(d) performing figure.

The Western theatre artists who have thus far approached the Chinese theatre have discovered in it aspects of alienation and universality which have confirmed and enriched their own theatrical experimentations. This study has attempted to recontextualise the Chinese performance art that it may 'speak' for itself. The Chinese spectator reads the performance against a contextual background filled with religious, philosophical, historical, aesthetic, social, even genetic information which changes the perspective of how *presence* functions on the Chinese stage. Moreover, the habit of reading is different, for the Chinese spectator reads in all directions – horizontally, vertically, and from without to within. Finally, the performance is almost unreadable without the contextual knowledge of the functioning of the Luo matrix of creation.

The performer's movements, as the manifestation of presence, or life, serve in the Chinese theatre to designate and connect, *articulate* and create the fictive, theatrical world. In doing so, the performer's body, at the central, axial position, is the locus of theatrical representation; the *incorporation* of another world. In this, the Western idea of the spectator as witness to the theatre event, is challenged. The Chinese spectator need not attend a performance to know that the correct moves were made by the correct person in the correct space. However, the Chinese spectator *does* attend theatre (although nowadays he may seldom attend *jingju*), and he is, moreover, an initiate in the fine details of the structure of the performance – *how* it is done (which sets him apart from his Western counterpart). This body of performance know-ledge means that the Chinese spectator *participates* in the reconstruction of the fictive world. The Chinese spectator goes to the theatre to be part of the represencing of the other world. The Chinese performer embodies all times, all spaces, all members of the community, by his presence on stage.

Chinese Dynasties

Xia		21–16 centuries BC
Shang		16th century to 1066 BC
Zhou	Western Zhou	1066–771 BC
	Eastern Zhou	770–256 BC
	Spring and Autumn Period	770–476 BC
	Warring States	475–221 BC
Qin		221–206 BC
Han	Western Han	206 BC –AD 23
	Eastern Han	AD 25–220
Three Kingdoms		220–280
Jin		265–420
Northern and Southern Dynasties		420–581
Sui		581–618
Tang		618–907
Five Dynasties		907–979
Song		960–1279
Liao		907–1125
Jin		1115–1234

The Chinese dynasties

Yuan	1279–1368
Ming	1368–1644
Qing	1644–1911
Republic of China	1912–1949
People's Republic of China	1949

Glossary of Chinese terms

bagua	the Eight Diagrams: eight combinations of three broken and unbroken lines used in divination
bamiaotang	(lit. Hall of the Eight Temples) name given to backstage area or tent in *nuo* theatre
Baolao	head-mask
biao	(lit. to manifest) to perform
biaoyan	(lit. to manifest and display) to perform
cai jiuzhou	stamping the nine provinces (a dance in *nuo* theatre)
chang	to sing, one of four skills required of an actor
Chi You	mythological God of Fertility and Agriculture associated with rain and the dragon; depicted as bear exorcist mask in tombs
chou	(lit. ugly) the comic role category
da	(lit. to fight) martial skill, one of the four skills required of an actor
dan	the female role category
daomadan	light martial female role category
dixi	form of *nuo* theatre
dong	paulownia wood used for masks, coffins, etc.
dou	bucket containing measure of rice known as *dou* (peck) used in initiation and burial ritual
dou	the Ursa Major (Big Dipper)
erhu	lower-pitch spike fiddle, second string instrument in *jingju* orchestra
erhuang	with *xipi*, a major melodic system of *jingju*
fa	method, doctrines, principles, way of doing things

Fangxiangshi	historical exorcist figure at court
Fashi	master of the *nuo* event
gui	spirit, ghost, foreign, other
Guifei zuijiu	*The Favourite Concubine Becomes Intoxicated*
guocheng	passage between movements in *jingju*
hao	(lit. to expend) hold a position in training for *jingju*
he	to unify
he	onomatopoeia for laughter
hua	flower, flowered, patterned
hua	to change, transform, metamorphose
huadan	(lit. flower *dan*) young, vivacious, female role category
huanjue	to make a series of hand signs
hun	the soul, spirit
huqin	high-pitched spike fiddle, main string instrument in *jingju* orchestra
jingju	(lit. theatre of the capital) Beijing style theatre, often misnamed Peking opera or Beijing opera
ju	theatre performance
jue	hand sign used in *nuo* event
kaiguang	(lit. open to let the light shine out) process by which artefacts are opened to presence
kuilei	puppet, marionette
kun	abbreviation for *kunqu* style of theatre
kundan	female role category in the *kunqu* style of theatre
kunqu	style of theatre deriving from south using flute as principal instrument
liangxiang	(lit. radiant, luminous appearance) pose held for period of seconds on *jingju* stage punctuated by percussion
longtao	(lit. dragon set) *jingju* chorus
Luo diagram	matrix of nine cells arranged in three rows of three accorded digits from 1 to 9 such that any straight line of three cells renders the total sum of 15. In mythology, the diagram was given to Yu the Great on the back of a tortoise as he stood at the Luo

	River. Yu used the diagram to separate the land from the waters during the Great Flood and thus created the world (China).
matong	horse groom; kind of *wuchou* (martial comic) role in *jingju*
mingqi	(lit. luminous, intelligenced, presenced vessels) mortuary goods
muou	sculpted image, puppet
nian	to recite, one of the four skills required by an actor
nuo	general term for fixed-masked theatrical event with exorcistic, regenerative, celebratory aim
nuogong	(lit. father of *nuo*) Patron god of *nuo* event
nuopo	(lit. mother of *nuo*) Patron goddess of *nuo* event
nuotangxi	style of *nuo* theatre
ou	counterpart, sculpted image
pao yuanchang	(lit. running in a circle round the stage) circuit of the stage to indicate passage of time or space
po	soul, spirit
pudu	ceremony of propitiation, cleansing and salvation of souls from purgatory
qi	air, breath, energy, spirit, presence
qingyi	(lit. blue or plain robe) female role category of high social status and dignified behaviour
qishou	'ugly head' exorcist mask hung in tombs
qitou	'ugly head' exorcist mask hung in tombs
shen	god, spirit
Tai Yi	(lit. The Great One) mythological god of the pole star, the Original Creator
Taotie	exorcist beast-like creature depicted on ritual mortuary vessels
tixian kuilei	marionette
tiyangxi	form of *nuo* theatre
wangzi	(lit. crippled, hunchbacked) puppet
wu	initiate in certain techniques or practices who can mediate between worlds
wu pusa	(lit. dancing the Buddha) dance with big head masks
wubaolao	dance with big head masks

wubolao	dance with big head masks
wuchou	comic martial role category
wudan	female martial role category
wusheng	male martial role category
wushu	martial arts
xi	theatre performance
xiao hualian	(lit. small painted face) another name for *chou* comic role category
xiaosheng	young male role category
xipi	with *erhuang*, a major melodic system of *jingju*
Yang	the male creative principle of light, life, warmth, etc.
Yin	the female creative principle of darkness, death, cold, etc.
yong	to leap
yong	moving mortuary figure
Yu the Great	mythological god of creation who created the world by dividing the land from the sea during the great flood with the help of the Luo diagram
yubu	(lit. the step of Yu) dance sequence over the Luo diagram said to repeat the dance of creation used by Yu the Great
yunshou	(lit. cloud hand) arm movement used to describe passage
zanghun	to deposit the soul
zaoxing	(lit. to build a form) small pose or posture
Zhong Kui	hunchbacked, crippled mythological exorcist figure. A scholar who gained the highest result in civil examinations but was barred from taking up a position because of his ugly looks. He committed suicide and was pitied by the gods who gave him the power to act as exorcist
zonghe yishu	(lit. total art form) syncretic art form that unifies different performance skills as *jingju*
zuo	(lit. to do) to act, one of the four skills required of an actor

List of Chinese characters

B

bagua	八卦
bai jia	摆家
baixi	百戏
bamiaotang	八庙堂
bangzixi	梆子戏
baoyueshi	抱月式
bawang kui	霸王盔
bazigong	把子功
bazikuayi	八字跨椅
beigong hua	背弓花
biao	表
biaoda tishen	表达替身
biaoyan	表演
bingdi	並蒂

C

cai jiuzhou	踩九州
caidan	彩旦
caiqiao	踩跷
chang	唱
cheshi	车式
chi	赤
chongzhangshi	冲掌式
chou	丑
chuan po bu chuan cuo	穿破不穿错
chuanju	川剧
chuling	刍灵

D

da	打
da wawatou	大娃娃头
dan	旦
daomadan	刀马旦
daqu	大曲
daxi	大戏
dazuo	大座
dingchangbai	定场白
dingchangshi	定场诗
dixi	地戏
dixia 32 xi	地下 32 戏
dong	桐
dou	斗
dou	豆
duan	端
duangong	端公
dui	兑

E

erhuang	二黄
ershisi shi men shen jiazi	二十四式门神架子

F

fa	法
fan yunshou	反云手
fangxiangshi	方相氏
fanshou	反手
fanu	发怒

324

fashi	法师	*huange*	换歌
fayi	法衣	*huanjue*	换诀
fengguan	凤冠	*huashan*	花衫
fenghuang	凤凰	*huiju*	徽剧
fusang	扶桑	*hukou*	虎口
G		*huqin*	胡琴
ge	戈	**J**	
gen	艮	*jia*	家
gong	公	*jian*	剑
gongzhuang	宫装	*jianjue*	剑诀
goujiao	勾脚	*jiazi hualian*	架子花脸
guanghan gong	广寒宫	*jiben wugong*	基本武功
guaziwu	卦子舞	*jiezou gan*	节奏感
gudeng	古灯	*jin*	金
gui	鬼	*jing*	净
guifang	鬼方	*jingchao pai*	京朝派
guocheng	过成	*jingju*	京剧
H		*jingtian*	井田
haitang nu	海棠女	*jiqi*	祭器
han sangzi	喊嗓子	*jiqi ren*	机器人
hanju	汉剧	*jiugong*	九宫
hao	耗	*jiuzhong*	九种
haotui	耗腿	*ju*	剧
he	合	*jue*	诀
he shang	和尚	**K**	
heheshen	和合神	*kai hongshan*	开红山
heitou	黑头	*kaiguang*	开光
hetu	河图	*kailushen*	开路神
hongsheng	红生	*kan*	坎
houpi jinr	猴皮筋儿	*kao*	靠
hu	胡	*kou shou yan shen bu*	口手眼身步
hua	花	*kuaijiao*	摔脚
hua	化	*kuilei*	傀儡
huabu	花部	*kun*	坤
huadan	花旦	*kun*	昆
huagai	花盖	*kundan*	昆旦
hualian	花脸	*kunqiang*	昆腔

kunqu	昆曲	*nufa*	怒发
kuqiang	哭腔	*numang*	女蟒
kuxiao	哭笑	*nuo*	傩
L		*nuogong*	傩公
lai	来	*nuopo*	傩婆
lanhua	兰花	**O**	
laodan	老旦	*ou*	偶
laogui	老鬼	*ouren*	偶人
laosheng	老生	**P**	
laoshi	老师	*paidai*	牌带
lei	雷	*pailian*	排练
leishi	雷式	*pao yuanchang*	跑圆场
li	离	*pi*	皮
li	利	*pihuang ban*	皮黄板
liang douxiu	两斗袖	*ping*	平
liangxiang	亮相	*pishou*	劈手
ling	灵	*posan*	破伞
linshi	临师	*pudu*	普渡
liuhua	柳花	*pufu*	搏拊
liujin	流巾	*pusa man*	菩萨蛮
liupai	流派	**Q**	
luoshu	落书	*qi*	气
lüzi	露滋	*qi*	魁
M		*qian*	乾
mang	蟒	*qianbian wanhua*	千变万化
mashi	马式	*qiba*	起霸
mei	美	*qing*	青
meiyou qi	没有气	*qingming*	清明
mi	米	*qingshen*	请神
ming qi	明器	*qingyi*	青衣
muou	木偶	*qinqiang*	秦腔
muzhu	木主	*qiqi*	傲傲
N		*qishou*	魁首
nanxi	南戏	*qitou*	魁头
naogui	闹鬼	**R**	
neichang	内场	*rankou*	髯口
nian	唸	*renji*	人祭
nongzi	弄姿	*renxun*	人殉

riyue ergong	日月二宫	*si da mingdan*	四大名旦
rou kuilei	肉傀儡	*sifang*	四方
ruhua	入话	*sigu*	司鼓
S		*siping*	四平
sa	洒	*songshen*	送神
saigong	赛公	*suona*	唢呐
san	散	**T**	
sang	桑	*tan*	坛
sangjia zhi yue	丧家之乐	*tang*	堂
sanji	三级	*tanzigong*	毯子功
sankuai war	三块瓦	*taotie*	饕餮
shahua	杀铧	*tianshang 32 xi*	天上 32 戏
shan	扇	*tiao bagua*	跳八卦
shanbang	山膀	*tiao shen*	跳神
shang changmen	上场门	*tiaotai*	跳台
shangu nuo	山鼓傩	*tiao wufang*	跳五方
shangxia zuoyou	上下左右	*tiefanwan*	铁饭碗
sharen xi	杀人戏	*tihetui*	踢盍腿
shene	伸萼	*tihoutui*	踢后腿
shenfen	身分	*tijia danshanbang*	提甲单山膀
sheng	生	*tipangtui*	踢旁腿
sheng	升	*tipiantui*	踢偏腿
shi	师	*tiqianghua*	提枪花
shi	尸	*tishizitui*	踢十字腿
shi	食	*titui*	踢腿
shifu	师父	*tixian kuilei*	提线傀儡
shigong	师公	*tiyangxi*	提阳戏
shou yan zhi fa bu	手眼指法步	*tizhengtui*	提正腿
shou yan shen zhi bu	手眼身指步	*tong*	同
shoubang weizhi	手膀位置	*tong*	铜
shouqi	收气	*tongchui hualian*	铜锤花脸
shuang douxiu	双斗袖	*tou*	头
shuangqiang fanhua	双枪反花	*touza*	头扎
shui	水	*tu laoshi*	土老师
shui kuilei	水傀儡	*tuanyuanxi*	团圆戏
shuixiu	水袖	*tuigong*	腿功
shuizhuan baixi	水转百戏	*tuipo jue*	推破诀
shuo gensheng	说根生	*turui*	吐蕊

W

waichang	外场
wangzi	尪仔
wawa jie	娃娃节
wei	畏
wenchou	文丑
wu	巫
wubaolao	舞鲍老
wubaoluo	舞鲍罗
wubolao	舞拨老
wupusa	舞菩萨
wuchou	武丑
wudou mijiao	五斗米教
wuhualian	武花脸
wusheng	武生
wushu	武术
wuxing	五行

X

xi	戏
xia changmen	下场门
xia huochi	下火池
xiama	下马
xianggong	相公
xiangpai	像派
xiaosheng	小生
xiaoxi	小戏
xiaozuo	小座
xima	洗马
xun	巽
xunzang	殉葬
xusheng	须生

Y

ya	压
yang	阳
yatui	压腿
yehua	掖花
yeye	爷爷

yingfeng	迎风
yingmian hua	迎面花
yinzi	引子
yiyangqiang	弋阳腔
yong	俑
yong	踊
yongantai junjun	永安太郡君
you jishu meiyou yishu	有技术没有艺术
yu	禺
yu	鱼
yuan	圆
yuanxiao	圆消
yubu	禺步
yudai	玉带
yunjian	云肩
yunshou	云手
yunshuang	陨霜

Z

zanghun	藏魂
zangshen zhou	藏身咒
zao	造
zaoxing	造型
zhangtanshi	掌坛师
zhangtou muou	杖头木偶
zhangxian kuilei	杖线傀儡
zhen	震
zheng yunshou	正云手
zhengxi	正戏
zhengyi pai	正一派
zhuanshen woyu	转身卧鱼
zonghe yishu	总和艺术
zoubian	走边
zouzheng	走正
zun wangzi	尊尪仔
zuo	作

328

Works in Chinese

Changsha Mawangdui yihao hanmu 1973 (*Han Tomb No. 1 at Mawangdui in Changsha province*), ed. Hunan sheng bowuguan, et al., Beijing.

Changsha Mawangdui yihao hanmu fajue jianbao 1972 (*Brief Report on the Excavations of Tomb No. 1 at Mawangdui in Changsha*), ed. Hunan sheng bowuguan, Beijing.

Chen Duo 1989. Gu nuoxi lüekao (Some thoughts on ancient nuo), *Xiju yishu* 3: 19–26.

Chen Xiaogao and Gu Manzhuang (no date). Fujian di puxianxi (Puxian theatre in Fujian), in *Huadong xiqu juzhong jieshao di er ji*, Fujian.

Cihai 1979 (*Sea of Words*), ed. Cihai bianji weiyuan hui, Beijing.

Daozang 1986 (*Daoist Scripts*), 36 vols., ed. Shanghai shudian et al., Beijing.

Dengxian caise hualu zhuanmu 1958 (*Dengxian Painted Brick Tomb*), ed. Henan sheng wenhuaju wenwu gongzuodui, Beijing.

Dongjing menghualu 1982 (*Record of the Dream of the Eastern Capital*), ed. Deng Zhicheng, Beijing.

Dong Weixian 1981. *Jingju liupai* (*Jingju Styles*), Beijing.

Fan Jingru 1991. Nuoyi 'tiao wu fang' zhong di yinyang wuxing shuo (The principle of yinyang and the five directions in the 'dance of the five directions' in *nuo* rite). Paper read to the International Nuo Conference, Hunan.

Gao Lun 1987. *Guizhou nuoxi* (*Nuo Theatre in Guizhou*), Guiyang.

Gao Mingbian 1980. *Gu wenzi leibian* (*Ancient Script*), Beijing.

Gu Poguang 1990. Fangxiangshi mianju kao (Thoughts on the Fangxiangshi mask). Paper read to the International Nuo Conference, Shanxi.

Guanghan sanxingdui guichi yihao jikeng fatu jianbao 1987 (Brief excavation report of the remains of no. 1 sacrificial pit at Sanxingdui in Guanghan), eds. Sichuan sheng, et al., *Wenwu* 10: 1–16.

Guanghan sanxingdui guichi erhao jikeng fatu jianbao 1989 (Brief excavation report of the remains of no. 2 sacrificial pit at Sanxingdui in Guanghan), eds. Sichuan sheng, et al., *Wenwu* 5: 1–21.

Guizhou nuo mianju yishu 1989 (*The Art of Guizhou Nuo Masks*), ed. Dai Dingjiu, Shanghai.

Guo Baoqun 1936. Xunxian xincun gucan muzhi qinglu (Record of ancient remains of tombs at Xincun in Xunxian), *Tianye kaogu baogao* 1: 167–200.

Hao Gang (no date). Gulai di Zitong yangxi (Ancient *yangxi* in Zitong), ed. Li Yuanqiang, in *Nuoxi wenxuan* (*Selected Essays on Nuo Theatre*) 84–8.

Hao Gang and Tao Guangpu 1993. Zitong yangxi di wenhua qianshi (Early cultural history of Zitong's *yangxi*), *Minsu quyi* 83: 149–69.

Hou Yushan 1984. Wo yan *Zhong Kui Jia Mei* (How I perform *Zhong Kui Marries off His Little Sister*), *Minsu quyi* 36: 17–33.

Hu Houxuan 1974. Zhongguo nuli shehui di renxun he renji 1 & 2 (Human killing and sacrifice for the tomb in China's slave society 1 & 2), *Wenwu* 7: 74–82 and 8: 56–68.

Huang Shengwen 1990. Xianxi di fasheng yu xingcheng (The origins and form of *xianxi*). Paper given to the International Nuo Conference, Shanxi.

Huang Weiruo, Josephine Riley and Michael Gissenwehrer 1991. Guanyu 'ban' yu yuan kanben *Dandaohui* di ruogan wenti (Some remarks on the relationship of the term *ban* to the Yuan play-text *Dandaohui*). Paper read to the International Nuo Conference, Hunan.

Huang Weiruo and Josephine Riley 1993. Yaofa kuilei kaolü (On chemically operated puppets), *Xiju*, 2: 86–9.

Hunan xiqu chuantong juben (47): nuotang xi (shidao) zhuanji 1982 (*Traditional Play Texts from Hunan (47): Nuotang (shidao) Theatre*), ed. Hunan sheng xiqu yanjiusuo, Changsha.

Jiang Wuchang 1986. Zhongguo chuantong juchang zhi guiju yu jinji

(Restrictions and prohibitions backstage of traditional Chinese theatre), *Minsu quyi* 40: 44–91.

Jin Weinuo 1981. Zhangxiong fusao muyong yu chutang kuileixi (Wooden mortuary figures from the tombs of Zhangxiong and his wife and early Tang puppets), in *Zhongguo meishu shi lunji* (*On the History of Art*), Beijing: 149–60.

Jingju erbai nian lishi 1974 (*The History of Two Hundred Years of* jingju), eds. Liu Shaotang and Shen Weichuang,vol. 2 of *Pingju shike congkan* (*Source Materials on the History of Pingju*) Taibei.

Li Changmin 1984. *Hunan muouxi* (*Hunan Puppet Theatre*), Changsha.
     1989. *Zhongguo minjian kuilei yishu* (*Folk Puppet Theatre in China*), Nanchang.

Li Fang, et al. 1962. *Taiping Yulan* (*Imperial Survey of the Taiping Era*), Taibei.

Li Fengmao 1986. Zhong Kui yu nuoli ji qi xiju (Zhong Kui, *nuo* rite and theatre), *Minsu quyi* 39: 69–99.

Li Hongchun 1982. *Jingju changtan* (*On Jingju*), Beijing.

Li Wei 1972. Zhonghua wudao yu taiji yuanli zhi shentao (Discussion of the origins of the taiji symbol and Chinese dance), *Huagang yishu xuebao* 3: 127–35.

Liao Ben 1989. *Song yuan xiqu wenwu yu minsu* (*Archaeological Artefacts and Customs of Song and Yuan Theatre*), Beijing.

Lin He 1990. '*Jiuge*' yu yuanxiang minsu (*The 'Nine Songs' and Folk Customs of the Yuanxiang Region*), Shanghai.

Liu Mingshu 1942. Han Wuliang sihua xiang zhong huangdi chiyou gu zhantu kao (On the depiction of the ancient battle of Huangdi and Chi You as part of the stone reliefs in the Han tomb at Wuliang), *Zhongguo wenhua yanjiu huikan* 2 (Sept.): 341–65.

Liu Shaotang and Shen Hanchuang 1933. *Fulian cheng sanshi nian shi* (*Thirty Years of the Fuliancheng*), Taibei.

Lo Chin t'ang 1970. Kuileixi di yulai (The origin of puppetry), *Dalu zhi* 41 (12 Dec.): 3–6.

Lu Jianrong 1983. *Xiqu bazigong* (*Weapon Training for the Theatre*), Beijing.

Lu Sushang 1952. Taiwan kuileixi jisha lu (On Taiwan puppet theatre and sacrificial rites), *Taiwan fengwu* 2, 6: 7–11.

Luo Zhenyu (no date). Gu mingqi tulü (Record of ancient mortuary artefacts), in *Luo Zhenyu xiansheng quanji* (*The Collected Works of Luo Zhenyu*), Beijing: 2415–555.

Luoyang jinmu di fachu 1957 (Excavations at a Jin tomb in Luoyang), ed. Henan sheng, et al., *Kaogu xuebao* 1: 169–87.

Ma Shutian 1990. *Huaxia zhushen* (*China's Many Deities*), Beijing.

Mei Lanfang 1985. Ed. Zhongguo yishu yanjiu yuan xiqu yanjiu suo, Beijing.

Mei Lanfang and Xu Jichuan 1961. *Wutai shenghuo sishinian* (*Forty Years of Stage Life*), 2 vols., Beijing.

Mei Lanfang changqiang ji 1983 (*A Collection of Mei Lanfang's Arias*), ed. Yu Zhongfu, Shanghai.

Mei Lanfang yanchuben xuanji 1959 (*A Selection of Mei Lanfang's Play-Texts*), ed. Zhongguo xijujia xiehui, Beijing.

Mei Lanfang wenji 1962 (*A Collection of Mei Lanfang's Writings*), ed. Zhongguo xijujia xiehui, Beijing.

Mei Shaowu 1984. *Wodi fuqin, Mei Lanfang* (*My Father, Mei Lanfang*), Tianjin.

Nansong gujikao 1983 (*On Ancient Relics of the Southern Song*), Hangzhou.

Nuoxi lunwen wenxuan 1987 (*Selected Articles on the Nuo Theatre*), ed. Dejiang xian, et al., Guiyang.

Qi Rushan 1979. *Qi Rushan quanji* (*Collected Works of Qi Rushan*), Taibei.

Qian Yi 1990. Shier shou – nuoxi di chuxing (The twelve animals and early forms of *nuo* theatre). Paper read to the International Nuo Conference, Shanxi.

Qiu Kunliang 1982. Taiwan jindai minjian xiqu huodong zhi yanjiu (Analysis of modern Taiwanese folk theatre events), *Guoli bianyi guankan* 11, 2: 1–44.

1983a. Taiwan di kuilei xi (Puppet theatre in Taiwan), *Minsu quyi* 23–4: 1–25.

1983b. *Xiandai shehui di minsu quyi* (*Contemporary Customs and Folk Performance*), Taibei.

See also Chu Kunliang in bibliography of Western sources.

Qu Yuan 1963. *Jiu ge* (*The Nine Songs*), ed. Wen Xiaoji, Beijing.

Quanzhou muou yishu 1986 (*The Art of the Puppet in Quanzhou*), ed. Chen Ruitong, Xiamen.

Ren Deze 1990. Quwo shangu bian (*Shangu* theatre in Quwo). Paper read to the International Nuo Conference, Shanxi.

Ren Erbai 1981. Ed. *Youyu ji* (*Records of the Jesters*), Shanghai.

Sato Haruo 1990. Ji zhi xue (A cockerel's blood). Paper read to the International Nuo Conference, Shanxi.

Shanxi Chanzi xian dongzhou mu 1984 (Eastern Zhou tombs in Chanzi county, Shanxi), ed. Shanxi sheng, et al., in *Kaogu xuebao* 4: 503–14.

Shen Zhongchang 1987. Sanxingdui erhao jijikeng qingtong liren xiang chuji (Initial report on the bronze statue in sacrificial pit no. 2 at Sanxingdui), *Wenwu* 10: 16–18.

Song Jinxiu 1985. Kuilei xi di zongjiao yishi (Religious aspects of puppet theatre), *Minsu quyi* 38: 88–111.

Sun Haipo 1938. *Xunxian yiqi* (*Findings at Xunxian*), Shanghai.

Sun Kaidi 1930. *Jindai xiqu yuanchu song kuileixi yingxi kao* (*On the Origins of Contemporary Theatre in Song Marionette and Shadow Puppet Theatre*), Beijing.

    1952. *Kuileixi kaoyuan* (*On the Origins of Puppet Theatre*), Shanghai.

Tang Degang 1981. Mei Lanfang zhuangao (Report on Mei Lanfang), *Li Yuan* 8 (10 June): 4–16.

Tuo Xiuming 1990. *Nuoxi, nuowenhua* (*Nuo Theatre, Nuo Culture*), Beijing.

    1992. Shaman wenhua yu nuowenhua di bijiao (A comparison of the shaman and the *nuo*), *Minsu quyi* 82: 145–78.

Wang Chunwu 1992. Tianshuaidao dui Sichuan nuoxi di yinxiang (The influence of Tianshuaidao on Sichuan *nuo*), *Minsu quyi* 82: 287–306.

Wan Fengmei 1982. *Xiqu biaoyan shenduan jibengong jiaocai* (*Basic Training – Teaching Materials for the Theatre*), Beijing.

Wang Gaoshan 1986. Ban xian yu zhen shen (Acting spirits and real gods), *Minsu quyi* 43: 109–32.

Wang Hongqi 1989. *Shenqi di bagua wenhua yu youxi* (*The Workings of the Trigrams and Games*), Beijing.

Wang Mingfang 1979. Shandong Laixi xihan muzhong faxian di tixian muou (A marionette discovered in a tomb of the Western Han at Laixi in Shandong), *Guangming ribao* Nov. 6: 4.

Wang Peifu and Lu Jianrong 1982. *Xiqu biaoyan tangzigong jiaocai* (*Teaching Materials for the Theatre – Floor Work*), Beijing.

Wang Yansheng and Wang Xingzhi (no date). Jiange yangxi (Yangxi theatre in Jiange), ed. Li Yuanqing, *Nuoxi wenxuan*, (*Selected Essays on Nuo Theatre*): 79–84.

Wei Shuxun 1959. Anyang chutu di rentou ji (On a human head found at Anyang), *Kaogu* 5: 272.

Wu Chunli and Zhang Zici 1983. *Jingju luogu* (*Jingju Percussion*), Beijing.

Wu Chunli and Zhang Ningzi 1983. *Jingju qupai jianbian* (*Introduction to Jingju Melodies*), Beijing.

Xiangxi nuo wenhua zhi mi 1991 (*Secrets of the Nuo in Xiangxi*), ed. Zhang Ziwei, Changsha.

Xinjiang chutu wenwu 1975 (*Archaeological Discoveries in Xinjiang*), Beijing.

Xinjiang lishi wenwu 1978 (*Historic Artefacts from Xinjiang*), ed. Xinjiang weiwuer zizhiqu bowuguan, Beijing.

Xiong Feide (no date). Shejian tiyangxi (Tiyangxi theatre in Shejian), ed. Li Yuanqiang, in *Nuoxi wenxuan* (*Selected Essays on the Nuo Theatre*): 77–9.

Yang Jingshuan 1960. Fangxiangshi yu da nuo (Fangxiangshi and the great exorcism), *Zhongyang yanjiu yuan, Lishi yuyan yanjiu suo jikan* 31 (December): 123–67.

Ye Yangxi and Lu Tian 1983. *Xiqu longtao yishu* (*The Art of The Chorus in Theatre*), Beijing.

Yijiuqisan nian Tulufan Asitana mujun fatu jianbao 1975 (Initial excavation report of the tomb finds at Asitana in Turfan in 1973), eds. Xingjiang weiwuer zizhiqu bowuguan, et al., *Wenwu* 7: 8–27.

Yu Yi 1990. Shier shou guichi xunzong (Some questions concerning traces of the twelve animals). Paper read to the International Nuo Conference, Shanxi.

Zeng Xiangjun 1991. Gudai shen ren shou mianju yu nuomian di guanxi (The relation between the masks of ancient deities, humans and animals and *nuo* masks). Paper read to the International Nuo Conference, Hunan.

Zenmo da luogu (How To Play Percussion), Shanghai 1982.

Zhongguo dabai ke quan shu. Xiqu quyi 1983 (*Chinese Encyclopaedia.*

Theatre and Performance), ed. Zhang Geng, Beijing and Shanghai.

Zhongguo fengsu cidian 1990 (*Encyclopaedia of Chinese Customs*), Shanghai.

Zhongguo jingjushi 1990 (*Chinese History of Jingju*), eds. Ma Shaobo, et al., 2 vols. (vol. 3 forthcoming), Beijing.

Zhongguo minzu minjian wudao jicheng 1980 (*Compendium of Chinese National and Folk Dance*), ed. Wu Xiaoreng, Beijing.

Zhongguo minzu minjian wudao jicheng: Dejiang xian ziliao juan 1990 (*Compendium of Chinese National and Folk Dance. Source Materials for Dejiang County*), eds. Li Shihong, He Zulan and Wei Wei, Guiyang.

Zhongguo nuoxi diaocha baogao 1992 (*Report on Research into Chinese Nuo Theatre*), eds. Gu Poguang, Fan Chaolin and Bai Guocheng, Guiyang.

Zhongguo shenhua chuanshuo cidian 1985 (*Encyclopaedia of Chinese Mythologies*), ed. Yuan Ke, Shanghai.

Zhongguo xiqu quyi cidian 1983 (*Encyclopaedia of Chinese Theatre*), ed. Shanghai yishu yanjiusuo, Shanghai.

Zhou Huawu 1991. Fangxiang. Taotie kao (On the Fangxiang and taotie). Paper read to the International Nuo Conference, Hunan.

Zhou Yibai 1980. *Zhongguo xiqu tongshi* (*A General History of Chinese Theatre*), 3 vols., Beijing.

1982. Zhongguo xiju yu kuileixi, yingxi (Chinese theatre and marionette and shadow play), in *Zhou Yibai xiju lunwen xuan* (*Selections from the Theatre Writings of Zhou Yibai*), ed. Li Shuji Changsha.

Zhu Jianming 1993. Langxi Dingbu di Wucang ji Wucang kao (On *Wucang* in Langxi, Dingbu), *Minsu quyi* 82: 197–215.

Works in western languages

Ahern, Emily 1973. *Cult of the Dead in a Chinese Village*, Stanford.

Ariés, Paul 1983. *In the Hour of Our Death*, Harmondsworth.

Artaud, Antonin 1970. *The Theatre and Its Double*, London.

Bagley, Robert W. 1988. Sacrificial pits of the Shang Period at Sanxingdui in Guanghan County, Sichuan Province, *Arts Asiatiques*, 43: 78–86.

1990. A Shang city in Sichuan Province, *Orientations*, November: 52–67.

Banu, Georges 1986. Mei Lanfang: a case against and model for the occidental stage, *Asian Theatre Journal* 3, 2 (Fall).

Barba, Eugenio and Nicola Savarese 1985. *Anatomie de l'Acteur*, Cazilhac.

Batchelder, Marjorie 1947. *Rod Puppets and the Human Theater*, Columbus.

Berglund, Lars 1990. *The Secret of the Luo Shu*, Södra Sandby.

Blake, Fred C. 1978. Death and abuse in Chinese marriage laments. The curse of Chinese brides, *Asian Folklore Studies* 37, 1: 3–33.

Bloch, Maurice and Jonathan Parry, eds. 1982. *Death and the Regeneration of Life*, Cambridge.

Bodde, Derk 1975. *Festivals in Classical China*, Princeton.

Brandon, James 1967. *Theatre in Southeast Asia*, Cambridge, MA.

Brecht, Bertolt 1964. Alienation effect in Chinese acting, ed. and trans. John Willett, *Brecht on Theatre: The Development of an Aesthetic*, New York.

Bulling, Annelies 1956. Die Kunst der Totenspiele in der östlichen Han-Zeit, *Oriens Extremus* 3: 28–56.

Cammann, Schuyler 1960. The evolution of magic squares in China,

Journal of the American Oriental Society 80, 2 (April/June):
116–24.

1962. Old Chinese magic squares, *Sinologica* 7, 1: 14–53.

1969. The magic square of three in old Chinese philosophy, *History of Religions*, vol. 1: 37–80.

Caroselli, Susan, ed. 1987. *Quest for Eternity. Chinese Sculptures from the People's Republic of China*, London.

Carr, Michael 1985. Personation of the dead in ancient China, *Computational Analysis of Asian and African Language (Ajia-Afurikago no keisu kenkyu)*, 24: 1–107.

Cervantes, Miguel de 1950. *Don Quixote*, Harmondsworth, Books 1 and 2.

Chan, P. 1972. Ch'u Tz'u and Shamanism in Ancient China, Ann Arbor (Ph.D. thesis).

Chavannes, Edouard 1913. *Mission archéologique dans la Chine septontrionale*. Paris.

Ch'en, Kenneth 1964. *Buddhism in China. A Historical Survey*, Princeton.

Cheng, Te K'un 1958. Chi You, God of War in Han Art, *Oriental Art* n.s. 4, 2 (Summer): 45–54.

Cheng, Te K'un 1960–3. *Archaeology in China*, vols. 1–3, Cambridge.

Chinese-English Dictionary 1981. Ed. Beijing waiyu xueyuan, Beijing.

Chu, Kunliang 1991. *Les aspects rituels du théâtre chinois*, (*Mémoires de l'institut des hauts études chinoises* 33), Paris.

See also Qiu Kunliang in bibliography of Chinese works.

Cohen, Myron 1988. Souls and salvation: conflicting themes in Chinese popular religion, in *Death Ritual in Late Imperial and Modern China*, ed. James L. Watson and Evelyn S. Rawski, Berkeley: 180–203.

Craig, Edward G. 1914. *On the Art of Theatre*, London.

Croissant, Doris 1964. Funktion und Wanddekor der Opferschrein von Wu Liang Tz'u, *Monumenta Serica* 23: 88–162.

Day, C.B. 1974. *Chinese Peasant Cults*, Taibei.

De Groot, J.J.M. 1982. *The Religious System of China*, vols. 1–6, Leiden 1892–1910, reprinted Taibei.

DeWoskin, Kenneth 1983. *Doctors, Diviners and Magicians of Ancient China*, Columbia.

Dohrenwand, Doris J. 1971. Jade demonic images from early China, *Ars Orientalis*, 10: 55–88.

Dolby, William 1976. *A History of Chinese Drama*, London.

 1978. The origins of Chinese puppetry, *Journal of the School of Oriental and African Studies* 4, 1: 97–120.

Dolby, William and John Scott 1974. *Warlords*, Edinburgh.

Doré, P. Henri 1936. *Manuel des superstitions chinoises*, Shanghai.

Eberhard, Wolfram 1968. *The Local Cultures of South and East China*, Leiden.

 1970. Oracle and theater in China, in *Studies in Chinese Folklore and Related Essays*, ed. Wolfram Eberhard, Bloomington.

 1986. *A Dictionary of Chinese Symbols*, London.

Eisenstein, Sergei 1986. *My Life on the Stage by Mei Hanfang to which is added The Enchanter from the Pear Garden by S.M. Eisenstein*, ed. International School of Theatre Anthropology, Rome.

 1988. *Yo ich selbst*, ed. Naum Klejman and Walentina Karschunowa, trans. Regina Kühn and Rita Braun, Frankfurt am Main.

Elliott, Alan J.A. 1955. *Chinese Spirit Medium Cults in Singapore*, London.

Erkes, Eduard 1914. *Das 'Zurückrufen der Seele' des Sung Yüh*, Leipzig.

 1928. Idols in pre-Buddhistic China, *Artibus Asiae*: 5–12.

 1950. Der schamanistische Ursprung des chinesischen Ahnenkults, *Sinologica* II.

Fenellosa, Ernest F. 1969. *The Chinese Character as a Medium for Poetry*, ed. Ezra Pound, San Francisco.

Finsterbusch, Kate 1966. *Verzeichnis und Motivindex der Han-Darstellungen*, 2 vols., Wiesbaden.

Fischer-Lichte, Erika, Josephine Riley and Michael Gissenwehrer, eds. 1990. *The Dramatic Touch of Difference. Theatre, Own and Foreign*, Tübingen.

George, David E.R. 1987. Ritual drama: between mysticism and magic, *Asian Theatre Journal* 4, 2 (Fall): 127–66.

Gimm, Martin, trans. 1966. *Das Yüeh-fu tsa-lu des Tuan An-chieh*, Wiesbaden.

Gissenwehrer, Michael 1983. Die Theaterlehre des Birnengartens. Die Ausbildung der Schauspieler für das jingju (sog. Pekingoper) in Beijing von 1800 bis 1949 und Taibei von 1949 bis1982, Vienna (Ph. D thesis).

 1987. *Peking Oper. Theaterzeit in China*, Schaffhausen.

Graham, D.G. 1954. *Songs and Stories of the Ch'uan Miao*. Smithsonian Miscellaneous Collections, vol. 123, no. 1, Washington.

1961. *Folk Religion in South-West China*, Washington.

Granet, Marcel 1959. *Danses et Légendes de la Chine ancienne*, 2 vols., Paris.

Gray, John Henry 1878. *China: A History of the Laws, Manners and Customs of the People*, London.

Hawkes, David 1985. *Songs of the South*, Harmondsworth.

Hentze, Carl 1928. *Chinese Tomb Figures*, London.

1932. *Mythes et Symboles Lunaires*, Antwerp.

1941. *Die Sakralbronzen und ihre Bedeutung in den frühchinesischen Kulturen*, Antwerp.

1943. Göttergestalten in der ältesten chinesichen Schrift and Ko-und Ch'i-Waffen in China und Amerika, in *Studien zur frühchinesichen Kulturgeschichte* 3, ed. Hentze and C.H. Kim, Antwerp.

Hopkins, L.C. 1920. The shaman or wu. A study in graphic camouflage, *New China Review* 2, 5 (October).

1945. The shaman or Chinese wu: his inspired dancing and versatile character, *Journal of the Royal Asiatic Society*: 3–6.

1943. The bearskin, another pictographic reconnaissance from primitive prophylactic to present-day panache, *Journal of the Royal Asiatic Society*: 110–17.

Hsu, Tao-Ching 1985. *The Chinese Conception of Theatre*, Seattle.

Huntingdon, Richard and Peter Metcalf 1979. *Celebrations of Death, The Anthropology of Mortuary Ritual*, Cambridge.

Idema, Wilt and Stephen West 1982. *Chinese Theater 1100–1450. A Source Book*, Wiesbaden.

Idema, Wilt and Stephen West, eds. and trans. 1991. *The Moon and the Zither: The Story of the Western Wing by Wang Shifu*, Berkeley.

Jennings, W., trans. 1969. *The Shi King*, New York.

Johnson, David, Andrew Nathan and Evelyn Rawski, eds. 1985. *Popular Culture in Late Imperial China*, Berkeley.

Johnson, David , ed. 1989. *Ritual Opera. Operatic Ritual. Mu-lien Rescues His Mother in Chinese Popular Culture*, Oakland.

Jordon, David K. 1972. *Gods, Ghosts and Ancestors: The Folk Religion of a Taiwanese Village*, Berkeley.

Kagan, Alan Lloyd 1978. Cantonese Puppet Theatre: An Operatic Tradition and its Roots in the Chinese Belief System, Ann Arbor (Ph.D. thesis).

Kanze Company 1982. *Ursprung von Theater. 600 Jahre altes japanisches noo-spiel*, Munich.

Kapferer, Bruce 1983. *A Celebration of Demons*, Bloomington.

Karlgren, Bernhard 1930. Some fecundity symbols in ancient China, *Bulletin of far Eastern Antiquities* 2: 1–67.

1946. Legends and cults in ancient China, *Bulletin of Far Eastern Antiquities* 18.

Karlgren, Bernhard, trans. (1950). *The Book of Odes*, Stockholm.

Kelly, Charles F. and Ch'en Meng-Chia 1946. *Chinese Bronzes from the Buckingham Collection*, Chicago.

Kleist, Heinrich von 1928. A marionette theatre, trans. Dorothea McCollester, *Theatre Arts Monthly*, July: 476–84.

1990. Über das Marionettentheater, in *Heinrich von Kleist. Sämtliche Werke und Briefe*, ed. Klaus Müller-Salget, Frankfurt am Main.

Laban, Rudolf 1991. *Choreutik. Grundlagen der Raum-Harmonielehre des Tanzes*, trans. Claude Perrottet, Wilhelmshaven.

Ledderose, Lothar and Adele Schlombs, eds. 1990. *Jenseits der Grossen Mauer. Der erste Kaiser von China und seine Terrakotta-Armee*, Munich.

Legge, James, trans. 1885. *Liji*, 2 vols., Oxford.

Li Ruru 1988. Chinese traditional theatre and Shakespeare, *Asian Theatre Journal* 5, 1 Spring 1988: 38–49.

Lim, Lucy, ed. 1987. *Stories From China's Past. Han Dynasty Pictorial Tomb Reliefs and Archaeological Objects from Sichuan Province*, San Francisco.

Loewe, Michael 1979. *Ways to Paradise. The Chinese Quest for Immortality*, London.

1982. *Chinese Ideas of Life and Death*, London.

Loon, Piet van der 1977. Les origines rituelles du théâtre chinois, *Journal Asiatique* 265, 1–2: 141–68.

Mackerras, Colin 1972. *The Rise of the Peking Opera 1770–1870*, Oxford.

1975. *The Chinese Theatre in Modern Times From 1840 to the Present Day*, London.

Mackerras, Colin, ed. (1983). *Chinese Theater from its Origins to the Present Day*, Honolulu.

Mahler, Jane Gaston 1959. *The Westerners Among the Figures of T'ang China*, Rome.

Mair, Victor H. 1989. *T'ang Transformation Texts. A Study of the Buddhist Contribution to the Rise of Vernacular Fiction and Drama in China*, Cambridge, MA.

Mathews Chinese–English *Dictionary* 1979 Cambridge, MA (originally printed Shanghai 1931).

Meister, P.W. 1956 Chinesische bronzemasken, *Ostasiatische Zeitschrift*, N.F. 14, 1: 5–11.

Mei Lanfang 1986. *My Life on the Stage by Mei Lanfang to which is added The Enchanter from the Pear Garden by S.M. Eisenstein*, ed. International School of Theatre Anthropology, Rome.

Misumi, Haruo, Gamo Satoaki and Hata Hisashi, eds. 1987. *Masked Performances in Asia*. Tokyo.

Needham, Rodney 1967. Percussion and transition, *Man* n.s. 2: 606–14.

Neher, Andrew 1962. A physiological explanation of unusual behaviour in ceremonies involving drums, *Human Biology* 34, 2: 151–60.

Nivat, Dhani 1947. The shadow play as a possible origin of the masked play, *Journal of the Siam Society* 37, 1.

Ortolani, Benito 1990. *The Japanese Theatre. From Shamanistic Ritual to Contemporary Pluralism*, Leiden.

Pound, Ezra 1955. *The Classic Anthology Defined By Confucius*, London.

Pronko, Leonard C. 1967. *Theater East and West*, Berkeley.

Rawson, Jessica, ed. 1992. *The British Museum Book of Chinese Art*, London.

Riley, Josephine and Else Unterrieder, ed. 1989. *Haishi zou hao. Chinese Poetry, Drama and Literature of the 1980s*, Bonn.

Riley, Josephine 1990. Dancing the gods, *Britain–China*, 43, Spring: 11–17.

Riley, Josephine, Michael Gissenwehrer and Huang Weiruo 1991. Exorcism by an ancient road, *Chime* 3, Spring: 4–20.

Rimer, Thomas and Yamazaki Masakazu, trans. 1984. *On the Art of the No Drama. The Major Treatises of Zeami*, Princeton.

Salmony, Alfred 1954. *Antler and Tongue. An Essay on Ancient Chinese Symbolism and its Implications*, Ascona, Switzerland.

Schafer, Edward H. 1951. Ritual exposure in ancient China, *Harvard Journal of Asiatic Studies*, 14: 130–84.

Schechner, Richard 1985. *Between Theater and Anthropology*, Philadelphia.

Schindler, Bruno 1923. The development of the Chinese conception of supreme beings, *Asia Major* 1: 298–352.

Schipper, K.M. 1966. The divine jester, some remarks on the gods of the Chinese marionette theater, *Bulletin of the Institute of Ethnology*.

　　1993. *The Taoist Body*, trans. Karen Duval, Berkeley, Los Angeles, London.

Schönfelder, Gerd 1971. Zum Gebrauch der Schlaginstrumente im traditionellen chinesischen Musiktheater, *Studia musicologica*, 13: 137–76.

　　1974. *Die Musik der Pekingoper*, Leipzig.

Scott, A.C. 1971. *Mei Lanfang. The Life and Times of a Peking Actor*, Hong Kong (first published as *Mei Lanfang. Leader of the Pear Garden*, Hong Kong 1959).

　　1982. *Actors are Madmen. Notebook of a Theatregoer in China*, Wisconsin.

Shen, Chien-Shih 1936–7. An essay on the primitive meaning of the character *kuei*, *Monumenta Serica* 2: 1–20.

Shi, Song 1976. Interview with Beiping opera actor Sun Yuan-pin, in *Echo of Things Chinese. Special Issue on Zhong Kui*, 6–7, ed. Linda Wu.

Smith, Richard J. 1991. *Fortune-Tellers and Philosophers. Divination in Traditional Chinese Society*, Boulder, Co.

Stalberg, Roberta H. 1984. *China's Puppets*, San Francisco.

Steele, John, trans. 1917. *The Yi-Li, or Book of Etiquette and Ceremonial*, London.

Tanaka, Issei 1972. Development of Chinese local plays in the 17th and 18th Centuries, *Acta Asiatica* 23: 42–62.

Teiser, Stephen F. 1988. *The Ghost Festival in Medieval China*, Princeton.

Thomson, Stuart E. 1988. Death, Food and Fertility, in *Death Ritual in Late Imperial and Modern China*, ed. James L. Watson and Evelyn S. Rawski, Berkeley: 71–109.

Thorp, Robert L., trans. 1978–80. Brief excavation report of the tomb of Marquis Yi Zeng at Sui Xian, Hubei, *Chinese Studies in Archaeology* 1, 3 (Winter): 3–45.

1980. Burial practices of bronze age China, in *The Great Bronze Age of China*, ed. Wen Fong, New York: 62.

Thorpe, W.A. 1930. Fang Hsiang Shih (Han to T'ang), *Pantheon* 5, 5 May: 234–8.

Trubner, H. 1968. *The Far Eastern Collection of the Royal Ontario Museum*, Toronto.

Waley, Arthur 1955. *The Nine Songs. A Study of Shamanism of Ancient China*, London.

Ward, Barbara 1979. Not merely players: drama, act and ritual in traditional China, *Man* n.s. 14: 18–39.

Warner, E.T.C. 1984. *Myths and Legends of China*, Singapore.

Watson, James 1982. Of flesh and bones: the management of death pollution in Cantonese society, in *Death and the Regeneration of Life*, ed. Maurice Bloch and Jonathan Parry, Cambridge: 155–186.

Watson, James and Evelyn S. Rawski 1988. *Death Ritual in Late Imperial and Modern China*, Berkeley.

Werle, Helga 1973. Swatow (Ch'aochow) horizontal stick puppets, *Journal of the Royal Asiatic Society. Hong Kong Branch*: 73–84.

Wichmann, Elizabeth 1991. *Listening to Theatre*, Honolulu.

Williams, C.A.S. 1976. *Outlines of Chinese Symbolism and Art Motives*, New York.

Williams, David, ed. 1991. *Peter Brook and the Mahabharata*, London.

Wolf, Arthur P. 1974. *Religion and Ritual in Chinese Society*, Stanford.

Wu Jingnuan 1991. *The Yijing*, Washington.

Wu, Linda ed. 1976. *Echo of Things Chinese. Special Issue on Zhong Kui*, 6–7.

Zung, Cecilia L. 1937. *Secrets of the Chinese Drama*, New York.

Index